CARBON DREAMS

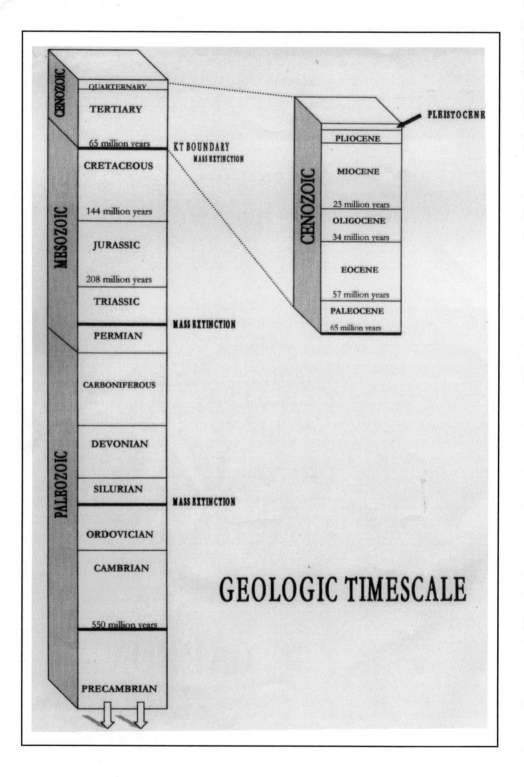

GEOLOGIC TIMESCALE

Susan M. Gaines

CARBON DREAMS

CREATIVE ARTS BOOK COMPANY
Berkeley ✿ California

For information contact:
Creative Arts Book Company
833 Bancroft Way
Berkeley, California 94710

Carbon Dreams is a work of fiction, and its characters and events are all creations of
its author's imagination. Though much of the science in the book is based on or
inspired by the published work of real scientists, the associated characters in the
book bear no relation to those scientists and any resemblance is entirely coincidental.

ISBN 088739-3063
Library of Congress Catalog Number 99-64937

Printed in the United States of America

Acknowledgements

Publications that were key in the writing of *Carbon Dreams* are mentioned in the Author's Note at the end, but I want to give special thanks to the dear friends and colleagues who conspired in its creation. Writers Jean Hegland, Ray Holley and Sean Swift nurtured this book through myriad revisions, and it would never have assumed its final form without their lively criticism and encouragement. I also want to thank farmers and nurseryfolk Carolyn and Terry Harrison for advice on things horticultural and for their comments on the manuscript, as well as geologist Dr. Juan Carlos Herguera, chemist Dr. Sabine Apitz, and biologist Dr. Sofia Gil Turnes for many years of stimulating conversations that contributed to the making of this book, and for their helpful comments on the manuscript.

CARBON DREAMS

Chapter 1

There was the cool nip of an offshore breeze, and the air was fresh, deliciously fresh, after ten hours in the lab. Cristina Arenas slowed her pace and took a deep, luxurious breath. Sweet offshore air and seaweed. Ocean rot. Slow, salty decay. She'd been hurrying, worried she'd miss the beginning of the seminar, but when she started up the hill and saw people still loitering outside the lecture hall, she turned to face the sun, the breeze, the sea.

The ubiquitous Northern California fog was nowhere in sight. She could see the edge of the beach below the bluff, BIO's long pier jutting out into the waves, a boat hanging off its side, and then ocean and sky, the great gleaming expanse of the Pacific stretching to the horizon and beyond. You could almost imagine, Tina thought as she walked backward up the hill, that mysteries still lurked out there. Simple, straightforward mysteries like uncharted continents, uninventoried species. . . . The hydrothermal vents, after all, were discovered just two years ago: entire ecosystems thriving in the desert of the deep sea, huge worms and mammoth crabs feasting on sulfur, unobserved and unimagined until 1980. And the three species of tiny phytoplankton that her own work depended on were unknown until just last year. The botanist who discovered them was indeed like an explorer who'd sighted land, Tina thought, always marveling over his luck, at the mere fact of their existence—though she was the only one who had shown any interest.

She sighed, edging slowly up the hill, gazing out at the blue horizon. No such straightforward discoveries awaited her, no simple mysteries beckoned. Nothing so tangible as a new species. She stopped walking, thinking of the grant proposal she was writing, and all the yet-to-be analyzed samples her technician had prepared. Her funding would run out in six months, and she had wasted the last two days in the instrument lab repairing a pump. She really shouldn't be wasting this Friday afternoon at yet another interesting-but-irrelevant talk. Some geologist was going to be theorizing about the origin of life. . . . Tina turned and hurried up the hill. Who could possibly resist a talk titled "Clay Crystals: the First Organisms"?

She joined the last stragglers filing into BIO's one large lecture hall, which was in the basement of the new geophysics building. Since the previous September, when she started working at the Brayton Institute of Oceanography, Tina had attended every one of these seminars. It was March now, she'd been there eight months, and yet she still felt a certain thrill when she entered that auditorium full of famous scientists and promising graduate students. She knew that she was too small, too fragile to seem like one of them, that in her bike shorts and sweatshirt she looked more like a twelve year old than a twenty-eight-year-old scientist, but she had long since given up worrying about it. She stepped off to the side at the back of the auditorium and stood up on her toes, scanning the audience.

It was more crowded than she had expected. There were a lot of people she didn't recognize from the university up the hill—a lot of BIO scientists she didn't recognize either, for that matter, people from all disciplines, a few still in lab coats, some in jeans and T-shirts, the older ones in sports shirts and slacks. Tina was still standing at the back, searching for one particular balding head she was sure would be in attendance, when she heard her name over the hubbub and saw one of the few women in the crowd beckoning to her from the middle of the auditorium.

"Do you think it happened in seven days and seven nights?" Katharine asked when Tina neared.

Tina laughed, stepping out of the aisle to stand by the seat next to Katharine. "It's a pretty outrageous title. But I've never seen this place so packed."

"Yeah, I had to fight for your aisle seat. I told them it was for a midget who wouldn't be able to see otherwise."

"Thanks a lot. What are you doing here, anyway? It's not exactly your kind of topic."

"Mark Jenner *is* a geologist, you know. Everyone from my lab came." Katharine swiveled around in her seat to peruse the crowd. "There must be two hundred people here. All the big names. Look, Conroy Decker even brought visitors from Scripps. I'll bet that's Charles Keeling with him. He's the one who started monitoring the rise in atmospheric CO_2 in the fifties, isn't he? Well look at that, they even dragged Harper Gibson out of his lair. That is Keeling isn't it?"

"Yes." Tina knew Conroy Decker and Harper Gibson by name only, but she recognized Keeling from her grad student days at Scripps—not that he'd ever talked to her. "What's Keeling doing up here?"

"He's working on something with Decker. I guess they decided to take a break, see what old Jenner has to say—though Jenner seems to have gone a little off the deep end this time." Katharine laughed and pushed a mass of blond hair back from her face. "It's a sure sign of senility when they start theorizing about the origin of life. Who are you looking for?"

Tina was still standing, looking for a man who had spent his entire adult life theorizing about the origin of life. "I'm looking for Garrett."

"Garrett?"

"Garrett Thomas, from the chemistry department up the hill. I want to see if he'll look over my proposal before I send it to NSF." Tina sat down. "Though I'm sure he'll say yes."

"Talk about senile," Katharine said. "That guy ought to retire."

"Who, Garrett? Garrett's not that old."

"Maybe not, but he hasn't done anything new since graduate school."

"Come on, Katharine," Tina said, annoyed. "He won a Nobel Prize. He was probably in your high school biology textbook."

"Sure. For an experiment he did when he was a graduate student. Fifty years ago. I hear he's been sitting on his laurels ever since."

"It was thirty years ago. Nineteen fifty-one, fifty-two? And he's done a lot since then."

"How do you know him anyway?"

"He was Jake's advisor—my graduate advisor's advisor. We've sort of become friends since I moved here. Now shush. They're trying to get started."

"Clay Crystals: the First Organisms" turned out to be a surprisingly apt title for a theory that was, indeed, outrageous. Jenner started with what was known about the origin of life: nothing, according to him. "After fifty years of research," he said, "all we know is that life exists." He paused for effect and leaned forward on the podium. "We have learned a lot about what life *is*: that it evolves, that it replicates, mutates, and metabolizes, and we understand many of the associated chemical processes. But the paradigm that has grown up around Garrett Thomas's Nobel-winning experiments, the so-called organic soup theory, is unwarranted. I'm not arguing with the significance of those experiments," he added, looking at Garrett Thomas, who was sitting in the first row. "They did prove that it was possible to create the stuff of life without first having life. But," Jenner said, "just because the chicken didn't *have* to come before the egg, doesn't mean that it didn't." He spoke briefly about conditions on the early earth, and then he turned on the slide projector to show a series of electron micrographs of clay minerals. "When life made its debut," he said, "these were the most readily available materials on earth."

What a lovely story, Tina thought, enthralled by the slides, the symmetrical molecular structures of the clay crystals which could grow, replicate, and even, through defects in the crystals, mutate and evolve. In Jenner's experiments organic molecules were adsorbed onto the surface of the clays, even incorporated into the crystals. But when he started speculating that the clay crystal "organisms" had "manufactured" simple carbon-based organic molecules and that these had eventually taken over and supplanted their clay masters, his story lost its nice, carefully-woven texture. His speculations were too vague, spun out of so much air without even a smidgen of evidence for ballast. But then, Tina thought, that was pretty much how it always was with origin-of-life research. It was *all* speculation, most of it pretty wild. And Tina didn't really see how it could be anything else. Life was, apparently, too old. They might find a few enticing clues in the rock record, but the evidence that could solve the mystery seemed to have been thoroughly eradicated by time. In a sense this was what made origin-of-life research so attractive: no matter how many theories there were, the field would always present scientists with a huge, seductively empty canvas on which to paint a new one.

Jenner was taking questions now, amiably entertaining some rather acerbic comments, responding philosophically—in the spirit, he noted, of his subject. When Garrett spoke, Tina thought his remarks were mildly phrased, considering. "This is a clever play on the semantic question, 'What is life?'" Garrett said. "But it doesn't tell us anything about the origin of life as we know it. Life has consisted of carbon-based organic molecules as far back as paleontologists can see, yet your scheme offers no mechanism for their introduction. Have you tried to synthesize the essential polymers on your clays? Nucleotides? Or even small peptides?"

Jenner grinned at Garrett, and Tina realized that they'd probably been friends for years. He was hoping, he said, to inspire organic chemists in the crowd to take up experiments of just that sort. There were some chuckles from the audience, and someone toward the back called out that the crystals must have been seeded with nucleic acids by extraterrestrial beings— a reference to the much-publicized theory of a well-known English scientist that life on earth had evolved from spores distributed by intelligent beings from elsewhere in the universe. Jenner's rejoinder was lost in the laughter, and a free-for-all ensued, the attacks becoming more directed and sarcastic. A biochemist from the university asked why, with the materials so ubiquitous, one didn't find societies of "clay organisms" thriving on the ocean floor. Since they were mineral rather than organic, the clay societies wouldn't be prone to destruction by modern life—why didn't they keep evolving anew? There were some snickers in the audience when Jenner answered that they had started a search for such new beginnings.

By the time Tina was acknowledged to speak, the room was humming and people were getting ready to leave. When she began, however, standing up and raising her voice to be heard, people turned to look and curiosity quelled the hum—because she was new, and young, and female.

"To get life as we know it," Tina said, "you've got to have organic molecules. As Dr. Thomas pointed out. The clay crystals may provide an ordered template for their formation, but you also need energy. You didn't really address this question, and I was just wondering what you're proposing. Some kind of chemosynthesis? Photochemical reactions by the organic molecules adsorbed onto the clays? Maybe even reactions that led directly to photosynthesis—early on, perhaps, from the very beginning of carbon-based life. Isn't there evidence of that? That photosynthetic organisms were among the earliest life forms, rather than evolving later the way we thought? In fact, didn't someone just find fossils of blue-green algae in the oldest sedimentary rocks? Over three and a half billion years old, or something?"

Tina was appalled at how long she'd gone on. She noticed Garrett twisted around to face her in the front row. Why was she proposing studies to verify a theory she didn't even find credible? She always did this. She'd get going on a line of reasoning and keep going just to see where it would lead. Jake used to accuse her of having a "philandering intellect," warning that it would lead to a life of "scientific wantonness" if she wasn't careful. She sat down, waiting to be ridiculed by some organic chemist's pronouncement that the reactions she'd just suggested off the top of her head were categorically impossible.

"This is an interesting line of inquiry, Miss . . . ?" Jenner strained to see her better.

"Doctor," Katharine spoke for her. "Dr. Arenas."

"Thank-you. Dr. Arenas. I don't know of any studies of the sort you are suggesting. Perhaps one of the chemists in the audience knows—" But to Tina's relief, it was a geologist who interrupted him now, the only woman at BIO with full professor status.

"Actually," Dr. Orloff said dryly, "those fossils of blue-green algae have not been verified. They were found in the Warrua formation which has been dated at 3.8 billion years, but whether or not they are truly fossils, let alone fossils of photosynthetic bacteria, is still in question."

"What about the carbon isotope studies?" someone called out from the audience.

Orloff turned, looking to address the speaker, but he—understandably, given her reputation—didn't identify himself. "Those studies were entirely inconclusive," she said hotly. "That work shouldn't even have been published."

"Yikes," Katharine whispered, scanning the room. "Phil Barrow and his group wrote that paper. Aren't they here?"

But Tina was caught up in the discussion, on her feet again. "Has anyone tried analyzing those fossils, or even the rocks, for specific organic molecules?" she asked. "So-called chemical fossils? That would at least tell us if there was life in the rock, if the fossils are real—"

"I don't believe such an analysis is feasible," Orloff interrupted her, "given the minute quantities of organics left in those rocks. I doubt that samples would even be made available."

Tina shrugged and sat down, blushing. The analysis was, in theory, feasible, that much she knew. Whether it would tell them anything useful was another matter.

"Geez, you're brave," Katharine whispered. "Come on, let's get out of here. It's almost six."

There was still some rather heated discussion going on, somone from Barrow's group rebutting Orloff's allegation, but the room had grown noisy again and people were hurrying out. Katherine headed for the door, but Tina hung back, waiting for Garrett. He'd gone down to the podium, however, and was immersed in an animated conversation with Jenner, so she gave up and followed Katherine out of the building.

Outside, the fog had drifted in, the offshore breeze had died down, and the air stank from the dairy ranch to the north. Tina joined Katharine, who was standing in the middle of the drive, waiting for her.

"Looks like old Jenner has never had the pleasure of meeting Dr. Cristina Teresa Arenas, alias Tiny Tina, otherwise known as the great Teeney-Weeney."

Tina laughed. She'd made the mistake of divulging the schoolyard names of her childhood to Katharine. By now everyone at BIO had probably heard them. "I guess he thought I was a grad student," she said as they started down the hill.

"These old guys think any woman they see around here is a grad student or technician. I wonder what they think happens to all those students when they finish their theses. Are we supposed to fade away into domestic bliss with our Ph.D.s? Spend six years of our lives as indentured servants subject to miscellaneous forms of psychological torture so that we'll make better wives and technicians?"

"State college professors. We're supposed to join the teaching ranks of the state colleges."

"Really? Are there a lot of women teaching in the state colleges?"

"Actually," Tina said, "I don't know. Not at the one I went to. But I did get offered two teaching jobs straight out of grad school."

"You did?" Katharine turned and looked at her. They were on BIO's main drive now, walking back along the bluff toward the chemistry and geology buildings. "Tenure track?"

Tina nodded. "But they don't give you a lab or anything. There's no research—all you do is teach." She hadn't even considered it.

"Well, but it's got to be better than soft money. I don't see how you stand it, not knowing from one year to the next if you have a job. And look at your salary—it's hardly better than a postdoc's." Katharine herself was still on a postdoctoral fellowship, working in Sylvia Orloff's lab.

"It's okay." Tina's researcher's salary seemed decent enough to her. If it weren't for all those undergrad loans to pay off, and her dead car, and worrying about her father, she would feel downright wealthy.

"You know, BIO doesn't exactly have a reputation for treating its soft-money researchers nicely when they run out of grant money. They don't care if you end up unemployed and homeless."

"Oh Katharine," Tina said, laughing. "Let's not exaggerate. I'm not going to end up homeless. And being on the fringe has its advantages." Tina's job was entirely dependent on the grants she got funded, and she was just a squatter in Max Lindquist's labs. Lindquist, however, was in Sweden for two years, leaving her free rein. Her work was actually flourishing in this no man's land of soft money research, thriving on the freedom of neglect, like a child playing out of doors, getting dirty and wet and climbing the most dangerous trees—but she didn't want to jinx her proposal by saying so.

"There's always industry," Katharine said. "I met this geochemist who works for one of the oil companies, and the labs he described make ours look like nineteenth-century artifacts. Not to mention the salaries."

"Yeah, but who'd want to work for industry? It'd be like . . . I don't know, like being stuck in one of those horrid undergrad chemistry labs for the rest of your life. 'Here's the experiment, and this is how it should turn out. Here's the product—make it, find it, whatever.' Talk about boring." No philandering intellects there, Tina thought. You'd have to tie your mind up in a straightjacket.

"Imagine what a fit Sylvia would have if I ended up in industry. She'd disown me completely— Oh," Katharine interrupted herself, stopping suddenly. "Did I tell you she's taking me on the big drill ship cruise this fall?"

"On the *Explorer*? That's great, Katharine!"

"Though I do wonder how I'll survive a month and a half on a ship with Sylvia Orloff as chief scientist. Working for her here is bad enough." Katharine sighed dramatically. "You should have seen how she tore into me at our last group meeting."

"You'll be fine," Tina said. "She wouldn't be taking you if she wasn't pleased with your work."

"I *am* the only one in the lab who's going." Katharine pressed her thin lips together in a smug half-smile. "I keep telling myself that she doesn't *really* think I'm an indolent moron. She just believes that the way to prepare a young woman for a life in science is to work her to death, encourage cutthroat competition and tell anyone who isn't ten times better than the best of the men that she will never amount to a heap of beans. At least I have some perspective, but imagine her poor students . . . ."

Half-amused, half-irritated, and a little envious because she would have liked to be included on the *Explorer* cruise herself, Tina listened to her friend run on about her famous boss. Katharine had some obnoxious affectations—a New England education that tyrannized her Texan drawl, a supercilious way of inclining her chin and tossing her hair back—but this arrogance collapsed at the slightest nudge, and she had pursued Tina's friendship with such eagerness and innocence, that Tina's initial aversion had given way to a guarded affection.

"Do you realize," Katharine was saying, "that Sylvia has never had a male student or postdoc? Just technicians. She likes to have male technicians, treats them like secretaries. She fancies herself a feminist, but I do believe the woman's got herself stuck in the sixties. Eighties-style feminism is beyond her comprehension. She doesn't get it that we need to do away with the superstar requirement. The problem is, Sylvia actually believes it herself, that there's no such thing as a good woman scientist, only a brilliant one. Just because that's how *she* made it. Though if the truth be known about Sylvia Orloff—"

"I should get back to work," Tina interrupted her. They had arrived at her building, but Katharine sounded like she planned to stand there in front of it gossiping all night. "I've still got a lot to do on my proposal. And I left the HPLC running."

Katharine stretched, pulling out of the slouch she acquired when she was with Tina, whose head didn't quite reach her shoulder. "Okay," she said, "go work. I'm meeting Fred for dinner pretty soon anyway. But Tina, tomorrow night we're going out dancing, and don't even think about saying you're too busy. There's a band playing Latin jazz at the Windjammer. 'Los Vagobundos.' You can get back to your roots."

"Latin jazz is Caribbean, Katharine. I don't know that they even listen to it in Uruguay." Actually, Tina had no idea what they listened to in Uruguay. All her father ever listened to was classical music.

"Fred's going to bring some of his mathematician buddies. And some people from my lab will be there. Male technicians and engineer included," Katharine added with a sly smile. "Lots of smart, handsome men for the beautiful midget to chose from."

"I think that's an oxymoron," Tina said, rolling her eyes. Men were more likely to call her "cute" than beautiful. She was pretty enough, and she'd been told that she had a dazzling smile. But her chin was too pointed, her cheekbones too steeply angled, her coloring as monotone as an old sepia photograph—hair, skin, freckles, eyes, all varying shades of brown—and she was just too small for beautiful.

"I'll pick you up at the Hovel," Katharine said, Hovel by the Sea being her epithet for the rundown duplex Tina rented in the midst of upscale North Brayton. "Seven? We can have pizza there."

"Yeah, okay," Tina said finally, laughing. She hadn't been out with any men since she moved to Brayton. And she couldn't even remember the last time she'd been dancing.

She would just run one sample, she thought, as she climbed the stairs to her office and labs, and finish the budget for her proposal.

The main lab showed signs of her technician having worked that afternoon, the glassware washed and sterilized, the lab benches cleared of paraphernalia, everything stashed neatly in its place. No denying that Michael was conscientious, Tina thought, despite his bright-boy cockiness. In fact, if there was a problem with Michael it was that he was too perfect. She picked out one of the samples he'd extracted for her and headed down the hall to her instrument lab.

This was the reason Tina had wanted the job in Lindquist's labs to begin with, this instrument lab, uncomfortable as it was. It was like a kitchen that had been designed for appliances with no thought for the cook—the room too cold and narrow, the counter crowded with instruments and tangled nests of connecting wires and tubes, the only window a square of shatter-proof glass in the door onto the hall—but Tina had coveted its almost new, impossibly expensive Mass Spectrometer. She had even coveted the geriatric, not-so-expensive High Pressure Liquid Chromatograph that she had spent the last eight months coddling, pampering, and repairing. Of the two instruments, new and old, she and an analytical chemist from the university had created an HPLC-Mass Spec that could detect and identify the tiniest traces of organic molecules. It was a bit jerry-rigged, assembled from the materials at hand—a UV detector older than the HPLC, a chart recorder filched from another instrument, a computer scavenged from a neighboring lab housed on a three-wheeled cart the janitor found in the basement—but it was state-of-the-art in what it could accomplish. Tina slipped into the narrow niche between counter and cart at the back of the lab and increased the solvent flow rate on the HPLC, smiling when she heard the quiet, steady beat of the pump she had rebuilt.

She rinsed the syringe and dipped the needle into her vial of extract, edging the plunger up with her thumb, forcing it down to expel the bubbles, and then up again, this time to draw a bubble-free microliter. This sample was an extract of a recent sediment, but she wondered what the system would turn up in something like the Warrua fossils they'd been talking about at the seminar. Sylvia Orloff had implied that it was a mistake and they weren't really fossils at all. Tina slid the needle into the injector and eased the plunger down slowly, forcing the sample out of the syringe and into the injector tube. She pulled the lever on the injector, pressed the start key on the microprocessor, hit "g" on the computer keyboard behind her, flicked the switch on the chart-recorder, and then she folded her arms and watched the instrument on the counter.

There wasn't much to see: two bottles of solvent sitting on top of a metal box, tubes running down to the injection valve and the foot-long steel chromatography column, the detectors—Mass Spec for identifying new structures and the simpler UV detector—and then the chart recorder to graph the signal and the computer to change it into numbers. She could hear the gentle thumping of the pump inside the box and watch the seconds ticking by on its tiny microprocessor screen, but she couldn't see the solvent moving through the tubes. There was nothing to see, and yet Tina watched, imagining the medley of molecules in her sample being washed out of the injector by a flood of solvent, moving swiftly into the column, encountering the silica packing and slowing, slowing...then caught in its siliceous embrace. With the solvents rushing steadily past, her heterogeneous sample would be separated into clans of molecules, and the clans into families, and then the families would be torn asunder by their preferential loves—for the silica in the column, for the blend of solvents rushing by—and left in lonely, individual, homogeneous clusters. If she stood there long enough, each cluster would yield to its solvent mix of choice and wash off the column into the detector, the recorder pen screeching suddenly up its bar, dropping as suddenly down for each clean sharp peak, each single compound. . . . Tina left the instrument running and walked back down the hall. It would be another half-hour before the first peak washed through.

The elderly Salvadoran janitor was down at the end of the corridor with his cart, and she waved and called out a greeting in Spanish as she went into her office. He had been especially kind and helpful to Tina in her first months at BIO, almost as if he'd taken one look at her and decided that she would need extra help to survive. His name was Esteban, and he was as much a fixture around the chemistry building as the flock of herons that lived in the grove of Monterrey pine outside—though Tina liked having Esteban around, and she wasn't sure how she felt about the herons. She had finally gotten used to all the bluster of their flapping wings and raucous take-off cries, but lately they'd taken to roosting on a branch just outside her window and being disconcertingly quiet. There were four lined up there now, not two feet from the glass, peering in at her with their beady red eyes, looking like a bunch of stodgy old men with their fat white necks tucked into black suits. She slid into the chair behind her desk and started shuffling through the chaos of papers, searching for the forms for her proposal budget.

She was still thinking about what Sylvia Orloff had said. If those were fossils in the Warrua rock—if there *had* been life and there were any organics left at all, she ought to be able to detect them. She had identified specific organic molecules, chemical fossils, in sediments as old as ninety million years. She'd just published a paper in *Geochimica* describing that work, but apparently Orloff hadn't seen it. And of course, the Warrua rock was forty times that old. It was older than old. Even if it had once contained remnants of life, the sturdiest of organic molecules might well have broken down or leached out by now. And even if you did find some resilient hydrocarbon, you would have to show that it hadn't leached in from later sediments. . . . Damn. Tina looked at the form in front of her. She should stop going to these talks. She was supposed to be thinking about money. Salaries. Supplies. A new HPLC. Not dreaming up some entirely irrelevant project.

When the phone rang twenty minutes later she had made good progress, though she'd decided to have the secretary type the forms. She knew it would be her father. She should have called him last weekend. That was what he expected, that she call every week. And she had, for a long time. First, because she was young and he worried about her, and then because she knew he was lonely, and for the past two years, because *she* had been worried about *him*. He'd bought a pizza franchise in 1980, in the San Fernando Valley not ten miles from the one he'd managed for most of Tina's life, but it was a bad year for such enterprises and by the end of it he'd been bankrupt, his house in foreclosure. For the past year he'd been managing an apartment complex. Tina thought he actually seemed happier than he'd been in the homely little tract house she'd grown up in. He had neighbors that he talked to now, even friends, there in the building.

"*Te llamé a casa.* But you weren't home. Friday night, I am thinking, maybe she has a date."

"So then why are you calling here?" Tina said, irritated by his hopeful prying, and sorry, already sorry, as soon as the words were out of her mouth.

"*Pues . . . ¿Te llamo despues, a casa?*"

"No, Dad, really. I didn't mean that." She softened her tone. "You can call me here any time you want. But it is cheaper on the weekend."

"*Te llamé el domingo pasado.*"

"I was here, at the lab."

"*Ah. Es lo que pensaba. Pero no te quise interrumpir. ¿Estás haciendo algún experimento importante, m'ija?*"

"No, not really. And it doesn't matter. Is everything okay?"

"Oh yes. Fine. I have a new tenant downstairs. I spent all last week getting the apartment ready. A very nice lady, *una bibliotecaria.* Maybe I can get a special extension on my books, no? I am reading a very strange book by a Mexican author, *a ver, como se llama* . . . Spota. A sort of mystery. I don't know if I will finish. It's from the downtown library and I have to take it back in one week."

"I've told you a million times, all you have to do is renew them. You can do it on the phone."

"I know. But it never seems right."

"And getting a special extension from your librarian neighbor does?"

"Oh I'm only joking. I think she works in a school. *¿Y allí, hija, como está todo?* You still like it? Are you going to settle in there?"

"I still like it, Dad," she said impatiently, ignoring what she knew to be the subtext of 'settle.' He made it sound like they hadn't talked in months, when in reality they'd had a very similar conversation a week and a half ago. They had talked, just as they talked now, about the weather in Brayton and the weather in L.A., about him making a trip to Brayton in the summer or maybe the fall when the weather was supposed to be nice. He asked about her car. She told him it was fine—a small lie, though she did mention that she was riding her bike a lot. For the exercise, she told him, and because it was a nice ride, which was true. The bike ride relaxed her, cleared her mind. Not so great when it was raining, but she didn't tell him she rode in the rain.

She knew he was proud of her. He'd been proud when she graduated from college, proud when she was accepted at Scripps, proud of the "Dr." in front of her name. He had encouraged her through all those years of education, sending money to supplement her small earnings from waiting tables and grading papers when she was an undergraduate. He'd supported her decision to take the loans when she got serious about chemistry, so she could work less, study more. Tina never had the heart to tell him that she was only now starting out, when as far as he was concerned she was at the zenith of professional success and it was time to get married and provide him with grandchildren. *Cuando tenga nietos,* he would say, his eyes glittering at the thought, and he would talk about the places he would take them, the toys he would buy, the books they would read. *You have some other daughter going to crank them out for you?* she'd said in a fit of peevishness last Christmas, and watched the hurt twitch across his face. It was always so much easier to hurt him than she thought it was going to be—than she wanted it to be. Not that he ever believed her, about not wanting children. He was just more guarded now about what he said. Tiptoeing around with words like "settled," convinced that she would change her mind, that it was just a matter of meeting the right man.

Pobre papá, Tina thought, hanging up the phone and heading down the hall to check on the HPLC. She had been his sole source of happiness since her mother died over twenty years ago. And now he was doomed to an unhappy old age, because she had absolutely no intention of ever providing him with grandchildren—right man, wrong man, or no man, as luck would have it.

Chapter 2

Tina loved mornings. She loved getting up in the predawn hours, drinking coffee and reading the latest *Science* or *Nature*, arriving at BIO when the buildings were still dark, the parking lots empty. The heaters would be on, her office warm, and she could peel off the extra layers of clothes that made the three-mile bike ride bearable. Morning was when things worked, when they made sense. When she *believed* that they made sense, anyway, when she had faith that the maze of technology in her instrument lab could turn an extract of sediments into a line on a strip of graph paper, and the line might mean something. A reductionist ride through an instrument, the rise and fall of a recorder pen, and from the merest of molecular remnants in the oldest of sediments, she might glean a story, an entire saga, might hear the faint, unlikely echoes of ancient life. Only in those first few strictly numbered hours of the day could science be so optimistic, so uncynical, that one could imagine knowing a thing as unknowable as how life had begun. By afternoon, she was usually more skeptical. Tired. More likely to fail. Unless, of course, she took a nap. Or drank the strong Uruguayan tea her father kept her supplied with. Or both.

It was almost noon now, and she had spent this entire Saturday morning in her office, the radio in the main lab across the hall tuned to the classical station. She had been munching on peanuts, and she wasn't particularly hungry, but she was tired and her concentration was beginning to fail. She was almost done with the project description for her proposal. There was just one more difficult section to write. She gathered up the typed pages she'd scattered across her desk, picked up a pencil, and started paging through what she'd written so far, most of it about developing her new method.

It all sounded so neat and logical, laid out in the proposal, after the fact, as if she'd known what she was doing. As if she hadn't done everything ass backward. As if she'd actually set out to find a way of telling the temperature of prehistoric seawater.

She'd come to BIO after a two-year stint as a postdoc in Santa Barbara, working on someone else's project, funded by someone else's grant to study the process of petroleum formation, analyzing the organic-rich sediments of continental margins and ancient swamplands. That was what most organic geochemists did. Petroleum was where the field had evolved, its bread and butter. But it wasn't what Tina wanted to do.

She'd had the vague idea that she could address oceanographers' questions—big sprawling questions about the dynamic history of oceans and continents, the evolution of climate and global chemical cycles—using an organic geochemist's techniques. She had been enjoying a maverick freedom at BIO, using her jerry-rigged HPLC-Mass Spec to study deep sea sediments from areas where life was so sparse and the sediments so notoriously low in organics that no sane organic geochemist would bother with them. Six months ago, she had just been exploring. She had analyzed an eclectic array of samples from the Deep Sea Drilling Project cores—sediments of various age, from various oceans—looking for traces of organic chemicals that might survive bacterial and chemical breakdown with enough structure intact to be traced to the organisms that made them, molecules that could persist in the sediments for millions of years and serve as "biomarkers" or chemical fossils.

There was a particular group of fat molecules, a group of lipids that had unusually long carbon chains and, oddly, a preponderance of double bonds. Once she'd identified them, Tina found traces of the lipids in all of the sediments she analyzed, from the most ancient to recent, from equatorial to Arctic. The double bonds were what really caught her attention, because double bonds were usually reduced to single in the early stages of decomposition and decay, and one didn't expect to find many in sediments as old as the ones she found the lipids in.

Even now, as Tina scanned the pages of her project description, the chromatograms and graphs where the story of finding the lipids was reduced to its result, its final chapter, she felt the little buzz, the nagging intuition those double bonds had roused.

Suspecting that the lipids originated in some kind of phytoplankton, she'd spent weeks filtering plankton from sea water and from laboratory cultures that she begged off of BIO's biologists—but she found no evidence of the lipids or their source in any living thing. She decided that she was wrong, that they must come from some sort of sediment bacteria, and she had given up hope of tracing them to any useful source—of tracing them at all—when she walked into the BIO library one day and picked up a journal that someone had left lying out on a table. It was an obscure botany journal that Tina had never heard of, which was probably why she picked it up and started leafing through it, lingering idly, the way her father used to do with mail-order catalogs at the breakfast table, without intending to buy anything.

There'd been a measure of intuition involved in the creation of this method, Tina thought now. A measure of pure stubbornness. A very large measure of luck. And love—she'd been bewitched by the pretty pictures in that journal, love at first sight.

The caption said they were electron micrographs of three new species of marine blue-green algae, or "cyanobacteria" as the author preferred to call them, and there was no reason but love at first sight to explain why Tina sat herself down to read that article. Written by someone named Roy Shimohata from the botany department of a small university in Illinois, it simply described the new species of phytoplankton, which were so small that he included them in a new size class, the picoplankton. Nothing was known about their ecology or abundance or distribution, but one thing was clear: these picoplankton were so small they went right through the finest plankton filter, which was why they had, until now, eluded discovery.

Tina, who had just spent three weeks hunting for her lipids in plankton filtered from seawater, went back to work. Using ultra fine-pored filters made for purifying solvents, she found her lipids in the first seawater sample she analyzed. When she called Roy Shimohata to request extracts from his cultures, he was overjoyed. Oceanographers had ignored his paper, he told her. Three new species of marine cyanobacteria, in a completely new size group, and marine biologists had written them off as a botanical curiosity!

Two of the beguiling portraits from Roy's article were taped to the wall behind her desk now, and she thought briefly about including them in the project description. She spun her chair around to look at them. One showed a cluster of spheres, the other several ovoids nosing up against each other. They always seemed happy to her, these transparent blue-green bits of life, joyful, almost festive. Sometimes she was envious of Roy Shimohata, whose job was to watch them live. All she ever got were solvent extracts of their carcasses. Tina turned back to her desk to read through the last pages of her manuscript. With Roy's article listed in the appendix, there was really no need to include the electron micrographs.

She'd found her entire contingent of sediment lipids in the first extract Roy sent her. They came from the picoplankton cell walls, as it turned out, but only when Roy sent extracts of cultures grown at different temperatures did the lipids reveal their true significance as biomarkers and give birth to Tina's "Saturation Index"—the star feature of her grant proposal. The picoplankton responded to changing temperature by increasing or decreasing the number of double bonds—the degree of saturation—in their cell-wall fats. They used the lipids like jackets, converting the lightweight windbreaker model into a wool coat when the water got a little nippy, beefing it up to the superduper down parka when they started seeing icebergs. They had, apparently, been doing this for eons. The sturdy jackets persisted long after their makers died or were eaten: in the slow rain of decaying particles and fecal pellets falling from surface to sea floor, the picoplankton lipids resisted decay, settled into the sediment, and were buried, remaining like artifacts to attest the climate of their time. Tina's Saturation Index was just a temperature rating for the jackets, the ratio of double to single bonds in the lipids. She'd used Roy's culture extracts to calibrate it, and she was proposing to augment that with analyses of the lipids in recent sediments, work she'd already started.

Tina pushed aside the pile of typed pages and set a tablet of lined yellow paper in front of her. She still needed to describe how she planned to use the Saturation Index to study paleoclimates. She needed to discuss the periods of time she wanted to study, and talk about how her work would relate to other studies. And she needed to write a conclusion expounding the virtues and universality of her biomarker techniques. She stared at the blank page for a moment, and then she stood up and stretched, eyeing the easy chair in the corner of her office. It was an ugly, musty-smelling thing left by some prior occupant, but it was big and comfortable, and Tina had gotten in the habit of curling up for an afternoon nap whenever she found herself doing things like staring at a blank page. The naps weren't necessarily a bad thing, given that she liked to get up at four in the morning, and they rarely lasted more than twenty minutes, but she usually tried to resist. Right now what she wanted was something to wake her up, clear her mind. She went over to the little table against the wall where she kept an electric burner and a kettle, a stash of coffee, and a bag of the *yerba mate* her father sent her from Los Angeles.

The problem with this part of the proposal, Tina thought as she waited for the water to boil, was that what she *wanted* to do was one thing—and what she could realistically do in the near future was limited by the samples she could get from the Deep Sea Drilling Project's collection of sediment cores. She wished she had known enough to put in a proposal for Sylvia Orloff's cruise on the new drill ship. But when proposals for the *Explorer* cruise were solicited, Tina was still a postdoc in Santa Barbara, her paleoclimate method not even a glimmer in her eye. Maybe, she thought, she would talk to Orloff anyway, maybe there was still some chance.

She filled her *mate* gourd with *yerba* and poured in the hot water, watching the foam rise and subside, thinking about the past hundred and fifty million years of global climate—what they knew, what they thought they knew, what they didn't know. Most of what they knew came from the carbonate fossil shells of phytoplankton and zooplankton, usually coccoliths or formanifera, in deep sea sediment cores. Different species preferred different water temperatures, and paleontologists could estimate past temperatures from the species they found in the cores. The other widely used indicator of paleoclimate, the oxygen isotope method, relied on the chemistry of the carbonate shells. The problem, Tina thought as she topped off the *mate* with more water, was that under certain conditions the carbonate dissolved before reaching the sea floor. There were periods of time and areas of the sea where the coccoliths and forams had left no record in the sediments. She slipped her silver *mate* straw into the gourd and sat down at her desk.

It was the big picture that was interesting, the progression from then to now, the why and wherefore of it. She sucked on the straw, relishing the intense bitterness of the *yerba*'s first wash, and then she'transferred the gourd to her left hand and nudged the tablet around to a horizontal position. She drew a line just below the top edge of the page, starting on the left and ending in the middle: the Cretaceous climate, homogeneous and unchanging, from pole to pole, ocean surface to ocean deep, moment to moment—a straight line, seventy million years of warmth—the monotonous world of the dinosaurs. Tina sucked the gourd dry and set it aside. She drew two short lines like an upended equals sign to mark the sudden end of that world, sixty-five million years ago. A mysterious holocaust. Life's most recent brush with demise. The latest theory blamed a giant asteroid. Tina sketched a little mushroom cloud. Added a question mark. A short dark age, the boundary between the Cretaceous and Tertiary periods, the KT boundary, as German scientists had named it. She colored in the equals sign, turning it into a black gash at the end of her line. That's how she imagined it in the sediments, a dark narrow band, a sudden lack of white carbonate fossils. She left the gash and slid her hand down to the bottom right-hand corner of the page, where she drew a two-million-year zigzag. The Quaternary period, a mere blip in time, so far. Man's world.

Like the Cretaceous line, Tina's zigzag sloped neither up nor down, but that was the only similarity. This Quaternary world was cold and unpredictable, a precarious balance of zigs and zags—a difficult place for survival. On average it was colder than anything that had come before, but how could one speak of averages in such a fickle world? It was dynamic and diverse in both time and space, with its freezing poles and steaming tropics, an ocean that moved in great impenetrable layers of warm and cold, glaciers that advanced and retreated in cycles. . . . Tina drew an ice cube over the zigzag. She tried to draw the earth orbiting around the sun to show the periodic variations in the orbit corresponding to the zigs and zags in climate, the periodic ice ages—and gave up. Everyone agreed now that it was only part of the explanation. She drew a bubble next to her orbiting planet and wrote "CO_2" in it. There was spectacular new evidence from ice cores drilled in Greenland and Antarctica that the greenhouse effect of CO_2 had played a role. Tina drew a little question mark in the bubble with the CO_2, because there were still doubts about the accuracy of the analyses.

She looked at the zigzag on the bottom right-hand corner of her tablet, at the black gash up near the top where she'd left the warm Cretaceous line hanging. You'd need some heavy duty cooling to connect the two. Of course, there was sixty million years for it to happen in. But where exactly did it start? Did it begin there at the gash, the KT boundary? Could you blame an asteroid for triggering all that change, forcing the climate system to reinvent itself? It was tempting. But they didn't know that the cooling had started there. Some people thought it started earlier, that the Cretaceous line shouldn't be so flat. Some thought it started later. Tina drew a question mark next to the gash. Then she slid her hand from gash to zigzag, sketching a light, tentative, sloping line. Actually, what data there was indicated that the cooling was stepwise. She drew a darker line over the top of the first, like broad steps leading down from a porch: a steep, three-million-year drop to a wide, gently sloping plateau, then another sudden drop, another plateau, three times. What triggered the drops? What stopped them? Separating continents, land drifting north, oceans divided and defined, deep sea circulation changing? Volcanism? CO_2? She drew a mid-ocean ridge with arrows for the spreading sea floor, the moving continents. She drew a volcano and a plume of dust and gas coming out its top. How did you separate out cause and effect, define the heroes and heroines of each change, on each time scale?

Tina leaned back from her desk. The *mate* hadn't worked yet and she was still sleepy. She pulled her feet up to the edge of the chair and hugged her legs, peering over her knees at the graph on her desk. She reached out and tilted the tablet up on edge. The best data available was for the zigzags down there on the right—they could tell from the oxygen isotopes, among other things, when glaciers had advanced or retreated. But they didn't know when ice had first appeared, when a permanent cover began to accumulate at the poles. It was probably before the zigzags really got going. Tina set the tablet back down, dropped her feet to the floor, and drew another ice cube during the last cooling step about fifteen million years ago. She froze a question mark in the middle of it because she was just guessing at where it should go. Actually, there were questions about everything. Some people were even saying that the Cretaceous really wasn't all that warm. Tina punctuated her Cretaceous line with more question marks, and then she set her elbows on the desk and leaned her chin in her hands, looking down at her handiwork. So many question marks. They looked like little seahorses dancing about the page. She sighed and laid her head down on the desk, her cheek flat against the tablet.

She's walking the line, one foot placed carefully in front of the other, like a gymnast on a balance beam, her eyes fixed on the line in front of her—and then it disappears. It's there, and then suddenly not there, not under, behind, or in front of her, not anywhere. Tina has no idea what to do, and she's just standing there like a fool when a seahorse comes up behind her and nuzzles her neck. She spins around, startled, but it seems friendly enough. There seem to be seahorses all over the place, moving toward her now, gathering round and inviting her to climb onto their backs, promising to take her wherever she wants to go. But that's the problem. She doesn't know where she wants to go. How can she know, if she doesn't even know what's out there? The seahorses are all vying for the honor of being chosen, and she tries to choose by color, thinks maybe she'd like a green one, or perhaps blue, but she can't tell what color they are, they seem to change, blue green red purple—transparent! They're all transparent, which seems a little risky, and they're not much bigger than she is, but she has to do something because there aren't any more lines to walk and she can't stand here all day balanced on this single, infinitely small point. She wraps her arms around the neck of the nearest seahorse and nestles up against its scaly back with her legs wrapped around its tail, its little fins fanning the water next to her breasts. It turns out to be great fun, riding piggy-back on a seahorse. She tosses back her head, laughing with pleasure, and the sudden motion sends her mount tumbling tail over head in a dizzying backwards sum-mersault—

Tina awoke with a start, suddenly lifting her head off the desk. She picked up her pencil and looked at the tablet peppered with question marks. She rounded a few noses, curled a few tails. And then she flipped back the page to a fresh sheet and launched into a brief overview of the doodles on her graph, an inventory of the DSDP cores to be analyzed, and the possibilities for future studies. By the time she started typing, the caffeine-like *mateina* had taken effect and she was sitting on the edge of her chair, wide awake and focused on choosing the words that would secure her job at BIO for the next two years.

Not only did her biomarker work expand the boundaries of her field and move it into the mainstream of the earth sciences and oceanography, Tina noted in her conclusion, but it was a whole new style of doing organic geochemistry. She described two novel uses for another of her biomarkers, a chiral hydrocarbon that petroleum geologists could use to divine the history of petroleum source rocks. This was an idea she'd had during a recent seminar on petroleum chemistry—an idle attempt to solve a problem she wasn't much interested in, not something she planned to develop—but it was clever, and it exemplified the broad base of interest for her work, one of the National Science Foundation's funding criteria.

Tina skimmed through the NSF guidelines pamphlet one last time and looked over her proposal. Paleotemperatures, petroleum geology, dating of sedimentary rocks—it was abundantly clear that her work would have "substantial impact" on progress not only in her own field, but across the board in the earth sciences. And the project's "intrinsic merit" was obvious. She typed the last few pages, and then she gathered up the manuscript and supporting materials, slipped the bundle into her knapsack, and headed downstairs to her bike. She had almost forgotten that Katharine was supposed to pick her up at seven.

She wanted to go sluicing along the bluff road and flying down the hill into town, but the afternoon fog was so dense that she could hardly see the pavement three feet in front of her. She geared down and spun the pedals with so much energy that she was bouncing up and down on the seat, the proposal thumping against her back with such satisfying heft that she had to remind herself it was just a plea for funds—not a culmination of anything, but a commencement. Shifting into a more reasonable gear she pedaled slowly along the flat bluff road, and thought about the work she had planned for the next few months.

BIO's small research ship, the *Rover*, was due back from the north Pacific at the end of April. Tina had convinced a shipboard biologist, John Carr, to collect water samples for a study Roy had designed, hoping to learn something about picoplankton ecology. And she had requested DSDP samples from a well-studied core so that she could compare her Saturation Index temperatures with data from the oxygen isotope method. These latter were ambiguous at best, Tina thought, drifting into the center of the narrow road to avoid the potholes along its edge. Carbonate shells incorporated the two forms of oxygen—the scarce O-18 isotope and more prevalent O-16—in a ratio that depended not only on temperature, but also on the background ratio of the two isotopes in the sea, which depended on rain and evaporation, and most significantly, how much ice there had been at the poles. She heard a car approaching and veered back to the edge of the road, bouncing over the potholes. Her Saturation Index was independent of all those factors. And it didn't require carbonate fossils . . . just lipids from picoplankton no one knew anything about. The car slowed alongside her, and Tina turned to see a huge, familiar white boat of an American car floating by, its headlights illuminating the mist like some sort of maritime visitation.

Garrett leaned over and rolled down the passenger window. "You want a ride?"

Tina smiled and waved him on, calling out thanks and shaking her head. But Garrett stopped the car in the middle of the road and got out.

It really wasn't necessary, Tina said. She was just going to North Brayton and she didn't want to put him out. But Garrett was headed to North Brayton as well. He opened the trunk and stood there waiting, a slope-shouldered, round-faced man with heavy black glasses, impressive eyebrows, and four lonely strands of black hair combed across his head. He was wearing a thin sports shirt, probably getting cold, Tina thought, and wondering why she was hesitating. She wheeled her bike around. The trunk was huge. She wouldn't even have to take the wheel off. Indeed, now that simple politeness had failed, Tina could think of absolutely no reason to turn down his offer—except the truth, which was that Garrett was an incorrigible speeder and his driving scared her to death. She'd even heard him boast about the number of speeding tickets he'd had, claiming that he was good for the town because he always paid them without a fuss.

At least it wasn't very far.

"I was looking for you at the seminar yesterday," Tina said, clinging to the armrest as they took off down the hill. "I wanted to ask you to look over my NSF proposal before I send it off."

"I'd be happy to. But you'd better send it in before Reagan's demolition crew goes to work on the National Science Foundation."

"Thanks. That's exactly what a person submitting her first major NSF proposal needs to hear."

"Oh, I don't really think they can do too much damage. But seriously, you'd better get that off if you need funding by fall."

Tina released her hold on the door long enough to open her knapsack. The small exploratory research grant she'd received when she began work at BIO ran out in September, and she knew she was going to be in trouble if NSF took more than six months to review this one. "I was going to read through it once more, but I might as well give it to you now." She set the folder on the seat between them.

Garrett took the manuscript out of the folder and started flipping through it, steering with his forearms as they ripped along at sixty miles an hour. "I read that last paper of yours," he said. "Some very interesting work you're doing. I don't think you'll have any trouble—"

"Garrett?" Tina interrupted him, her eyes on the road. "I think the speed limit's thirty-five through here. Sometimes there are cyclists."

He slowed down a little, and Tina slipped her proposal out of his hand and tucked it under his briefcase in the back seat. She asked him what he'd thought of Jenner's seminar the day before. Listening to his deconstruction of the clay crystal theory, she could almost ignore his driving.

She loved talking science with Garrett, though when they first met she'd been a bit in awe of him. He had the most extravagant eyebrows she'd ever seen, angling up from the bridge of his glasses like a soaring vulture's wings, and Tina had imagined him swooping down, tearing her ideas into ragged pieces. But Garrett Thomas was no vulture. He might helpfully accompany one through the destruction of a pet theory, but he would never gloat over dead meat.

"You certainly threw Mark Jenner for a loop with your speculations about photoreactions," he said, chuckling. "And Sylvia Orloff wasn't about to let you get away with using the Warrua fossils as justification—"

"I wasn't trying to justify anything. I just heard something about those fossils, you know, and I was wondering. I didn't realize it was so controversial."

"She's right that the evidence is skimpy. It could be a lot of hullabaloo about some symmetrical mineral formations."

"Well, when you think about it. . . . For something as complicated as photosynthetic bacteria to have evolved so soon after the earth— Garrett!" She turned and looked over her shoulder toward the intersection they'd just floated through. "That was a red light!"

"Yellow. It was yellow when I saw it."

Fond as she'd become of him, there was no doubt that the man was a menace. This was only the third time that she had been in his car and, just as she had the first and second times, she vowed that it would be the last.

Garrett got out to help her unload her bicycle in front of the duplex, and she invited him in for coffee, but he declined, saying it would make him late. Late for what? Tina suddenly wondered as he drove off. Where would Garrett be going on a Saturday evening in North Brayton? She knew he lived somewhere in Brayton's eastern suburbs, though she'd never been to his house. What had Jake told her about Garrett, years ago? Called him an old-fashioned diehard bachelor, or some such. How old was he anyway? Late fifties, maybe sixty?

Was Garrett ever lonely? Tina wondered, peering down the street toward the ocean. The beach was only six blocks away, but even when it was clear all she could see was a narrow patch of distant blue horizon. Today, she couldn't see much beyond the duplex's large bare yard, the pale sickly green of painted gravel, the border of chalky pink along the sidewalk and walkway. She wheeled her bike up the walk and locked it to the drainpipe on the side of the building.

Garrett didn't really seem lonely, not like her widower father. There was something compelling about Garrett's aloneness. Not loneliness, but the fact of being alone—his staunch satisfaction with that fact, with his work, his own imagination. Of course, her father had never had work that was satisfying in the big way that Garrett's was. She went into her apartment and moved through it opening the windows, airing out the smells of mildew and foggy beach, the aura of soured vacation dreams that seemed to emanate from the carpet. But her father had her, a daughter to keep him company. And Garrett? Well, Garrett had friends and colleagues, and there must have been women when he was younger. She went into her bedroom and stared at the small assortment of dresses hanging in her closet. For all she knew, there were women still, girlfriends. She wondered what they were like, what it would take to impose on all that stalwart aloneness. The flattery of a young woman's attention, perhaps? Would that be enough, that cliché? A slender, agile body to hang on his soft, pudgy middle-age. . . . Tina smiled and shook her head, embarrassed by her own thoughts. She chose a short cotton shift, laid out the wool coat her father had given her when she went away to college, and went into the bathroom to shower.

She had forgotten how much she loved to dance.

It was as though her limbs were being released one by one, muscles freed from the confinement of their bones. The syncopated rhythms found her feet and hips, her arms and shoulders and head. She looked at the man moving stiffly from one foot to the other across from her, a friend of Fred's, a postdoc in the mathematics department at the university. He was thin, tall and wiry, which she liked. Alan. Katharine had introduced them.

"You dance well," he said, leaning over to speak into her ear.

Tina smiled and spun away. She looked around for Katharine, but Katharine was up near the stage, dancing with Fred.

The band was Puerto Rican, surprisingly good to be playing at a bar in Brayton, but when the song ended they switched from salsa to a crooning love song. Couples moved out to slow dance, and Tina and Alan walked back to their table, where two of the grad students from Orloff's lab were still sitting, deep in conversation. Tina found her wine and sat down across from them.

"So, what do you do down at BIO?" Alan asked her, sliding his chair closer. "Katharine tells me you're from Paraguay."

"Uruguay. Not me, my father. I've never even been there." She wondered what else Katharine had told him. "I'm a research associate. Organic geochemistry."

"Organic geochemistry?" He held his empty beer bottle up, gesturing for a waitress, then turned back to Tina. "I'm not sure I even know what that means."

"It's a mix of chemistry, geology, and biology." The waitress arrived, and Tina paused while Alan ordered another beer and more wine for her. "It's a young field," she said then, "still evolving. We use organic molecules the way a geologist might use a rock, or a paleontologist a fossil—as clues to the age of a sediment, what kinds of organisms existed, what the ecology was like, the climate. . . . At least that's what I'm doing at BIO. I work with marine sediments from deep sea cores, studying paleoclimates." Alan didn't say anything, but he appeared to be interested, so she went on. "I found a group of lipids that contain the imprint of seawater temperature in their structures. They come from these microscopic algae that no one even knew existed until last year."

Alan nodded thoughtfully. "How'd you get into that? Organic geochemistry."

Tina looked at him and laughed. "God knows. How'd you get into mathematics?"

"Oh. Well . . ." He seemed nonplussed, as if he'd never been asked that, as if it were obvious. "I was just good at it. From the time I was small, all through high school. It seemed almost . . . Preordained."

"I guess I can't say that," Tina said. "I didn't even know what chemistry was until college." She had been studying with the same reckless abandon that graced her relationships with men at the time, aimlessly taking whatever classes sounded interesting—not an unusual thing to be doing at a small college in California in the seventies. Astronomy, ecology, world history . . . hoping, she supposed, to glimpse an earth that was bigger, grander, more vital than the flat one of her suburban childhood, with its disorienting smog, its limited depth of field. But the classes had been disappointing assemblies of facts to be memorized, and Tina was never very good at memorizing things. Then she started taking chemistry classes, and by the third quarter she was hooked. Instead of stepping back for some great god's-eye view of the world, she'd found herself taking it apart to see how it worked.

"There was a good chemistry department where I went to school," she told Alan. The challenge of excelling in that small, demanding department had indeed been one of the attractions. "I got really into physical organic chemistry," she said. "But luckily I saw the light. All that theory—it's too clean. Too tame and constricted, like a puzzle, or a game." She paused and flashed him a smile. "Too much like mathematics," she said, "to really explain anything."

Alan laughed, clearly too confident of his calling to take the jibe personally.

"So I went to grad school in oceanography," Tina went on as the waitress arrived with their drinks. "Which is about as big and messy as you can get." She made a move for her purse, but Alan touched her wrist and shook his head. He already had his wallet open and Tina watched him count out the money. His hands were fine, the fingers long and graceful— she could imagine them manipulating tiny wooden numbers, lifting them into the air and floating them there, arranging sequences and equations. "Tell me something," she said, when the waitress had gone and she had thanked him for the wine, "about mathematics. I can't think of it as anything but a tool for doing something else. How exactly does one go about 'doing research' in mathematics?"

"Sitting at a computer, usually."

Tina smiled, feeling silly. "I asked for that, didn't I? But I'm serious. You can't just say 'mathematician' and expect people to know what you do."

"It's funny, but that's usually the way it is. I say I'm a mathematician, and that's that, end of conversation." He laughed. "It's not like saying you're an 'organic geochemist.'" He poured beer into his glass and drank the foam off the top, his eyes on Tina. "Do you know about chaos theory?"

"No. Should I?"

"Maybe," he said, and went on to explain how chaos theory was revolutionizing mathematics, how every field of science would be affected. Tina was chagrined to learn that fundamental principles of mathematics and physics had been in upheaval for the past decade, and she'd been completely unaware of it. But Alan assured her that she wasn't alone, that chaos theory had been slow to catch on. The math was difficult to understand, he told her. And scientists seemed to see it as a threat, a renunciation of inductive reasoning. What he'd described did sound a little like science without rhyme or reason, effect without cause, though Tina wasn't sure she really understood. She was about to question him further when Katharine came over from the dance floor and pulled her out of her seat to dance. Fred collapsed next to Alan.

The band was back to its seductive syncopated rhythms, and Tina and Katharine danced at the edge of the dance floor, where there was plenty of room. Tina saw Alan turn his chair so that he could watch her while he talked to Fred. She liked him. He was nice. Interesting. Good-looking. She was attracted to him, or at least she thought she was, or at least she thought she ought to be. When he offered to drive her home, she said yes. When he asked where to park, she pointed to a spot on the street behind her old red Toyota, which she'd been meaning to get repaired for the past three months. When he turned off the ignition and got out of the car with her, Tina knew he had more in mind than walking her to the door.

She hated arriving home at night to her dark, slightly dingy building; the other half of the duplex was unoccupied, in such bad repair it couldn't be rented, and she hated that lonely moment, that little flutter of fear before the lights went on and she walked into her apartment and staked her claim. Perhaps that was the reason she invited Alan in—because by the time he bent to kiss her, standing just inside the door, his narrow hands sliding into her unbuttoned coat, she was feeling more ambivalent than seemed reasonable if she was going to spend the night with him. She wedged her arms between them and ducked out of the embrace.

He smiled sheepishly, and Tina realized—with some relief because she didn't want to hurt his feelings—that he thought he was just going too fast for her. And maybe that's what it was, she thought as she bid him good night and promised to get together some other time. Or maybe she was just too tired to be enthusiastic. She thought about the last man she'd had a long relationship with, a physical oceanography student she met during her first year in graduate school. It lasted a year and a half, and then the relationship had faded gradually into non-existence, and he'd married his friend's little sister. The last Tina heard of him, he was doing a postdoc at the Lamont Doherty labs and his young wife had just had a baby.

It wasn't that she avoided getting involved. But none of her involvements of the past few years had lasted more than six months. And now they seemed to be petering out before they even got started. Suddenly hungry from all the dancing, she went into the kitchen and opened the refrigerator, peering in at its contents as if there might be something new and exciting to eat in there. Cheese. Butter. Lettuce. Ham. Orange juice. Her usual limited fare. She took a slice of bread from the loaf on the counter and stuck it in the toaster. So what was wrong with Alan? He was the perfect guy. Maybe she was just getting too old to be jumping into bed on the first date, maybe that was it.

Chapter 3

All Tina knew about Sylvia Orloff's cruise was that it was a big international, multi-institution affair, the first on the new drill ship. And that it would be leaving from Guam and ending up in New Zealand. She had been hoping that Katharine would fill her in on Orloff's research plans, but instead Katharine was enthroned in Tina's easy chair, regaling her with gossip. It was late Thursday morning and they hadn't talked since Saturday night, but Katharine already knew that Alan hadn't spent the night with Tina, and that when he'd called her earlier in the week Tina had made "lame excuses" not to go out again. Tina leaned against her desk now, waiting for Katharine to hand back the *mate*, listening with a mixture of amusement and annoyance to the news that a BIO paleontologist wanted to take the French graduate student he was having an affair with on the cruise.

"You're bogarting the *mate*," Tina said finally, interrupting Katharine's story. She reached for the gourd, but Katharine wouldn't relinquish it.

"I haven't even had any yet! It was too hot." She sucked at the straw and grimaced. "Oh yuck. It didn't taste this rank last time you made it for me."

"Because I made you *mate dulce*, with three tons of sugar. The way my dad used to make it when I was a kid." Tina took the gourd, sucked it dry, and stepped over to the table where she kept the tea kettle. According to her father, *mate* drinking was supposed to be a social activity, the gourd passed from friend to friend and refilled by the host or hostess—no matter that the host was just a father, the friends a single little girl, as long as the

31

gourd was shared. Katharine's gossip was entirely appropriate to this ritual and, Tina had to admit, some of it was pretty entertaining.

"I was thinking about requesting samples," she said, pouring sugar into the gourd. "I was even imagining that there might still be openings on the scientific crew, a way to submit a late proposal." She handed the *mate* back to Katharine. "But it sounds like I don't stand a chance. Everybody you've mentioned is a big name senior scientist."

"Or one of their grad students or postdocs . . . Now let's see . . ." Katharine pursed her lips and looked Tina up and down. "Harper Gibson is probably the most famous and disgusting of the possibilities. You could try an affair with him."

Tina laughed and shook her head. "Seriously, Katharine. I would like to talk to Orloff and—"

"It would be great to have you along, if we could swing it," Katharine interrupted her. "A little moral support in the midst of all the old crony big egos. The question is what can you do that Sylvia might want? The cruise is almost full, and unless she thinks your work will be particularly useful . . ?"

"How would I know what she considers useful? I didn't see any of the cruise proposals and you still haven't told me what—"

"Oh, I just thought of something. You *have* to go. There's this paleontologist who would be perfect for you. He's from Woods Hole, I met him at a conference—"

"Katharine!" Tina exclaimed, exasperated. "Just five minutes, okay? Let's just be serious for five minutes."

"I *am* being serious." Katharine gave her an innocent smile and took a sip of the sweetened *mate*. "If you turn up your nose at this guy you're truly a lost cause. Though I never know about you. Look at Alan . . . But I *know* you'll like Nigel Martinelli. He's in his early thirties, but he's already got tenure. Not only that, but he's tall, dark, ruggedly handsome—"

"Great. Now she's got me starting an affair on the cruise."

"Why not? There's always an affair or two started on cruises. They usually end as soon as you get off the ship, but then that's the beauty. I even heard about one between a graduate student and a crew member last year. It adds a little suspense, you know, everyone speculating about who the women are going to end up with. We're talking over twenty men, not counting the technical staff and crew. And three women, counting you. Not counting Sylvia, which, of course, we don't."

"Two women, Katharine. I'm not slated to go on this cruise, remember? The topic of this conversation? Give me that—" Tina snatched the gourd back from Katharine. "You want more?" Katharine shook her head, and Tina refilled the gourd and drank it herself. She glanced at the clock on the corner of her desk. "Do you realize that I've been trying for over a half-hour now to get you to give me some small insight into what your lab is up to so that I can talk to Sylvia Orloff without sounding like a total fool, and I still don't even know what the focus of this cruise is? Besides sex."

"Oh, well." Katharine gave a little sniff. "You know, this is only the second cruise on the *Explorer*. They can drill through over a thousand meters of sediment, and everyone has high hopes. Sites were chosen with an eye for thick sediments on old basalt, places where the crust formed in the Cretaceous or earlier. People are dreaming of a continuous sediment record from the Neogene all the way back into the mid-Cretaceous. Sylvia is mostly interested in the Cretaceous and Paleogene. And totally apart from the cores, Harper Gibson and Conroy Decker are building some contraption for taking water samples while we're in transit between sites. Lord Almighty, I wish I could've seen the fireworks when they got *that* approved. No one has ever tried anything like that on a drill ship and Sylvia absolutely hates Harper Gibson—"

"What are you going to be doing?"

"Me? I'm doing strontium isotopes in the Cretaceous sediments."

"Strontium?" Tina moved around her desk and sat down. "What's that tell you?"

"We're using it as a measure of hydrothermal activity. Sylvia has a new theory about why the Cretaceous was so warm. Until recently, the thinking has been that it was because of the position the continents were in, the geography, right? But now we have these sophisticated computer models that combine everything we know about continental drift with what's known about atmospheric circulation, and the simulated temperatures just aren't that high. So there must have been something happening that's not in the models."

"I saw those papers," Tina said. "They postulated a greenhouse effect from excess CO_2 in the atmosphere. But when they tried it in the models, they found that even that wasn't enough, unless CO_2 was unbelievably high, something like five times the modern level."

"And if that was the case, then where did it all come from? Sylvia thinks that there was more hydrothermal activity. At first she thought there was a faster sea-floor spreading rate, with more hydrothermal vents and under-water volcanic activity along the spreading centers, all churning out CO_2. Now she's thinking it might have been mid-plate hydrothermal activity."

"Could be," Tina said, considering. "And then again it could have been a lot of other things too. Some people say we should re-examine the data, that maybe the Cretaceous wasn't really all that hot."

Katharine nodded. "Sylvia's hoping we'll get good enough cores for the paleontologists to sort all that out. And her students are going to do the oxygen isotopes on the carbonates. She just decided last week to take one of them along on the cruise, our one other woman." Katharine laid her head back on the top of the easy chair. "It makes me tired just thinking about it," she said. "Not just the cruise, but afterward. The forams for the O-18 all have to be hand-picked—surface-dwelling species for surface layer temperature, benthic for deep sea. And guess who's been elected to help? I'll probably be blind by the time we finish. I argued that the stu-dents should sort their own bugs, but Sylvia says she wants someone 'experienced' working with them." Katharine lifted her head and pushed her hair up so that it fanned out over the back of the chair. "I don't sup-pose it has occurred to her that I got that experience as a grad student myself—"

"I didn't realize," Tina interrupted her, "that you guys were doing so much work with paleoclimates. I mean, I knew Orloff was studying sea-floor spreading centers and volcanism..."

"She was. Is. This is a recent—"

"Anyway, it's obvious where I could be 'of use,' as you put it."

"What, sorting bugs? I don't think—"

"God no—I wouldn't know a foraminifera from a coccolith, let alone surface from benthic. But I have a way to determine sea surface tempera-tures. It doesn't require carbonates. And it's less ambiguous than O-18."

"Less ambiguous?"

Tina waved her hand impatiently. "Ice. How much O-18 you find in the carbonates reflects temperature *and* ice, remember? And since we don't know how much polar ice there was at any given time . . . or exactly when it began to form . . . And now, with people postulating that there might even have been ice way back in the not-so-warm Cretaceous . . ." Tina took a reprint of her latest paper out of a desk drawer, rolled it into a tube, and launched it across the desk at Katharine. "I'm sure I've told you about this."

Katharine snatched the reprint up from the floor and glanced at the title. "Oh yeah," she said. "Paleotemperatures from sediment organics. I forgot you were doing this." She read the abstract and then flipped to the last page and read the conclusions. When she was finished, she looked up and smiled. "If Sylvia thinks this will work, she just might find room for you on the cruise."

"If she thinks it will work? I'll go talk to her, show her what I've got. Though actually . . ." Tina sighed. "From what she said at that seminar last week, she thinks what I do is impossible. Maybe I'll wait until I can show her a curve from these DSDP sediments I'm expecting—"

But Katharine was shaking her head. "That's not the way to go about it."

"What? You think I should just send her a proposal?"

"No, no. It has to be her idea."

Katharine thought for a moment. Then she leaned forward on the sagging edge of the easy chair and waved Tina's reprint in the air like a flag. "I'll just make sure I'm reading this when Orloff walks through my office," she said. "Which she does regularly. And I'll say something like, 'Hey have you seen this? Looks like this Cristina Arenas has a new way to determine paleotemperatures.' Then she won't be able to stand it that there might be something interesting in the literature that she missed, and she'll want to read the reprint."

"And then I stop by her office and—"

"No. Then you sit back and wait until she contacts you and says how she thinks it might be interesting to try your method on cores from the cruise, and you can say, as if you never thought of it, that it's a good idea, etc., etc."

"But—"

"Tina, just play the game, okay? If you want to get on the cruise."

"It just seems so ridiculous—all this intrigue. I can't believe Orloff's as bad as you make her out."

"To tell you the truth," Katharine said, pushing herself up out of the chair and stretching, "I am beginning to think she might be worse. You want to go get something to eat?"

Tina shook her head, and when Katharine left for the snack bar, she fished an apple out of her knapsack. She had finally finished the paperwork for her proposal that morning, assembled the twenty requisite copies of everything and, with a silent benediction, laid the packet in the department mail drop. When Katharine stopped by, she had been readying the HPLC for a run, and now she was eager to get back to work. Still chewing on her apple, she headed down the hall to the instrument lab. Michael had been extracting some recent Santa Barbara Basin sediments she was using to calibrate the Saturation Index, and she wanted to finish running them before her DSDP samples arrived—but when she opened the door of the instrument lab and heard the pump, she realized that the HPLC had other plans, and her heart sank. She tossed her apple core into the trash can and moved to the back of the lab, the frustration so palpable she wanted to kick something. The pump sounded like it was about to explode. The needle on the pressure gauge was quivering at the edge of the red. Tina jabbed at the microprocessor keys, lowering the flow rate.

"Damn." She glared at the instrument on the counter. Sometimes she felt like the thing was alive, manipulating her every move. Even with the flow rate on low it sounded bad. Too loud. Threatening. She almost wished it would explode. But, of course, it would never do anything that heroic. It would just burn out, leading her on, tormenting her to the very end. She closed her eyes and took a deep breath, exhaled, and suddenly found herself thinking of the dog she and her father had when she was a child. Canela. It was an ugly little mutt, always vying for attention, a downright nuisance. But, oh, how they'd grieved when it died! Tina remembered sneaking around the cemetery with her father, the dead dog in a box tucked under his arm. He wanted to bury it near her mother, who died when Tina was four. Canela, he told Tina that day, was her mother's puppy . . . and Tina, at ten, had been filled with regret.

Tina went back to the main lab to get tools and a clean beaker. And the radio. She was a scientist, not a little girl. It was a machine, not a dog. But if it died before she had money for a new one, her grief would be boundless.

The music made her patient. She started at the detector and worked backward, struggling stubbornly with the miniature wrenches and frozen fittings, pausing to listen as a symphony swelled to a familiar-sounding climax. Mahler? Beethoven? Relieved to find that her rebuilt pump was not the culprit, she carefully removed a clogged filter from the end of the column and dropped it into a beaker of solvent to clean. Wagner? She had no idea. She always had this vague feeling that she wasn't entitled to enjoy the music if she didn't know anything about it, which she never did. Sometimes she listened to the announcers, tried to learn, but it was just names and dates, and she never remembered any of it.

By the time she had cleaned both clogged filters, filled a worrisome void in the silica packing at the head of the column, and run a standard solution of lipids, it was after five. "Thank you, thank you, thank you," Tina said aloud as the test chromatogram rolled off the chart recorder. "Now just give me six months with no hysterics. Then you can retire." She hadn't even started on the samples Michael had prepared. But, she reminded herself as she locked up the labs, she had mailed her proposal. And maybe, just maybe, there was a chance she could go on Orloff's cruise. Or at least get samples.

It was still light outside, still clear, and there was no traffic on the bluff road, nothing to stop her from letting fly down the hill. She loved this: the cold rush of air, watering eyes, taut muscles, the edge of danger as she leaned into the curves, fleet and graceful as an athlete in a race, body and bike frame united. She swerved around a pothole, held steady through a patch of gravel . . . Not that you'd find too many athletes riding around on junior ten speeds, Tina thought, slowing for the turn at the bottom of the hill. With fifteen pounds of books and papers on their backs. She tossed a glance over her shoulder and merged onto the four-lane thoroughfare that led into North Brayton.

She had never been on a cruise, let alone on a big drilling operation like the one Orloff was leading. In fact, she'd only seen intact cores once, in the repository at Scripps where they stored the archive halves of the DSDP cores. She sped up, trying to get to an intersection before the light changed. Imagine seeing the cores when they were first split open, unstudied, pristine! A van started to turn in front of her and Tina touched her brakes, which let out a horrendous, intimidating screech. She swerved around the stopped van, its stricken driver waving apologetically, and at the next light, she turned onto one of the quieter side streets that paralleled the beach.

Katharine said they were hoping for a continuous sediment record all the way back into the mid-Cretaceous. How far back? The oldest sediment she'd analyzed was ninety million years, and her lipids had been in full force. She had no idea when the picoplankton first came into existence, but she imagined they'd been around since the beginning of the Cretaceous at least. And its end, at the KT boundary? Imagine if they actually got a good sediment record there, what a thrill that would be, just to see it! The Saturation Index was so sensitive that she might be able to tell what had happened with the climate then, during the die-out. Of course, it depended on how her picoplankton had fared. Obviously they had survived. But to what extent? Had they, like most of the plankton, died back almost completely? Would the lipids disappear from the sediments at the KT boundary, then reappear in the Paleocene. . . ?

Tina cut short her daydream and turned onto her street. She wasn't sure what to think about Katharine's scheme to get her invited on the cruise, but at least she could request core samples. She eased her bike between her Toyota and a truck that had parked behind it, scooted across the sidewalk—and stopped on the path to her door.

There was a man climbing down a ladder from her roof. Another man was standing above him, waiting to follow. The roof was half-covered with new tar paper shingles.

Tina stood in the path with one foot on the pavement, the other still in its toe clip, and stared. She glanced around the yard. The colored gravel had been raked into piles exposing the hard-packed soil, and the area in front of the apartment next door looked as if it were being prepared for construction. When had all this started?

"They're really getting the place fixed up, huh?"

Tina started and almost lost her balance as she looked over her shoulder toward the voice. A rather large, husky workman in a faded red baseball cap was leaning on a metal rake next to one of the gravel piles, looking at her. "Oh—hi," she said. "I didn't even know they were planning to fix it up."

"Really? You're the tenant, right?"

Tina nodded.

"The owners said they were going to call you, let you know there'd be people around working on the place."

"Owners? You mean that guy in L.A.? I thought he was never going to do anything with this place."

"No, that guy sold it. Didn't you know any of this? A couple from New Mexico bought it. I think the rental agency was supposed to contact you."

"Oh. Well maybe . . . I've been kind of busy— Oh god, am I supposed to be moving?"

"I don't think so." The workman laid his rake against the gravel and walked over to Tina. "I'm Chip Stevenson, by the way. Landscaper, nursery man, and farmer in my spare time." He took out his wallet and handed her a card. "I've agreed to be a caretaker for the gardens here, since these folks won't be around much."

Gardens? Tina glanced at the bare dirt in the yard.

"They told me I should be careful not to disturb the tenant," the man went on, "but I was beginning to think their tenant might have skipped town or something."

He turned to say something to the roofers, and Tina looked at the card he'd given her. A drawing of trees woven together to form a fence ran across the middle of it. The man's name and phone number were along the top, and below the trees were the words TREE SCULPTURES AND EDIBLE LANDSCAPES.

"Let me get you the owners' number," the gardener said, turning his attention back to Tina. "You can give them a call." He went out to his truck, and Tina got off her bike and walked it around to the side of the house. The weeds had been cleared from around the exposed pipe where she always locked it.

It was great that they were fixing the place up, Tina thought, but what if they raised the rent? What if she had to move?

"Nice bike you got there." The gardener was back, holding out a slip of paper.

Tina snapped her bike lock into place and stood up. "Thanks." She looked at the number on the paper he'd handed her. "Where did you say they're moving from?"

"Santa Fe. But they're not moving. This is just a second home. And an investment, I guess. They seem like nice people. I've spent a lot of time on the phone with the woman, Sherri, planning the gardens." He glanced around the yard. "I'll be around a lot for the next few months."

Tina nodded and started to move away, fishing in her knapsack for her keys. "I'll call them," she said. "Thanks."

"No problem. See you . . . What's your name?"

She told the gardener her name, and then he went back to his rake and she climbed the steps to her porch. She was just opening the door, when he called after her. "Hey Tina," he hollered across the yard, and she turned.

"You wouldn't happen to know anyone wants a couple yards of pink and green gravel, would you?"

She shook her head. "I don't think so," she said politely, before she realized that the man's mustache was camouflaging a smile. She laughed, feeling a little foolish, and went into the house to call her new landlords.

To her relief, they had no intention of raising the rent or making her move. She talked to the woman, Sherri, who immediately decided to do away with the rental agency and deal directly with Tina. True to the gardener's assessment, Sherri was very friendly. She chatted at length about the improvements she and her husband had planned for the duplex: about shingling the side walls and building a deck, about the contractor they'd hired and the wonderful landscaper their friend had recommended, about pergolas and herb gardens and all sorts of things that Tina had never given much thought to. When she hung up the phone, Tina went to peer out the living room window at her naked yard, trying to imagine it with all the things the landlady had described. It might be nice to have something green to look at out there.

Chapter 4

When Tina got home on Monday, the cement walkway had been broken up. On Tuesday, the chunks of concrete were gone. The piles of gravel disappeared. The roof was completed. Posts were set into the ground in front of the apartment next door, and by Friday, beams had been assembled to frame the deck. The following week she got home to find the entire yard plowed up. Even the narrow backyard had been cleared of weeds and plowed. Two days later a dirt path appeared, the soil raked smooth and tamped down in a graceful, asymmetric curve from the sidewalk to the edge of the new deck, with a branch arcing over to Tina's apartment. Tina's DSDP samples had arrived, and she was busy in the lab, but she found herself looking forward to getting home before dark and seeing what was new around the duplex—there was a certain mystique about the whole operation, facilitated, as it seemed, by invisible hands.

The HPLC was holding up, results from the Santa Barbara sediments were excellent, and the first few DSDP samples looked so promising that Tina almost threw Katharine's ridiculous scheme to the winds and walked into Orloff's office to request a place on the cruise. But she had only run three samples from the DSDP series, and there was really no reason for such confidence. No reason at all, Tina thought, as she stood above her desk looking at the chromatogram from the fourth sample.

Tina sometimes felt she understood the language of chromatography better than she understood English or Spanish, but what was on the strip of recorder paper in front of her was a bunch of meaningless gibberish. It looked like the outline of an old, worn-down mountain range, its peaks more like hills than mountains, each flowing into the next. The peaks represented different lipids, the clump of peaks near the end of the chromatogram the picoplankton lipids that she used to calculate her Saturation Index—but the peaks should be more precipitous. Clearly separated. Steeper. Cleaner. More resolute.

It looked dirty. Contaminated. It looked like a chromatogram from hell. She glanced warily at her open door, as if Sylvia Orloff might choose this moment to come by for a chat, as if Sylvia Orloff would even be working on a Sunday afternoon. It could just be the HPLC, she reminded herself, with some creative new way of tormenting her, but the thought was no comfort.

She slumped into her chair, disgusted, filled with malaise, with all-encompassing doubt. She thought of the grant proposal she'd sent off a few weeks ago, and wondered if it wasn't a lie, a misrepresentation. She thought of the idea she'd been forming for Sylvia Orloff's cruise. But who would allocate sediment samples, let alone precious shipboard space, to a scientist whose data looked like this? It made her tired just looking at it. The fine grid lines of the paper blurred into a blue haze, and she felt the familiar, irresistible sense of falling forward into sleep, the unpleasant jerk as she caught herself.

She pressed her hands flat against the chart recorder paper as if its cool touch might rid her of this torpor, focus her mind on what she needed to do next. It could be that the HPLC column was shot. It could be that this sample was contaminated. Or it could be that, despite all their precautions, contamination had crept into her extraction procedure, or there was something used in sample retrieval or storage, something that would make all her data questionable, unpredictable, useless. . . . She turned away from the chromatogram and gazed out the window, at the bright rays of spring sun filtering through the branches of the pines. It was quiet out there, the herons nowhere in sight.

Doubt could come from any direction. It could trip you up at any time, overtake you, catch you unawares. Immobilize you. Contamination in your samples, data that you couldn't reproduce or explain, conflicting results, even a malfunctioning piece of technology. Doubt was, of course, one's stock in trade. It made for good science. But there was an element of faith involved as well, faith that there was something irrefutable to be discovered, that answers did indeed exist, if not the possibility of knowing them absolutely. It was this faith that sometimes failed Tina, left her feeling like an imposter on her own turf, a secret disbeliever, a charlatan among the pious. There would always be another question lurking just offstage, waiting for her. Another doubt.

She turned to look at the picoplankton portraits on the wall. What did she really know about her tiny chroniclers of ancient climate? Nothing. Why were their lipids in the sediments so widespread, how plentiful were they now, in the contemporary ocean, what was their ecology in the open sea? The *Rover* was due back in ten days, but even the biologist bringing her samples didn't believe the study would reveal anything. She stared at the electron micrographs. How long had these picoplankton been around, when did they first appear, could she trust what they had to say? Even if she succeeded in answering one question, it would only lead to another— really no answer at all. Sometimes she worried that her soul was just one endless, hopelessly tangled string of inquiry, of question upon question. What kind of soul was it that had no more substance than that?

She got up and stepped out into the hall. The building was dead, doors closed, lights off, quiet, except for the music from her radio. Where were they anyway, all the faithful? She went back into her office and closed the door. A quick nap, just a few minutes, and then she would walk down the hall to the instrument lab and run a standard, figure out what was going on. She toed off her shoes and curled up in the soothing mustiness of the easy chair . . . *and she is running down the corridor, slipping and sliding across the linoleum in her socks, out of control, grabbing onto a doorknob to stop herself. The door flies open, and she swings around it into her instrument lab. Closes the door. Stares. The lab looks as if it has been the victim of a suburban teenager's prank. Chart recorder paper fills the entire room in great billowing white swaths from floor to ceiling, like a giant roll of toilet paper come unwound. Tina looks at the section of chromatogram hanging in front of her face. She pulls another section down from over her head, and then another, and then she pushes her way into the lab, searching for the chart recorder, swimming through miles and miles of rustling graph paper, catching glimpses of this single, endless chromatogram, with no pattern no rhyme no reason, only random black tracks in an ocean of white and blue. Nonsense. Hieroglyphics. She glimpses the corner of the chart recorder and reaches to turn it off, to put a stop to this before someone notices, but her arms are entangled and she is trapped, even her neck wrapped and tied so that she can't turn her head to see who is at the door—*

"Tina?"

She bolted upright, shoved her feet into her tennis shoes, and stood up in one motion. Michael had pushed her door open a crack and was leaning through the opening.

"Sorry," he said, opening the door the rest of the way and stepping through it.

Tina reached out a hand to steady herself against the wall. Her heart was pounding and she was dizzy from standing up too fast. "What are you doing here? You never work on Sundays."

"I'm not really here. I'm on my way to a volleyball game down by the pier, and I just thought I'd stop by and get those last extractions started. You mind if I turn the radio down a little? You can hear it all the way downstairs."

"Go ahead." Annoyed, and a little embarrassed, Tina leaned over to work her heels into her shoes. It wasn't the first time Michael had interrupted a nap.

"How's the HPLC doing?" he asked.

She sighed and glanced at the chromatogram on her desk. "We might need a new column," she said. "I *hope* we need a new column, since the other possibility is that we have a contamination problem. I'm about to go find out." She made a move toward the door, but Michael showed no indication of leaving. Tina paused and looked up at him, waiting to see what he wanted. Volleyball? Michael looked more like he would play football.

"I guess this is bad timing," he said. "But I was wondering when you're going to teach me to use it."

"Oh. I don't know."

"Think how much time you could save."

"Of course. But—" Tina paused. She didn't know how to explain why she liked to run the samples herself. Michael was quite capable of using the HPLC. And it was probably something he should be learning in her lab. "Look Michael, I'm sorry, but you're right—this really is bad timing. We may not even have an HPLC, the way things are going." It wasn't as if he was her grad student, Tina thought as he turned away. He was her paid technician, an undergrad from the chemistry department at the university.

She followed him into the main lab, retrieved the vial of standard from the refrigerator, and went down the hall to the instrument lab.

She had been only too happy to delegate the other tediums of the lab to Michael, all the washing and organizing, measuring and weighing and labeling, even the extractions. But it was different with the instruments. They were what set the limits of what she could know—limits that were still expanding. She needed this physical contact—the firm grip of the membrane as the needle slid into the injector, the imperceptible little thunk as it came up flush against the hole inside, her own hand in control of the plunger descent—she needed this connection to the data. Even worthless data. Especially if the data were worthless, Tina thought, pulling the lever on the HPLC injector. She stood there staring at the column for a moment, and then she went back down the hall to give Michael an answer to his question.

She stopped in the doorway to the lab and watched him work, waiting for him to look up, marveling at the perfect order he had assembled around him: the flasks, each with its tiny plug of sediment, arranged in perfect rows in the basin he was using for a tray, labeled in his impeccable printing; the bottle of methanol, a sterilized beaker, and a graduated cylinder at the ready; the scissors religiously returned to their place atop the box of parafilm after each use . . . She walked over and turned the radio off. Michael was ignoring her.

Tina leaned against the lab bench and waited while he measured methanol into the flasks; even angry, even with his boss standing there watching him, his hand was steady, his measurements precise—no back and forth, a drop more, now less, too much, now too little, he got it right the first time he poured. How could she tell this humorless, efficient young man that she liked to stand around imagining her sediment extracts moving through the HPLC column as if they were societies of love-crossed elves? That it helped her understand the data, develop new methods? Intuition was not something she wanted to discuss with Michael. Especially not today.

"When we get a new HPLC," she said when he'd finished pouring, "that's not so temperamental, you can start doing some runs."

He covered the last flask and turned to face Tina, his white-gloved hands suspended like ghosts in the air between them. "When are we getting a new HPLC?"

"As soon as I get more funding."

"Which will be . . ?"

"By September, I hope."

Michael nodded and carried his tray of flasks to the sonicator at the back of the lab. By the time Tina tossed the chromatogram of the standard onto her desk, he had gone off to his volleyball game.

It was even uglier than the sample chromatogram.

She ought to be relieved that the problem was with the instrument, not with her method, that it wasn't some insidious, untraceable contamination problem, that it was so easy to explain, so readily solved. But the doubt was still with her, the feeling from her dream, unreasonably profane . . . as if this trickster of an instrument were the ultimate source of the data, rather than its means of expression; as if the data sprang from the technology itself, from the medium, the intermediary, rather than from the nature it was intended to give voice to; as if the instrument were an experiment too complex to understand, hidden from scrutiny in a black box and churning out data that she had no means of assessing . . .

Well it wasn't. Tina turned away from her desk and started grabbing catalogues off her bookshelf. For god's sake, she thought, it's just a worn out HPLC column. A deluxe version of something chemists had been using for ages. She plopped several telephone-book-sized catalogues onto her desk and started scanning the specs and comparing prices for columns. Two hundred and forty dollars. She filled out a purchase order and left it on the department secretary's desk for Monday, and then she headed for home— walking. She set out walking, along the bluff road and then down the hill to the beach, because the back tire of her bike was flat. And because, despite the patch kit in her knapsack and the pump on her bike frame, she did not want to fix it. Not now. Not today. And because walking, on this warm April afternoon, was not unpleasant.

Indeed, Tina thought, when she turned onto the boardwalk along the beach, walking seemed to be the thing to do in North Brayton on a Sunday afternoon. There were university students and Mexican men in their respective coteries, sauntering wetsuit-clad surfers, a man and a little girl collecting aluminum cans, old folks sitting alone on benches. There were runners and skateboarders and some serious walkers. A group of women in shiny, multi-colored tights overtook Tina, parting behind her and coming together in front like a wave washing around a rock, and she picked up her pace, tumbling along in their bright, companionable wake. A cluster of Mexican men were discussing the weather, and Tina slowed again, lingering, listening to their easy, fraternal exchange, their slurred Oaxacan Spanish. It was supposed to rain again. The men came from a town a few miles to the east, and they were worried about the grapes flowering, the rain ruining the crop—they lowered their voices and turned to look at Tina, and she hurried on, suddenly self-conscious in her bike shorts with no bike. She passed a couple sitting out on the terrace of their condo drinking beer, and then she turned inland and walked the four blocks to the market.

Eggs, cheese. Bread. Toilet paper. Tina pushed her cart haphazardly down the aisles. She picked up a six-pack of beer. She would go home and sit out on her front steps, like the couple on the terrace, enjoy the sun. Milk. Eggs. Chicken breasts. Lettuce. Bananas. Orange juice. A bag of chips and a jar of salsa to go with the beer. She watched a woman in a tailored blue business suit pluck a magazine off the rack, and on a whim she did the same. Tina looked at the cover curiously: a photograph of a blonde in a low-cut blouse smiling lasciviously over a dark chocolate torte. Tina felt a little self-conscious when she got to the front of the check-out line, as if she were buying tampons or birth control, and it took her a moment to understand why the clerk was holding the six-pack, looking at her expectantly. "I'm twenty-eight," she said impatiently, throwing open her wallet. He shrugged and rang up the beer.

The sun was lightly swaddled in fog by the time Tina got home and settled on the top step of her porch with her beer and chips. She surveyed the yard. The wooden deck in front of the neighboring apartment was finished. Piles of fragrant cedar shingles had been set out at intervals around the duplex, and for the past few days they had been progressing up the walls in long, even rows. Tina dipped a chip in the teacup of salsa she'd set out and turned her attention to the magazine on her lap.

She couldn't remember ever looking through one of these women's magazines. Certainly she had never read one page by page like this, pausing only to sip at the beer or fish out a handful of chips. She read the advertisements for anti-wrinkle cream, and eye gel, and firming cream . . . and wondered how vitamins applied to the surface of the skin became biochemically involved. Examining the photographs for an article about how to dress for "the office," Tina decided that the model with no make-up on the "don't" side was still beautiful, and discarded her notion that it was the make-up that did it. There was an interview with an actress who said that nothing in her life measured up to having the baby she had at forty, calling it the "ultimate creative act," the ultimate fulfillment. Maybe, Tina thought skeptically, ferrying a chip to her mouth. She thought of the wave of women on the boardwalk, her brief urge to join them, thought of the foam left on the sand when a wave has passed, how it sank away and disappeared, its brightness hollow and illusory. A baby was anything but illusory. A baby would sit there on the sand screaming and pooping helplessly, its need a justification of its mother's existence, its inexorable growth her fulfillment. Maybe that was why people wanted it, an automatic point in pointless lives. She imagined a graph of the data, an endless sawtooth pattern of pointlessness leading on into infinity. . . . She turned the page. "How to Warm Up a Cool Marriage." "Nancy Reagan's Wardrobe." "Amazing Two-Day Diet." A story about a child being hit by lightning. Ten favorite recipes from chocolate-loving movie stars. "Superwoman: How to be Mom, Wife, and Corporate President Without Burn-out." An article about fingernails.

It was getting too dark to see. The fog had thickened and settled in for the night, and Tina was shivering, hunched down over the magazine. She felt a little sick, as if she'd just eaten the results of all ten chocolate lovers' recipes. Had she discovered some sticky new kind of self-indulgence? All kinds of people read these magazines, Tina thought, tossing it into the trash. Well, women. She tried to remember if Sylvia Orloff wore make-up. She dressed a little like the woman in the Superwoman article. She wasn't a mom, but she did have a husband. She probably cooked dinner for him. Tina poured the rest of the salsa back into the jar. Try as she might, she couldn't imagine someone like Sylvia Orloff reading magazines like that. Wasting time. Questioning her faith in the science god. Like Orloff? There wasn't anyone like Orloff. No one that was a woman, anyway.

Maybe she ought to write an article for *Redbook*, Tina thought when the accounting office informed her that her new HPLC column had left her with forty dollars for supplies. "How to Run a Geochemistry Lab on a Shoestring." May, June, July . . . eight dollars a month? But then, who was counting? She had no idea when she would hear from NSF, but her HPLC column arrived within the week, and she could borrow solvent from the neighboring lab if things got that bad. With the new column in place, the DSDP series was looking as good as the initial results, showing precisely what she had hoped and expected it to show.

As for the *Rover* samples that John Carr told her to pick up the following week, Tina didn't know what to expect, either from the samples or from Carr. When she had first approached him about the study, he'd told her to her face that he thought she was a little deranged. The picoplankton were just a rare botanical curiosity, he'd said. She wasn't going to find them growing in the middle of the north Pacific. He had been unconvinced by Tina's meager evidence of their lipids in sediments from similar environments, but he had been amused by her eagerness and persistence. He had agreed to bring her samples and help her with the analyses in his lab, but he'd made no promises to spare her his sardonic English wit if he was right and it all turned out to be a waste of time.

Tina was the one who'd had to convince John Carr, and it had been her idea to get someone on the *Rover* cruise to study natural populations of picoplankton, but Roy Shimohata had designed the study. He had been the one with all the questions and ideas. The picoplankton were his darlings, after all, his neglected, underappreciated prodigies. How did they respond to environmental changes? To nutrients? To light? What of their ecology, their niche in the food chain? Tina had laughed to hear him go on. Something simple, she'd admonished him, because John Carr had his own agenda for his time on the *Rover*. And so Roy had devised a way of including the picoplankton in Carr's routine study of photosynthetic rates, a study designed to answer his most basic question: how abundant were the picoplankton?

Carr's analysis of primary productivity was a standard one: he collected water samples from various depths, injected them with radioactive CO_2 and left them under grow lights, then calculated the rate of photosynthesis by filtering out the plankton and seeing how much radiocarbon they contained. Tina had simply asked him to save his filtrates so that she could pass them through her small-pored filters and run a second set of radiocarbon analyses. When she went to get her samples, John Carr was still skeptical.

"You want to save yourself some time?" he said, leading her over to the Geiger counter he used for the analyses. "This is what a zero reading looks like. This is what you're going to find in those filtrates." But he had been true to his word and saved all his filtrates, and Tina loaded the boxes onto a cart and wheeled it back to her building.

When she returned the next morning with her dried filters, and he saw the result of the first radiocarbon analysis, he was contrite. And by afternoon, John Carr was converted, transformed, in the space of a few hours, from skeptical onlooker to the third collaborator on the paper Roy would be writing.

The *Rover* results shocked John Carr, and they surprised Tina. The picoplankton were more numerous and active than even Roy could have imagined—and this in the barren open ocean, long considered the unproductive desert of the sea. In the nutrient-poor center of the North Pacific Gyre, Tina's values for picoplankton productivity were nearly half as high as John Carr's values for all the larger classes of phytoplankton combined. And while Carr's numbers decreased with depth, picoplankton productivity remained high down to a hundred and fifty meters, where the light was so dim that most phytoplankton couldn't even survive. In the richer subpolar waters where spring phytoplankton blooms were in progress the picoplankton were outcompeted at the surface, but actually increased at depth.

When Tina called Roy Shimohata with a preliminary report, he fell into a fit of inarticulate ecstasy. *You're kidding. You're kidding. You're kidding. Can you believe it? That's incredible. That's incredible. . . .* His tiny plankton were finally going to make a splash. Clearly, estimates of primary productivity and its distribution throughout the world's oceans, based on decades of measurements, needed to be reassessed. Clearly, the overall primary productivity of the open ocean had been underestimated—though until more studies were done, they couldn't even guess by how much. Clearly, there were implications for biologists studying the structure of plankton communities. Roy set up experiments to study the effects of light and nutrients on his picoplankton cultures, and John Carr and Tina agreed to wait for his results to publish the *Rover* findings.

By the time the *Rover* returned, the construction around Tina's duplex was complete. Nothing had been done to the inside of Tina's apartment, but they had apparently remodeled the one next door. Outside, an odd Tinker Toy-like construction had been assembled over the deck, and Tina figured it must be the "pergola" the landlady had gone on about. The yard itself was a much slower, more evolutionary process, and no end seemed in sight. The path had been lined with large stones. Two huge piles of rich black soil had appeared suddenly, then diminished gradually, the soil spread and arranged about the yard. When plants started appearing, they did so gradually, almost haphazardly. It was as if the yard were undergoing some sort of colonization, rather than simply being landscaped. Tina was a little disappointed when she got home early one day in May and found the gardener there, spoiling the sense of mystery and mystique, the illusion that it had all been accomplished by magic. There was certainly nothing mystical about the burly workman in the faded red cap kneeling in the dirt. It was almost six o'clock, but he was still working, planting seedlings along the new path. He sat back on his heels and greeted her by name as she wheeled her bicycle up the path. "You ever get hold of Sherri?" he asked.

"Uh, yes, thanks," Tina said, trying to remember the man's name. "She's very nice," she added.

"Nice and talkative." He turned back to the flats and six-packs of seedlings he had strewn about. "Ever try this stuff?" He pulled a flat toward him and sliced out a small clump of plants.

Tina shook her head, amused by the tender way this rather bear-like person cradled the delicate bundle of roots in his palm. He parted the soil with the trowel in his other hand, slipped the seedling into the hole, and pressed soil around it, gently but firmly, as if it were a child he was sending off to school. He looked up, and Tina realized that she hadn't answered his question. "I don't even know what it is," she said.

"Lime thyme." He pinched a sprig off a plant in the flat and stood up. "Smell," he said, crushing the tiny leaves between his fingers and holding them in front of Tina's nose.

She pulled her face back slightly and inhaled.

"Great stuff, huh?"

Tina nodded and smiled, surprised by the fresh clean smell of lime on his dirt-caked fingers.

"I hardly even cook with the other thymes anymore. But the different colors and textures are great for a garden like this." He pointed out the various kinds of thyme he'd planted in an irregular pattern along the rocks lining the path. The lime thyme was not only lime-flavored, but lime-colored. "That yellowish one is lemon thyme," he said. "That gray-green one is wooly thyme. It grows into a thick, soft mat, sort of fuzzy. That one there with the bigger leaves is oregano thyme. And then I thought I'd put in some violets and pansies," he said, bending over a tray of six-packs with flowering seedlings. "Give you a little color." He pinched off some of the flowers and offered them to Tina, who was still standing in the path, trying to figure out how she was going to get her bike over to the drainpipe without wrecking his newly planted border. "These're great in a salad," he said, tipping the flowers into Tina's palm.

"You eat them?" Tina looked down at the flowers in her hand. A yellow pansy. Purple, burgundy, and pink violas.

"Yup. Go ahead. They're clean, no chemicals."

Tina put the pansy in her mouth, chewed. It tasted like a flower. Pungent. Not particularly edible. The man was going on about the culinary uses of the flowers, watching her expectantly. "Kind of bitter," she said, closing her fist on the rest of the flowers.

"These fancy restaurants in San Francisco have started using them. To spice things up, you know, make the food pretty. Maybe cooked—"

"They are pretty," Tina interjected, afraid she'd insulted him.

"I guess it's an acquired taste," said the gardener, sounding more disappointed than insulted as he turned back to his work.

Tina slid her forearm under the frame of her bike and lifted it awkwardly over the rocks and new seedlings of the border.

She was making dinner, beating the eggs for her omelet, when she remembered the flowers. He'd said that they were good in scrambled eggs. Tina retrieved the little clump of bruised flowers she had left on the table next to the telephone when she came in. The gardener's card was still tucked under the corner of the phone with the PG&E bill and the landlady's phone number, and she paused to look at it. TREE SCULPTURES AND EDIBLE LANDSCAPES, that was what it said, and then in small print along the bottom "Organic methods only." She went back to the kitchen and chopped up the clump of flowers, imagining her yard as a latter-day garden of Eden where one strolled about nibbling giant flower petals and sipping white wine and admiring the pergolas. She poured her eggs into the pan and sprinkled the bits of flowers over them, admiring the pretty purple and red and pink specks. But by the time she'd flipped the omelet and put in the cheese and folded it over, the specks had all turned to brown, and when she slid it onto a plate and tasted it, expecting something piquant and exotic, she found she couldn't taste the flowers at all.

Chapter 5

No matter how familiar the face, however gentle the intrusion, no matter that she sensed the approach and carefully finished pouring and set down the heavy bottle of solvent before looking up—no matter how mundane the activity or trivial her thoughts, Tina always came jerking out of them as if she'd been deep in reverie and someone stepped up behind her and screamed "boo" in her ear. She gasped and started, though it was just Garrett, standing there with his nose flattened against the window of the instrument lab door, waiting for her to look up. She laughed and motioned for him to come in.

"I have a surprise for you," he said, holding something behind his back as he pulled the door shut.

Tina eyed him suspiciously. Garrett wasn't in the habit of dropping by unannounced. She hadn't seen him in well over a month, since that day he'd given her a ride home. He was wearing a blue-and-white striped sports shirt, black slacks, a cardigan sweater. Black shoes. "What?"

Garrett bowed with studied formality, and then he brought forth a small brown cardboard box with a large red bow on top.

"What in the world?" Tina peeled off her gloves and took the box from him. She stuck the bow on the side of the Mass Spec and lifted the cardboard flaps. There was a single vial inside. She examined the bit of pulverized rock it contained and read the label, in Garrett's cryptic scrawl: "WAR548D." Puzzled, she looked at Garrett, who was buttoning his sweater. "Did I ask for this? I don't remember asking you for samples."

"You didn't exactly *ask* for them." Garrett grinned. "But you did refer to them rather wistfully at that seminar of Jenner's back in March."

Tina looked down at the vial in her hand. Suddenly the label made sense. She was holding a sample from the oldest sedimentary rock formation, the 3.8 billion-year-old Warrua rock. She might even be holding the first evidence of life. "Garrett— What am I going to do with this? How did you even get hold of it?"

"I haf my vays," he said, rubbing his hands together and flexing his eyebrows.

"I'm sure you do."

Garrett smiled. "I know the paleontologist whose group found those fossils. I told him I wanted rock samples to analyze for amino acids. I thought I'd see if I could shed any light on the situation." He nodded at Tina's star child, the HPLC, pumping away dutifully as if it had never given her a single problem, and the red-bow-adorned Mass Spec, which she hadn't used in months. "And I just got to thinking," he said, "that you might have some luck with this set-up of yours."

Tina put the vial back in the box and motioned Garrett toward the door. "Let's go to my office. It's freezing in here."

"To tell you the truth," he said over his shoulder as he stepped into the hall, "I think lipids and hydrocarbons are much more promising than the amino acids."

"Promising?" Tina glanced down at the box in her hand. "I've never run samples this old."

Garrett laughed. "Who has?"

"I've never even seen rocks this old," Tina mumbled, leading him into her office. She set the box on the corner of her desk and sat on the arm of the easy chair, leaving Garrett to sit in the chair behind her desk.

"You can detect sub-picomolar quantities, can't you?"

"Yes." Tina stared at the box, resisting the temptation to take the vial out and look at the powdered rock again. This was a project that would most likely lead nowhere. A project that would get her hopelessly sidetracked. She dragged her eyes away from the box and looked at Garrett. He was exuding enthusiasm. She could feel it floating in the air around him, drifting toward her like a cloud of intoxicating gas. Damn. It was irresistible.

"Sylvia Orloff was right," Garrett was saying. "There's no proof that the marks in the rock are fossils. The isotope study was refuted." He held up a manila folder he'd had tucked under his arm. "We're back to what the paleontologists say, that they *look* like blue-green algae—"

"Cyanobacteria. 'Blue-green algae' is passé," Tina said.

Garrett shrugged and pushed the folder across her desk. "Cyanobacteria, blue-green algae, whatever you call them . . . any organic molecules in this rock would at least be evidence that there was some form of life—if, of course, we can be reasonably certain that they're from the original deposit, the same age as the rock."

"Oh, right," Tina said, rolling her eyes. "A piece of cake."

"That's the problem with the amino acids. They're too small, too mobile. Whatever might remain from 3.8 billion years ago is likely to be contaminated by amino acids leaching in from more recent deposits. But something like those long-chain lipids of yours—"

"Oh, that's pretty unlikely, Garrett. For one thing, those lipids are only produced by a few species of picoplankton, planktonic cyanobacteria. And—"

"Do you know that?"

"Well, to qualify: I know that there are only three species that produce those lipids in the contemporary ocean. I don't know when they started producing them or how long the lipids persist without breaking down. The oldest sediment I've analyzed is only ninety million—"

"Anyway, I said something *like* those lipids. Big, inert, relatively immobile hydrocarbons."

"Maybe steranes, then."

"Or isoprenoids."

"Pristane."

"Cholestane?"

"No . . ."

"What about that chiral hydrocarbon you mentioned in your proposal?" Garrett asked. "In the conclusion, where you sang the praises of your biomarker techniques." He chuckled. "It wasn't totally clear to me how petroleum geologists would find it 'useful.' But you also said something about using it to date organics in sedimentary rocks? So maybe . . ?" With a little wave toward the box on the desk, he left the question dangling, eyebrows raised.

"That's just an idea I had at a seminar I went to, on petroleum forma-tion," Tina said, brought back to earth by the reference to her proposal. "I wasn't planning to develop it. You know, Garrett, we're not talking about something I can just whip out in a few days. Just doing the extractions, identifying the hydrocarbons—"

"Oh well," Garrett said, leaning forward and reaching for the box. "If you don't think it's worth the effort I certainly won't waste this sample on you."

"No," Tina said quickly, launching herself out of the easy chair and laying a hand on the box. "No, let me try. There might be something."

Garrett smiled and stood up.

"I've got some things I want to finish up first."

"Fine," Garrett said cheerfully. "Just give me a call." He moved toward the door, and Tina took her hand off the box.

"Thanks," she called after him. "I guess."

It was like Christmas, Tina thought when she got home that evening and saw the tree by her living room window. A day for useless, but intriguing, acquisitions. She lifted her bike over the rock border and rolled it across the fresh-turned soil, pausing to examine this latest arrival. Just like that, a whole tree, where there hadn't been a tree. It wasn't that big, but the shape was oddly contrived, flat against the wall, with two branches that sepa-rated just below the window and looped around to cross above it. There weren't any leaves yet, but the branches were festooned with clusters of white flowers that gathered the declining light, so that they seemed to glow like a halo around the window. Like white Christmas lights, Tina thought. Christmas in May.

By the end of the month Tina had given in to the lure of Garrett's gift and was beginning the first extraction. She held the flask up, and with a single, delicate motion of her wrist started its contents swirling. She watched the bit of 3.8 billion-year-old powder lift off from the floor of the flask to ride the solvent eddy, and as it began to settle, she moved her wrist again. And then again. And again . . . all the while watching the swirling contents of the flask as if she could see the hydrocarbon molecules danc-ing free of their stone prison, long strings of carbon atoms rising and dip-ping and stretching out their kinks in the liberating solvent, twisting and turning, teasing and eluding her with hints of primeval origins. . . . She was about to walk down to the end of the lab bench and set the flask in the vibrating water bath of the sonicator, where an entire day of shaking was required to free the organics from the rock matrix. Any moment now, she would leave off staring at this swirling bit of dust with such unreasoning and unscientific passion—simultaneously excited and skeptical, knowing she was going to make a fool of herself, like a woman caught in the spell of an exotic and unattainable man, egged on by the mystery, the very unlikelihood of success. She gave the flask another swirl—

"Cristina Arenas?"

Tina gasped and jerked, but she held the flask level as instinctively as a mother protecting a baby from a fall. She turned to look at Sylvia Orloff standing in the doorway.

"I'd like to speak to you, if I may."

"Sure, of course," Tina said. "I'll just be a moment." There was something about this imposing, handsomely groomed woman, in her dark tweed dress and nylons and low-heeled pumps, her heavy earrings and well-cut black hair, something besides her achievements and renown that made Tina, in her bike shorts and dirty lab coat, feel small and self-conscious. She went to the back of the lab and put her flask in the sonicator, wincing as its dental drill buzz filled the lab. Suddenly the project seemed frivolous, and she was relieved that Orloff showed no curiosity about her activities, but rather waited in the doorway for her to come to a stopping point. Tina peeled off her gloves and washed her hands. The woman's stance made it clear that she didn't expect to wait long.

"I was interested in a recent paper of yours," Orloff said as they stepped into Tina's office. "A method of determining paleotemperatures."

No introduction, no explanation, just this tacit request for information. But then, Tina didn't need an explanation from Sylvia Orloff.

She pulled a large notebook off her shelf and laid it open on her desk. Orloff had disregarded Tina's invitation to sit down, so they both stood over the desk as Tina flipped through the notebook, unfolding the chromatograms and their accompanying mass spectra, pointing out the most prominent picoplankton lipid peaks, showing off the mass spectra where she'd identified the molecular structures. She showed a chromatogram of a recent sediment from near the south pole, and one from the equator, pointing out the dramatic difference in the sizes of two prominent peaks, the one from a more saturated lipid than the other.

Orloff didn't say anything. She was more geologist than chemist, concerned with the inorganic chemistry of minerals and salts—she wouldn't know much about HPLC, Tina realized, and the organic mass spectra wouldn't mean anything to her. Tina closed the notebook and hunted for the calibration curve she'd done to correlate Saturation Index and temperature. The original curve, using Roy's culture extracts, was in the paper Orloff had seen, but Tina had added data from the Santa Barbara Basin sediments and from extractions of the *Rover* water samples. She was particularly pleased with the sediment data. There was so much biological activity in the basin and the sediments accumulated so rapidly that a mere five years produced a layer thick enough to sample; the Saturation Index in sediments from the past twenty years correlated perfectly with the recorded temperatures of the surface water above. Sylvia Orloff, however, seemed unimpressed.

"I've been working on this segment of DSDP core," Tina said, rifling through the papers on her desk for the sheet of graph paper where she'd been plotting the results. "The temperature estimates from the O-18 method were published a few years ago." She laid her graph out in front of them, the Saturation Index and the O-18 temperatures both plotted against the age of the sediment. "You don't get an exact correlation, of course, because the O-18 is affected by ice. But you can see that the trends are consistent. And look at the small margin of error, the greater detail possible from the Saturation Index."

Orloff leaned closer to get a better look, and, encouraged, Tina talked on about the older cores she wanted to study and how she hoped to be able to elucidate the climate shifts from the Cretaceous to the Miocene.

"And what," Orloff interrupted her suddenly, "makes you so confident that these picoplankton are going to provide such a reliable record of sea surface temperature all the way back to the Cretaceous? I take it not much is known about them—and all you've shown me is this bit of Miocene core."

Tina looked up to find the woman's eyes on her, an intense green gaze that held her own so that she felt herself unable to respond, frozen like an animal staring into the headlights of a car. "Well," Tina said, forcing herself to look away, turning to the data spread across her desk. "These lipids have been present in every sediment sample I've had access to since I set up this instrument." She brushed aside the graphs and began to turn the pages of chromatograms in the notebook. "Here," she said, unfolding the chromatogram from her oldest sample and pointing to the caption scribbled on one side. "DSDP Site 389. Late Cretaceous, eighty-nine million years." She started flipping pages again. "And here," she said, turning to another. "Site 139. Mid-Miocene." Tina started turning the pages more rapidly. Of course she didn't know, at this stage of the work, if she was going to find a continuous record of the lipids. If they would be consistent and reliable temperature indicators. But she had some damn good evidence. "We don't know a lot about the picoplankton," she said, "but we just did a primary productivity study on the *Rover* cruise, and they are clearly widespread in the modern ocean—responsible, in fact, for over forty percent of the total primary productivity—"

"We may be getting some very good cores this fall," Orloff said calmly, her eyes still fixed on Tina. "We're studying the links between sea-floor hydrothermal activity and climate during the Cretaceous and early Tertiary. We suspect that excessive hydrothermal activity during the Cretaceous might have released enough CO_2 into the atmosphere to explain the warmth of the period, which has recently been called into question. I've got a student doing the O-18 on the carbonates. But perhaps this Saturation Index would give us a better temperature record." She went on to talk about the sites they planned to drill and the types of cores expected, and it was a moment before Tina realized that she was being offered samples. She interrupted then, bursting forth with the idea she had started formulating when Katharine first told her about the cruise.

"If we can get both Saturation Index and O-18 for the same samples," she said, "we'll have more than a firm record of temperatures. In the Cretaceous and early Tertiary, when there was no ice, the O-18 and the Saturation Index should correlate closely. But the formation of ice at the poles changes the O-18 in the sea, which affects the O-18 in the shells, right? So once permanent ice masses began to form at the poles, the two data sets should diverge—not only can we pinpoint the beginning of the polar ice masses, but we might even be able to figure their rate of formation! Assuming," Tina went on, excited now, "that the Cretaceous actually was free of ice, because hasn't there even been some doubt about that?"

"Assuming we get cores that good," Orloff said. "Which we shouldn't assume." But she was nodding, and it occurred to Tina that she might actually be enthusiastic about the project. The woman was so incredibly taciturn it was hard to tell—she was standing there with her arms folded, nodding like a marble statue come to life. "Perhaps you would like to join the shipboard scientific party," she said, but it was more statement than question. "I'll need a brief description of the work you're planning, a few pages. And some assurance that you'll have funding to complete it?"

"I've got an NSF proposal in," Tina said. "But I haven't heard yet."

"Include a copy of the proposal then," Orloff said, moving toward the door. "They have all the forms at the director's office."

"Don't you want to see the instrument? It would be great if I could set up in the ship lab. Actually, I'd just need the HPLC—"

"Lab space is limited," Orloff said, actually smiling. "You've never been on a drill ship?"

Tina shook her head.

"Well, you'll find you have your hands full just doing the routine core descriptions and analyses. Take a look at the handbook that the *Explorer* staff puts out for shipboard scientists—they'll give you a copy when you pick up the forms. But do show me your set-up," she added, and Tina took her down the hall to the instrument lab.

It was almost two o'clock by the time Sylvia Orloff left. Tina was ecstatic. Michael had arrived while they were talking, and she went into the lab to tell him the news. He was leaving in a week, going off to Europe for the summer, but he had agreed to work for Tina in the fall, and he seemed interested and pleased when she told him about the cruise. Maybe she'd make a geochemist out of him yet, Tina thought, though she'd always imagined him in some hot new field of biochemistry, working in a big well-funded lab with whole battalions of postdocs and grad students. She went looking for Katharine to tell her the news, but Katharine was not to be found, so Tina spent the rest of the afternoon preparing her cruise proposal, then headed for home.

It was still clear out, sunny and warm, when she turned up the path to her apartment. There was a truck parked out in front, but no one around. Tina surveyed the yard, but she couldn't see anything new. The best thing that had happened in the past two weeks was this new branch in the path, so she didn't have to step over the rock border. She locked her bike to the drainpipe and followed the path around to the backyard. She hadn't seen the gardener since the day he'd given her the flowers to eat, but a huge pile of steaming, odoriferous manure had appeared in the backyard a few days ago, and he was there now, spreading it around the narrow yard, his back to Tina. What was the man's name again? Hank? Chad? It was something short like that. Chuck?

"What are you going to do back here?" she said finally, bypassing the name altogether.

He turned around calmly, as if he'd known Tina was standing there and had just been waiting for her to speak. "A belgian fence," he said. "Block off that alley." He lifted the bill of his cap slightly and surveyed the strip of soil between the duplex and the back alley. "Some herbs in this little area in front here. Rosemary, a few sages with nice flowers—pineapple sage, Mexican sage. Think I'll put in some leeks too, let them naturalize and reseed themselves. Little clumps of chives. Got some pretty chives. Striped leaves, nice flowers. There's one where you just eat the flowers, nice purple flowers that taste like garlic." He squinted at the bare yard. "Might put in some leafy stuff with color—red mustard, curly kale, some chard—stuff that doesn't need too much care. It'll look nice back here, outside the kitchen windows—smell nice too, once this manure cools down. Sherri was all gung-ho about it," he said, turning his attention back to Tina. "But between you and me, I think you're going to get to eat most of it. You like kale?"

Tina laughed. More edible landscape, as advertised. She had no idea what a "belgian fence" was. "I'm not sure I've ever tried it," she said. "But I like most vegetables. Except maybe brussels sprouts. I'm not too fond of brussels sprouts."

"I wouldn't plant brussels sprouts here. They're too ugly. And they don't reseed." He turned back to spreading the manure, using the back of the rake to push piles of it around the yard.

It was such a beautiful day, a brilliant day—no rain, no fog and not even windy—that Tina just wanted to stand out there with the sun on her face in her manure-scented, soon-to-be-Garden-of-Eden backyard, exulting in her success at getting a spot on Sylvia Orloff's cruise. But she didn't have anything to do in the yard and she felt silly standing around watching the gardener work. She went inside to look for something to eat.

There was some cheese, only slightly moldy. Salami. A jar of pickles. A head of lettuce. Beer. That's what she'd do, she thought, setting a bottle of beer on the counter next to the cheese. Celebrate. She loaded up a plate with cheese, crackers and salami, grabbed an issue of *Nature* that she'd been wanting to read, and went outside to sit on the steps in the sun. She had just opened the journal, when the gardener came around the corner of the house with a wheelbarrow full of tools.

"Nice day, isn't it," he said, "after all that rain." Tina nodded, and he stopped and set the wheelbarrow down in front of her. "Why are you sitting on these funky steps when you've got that beautiful new deck next door? Hell, someone might as well get some use out of it."

Tina looked over at the deck and shrugged, her mouth full of crackers. She picked up the plate and held it out to the gardener.

"Thanks." He rubbed his hands vigorously on his jeans and politely picked a cracker and a piece of cheese off the plate. Then he stood there, eating slowly and waiting, it seemed, for Tina to get up and move to the deck.

She closed her *Nature* and stood up. She glanced at the gardener, who was apparently in no hurry to go home. "You want a beer?"

"Sure." He smiled. "Never turn down a beer."

When she went inside, Tina stopped to look at his business card again. Chip. His name was Chip Stevenson.

He was already sitting on the edge of the new deck when Tina stepped outside. The plate of food and Tina's bottle of beer were set out next to him. He'd left the journal on her porch.

Tina handed him the beer and sat down next to the food, her legs hanging over the edge of the deck.

"Cheers," he said, saluting her with the bottle before downing half of it.

Tina took a sip of her own beer, picked up a cracker and topped it with a pickle.

"How do you like the Chojuro," he asked her. "Now that it's leafed out."

"The what?"

"The Asian pear. The tree." He gestured with his bottle toward Tina's side of the duplex.

She turned to look. "The tree by my window?" It had filled out with fluttering young leaves in a tender, radiant shade of green, its looped branches forming a green porthole into Tina's living room. "It looks nice," she said, and asked him how he'd done it, got it to grow that way. He went on at some length about how he'd "trained" the tree, pruning the branches to grow the way he wanted, and tying them into place while they were young and flexible.

"So is that a 'tree sculpture'?" Tina asked, recalling the expression from his card.

He chuckled and glanced at Tina. "It's really just an espalier," he said. "But 'tree sculpture' makes it sound like a work of art. These rich customers, see, they like to think they've hired an artist to dig around in their yards." He helped himself to more cheese and appraised the yard in front of them. "I have a few that are three-dimensional, that you might really call sculptures. I'm growing an apple tree for some folks down in Marin that looks like a chandelier—one of those ones with the little candles sticking up in a ring. Speaking of apples, what kind do you like? I'm gonna do the belgian fence with apples." He looked at Tina appraisingly, as if he could tell the answer to his question by looking at her.

"I don't know. Any kind, I guess. What I really like are apricots. And plums. I love plums."

"Too much spring rain for apricots," he said seriously. "But I know just the plum. Fact, I know where I can get one in a pot, put it in now." He took his eyes off Tina and looked around the yard again. "The rest won't go in until January, when I can bareroot them. I've got 'em in the ground up at the farm."

"Farm?" Tina said, reaching for a slice of salami. "You have a farm?"

"Yup. One of the first certified organic farms in California. Been at it nine years now. Tomatoes, peppers, lettuce . . . a little of everything."

"I thought it was too foggy around here for anything but cows and redwoods."

"Oh, you could probably grow artichokes on these bluffs, if you had the water, like they do down south of the City. And brussels sprouts," he added, grinning. "But our place is up out of the fog belt, in the hills on the east side of town. We can grow almost anything—me and my partner, Jorge Mendez. Fact, that's the problem, one of the problems. Probably growing too much different stuff to make any money. But, what the hell—damn landscaping business subsidizes the whole operation anyway." He glanced at Tina, then back at the yard. "Couldn't turn down this job, even though they want me to take care of the place all summer. Least it's not as long a drive as some of them. I hate all the driving around. If I had my druthers I'd ride my bike everywhere the way you do." He gestured in the direction of Tina's bike on the other side of the duplex. "You commute to work on that, don't you? How far you go?"

"Just down to BIO," Tina said.

"You work at BIO? What do you do?"

Tina nodded, her mouth full of cracker and salami. "I'm a chemist," she said after a moment.

"You're a what?"

"A chemist. A researcher at BIO."

He stared at her. "A chemist?" He wrinkled his nose as if he'd just now caught a whiff of her toxic perfume. "You don't look like a chemist," he said.

Tina rolled her eyes in mock indignation. "And what, pray tell, do chemists look like?"

"No, I didn't mean—" He shrugged, and looked down at the empty beer bottle in his hand. "I thought BIO was oceanographers."

"Oh, and do I look like an oceanographer?" Tina flashed him a smile, but he didn't look up. "I am an oceanographer of sorts," she said then. "In fact, that's what inspired this beer." She lifted the bottle up to the sun. "I'm celebrating that I got a place on a big cruise this fall."

"I think of a chemist," Chip said, "I think of someone in a little white coat in a laboratory concocting chemicals—insecticides or cleaners. Or maybe pharmaceutical drugs or something." His gaze shifted to Tina's bare legs, as if he were loath to clothe them in this imagined white coat.

"I do work in a laboratory," she said, amused. "And wear a white coat. Which you would probably consider little. But I don't 'concoct' anything. I work with deep sea sediments, ocean plankton. I find chemicals that nature made."

"And what do you do with them?"

"'Do' with them?"

"These chemicals you find. What do you use them for?"

"Oh. I extract information about climates, ocean environment, early life-forms. . . . Climate is what I've been working on at BIO. " Tina finished her beer and looked over at the gardener. He'd stopped eating and he was chewing on the ends of his mustache, rotating the empty bottle in slow circles on his knee. "You want another beer?"

"No. No, thanks." He set the bottle on the deck and stood up. "I'd better get going. I need to get back to the farm before dark."

Tina waited for him to wheel his tools out to his truck and drive off. Then she yielded to the lazy, pervasive warmth of the afternoon and lay back on the deck, her arm folded across her forehead, her legs dangling over the side.

She thought about her conversation with Sylvia Orloff, about Orloff's hypothesis that hydrothermal activity was the reason the Cretaceous was so hot. The idea was that so much CO_2 had been released that it had caused a greenhouse effect—and that erosion and weathering of the continents, which used up CO_2, hadn't been able to keep up. One had to assume that the fluxes of CO_2 from hydrothermal activity and weathering were so large that you could ignore the rest of the complex web of inputs and outputs that constituted the carbon cycle—a common enough ploy when working with geochemical cycles. You assumed that a large flux overshadowed all the small ones, so that something as intractably complex as the carbon cycle could be simplified into a useful model. It was a reasonable hypothesis. And the assumption might well turn out to be warranted—and necessary if one were to make sense of things. But she did find it hard to ignore all that required ignoring.

If you were a geologist, she thought, you might be able to think about CO_2 without worrying explicitly about photosynthesis and respiration. You might be able to convince yourself that, on certain time scales, life was just an insignificant scratch, a minor irritant, on the surface of a mineral planet. A geologist might be able to do this. But not an organic geochemist. An organic geochemist would be incapable of ignoring the very source of her information. If she was going to think about CO_2 as the determining factor in the warm climate of the Cretaceous—and perhaps even in the cooling that followed?—then she couldn't help but be thinking about primary productivity, about photosynthesis.

Tina let her arm slide down onto the deck and turned her face toward the west. A rosy heat lay seductively on her eyelids. If she was thinking about photosynthesis, then she was thinking about nutrient cycles and decay—about how much of that organic material created out of light and CO_2 and nutrients was consumed by bacteria and burned back to CO_2 and nutrients in the surface layer of the ocean so rapidly that it had little effect on atmospheric CO_2; and how much might have dropped to the sea floor and fallen prey to the bacteria in the sediments, yielding up its treasure of nutrients and CO_2 to the deep sea where it would reside a thousand years before circulating back into the action at the surface; and how much might indeed have fallen to oblivion on the sea floor and been buried and lost to the cycle for tens of millions of years . . .

She is floating on her back, bathed in friendly green light, submerged, but suspended in the surface waters of the sea. She can sense the great mass of cold water that holds up her warm, well-mixed layer, but it's distant and inaccessible, a slow dark foreign deep-sea world. Somewhere, off at the ends of the globe, these few hundred meters of surface water get so icy cold that they sink into that world. But not here in the open reaches of the great Pacific, where she basks. She rolls her head to the side and sees a molecule of phosphate bobbing just within reach, oxygen atoms sticking out like floats around the precious phosphorus at its core—she reaches out and grabs it, pops it into her mouth. Nutritious food is a little scarce up here in the sun. Especially phosphate. You have to snatch it up the moment it appears to keep from starving. If only one could live on CO_2 alone. There's plenty of CO_2, a never-ending supply. You could guzzle CO_2 all day all week all year and never move and never run dry—never-ending? How can that be? Is she supposed to belch it back every time she takes a sip? What if she clings to it even when she sinks, falls away from the sun, drops into the dark cold depths and settles into oblivion in the sediments below? What if she wants to keep her carbon forever? Be buried with it like the pharaoh in his tomb with all his favorite liquors, keep it in stock for her immortal soul— Soul? What soul is that? Made of what? A pure carbon soul? She doesn't know. She doesn't know anything, and realizing this she panics, and panicking she begins to sink, glancing down like the fox running off the cliff, and dropping, falling, out of the sun, out of grace.

Chapter 6

Tina had been sitting at her desk in a very proper position, her thighs flat on the chair and her feet on the floor in front of her—sitting as still and upright as the herons outside her window—staring at the letter for a full fifteen minutes now, and she still couldn't quite believe that they had turned down her proposal. Less than three months after she sent it. Record time.

Michael had left for Europe at the beginning of June, and for the past two weeks Tina had been concentrating on the project with Garrett, working at the relaxed, contemplative pace that the ancient Warrua rock seemed to dictate. The yellow pad on her desk was full of notes about the compounds she was finding, their structures and possible origins, which ones had leached in from later sediments and which might be resistant products of 3.8 billion years of biological and chemical breakdown, relics of life's earliest manifestations. She had been leaving the lab by five most days, doing a lot of reading, even taking an occasional walk on the beach. She had been content. Unsuspecting.

She got up and opened her window, as if the ocean air might help her think more clearly. Think clearly? She had been thinking more clearly than ever in her career. She had a new technique of undeniable power, with good, solid support data. She had the rich prospect of the cruise samples, the possibility of a collaboration with Sylvia Orloff . . . her wonderfully symbiotic relationship with Roy Shimohata . . . Garrett's sample. It was unbelievable, with so much happening, that she should be without funding. "I don't believe it," she said to the herons perched outside the window. She tapped on the window ledge, but the birds ignored her. She curled her hand into a fist and knocked on the glass until they finally responded with an outburst of offended shrieks and took flight.

She went back and sat down, set her elbows on the desk, propped her face between her fists, and read the letter again. According to the program director, the reviewers felt that, though Tina's methods were novel, the paleoclimate questions she was posing were already receiving ample attention in other labs. Several reviewers thought using a chiral hydrocarbon to study petroleum formation was a promising line of inquiry, but they said the idea was not sufficiently developed.

Of course it wasn't developed, Tina thought. It was just the sideshow. Not even. It was the sideshow of the sideshow.

"I don't get it," Tina said, handing the letter to Garrett the moment he stepped into her office. He sat down in the easy chair, and Tina went to sit behind her desk, resisting the temptation to peer over his shoulder while he read the letter. "How can they say that I don't have anything new to offer paleoclimate research?" she said. "There isn't any other method for determining paleotemperature that's anywhere near this good. And next to nothing has been done for the Cretaceous and early Tertiary. Even Brian Maitland, who has his nose in everything, has concentrated on the Quaternary ice ages. None of the reviewers even mentioned the picoplankton. A significant aspect of this proposal, after all, is that we learn more about them. And *no* one is working on that—"

"This program director," Garrett said, looking up from the letter, "Joseph Chaplinsky. He's a mineralogist—does something with oil maturation or migration, or some such. It appears that he doesn't see paleoclimatology as a big funding priority." He stood, stepped over to Tina's desk, and set the letter down in front of her. "The way I read this, he saw a few very well-respected researchers already working in this area and funded by NSF, and decided there was no need to spend money on a newcomer."

"But what about the reviewers? He must have sent it to Maitland, and I'll bet you anything that Maitland would find this work interesting." Tina had never met Brian Maitland, but he'd been one of her heroes since graduate school. He worked at Woods Hole, broad-jumping across the entire spectrum of oceanographic disciplines and blithely publishing the most radical new ideas wherever he touched ground. "Maitland's not the type to shoot down a new idea," she said.

"No. But there were six reviewers, all chosen by Chaplinsky. And Maitland, if he was one of them, was only one." Garrett returned to the easy chair. "I'm just guessing about this Tina. I don't know much about this fellow Chaplinsky. Most program directors try very hard not to let their own interests bias them—but it seems to me that is exactly what has happened here." Garrett sighed and shook his head. "Research funds are threatened from all sides, and competition for what little is available is getting desperate. Basic research now has to defend its existence on the same terms as applied research and technology, using task-oriented language. Colleagues and collaborators have become competitors. 'What *they* do in *that* lab is just academic twaddle, but what *we* do is of immediate and recognizable *use* to society.'" Garrett settled back in the chair. "I don't suppose basic research was ever really funded just for its contribution to culture," he said. "For enlightenment. But that's how it seemed back in the fifties and sixties." He made a little wave with his arm, as if to absolve his own nostalgia. "There was this faith that science as a whole, if encouraged, would give birth to new knowledge, and knowledge was always useful. After all, we had just seen the most basic theoretical research give rise to incredible—if horrific—results. The point is that science was viewed as a body with interconnected parts and organs, and no one would think of cutting off the blood to—" He lifted a hand and wiggled his little finger. "To the pinky, say, just because we didn't yet understand what use it was."

Tina was only half listening. She wondered why she'd asked Garrett to stop by. For advice, she supposed. She was hoping he'd have some miraculous cure, that he'd say oh, not to worry, tell her what to do. She picked up the letter, holding it by the top two corners. "There's a way to appeal this, isn't there?"

Garrett came out of his reverie. He pulled himself up in the chair, crossed his legs, and focused his gaze on Tina. "Yes," he said. "But I think I've only heard of one person ever winning such an appeal. And he spent so much time and energy and made so many enemies that it wasn't worth it in the long run. But program directors only have a two-year appointment, and I think this is Chaplinsky's second year. You're probably better off finding some other source of funding to tide you over."

"Such as?"

He thought for a moment, pressing the tips of his fingers together to form a tent in front of him. "What's this 'petroleum application' that Chaplinsky mentions. I don't remember that from your proposal."

Tina rolled her eyes. "That's because I hardly mentioned it. It has to do with that chiral hydrocarbon, the one I said might be used for telling the age of organic residues in sedimentary rocks. I mentioned that it might also be of use to petroleum geologists."

"Ah yes, I remember now—a bit of frosting on the cake, wasn't it? At the end?"

"I was just trying to establish a broad base of interest. For all the good it did."

"Well, it got the reviewers' attention."

"Right. The message being that petroleum geochemistry would be more in keeping with an organic geochemist's talents than fooling around with paleoclimatology."

"A lack of imagination on their part. But I take it there really is some biomarker use for that hydrocarbon in petroleum geochemistry?"

Tina shrugged. "Maybe. That's actually where the idea to use it for dating organic residues came from to begin with."

Garrett folded his hands on his knee and looked at her expectantly.

Tina sighed. "I went to a seminar," she said. "Up the hill, in the geology department. This geologist presented a model that used the thermal history of a rock to tell if conditions had been right for petroleum formation, a way to find oil without drilling exploratory wells. The seminar was misleadingly titled," she explained, with a chagrined little shrug, "or I wouldn't have gone. Anyway, they got into this big argument in the middle of the guy's talk. Apparently, there isn't any way of *knowing* the thermal history of these rocks, which makes his model pretty useless—as someone kindly pointed out. They can estimate pressures, but they don't have a good way of knowing temperatures." While the geologists were arguing about the effects of pressure, temperature, and time on petroleum formation, Tina had been doodling on her tablet, indifferently sketching the structures of organic molecules that might be found in the rocks the speaker had described. A certain common hydrocarbon came to mind, the severed tail of the chlorophyll molecule. Tina had identified it in sediments not long after setting up her HPLC-Mass Spec. While the debate raged around her, she sketched the four configurations of this hydrocarbon, for it was a chiral molecule, one with two centers of asymmetry.

A chiral organic molecule contains a carbon atom with four different atoms or groups attached—switching the positions of any two groups gives the mirror image of the original molecule, creating a left hand and a right hand that appear identical except for the thumbs sticking out in opposite directions. Tina's hydrocarbon, with its two asymmetric carbons, could form four configurations or stereoisomers, two sets of mirror-image twins with nearly identical chemical properties. Life, however, was picky and invariably used only one. Algae manufactured a single stereoisomer of the hydrocarbon for its chlorophyll, but over time—long after the algae died and the hydrocarbon was buried in the sediments—thumbs popped off and switched sides to form the other four. Theoretically. Popping off thumbs was no easy task, and these non-biological stereoisomers were bound to be slow in coming—exactly *how* slow depended on temperature and pressure. Tina had spent the last half of the seminar scribbling kinetics equations in her tablet. Theoretically, you could determine the rates and temperature dependence of the thumb-switching reactions in the lab. Then, if you wanted to know the temperature history of a rock, you could measure the concentrations of the various stereoisomers in it and feed the numbers into the kinetics equations. Or, if you had an idea of the temperature history and wanted to know the age of the organic matter in the rock, you could flip the equations around and find out how long the hydrocarbon had been hanging out doing its thumb-switching routine.

Tina was only halfway through her explanation when Garrett saw where she was leading and interrupted her. "A nice twist on the stratagem," he said. They both knew that the idea was heir to work that Tina had done as a graduate student with Jake, and that Jake had started with Garrett when he was Garrett's student and they'd used the thumb-switching reactions of chiral amino acids to date fossils and bones. "Of course." Garrett nodded and smiled warmly, as if acknowledging some familial talent in a grandchild.

"It was just an idea," Tina said, punching at the button of the pencil she'd picked up while she was talking. "Theoretical."

"Mmm."

"Mmm what?"

"I think you can get it funded—"

"What are you talking about?" The lead dropped off the end of Tina's pencil and onto her desk. "I don't want to get that funded. I don't even want—"

"The American Chemical Society has a special fund called the Petroleum Research Fund. They offer a one-year grant, and the application procedure is much simpler than NSF's, not to mention quicker. NSF takes at least six months," he added, "when your proposal gets proper attention. Anyway, the designation is pretty broad. They take proposals on just about anything in organic geochemistry—"

"Damn it, Garrett, I don't want to do petroleum geochemistry." Tina tossed the pencil aside. "If that's what I wanted I sure wouldn't be here begging NSF for grant money to buy a new HPLC. I'd be working for Exxon or Chevron with whatever fancy instruments I wanted. And making $60,000 a year to boot."

"Calm down. All you'd have to do is develop the kinetics of this hydrocarbon isomerization, maybe analyze a few petroleum source rocks."

"God Garrett, I don't even know if I can *separate* the stereoisomers. Minor detail, right? And the kinetics experiments—how am I going to crank up the temperature and pressure enough to get that reaction going in the lab?"

"I think Mark Jenner has an apparatus that can do that."

"And my paleoclimate work? I might as well forget going on Orloff's cruise this fall." She pressed her lips down hard on the disappointment and swiveled her chair around to face the window, her back to Garrett. The herons had returned.

"You can still do your paleoclimate work," Garrett said patiently. "And go on your cruise. You write it into the proposal, same as before. You have to move this hydrocarbon work to the fore, develop it more—but that doesn't mean you have to eliminate the paleoclimate study."

Tina didn't say anything. She stared out the window. The frustration she'd been feeling all afternoon was beginning to border on rage—a need to cry, to kick a wall, to throw her stapler through the window and knock the birds off their perches.

"What do you want me to say, Tina? That this isn't how it's supposed to work at NSF? It's not. That it's ugly and unfair, perhaps even unethical? It is. But I don't know that it's going to do any good for Cristina Arenas's projects to go unfunded." He paused, then added wistfully, "It would be such a waste."

Tina spun her chair back to face him. He was sitting on the edge of the easy chair.

"This *is* an interesting idea," he said when he saw that he had her attention. "After all, you'd be developing the dating method at the same time . . . and didn't you identify that hydrocarbon in the Warrua samples?"

"You know I did." Tina narrowed her eyes. The look on his face irritated her. His zeal for her work taunted her. "What, you think ACS wants to spend its money on our burning questions about the earliest forms of life? On a rock with a few ambiguous scratches, a few organic chemicals that came from god knows where?" She lifted her pad of notes and let it fall back to the desk with a thud. "Maybe if the world-famous Professor Garrett Thomas sent them a proposal, but—"

"Tina. You know full well I'm not suggesting you center the proposal around the Warrua sample. All I'm saying is that this kinetics study is of interest, as you yourself pointed out, to more than just petroleum geologists. Petroleum is just the buzzword, a front for some very solid, even eloquent, geochemistry. It's a way of appealing to the technological imagination, which happens to be the vogue. But then you know all this, don't you? That's why it was in your proposal to begin with. It was a good instinct you had, a survival ploy for the eighties. You just need to toss the buzzword around a little more."

There was something infuriating about this sort of talk from Garrett. The cynicism in his voice didn't belong there, seemed foreign, unnatural. Tina met his gaze. "I bet you've never done that. Tossed around buzzwords. Applied to the 'technological imagination.'"

"I never had to. You know that."

"Right. You were lucky. One experiment."

"That's true. I was lucky. And things were different. I wasn't vying with the most respected researchers in my field for a slice of a shrinking basic research pie. There was plenty to go around for a young researcher."

"Garrett," Tina said suddenly. "Why did you bring me that Warrua sample?"

Garrett ignored her acrimonious tone. "Oh," he said casually, "I just had to see what you'd come up with." He smiled and flexed his eyebrows at her, a balding demon-faced clown trying to lighten her mood.

"That sample is just a tease. I could work on it for a year and not end up with anything publishable." The pitch of Tina's voice had risen beyond its normal range. "Or I could publish a bunch of ambiguous results and get ridiculed out of existence like everyone who theorizes about—"

"Tina." Garrett had stopped smiling. His eyebrows descended to a dark ravine beneath his glasses.

"I don't have tenure and a name so big it doesn't matter what I do. Isn't that what you've just been telling me?" Tina picked up the letter and waved it at him. "That I can't compete with the big fish in the small pond of paleoclimate research?" A rare red glow was showing in her face, a deep burgundy red beneath the pale brown skin, a slight inflammation of the freckles on her cheeks. She was standing up. "Goddamn it—" The letter crumpled in her fist. "I don't want to run around divining for oil! I don't want to toss around your goddamn buzzwords!" The letter landed at Garrett's feet. She ripped the sheaf of notes off the pad on her desk and crumpled it awkwardly; the loose wad of paper she threw hit the edge of the desk and tumbled ineffectually to the floor.

Garrett stood up. "They're not my buzzwords," he said coolly.

Tina stared at him. She was close to tears. "Oh shit," she said, "I can't do anything without a fucking grant."

"That is precisely the point, Tina," he said, and walked out of Tina's office, just as Katharine was arriving—she backed into the hall to let him past.

"What was *that* all about?" Katharine stepped into Tina's office.

Tina looked at her blankly for a moment. "Oh," she said with an abrupt laugh, "just a little temper tantrum." Her voice was unnaturally shrill, her lungs filled like an overinflated tire: she sighed, the air escaped, and she sat down. Her freckles cooled, her color faded to a more subtle hue. "My grant," she said. "My grant is a no go. As in no cruise. No lab tech. No HPLC. No job. Etcetera."

Katharine closed the door and moved to the easy chair. "They turned it down flat? They say why?"

"They implied that the bases are already covered. Which is total bullshit. Garrett thinks that the program director didn't give it a fair chance because it's not his field and he'd rather direct more money into something closer to home." Tina shrugged. "I don't know."

"So why were you screaming at him when I walked in? That was Garrett Thomas, right?"

"I was screaming?"

"Well, speaking loudly. And using some pretty amazing language."

"I don't know," Tina said, sighing. How could she explain her devastating disappointment that no one was jumping up and down cheering on her paleoclimate research? That the intrinsic value and promise of her science was unrecognized, a low priority, the two-year NSF grant she'd expected to be part and parcel of life at BIO, not to be? "I guess he was giving me advice I didn't want to hear. Suggesting I pursue a project I don't want to pursue. To get funding."

"Boy, remind me never to give you advice."

"Yeah, right, that'll be the day." Tina laughed in spite of herself. "You're always telling me what to do."

Katharine grinned. "Just about your personal life. And you never listen to me anyway. What're you going to do, then? What did Thomas suggest that set you off?"

Tina explained briefly about the petroleum geochemistry project and the ACS grant.

"So what's wrong with that?" Katharine said. "It sounds like pretty good advice to me."

Tina opened her mouth to speak and then closed it. She looked at her friend sprawled in the easy chair, the essence of worldly pragmatism, her outlook concrete, concisely framed. What could she say that would make any sense to Katharine? That the hydrocarbon project was narrow-minded, its goals trite? Wasn't that obvious? Not even the how and why of petroleum formation, just the where? "It's such a banal project," she said. "It's almost worse than the stuff I did as a postdoc. . . . And I haven't done any of the background work for a proposal like that."

"You mean, you don't think it will work?" Katharine said.

Tina shrugged. "The idea is sound. Theoretically, I can separate these stereoisomers on the HPLC, and do a series of kinetics experiments to determine the rates and temperature dependence of their formation. As for petroleum geologists actually using it to find oil, who knows?" Tina paused. "Well, I suppose I can leave that to the geologists," she said, and suddenly realized she was about to parrot what Garrett had been saying, that she only needed to study the kinetics of the hydrocarbon and try it out on a rock or two, no big deal. Talking to Katharine, it all seemed perfectly natural. But Garrett! Coming from Garrett, it sounded like—like sacrilege. With all his sad talk about basic research being out of vogue, having to masquerade as something else to get funded.

"What about the cruise? Can you still go?"

"I don't know. . . . There are some major hurdles, before I could even write this proposal. Like the chromatography, for starters. Who knows how long that will take. If I can even get it to—"

"You know what you should do? Once you submit the proposal, you should go talk to the director and see if BIO will cover you until it gets funded. There's this tide-you-over fund that you can borrow against if you've got a proposal under consideration."

"I've never heard of that."

"They don't exactly advertise it. You have to talk to the director—"

"How do you know this stuff?" Tina shook her head. Katharine was still a postdoc, after all.

"I heard about it somewhere . . . I think Don Hansen over in Applied Ocean Science knew someone who got one." Katharine stretched and sank back into the chair. "What an odd duck that Garrett Thomas is. What'd you tell me? That he was your graduate advisor's advisor or something?"

Tina nodded. "We've been collaborating on a small project," she said.

"Oh? I doubt that collaborating on small projects with Garrett Thomas is going to help your grant situation much. Even if he does give good advice. I must say, that's the one good thing about working for Sylvia. People start associating your name with Sylvia Orloff and you've got it made. Speaking of whom, I suppose I should get back to work." Yawning, she made no move to leave.

"Katharine," Tina said, interrupting the yawn. "Don't you dare mention any of this to Orloff. About my proposal being turned down."

"You think I'm crazy? I wouldn't tell Sylvia something like that."

"It's just sometimes you get to talking about people. . . ."

Katharine straightened up. She pursed her lips and swept her hair back from her face. "If this is all such a big secret, Tina, you shouldn't be scream- ing it at the top of your lungs with your office door open."

Tina grimaced. "Right. I'm sorry, I just thought . . . well, you know, in case I can still go on the cruise."

"Maybe I do talk a lot, but I'm not indiscreet." Katharine's voice wav- ered, and Tina was sorry she'd said anything. "After all, if I didn't talk to people you would never have gotten on that cruise to begin with."

"That's true," Tina said, though she wasn't really sure it was.

When Katharine left, Tina got up and retrieved the letter she'd thrown at Garrett. She smoothed it out and laid it on top of her proposal. She picked up the wad of notes with her ideas for the Warrua project and, without checking to see exactly what she was throwing away, dropped them in the wastebasket—something Tina, with her insecurity about her poor memory, never, ever did. Building momentum in the few steps across the hall to the lab, she opened the refrigerator and took out the vial of extract she had been working with for the past couple of weeks. She paused. She couldn't very well throw it away. She dried it under a stream of nitrogen and put it in the freezer. Then she went back to her office and hunted through the Merck Index until she found a commercial source for the chiral hydrocarbon—at least she didn't have to synthesize a standard. Just separating its four nearly identical stereoisomers on the HPLC would be hard enough. She walked over to the library, to see if anyone had tried a similar separation of chiral hydrocarbons. There was nothing. It would be worth a paper in the *Journal of Chromatography*, if she could pull it off. And if she couldn't, then there would be no project.

When Tina returned from the library, Esteban was just stepping out of her office with the wastebasket. He greeted her with his usual good cheer, and Tina paused to exchange pleasantries, but she was staring at the wastebasket hanging from his hand. Finally, she stammered an excuse and reached into it to retrieve the wad of yellow paper in the bottom. Esteban looked amused and a little concerned, but he didn't say anything, and for the first time in an afternoon rife with embarrassing behavior, Tina was thoroughly embarrassed. She retreated into her office and unwadded the notes, added two pages that she'd left on the pad in her haste, secured the pile with a butterfly clip, and stuffed it into a drawer of her file cabinet.

Chapter 7

Tina was mad. Frustrated. Pissed off. Not at Garrett, not at anyone or anything that she could name, just mad in general, poisoned with a vague, unfocused anger. She knew she should call Garrett and apologize. She knew that she'd been totally out of line, that he had only been trying to help her. But she couldn't bring herself to call him, to pick up the phone and say, 'Hi Garrett, I'm sorry I was such a jerk. I'm following your advice after all.' Because that was what she was doing. She was in a working rage, a productive rage. She hardly talked to anyone for three weeks, didn't go to any seminars, snubbed Katharine's attempts to lure her down to the pier for the summer TGIFs the graduate students had organized. With tight-lipped determination, she was laboring to separate four versions of a single boring hydrocarbon, her anger like air blown on a fire, keeping the work ablaze—work that was become a job, a senseless chore, a task to be done, to be got done, to be finished as quickly as possible. That the chore happened to be a great challenge, however, took some of the sting away.

A mix of the hydrocarbon's four stereoisomers appeared as a single peak in Tina's chromatograms, the twins within each mirror-image pair of hands chemically identical, the two pairs nearly so. To distinguish them, Tina needed to introduce another chiral molecule, a foreign pair of hands, and hope that the new shapes formed of left and right hands joined with right and left would be unique enough to separate. If she added a chiral substance to the HPLC solvent, each stereoisomer would be clasped in its singular grip and washed off the column independently, yielding four peaks instead of one. That was the idea anyway. The reality involved a lot of trial and error. Various additives, with various combinations of solvents, and varying gradients for pumping them into the column for varying lengths of time. Perseverance. Luck. Many hours, days, weeks, even months, depending on the luck, in the lab. Of course, what one tried and how one read one's misses had a lot to do with the luck.

When the first hint of the hidden quadruplets began to show in a chromatogram of the hydrocarbon, Tina nearly forgot her ambivalence about the project she was working on. It was just a small notch in the top of the single peak, but it thrilled her. This was chromatography at its most refined and, for all her frustration and rage, she couldn't help but take pleasure in it. Like a pianist's joy in the smooth surface and gentle action of the keys, or an artist's delight in the act of placing paint on canvas, this was a sensual pleasure apart from the larger satisfaction of music or art or knowledge. She started spending nights in her office, catnapping in the easy chair, waking every few hours to inject another sample. She used the divers' shower in the marine biology building, relied on junk food from the snack bar and vending machines. Four days after that first hint, she had the notched peak divided into two, and the two were hinting at four. She went home and slept one night, picked up a change of clothes, and returned to the lab. After two more marathon days of making infinitesimal changes in the solvent gradient, she had it: four beautiful narrow peaks, where there had been only one fat one.

It was early afternoon when that perfect chromatograph rolled off the chart recorder. Tina slipped her hand under the paper and lifted it up to admire . . . but the thrill was ephemeral. By the time she had sliced the chromatogram off the roll and carried it down the hall to her office, she was simply exhausted, burned out—the thrill gone, her rage used up. She sorted through the week's mail, and then she went into the main lab to clean up.

The sinks were full of dirty glassware, the counters littered with notes and wads of used parafilm and vials of leftover solutions. There'd been a postcard from Michael, which was probably why she was noticing the mess. Corfu, Greece, a picture of a tiny goat-bedecked island in a turquoise sea. "Run out of clean glassware yet?" the note said. "Hanging loose with the locals. See you in September." Tina found it hard to imagine Michael hanging loose. Wasn't his life as meticulously mapped out as his laboratory paraphernalia? She was not looking forward to telling him that her grant hadn't been funded and he no longer had a job, though she knew it was just pocket money for him. There weren't any clean flasks, Tina noted. She covered the acid bath, checked the valve on the nitrogen tank, and locked the door on the rest of the mess.

She coasted down the hill. The task was anything but completed. She needed to design a set of kinetics experiments to determine the rates of the thumb-switching reactions and do a quick estimate to include with the proposal. She should probably start thinking about obtaining some suitable rock samples. But not now. Now she was too numb and hungry, making her way home like a robot following its programming, pedaling desultorily, turning right, then left, then right, thinking vaguely about food . . .

"Tina!"

She stopped so abruptly she almost fell over, yanking her foot out of the toe clip just in time to catch herself.

"Sorry," she said. She had almost ridden into Chip, who was hurrying down the path as she turned up it. She hadn't noticed his truck parked at the curb. Indeed, she had ridden the whole way from BIO without noticing much of anything. She looked down at her thin bare leg and her foot in its blue tennis shoe resting on the hard-packed soil of the path, and realized that she could not even recall pedaling, or braking, or crossing the several busy intersections she must have crossed in dense fog. She forced herself to remember locking the labs, checking the nitrogen tank, turning off the computer and the chart recorder. She took a deep breath and looked up at the gardener, who was not moving out of her way or even taking the step back that would have been natural, but standing there flat-footed, like a huge boulder planted in her path.

"Hey," he said, "I thought maybe you'd been lost at sea."

"What?" She might have been intimidated by the dense bulk of him hovering above her if it weren't for the smile that spread his mustache into a broad fan across his face.

"Nothing. Just that I haven't seen you around."

"I've been at the lab a lot," Tina said. "Getting home late." Her tongue felt thick and uncoordinated, as if she'd just woken up. She hadn't, in fact, done much talking lately. She took her other foot out of the toe clip and awkwardly dismounted her bike.

He looked at her curiously for a moment. Then he unplanted his feet and moved to the edge of the path so that she could get by.

The air in her apartment was stale and rank smelling. The refrigerator was even worse. Tina threw out the culprit can of tuna fish, the half-carton of sour milk, a slimy bag of lettuce, fermenting tomato. After three weeks of snack bar and vending-machine food, she was craving vegetables—salad, broccoli, carrots. And chicken. A baked chicken. She headed back outside. She would walk to the store, while she still had a little energy left.

"That's your plum," Chip announced as she stepped onto the sidewalk. He was standing by the tailgate of his truck, sliding tools into the back. He gestured behind her.

Tina turned to look. A new tree had been planted in the curve of the path. It was a spindly thing, the trunk curved near the top like an old woman's bent back, the three weak branches likewise bowed—a sad looking tree.

"A weeping Santa Rosa plum," Chip said.

Tina looked back at him. "A 'weeping' plum?" She giggled.

He nodded and slammed the truck tailgate closed.

Tina was laughing now, as if that first giggle had jogged something loose and released three weeks worth of unlaughed laughter.

Chip looked at her. "What's so funny?"

But Tina was laughing too hard to say anything, laughing much harder than was warranted, which made her laugh even more, laughing at herself for laughing. She sat down on the curb.

Chip took a step toward her and squatted down to peer into her face. "You okay?"

Tina bit her lip and nodded, trying to catch her breath. "It's just," she said, finally, "the idea of a weeping plum. Purple cheeks with tears running down, and then that sad-sack tree." She motioned weakly toward the plum tree.

He stood up and looked at the tree, then back at Tina.

"Okay, so it's not that funny," Tina said, wiping at her face with the heel of her hand. "I'm a little punchy from lack of sleep. I take it you mean it's like a weeping willow?"

He nodded.

"But it has plums?"

He nodded again. "Will have. A few next year, maybe. A lot after that."

"Got it." Tina stood up and stepped onto the sidewalk, only to find that

Chip was standing in her way again, leaning back on his heels with his arms folded across his chest, as if he planned to stand there on the sidewalk in front of her apartment all day. She glanced up at his face, and then quickly away, caught off-guard by a sudden physical, almost sexual, awareness of him. "I'd better get to the store," she said. "Buy some decent food." She hardly knew him. He wasn't even attractive. He was too thick—thick forearms, shoulders, waist—for her taste.

"Seems like you work an awful lot."

Tina shrugged, her eyes on the sidewalk, the cracks in the cement, his huge work boots with the manure clinging to the laces. There was something about the way he was standing, a quietness or a denseness, that made him seem immovable, rooted. She waited for him to step aside.

"You know," he said, slowly, "I'm about to head out to the farm. Where there happens to be an overabundance of decent food." He paused, shifted his weight. "You could drive out there with me," he said. "Have dinner."

Tina looked up from his boots. His mustache was blonde touched with gray, and so thick she could only tell he was smiling now by the way his eyes crinkled at the corners.

"I'll cook," he said. "I like to cook."

She glanced at his truck.

"I'll drive you back," he said quickly. "After dinner. I can bring my tomato delivery down, leave it off tonight instead of in the morning."

He met her eyes, and Tina felt herself suspended between an uneasy caution, a faint distaste—for this bear of a male stranger who could scoop her up with one swipe of his clumsy paw, swallow her whole—and a maverick attraction. How limited, how narrow her world had become, with its pale, thin, predictable and probably brilliant paper-doll men. And it was just a dinner invitation, after all, at this rather ordinary, wholesome-looking man's home. "How far is it?" she said.

"'Bout a twenty-minute drive." Chip had stopped smiling and started chewing on the ends of his mustache, waiting for her answer.

"Okay," Tina said, when she saw how easily she'd made him nervous. "Hang on two minutes."

She turned with a little skip and ran inside to change into jeans and a sweater, her exhaustion forgotten. She was going on an adventure, a lark! An unplanned experiment! A farm?

There was a large, pale yellow apple nestled in the crevice of the seat, and he picked it up and polished it on the front of his shirt as Tina climbed into the truck. "To hold you over," he said, handing it to her. "Until dinner." Then he started up the truck and turned his attention to negotiating Brayton's bit of rush-hour traffic.

Tina bit into the apple, wincing at the tartness. She looked at it more closely—beneath the yellow skin the flesh was streaked, bright pink and white. She took another bite, half-expecting the thing to taste like a candy cane, and was surprised anew by the extraordinary tartness. She consumed the entire apple, scrutinizing the pink flesh between bites, shocked each time by the sour nip, and when she got to the core, she still didn't know whether she liked it. They were out of town now, and she rolled down the window and tossed the core into the brush along the road, blinking at the brightness as they emerged from the fog. They rounded a curve at the top of a low ridge, in full sunshine now, and Tina looked back toward Brayton. The fog looked disconcertingly inconsequential down there, a pale gray fringe at the base of the hills, hiding the coast and the town, though it didn't seem like they had gone very far.

They turned onto a rough gravel road, and had been following it for about five minutes when Chip suddenly announced: "This is it." They descended into a tiny valley and continued on past a small house and across a creek. The road ended in front of an old clapboard house, on a knoll halfway up the hill on the far side of the valley.

"It's beautiful," Tina said, climbing down from the truck. A huge bay tree grew up from the bottom of the knoll, its branches curving possessively over the roof and porch of the house, its pungent medicinal odor hovering in the air like a protective shield. She turned to look out at the little valley.

Chip came around the truck to stand next to her. "Yup," he said. "It's beautiful. And you can't even see the best part from here." He gestured behind them, toward the hills behind the house. "There's a little grove of second-growth redwoods up there. Most of this area was turned into pasture long before we got here, but I guess that ravine was too steep to bother with. We planted some trees back in there to expand the grove. And seeded native grasses up above, on the hill." He turned back to the cultivated fields that nestled on the floor of the valley. "These fields," he said, "were all overgrazed pasture when we bought this place. All along the creek there, where we have the lettuce, was covered with blackberry brambles and poison oak."

"How long have you been here?" Tina asked, wondering who the "we" referred to.

"About eight years. Moved up in '74. Done a lot of work on the house too, though I suppose it doesn't show. We fixed up my partner's place first, that house we passed coming in." He led her around to the side of the house, where there was a porch and a steep, rickety wooden staircase that led down to the base of the tree at the bottom of the hill. "There's the latest addition," he said, moving to the back edge of the porch and pointing to two black panels on the far side of the house, beyond the bay tree's shade. "Solar water heater. Someday I want to convert the whole house to solar," he added, moving back across the porch to open the door. "But it's so damned expensive."

They entered a large old-fashioned kitchen, and he told her to make herself at home while he called the guy who took his produce down to the city. The house renovations didn't seem to have included the kitchen. The appliances had the heavy, round-cornered look of the forties, the counters were covered in tiny impossible-to-clean tile, and the linoleum had a yellow cast, the floor sloping noticeably downhill toward the back porch. Tina sat down on a bench built into the corner around a big rough-hewn wood table. The place was clean, but cluttered, clearly a well lived-in kitchen—two small zucchinis on the counter, a stray tomato, a bowl of peaches and hovering fruit flies, the table strewn with papers and paraphernalia. The *Brayton Bee*, a *New York Times*, seed catalogues, a Sierra Club newsletter, an advertisement for bird guano from Chile. A small cardboard box. A pair of red-handled pruning sheers.

When Chip finished his call, he went to the dish drainer and picked up a big metal bowl. "I forgot to mention," he said, holding the bowl aloft, "that the 'decent food' has yet to be harvested. We can walk down and get some stuff for a salad. My partner's down there with the guys, picking tomatoes, and I want to check in with him—if you don't mind," he added, lowering the bowl to his side. "Or maybe you're too tired. If you want, you can wait here and I'll—"

"Oh no, I'd love to go for a walk. I've been cooped up in the lab for weeks."

"You want a piece of cheese or something before we go?" He set the bowl down and hurried over to the refrigerator.

"No, really," Tina laughed. "I'm fine. That was a big apple."

He shrugged and closed the refrigerator, retrieved the bowl, and led her down the hill to his fields, which had the same disheveled-but-well-loved look as his kitchen. Lush weeds grew between the rows and fields, the plants rising above them, lusher still. They crossed the creek to a dirt lane that bordered a field of neck-high tomato plants, and Chip started telling her about the different varieties of tomatoes. Most weren't ripe yet, but he described them with a connoisseur's eloquence: there were bright orange cherry tomatoes, and pear-shaped yellow ones, egg-sized purple ones, huge "old-fashioned" lobed ones, and tiny yellow ones that grew in clusters like grapes; there were green-striped, and orange-striped and even black ones. Tina hadn't realized they came in any color but red. Black tomatoes?

"They're called Black Krim," Chip said as they came upon a truck parked in the tractor swath between fields. "But, actually, they're dark brown." He turned into one of the rows, and Tina noticed a red baseball cap bobbing in and out of view at the far end. "I always get carried away and plant too many varieties," he added, ruefully. "I'm a total sucker for the weird ones, anything with a different color or shape . . . It's not the most effective way to farm. And Jorge here's no help at all," he said, grinning, as they came upon the bearer of the red cap. He introduced Tina to his partner, a small, handsome, sun-wizened man, who stopped picking to greet them.

Tina shook the hand that Jorge proffered, and he leaned toward her conspiratorially. "It's not true," he said in heavily accented English. "About the tomatoes. I told him. I said it was too many tomatoes."

"Oh, yeah," Chip said, "you should talk. You're just as bad with the chiles. And flowers. Talk about over-diversification, not to mention lack of demand and— Hey!" Chip snatched the cap off of Jorge's head and set it on his own. "Where'd you find it?"

Jorge picked up a blue nylon cap that was hanging on a tomato stake and put it on without answering. With a smile, and a nod to Tina that had something of a wink about it, he turned back to his picking, and Chip fell in alongside him while they talked about the work schedule for the next day. Apparently they had one regular employee and one temporary, both of whom had already gone home. When they started arguing about how much water the tomatoes should be getting, Jorge switched to Spanish, and

Tina was surprised to hear Chip answer in thick, plodding, but competent, Spanish. Not letting on that she understood, she started to wander back down the row, leaving them to their argument, which was apparently an old one. She stopped when she heard Jorge interrupt it to ask somewhat incredulously if she was the woman, the chemist, who rented the place in North Brayton.

"*¿Esta es la química?*"

"Yes," Chip told him in Spanish. "That's her. Works at that oceanography institute."

"Well, it's a very pretty scientist that you've found. What a shame that she can't be rich too, something extra for the farm jar."

They laughed, and Tina wondered what the farm jar was.

"*Vamos, hombre,* I don't know what you are so worried about. This is a nice girl you have here, I can tell."

"I don't have her, Jorge. I just invited her to dinner is all. I'm not even sure she's to be had."

"Oh, but tonight, no?" He offered to deliver the tomatoes in the morning, but Chip told him he'd arranged to take them after dinner, give her a ride home.

"*¿Qué, estás loco? Aquí tienes—*"

Tina stepped out from among the tomato vines to stand in a swath of sunshine, out of earshot. She tried to remember her other encounters with the gardener. They'd had that one beer together on the neighbors' deck, over a month ago, when Orloff invited her on the cruise. Certainly she hadn't, until today, ever looked twice at the man. It was a little unsettling to hear that she'd been a topic of conversation here, though she wasn't entirely displeased to learn that this invitation to dinner was slightly more complicated than the friendly, spur-of-the-moment offer it appeared to be.

Chip came up alongside her, the red cap firmly ensconced on his head. He handed her the bowl, now containing several small orange and red tomatoes, and led her into what he called the "salad bowl field." None of the assorted leaves and lettuce he filled the bowl with looked familiar to Tina. Pale green, dark green, red and green leaves; smooth, ruffled, flat, and curled leaves; a small round soft-leafed head, iridescent magenta-colored swirls, cream-colored hearts. Serrated leaves from a weedy plant that grew in random patches scattered around the field. "That's arugula," Chip told her when she asked. "Looks like a weed, and after you plant it once, it grows like a weed forevermore. Stuff is so damn easy to grow it's hard to believe we can charge as much as we do for it. 'Course it's also hard to believe it tastes as good as it does. It's really starting to catch on with the gourmets in the city. If we were smart we'd let it take over these fields, make a fortune. But god forbid," he said cheerfully, "we should make any money on this operation."

When his back was turned, Tina fished one of the leaves out of the bowl and took a tentative bite. It tasted like walnuts. And radishes. But it was green and leafy and tender.

He added herbs and flowers from a border along the creek side of the field, added carrots and radishes from the "garden" farther down the creek, and then they headed back across the bridge. He paused when they got to the gravel road, glancing first at the sun, which was low over the hills, and then at Tina. "You want to see the trees?" he asked her, but she was slow to respond, and he answered for her. "No. Why would you want to see the trees? Let's go make dinner."

They were starting up the drive to the house when it dawned on Tina that he'd meant the fruit trees he grew, that she hadn't seen the "tree sculptures." Dinner, however, was beginning to seem like a good idea, so she kept walking until, midway up the hill, Chip stopped again. He didn't say anything, just tucked his chin in and made a series of hollow-sounding noises deep in his throat. He paused as if listening for an answer, then did it again. This time Tina heard the answer, from somewhere back in the hills. Chip called again. Then the owl. Then Chip, and they went on like that for a couple of minutes, the owl sounding a little closer each time, until suddenly there was a soft rustle over their heads, and Tina looked up to see it flying like a huge moth into the oak tree they were standing next to. She glanced at Chip, who was gazing up at the owl as if in earnest conversation—though it was hard to imagine what could be said with this single series of hoots repeated over and over, back and forth, their voices echoing in the premature dusk on the east side of the hill. Just when Tina realized that the echo was a second owl calling in the distance, Chip started walking again, continuing up the hill.

"That's his mate," he said. "Wondering who the hell he's gabbing with down here."

Tina hurried after him. It was unclear whether it was the man who enhanced the place, or the place the man, or if the symbiosis was absolute and equal, or if lack of sleep had made her overly vulnerable to enchantment, but she was, for the moment, enchanted. She looked over her shoulder at the valley, then turned and continued backward up the drive. The crowns of the surrounding hills shimmered like bald men's heads in the afternoon sun, their golden swathes of pasture set off by dark sheaves of oak and madrone on the steeper sides and in the notches between hills. This place could easily be the stuff of dreams, Tina thought, except her dreams were always made of the same stuff as her life. She turned around, just in time to avoid colliding with Chip for the second time that afternoon.

She had the feeling that he had been watching her, that he had only now shifted his gaze to the view of his farm below, but she was too close to tilt her head back and see his face. She stared instead at his broad, looming chest, the gray hair that curled from the top of his work shirt, the belly straining slightly at the button of his jeans, the metal bowl full of greens clutched against his hip . . . the two of them frozen in a stand-off like two creatures deciding which should be victim and which hunter, or whether to sidestep the confrontation and pass in mutual disinterest, like bear and porcupine.

They moved simultaneously. Chip turned aside, Tina stepped around him, and they almost collided again, but neither laughed nor said a word. Tina inhaled the bay tree's sharp, mind-clearing scent, and followed him into the kitchen. She wouldn't say that she found the hairy chest attractive. Or the belly. Or even the curly blonde hair, pressed flat on top where his cap seemed to have permanently straightened it. He directed the making of the salad, reaching around her to set carrots and radishes and a pale green globe with leaves like antennae on the cutting board in front of her. She could smell the stale musk of sweat dried in his shirt. She anticipated the tickle of his forearm against the back of her hand, or the slight pressure of his chest against her head, or the belly, now dusted with flour from the biscuits he was making, brushing past her back—without knowing how she would respond when they came.

She didn't have to decide. She finished slicing the vegetables, and Chip banished her to the bench at the dining room table without having made use of any of a half-dozen opportunities to touch her. He swept the papers and magazines into a pile and set it on the end of the bench, set a glass of white wine in front of her, and turned his full attention to making salad dressing with the herbs they had collected. Tina sipped at the wine and gazed out the window, which faced the driveway and overlooked part of the valley. She watched Jorge drive up in the truck full of tomatoes. Her ride home, she thought, when he left the tomato truck and drove off in Chip's, announcing his departure with two beeps on the horn. By the time Chip finally set the pan of biscuits on the table and sat down across from her, she was starving.

"I just saw this article about the climate," he said, as if he'd been saving the topic for their dinner-table conversation. He filled a bowl with salad and handed it to her. "These scientists were saying that burning coal and oil creates carbon dioxide, and they think it's accumulating in the atmosphere. They have this theory that it might be changing the climate, making it warmer. They call it the Greenhouse Effect." He paused and looked at Tina expectantly. "The article said it's controversial," he added. Scientists have been working on it for a couple of years, since seventy-nine. But they don't agree."

"We've known about the greenhouse effect for almost a century," Tina said, examining the biscuit she'd just bitten into. It contained bits of something green and tasted strongly of garlic. She took another bite and glanced up at Chip, who was holding a forkload of salad frozen in mid-air above his bowl, staring at her as if she'd just revealed some horrible secret.

"You're kidding." He lowered the fork. "This article made it sound like it's something they just discovered."

Tina shook her head, swallowing. "Arrhenius put forth the theory in the late eighteen hundreds. Someone had the idea even before that, but Arrhenius was the first one to formalize it."

"You're telling me that they've known since the eighteen hundreds that we're heating up the planet? Tampering with the *climate*?"

"No, no. We've known that changing the amount of carbon dioxide in the atmosphere would, theoretically, have a warming effect, that's all. The gas is transparent to short-wavelength radiation, visible light—to sunlight. But CO_2 molecules absorb and reradiate the long wavelength infrared radiation that the earth transmits back into space. So the gas acts like a one-way screen, letting energy in but not out. Well, like a greenhouse."

"But the article said that burning anything—gas, oil, wood—creates carbon dioxide. They knew *that* a long time ago didn't they? That we were producing this gas?"

"Sure. But people thought that CO_2 generated by industrialization would be taken up by the oceans, removed from the atmosphere. Which seems reasonable when you think that the oceans contain sixty times more CO_2 than the atmosphere. People thought that proportion would remain constant—until Revelle and Seus came along in the fifties and showed that it wouldn't. Most of the CO_2 in the oceans is in the form of carbonate and bicarbonate ions with a tiny percentage as the dissolved gas, and— Well, because of the complicated chemical equilibria between carbon species, and because gas exchange is limited to the surface layer of the ocean, atmospheric CO_2 can increase dramatically, with only a small increase in oceanic CO_2. And as atmospheric CO_2 rises, that oceanic percentage gets even smaller."

"That was in the fifties?"

"Fifty-seven, fifty-eight? I think that was when Keeling set up his instruments in Hawaii, to measure atmospheric CO_2—when they first realized that it might actually be accumulating."

"So twenty-five years. They've known for twenty-five years. And here we are, 1982, and nothing's been done."

"I don't know," Tina said, concentrating on her salad, trying to get a little of everything on her fork at once. "I think atmospheric scientists have done quite a bit of research, but I'm not that up on it."

"I wish I could say I can't believe it, but it's only too easy to believe. Here we are the biggest, richest industrial nation in the world, we've known since the fifties that we're screwing up the climate, and—"

"Actually, I don't think we can say, even now, what the effect on the climate has been."

"But you just said they knew a hundred years ago that more CO_2 means a hotter earth."

"I said that it has a warming effect. CO_2 is just one factor in a whole slew of intertwined cause and effect that determines climate."

"This article said that scientists were predicting global warming in the next fifty years."

"Really?" Tina thought for a moment. "They're actually making two predictions when they say that. First, you need to predict the actual change in atmospheric CO_2. We have Keeling's measurements, an incredible record of the increase since the fifties. But as for what it's going to look like in the future? They have to estimate how much fossil fuel we'll use. And quantify the uptakes by ocean and plants, the rates, and the feedbacks . . . Then they use these complicated computer models of atmospheric circulation to predict the climate's response to the predicted change in CO_2. Of course, how much CO_2 stays in the atmosphere is affected by the same climate changes that its increase causes, so it all gets pretty messy." She paused, trying to remember a review article she'd read in *Science* a few months ago. She was beginning to find the conversation frustrating, precisely because of all that she didn't know, or half-knew, or knew but couldn't remember. It made her feel guilty for not keeping up on the literature, like she ought to jump up from the table and go read the last five years of *Science* and *Nature* and *Geochimica et Cosmochimica*, issue by issue, page by page.

"But, so what do you think?"

"What do *I* think? Those predictions were made by atmospheric scientists. I don't know enough about atmospheric physics or these computer models to say how reliable they may or may not be."

"But do you think that we're changing the climate? That we're making it hotter? In this article, they said that there's a lot of controversy among scientists. Some are saying that winters are actually going to get colder. The winter of '82 was the coldest on record back east, and some scientists say that's a trend, because of these spots on the sun or something."

Tina shook her head. "There may be some controversy about the warming predictions," she said, a little impatiently. "But nobody buys that theory about the sunspots. Where'd you read all this, anyway?"

"*Organic Gardening and Farming*. They always have these articles about the weather."

"I see." Tina toyed with the last bit of salad in her bowl. The kitchen had grown too warm, heavy with the odors of garlic and overripe peaches, and she felt her body sinking back into its fatigue, the wine taking its toll. Chip was quiet, eating slowly, apparently still waiting for her to offer some sort of opinion. As if the climate were a matter of opinion. What was it they'd said in the review she'd read? That they still couldn't discern a warming trend in the general noise of the natural climate fluctuations? They didn't have a very good record of average global temperatures to work with—she remembered that. She pulled the big bowl of salad over and served herself more. She hated trying to talk around gaps in her knowledge. What was the point? She loved a nice bit of speculation, of course, engaged in it all the time. But if you didn't even have the available information to work with? If you didn't know what you were talking about? And then trying to pare down such a complex problem—problems—into a single yes or no question was, well, ridiculous. She took another biscuit from the pan. "What's in these?" she asked, changing the subject. "They're good."

Chip looked at the biscuit she held up, and smiled. "Pineapple sage. Sharp cheddar cheese. And garlic chives."

"This is the first real dinner I've had in weeks," Tina said, stifling a yawn. "It's wonderful." A little weird, she thought, but not bad.

"You eat out a lot?"

"I don't know if you can call it eating out. There's a pretty awful little snackbar down at BIO. Hamburgers and sandwiches and the like."

"Sounds like you practically live down there." He looked at her curiously and leaned forward to take a bite of salad, his eyes on her face.

"Sometimes it's just easier to stay over. I think I actually get more sleep than when I ride home every night."

"They have some kind of dormitory down there or something? At BIO?"

Tina shook her head. "There's an easy chair in my office."

"You spend the night in a *chair*?" He stopped eating and rested his forearms on the table, looking at her.

"It's a big chair," Tina said, feeling foolish. She'd never thought of it as strange before. She concentrated on the biscuit in her hand, picking at the orange-and-green-flecked crumbs, tucking them into her mouth. He laughed, and she looked up, startled.

"I guess you're not very big, are you?"

"Right," Tina said, and looked away, because he was staring at her openly now, his face serious, despite the laugh.

Was she actually blushing? Since when did she blush at comments like that? And was this it? Was this how he was going to come on to her? Now? After that tedious and pointless discussion about the greenhouse effect? With the dinner table and all these half empty dishes between them, and this lethargy descending so rapidly around her that it was all she could do to lift fork from bowl to mouth even though she was still hungry? And why was he suddenly looking so serious, as if he were pondering life after death, instead of contemplating making love to her? She wished she could start the evening over, step outside and get some fresh air, a whiff of that bay tree's smelling-salt scent. She risked another look at his face, but he'd ducked his head down over his bowl, and all she could see was his thick beginning-to-gray hair. She wondered how old he was. Thirty-five? Maybe older. It was hard to tell.

She was relieved when they finally finished dinner, and he sent her into the living room to put a record on the stereo, said he would make tea and heat up some pie. He hadn't mentioned the truckload of tomatoes to be delivered, and so she went into the living room and started the album that was on the turntable and sat down on the couch to wait for him . . . but by the time Joan Baez was halfway through her first song, Tina was sound asleep.

She's walking in the dips between hills, steep hills, more like mountains than hills, as steep as spires or minarets, and they all have names, each peak has a name. She's looking for a particular one but she can't remember which, and suddenly she's not in the dips anymore but standing at the apex of the tallest peak, looking down from a great height at all the others—hoping, she explains to Garrett, who is comfortably ensconced in a shallow trough below her left foot, to get the big picture, the Whole Picture. . . . But the damned mountains are moving, won't stop moving, melting, disappearing—not mountains, not spires, not even hills, but waves, rising and falling, cresting and breaking, and she's riding a crest, looking for Garrett now, but he's gone. Whether he raced off without her in his old boat of a car, or sank beneath the waves while his hand flailed, trying for a hold on her foot, Tina isn't sure, but she is definitely alone now, riding the top of a swell and sliding down into its trough, rising again as a new swell forms. The waves are carrying her out beyond the fog toward the faint line of the horizon, taking her someplace that she's too tired to go, and she'll never make it there, wherever there is, she's just too tired to stay afloat out here all alone, sinking. Then she sees the rock. A big rock, a huge rock, an island jutting out of the sea at an unlikely angle. Tentatively, with the last of her strength, she starts to swim. If she can only reach the rock she might rest there, if only if only if only the rock doesn't know her, it might allow her to rest, for a minute, a moment, a short while, on its shore.

Maybe it was the light that woke her, the almost-full moon shooting its last rays through the window as it dropped behind the hills. Or maybe it was the discomfort of the couch or the itchiness around her neck from the wool blanket that had been placed over her during the night, or perhaps it was just the familiar predawn hour. There was a wedge of pie half submerged in a pool of pink ice cream directly in her line of vision when she opened her eyes. She lay still for a moment, alarmed, then embarrassed as she realized what had happened. Had he tried to wake her, perhaps, not been able to? She got up and walked over to the window. The drapes, Mexican blankets on curtain rings, had been left open. Tina could make out the truck parked in the drive and beyond it the little valley, swathed in the subtle light of the setting moon and the not-quite-rising sun.

She went to the bathroom, moving quietly past what she assumed was his bedroom, the door ajar, but not enough that she could see in. Then she returned to the living room and looked around. There was a loft above half the room, with steep ladder-like steps leading up to it. There were several faded color photographs of mountains and rivers hanging on the wall. She went to the couch and folded up the blanket, stared at the pie and the mug of cold tea on the coffee table. When she realized that the pie was made from pink apples like the one she'd eaten in the truck, she picked up the plate and took a tentative bite. It was definitely sweet. Unlike the apple. Decidedly delicious.

She was still standing there eating the pie when Chip emerged from the bedroom. He had a sweater slung over his shoulder and a pair of socks in one hand, and he seemed to be in a hurry, as if he'd overslept. He bid her good morning, apologizing that he didn't have time to make coffee.

"I've got to get the tomatoes into town before this guy takes off for the city," he said, hurrying past her into the kitchen.

"I'm sorry I fell asleep like that," Tina said, following him. He was gathering up work gloves, clippers, a wallet, keys, a dirt-encrusted notebook, and various loose papers, piling everything on a corner of the table. He took the sweater from his shoulder and glanced over at Tina—then stared as she forked the last bit of pie out of the melted ice cream on the plate.

"Don't tell me you ate that soggy mess."

Tina nodded and laughed. "It was wonderful," she said, but he looked annoyed. He walked over and took the plate from her, set it in the sink. Then he laid his sweater on the counter and retrieved a pie tin from the refrigerator. "Here," he said, handing it to Tina. "Take it home and try it when it hasn't been soaking in ice cream all night. Heat it up a little."

There was almost half a pie in the pan. Tina tried to tell him not to give her so much, but he pressed it on her.

"Hell, I don't need it," he said, suddenly grinning and patting his belly, which extended just enough for his jeans to press a dent.

Husky, Tina thought, he was just husky. And when he picked up his sweater and pulled it over his head, she was jolted by a yearning to ease herself up to that belly, wrap her arms around it and squeeze, letting the sweater—an old brown wool thing covered with fuzz balls—slip down with her inside of it. But when Chip's head emerged from the sweater, he was already moving toward the table. He pulled on socks and boots, took his hat from the back of the chair and settled it onto his head, scooped up the pile from the table, and led Tina out into the bay tree's pungent morning embrace.

Chapter 8

Garrett's sample lured Tina back to it as soon as she recalled its presence in her freezer, a week after she perfected the HPLC separation, when she had completed an estimate of the thumb-switching reaction rates. The Warrua rock was certainly not the sort one would be studying if one were looking for petroleum. But she already had an extract of it. And it did contain the chiral hydrocarbon. And it had undergone the heat and pressure of burial, all thoroughly studied by geologists. And it was old—so old that she might use it as a limiting case for the usefulness of the thumb-switching reactions, which was what she needed for the ACS proposal. If, of course, any of the organics in the Warrua sample, the hydrocarbon in particular, were as old as the rock that contained them. The big question. The question Garrett wanted answered.

It was nine o'clock in the morning when Tina injected the sample, a little after ten when the hydrocarbon peaks started coming through the detector. She returned to the instrument lab just as the chart recorder pen scratched upward to mark the first of the non-biological stereoisomers. Yes, yes, yes! She jumped up and down in the constricted space, petroleum geology and the ACS proposal forgotten as the pen continued upward, implying an excess of slow, difficult thumb-switching— an extravagance of time. The pen reached an apex, paused, and dropped swiftly down to a neat baseline. Tina reached over and patted the side of the HPLC casing. She stood by the chart recorder, bouncing up and down like a cheerleader, watching the other peaks appear.

There was a lot to be done before the peaks really meant what Tina felt in her keyed-up shivering bones they meant, and once she had cheered the last of the four through the detector, she set to work. By mid-afternoon, however, she couldn't stay put any longer. She rolled up her chromatograms, grabbed the tablet where she'd scribbled her calculations, stuffed everything into her knapsack, danced down the stairs, jumped on her bike, and headed up the hill.

"Garrett, you gotta see this!" Tina said, barging into his lab—and only then recalling just how rudely she'd spoken to him about the very subject of her present exuberance the last time she saw him, and that she had not, in the intervening month, called to apologize. She stopped just inside the threshold, her knapsack already off her shoulder and unzipped. Garrett was at the bench, adjusting the drip from the bottom of a desalting column. She couldn't very well bring it up now. "Sorry," she said, apologizing instead for the heedless way she'd disturbed him in his lab. "Uh—I've got something to show you. If you have a minute," she added contritely. She waited there in the doorway, still breathless from her ride up the hill, her hair damp from the fog.

Garrett finished adjusting the stopcock. Then he straightened up and turned to look at Tina.

"Let's see it," was all he said. He motioned her over to the lab bench.

Tina unfurled a chromatogram of the commercial standard and explained how she had separated the four stereoisomers. She had drawn a three-dimensional sketch of each conformation above its corresponding peak.

Garrett made an appreciative noise in the back of his throat. "I've never seen anything like this," he said, looking at the perfectly resolved peaks. "Not with hydrocarbons on an HPLC. Weren't you complaining that the one Lindquist left you was on its last legs?"

"I gave it a wheelchair," Tina said, and covered the chromatogram with the one she'd just run of the sample he'd given her. "But look at this. This is what I wanted to show you."

"What am I looking at?"

"The Warrua sample." Above the chromatogram, Tina set out the four mass spec traces that she'd run to verify the hydrocarbon peaks. All four thumb-switching siblings were in attendance. She pointed to a tall peak in the last half of the chromatogram. "Here's the original stereoisomer," she said. "The biologically derived one. Here—" she said, tracing its twin, just in front of it and almost as tall. "And here—" she skipped to the half-pint sibling trailing along behind. "And here—" she tapped the last and smallest of the four. "Are the non-biological stereoisomers."

Garrett didn't say anything. Tina had the feeling that the pudgy body alongside her was gaining buoyancy, that if he weren't wearing those heavy black shoes he always wore, Garrett might actually lift off his heels and float upwards until his spine brushed the ceiling of his lab and held him suspended like a balloon between tubes of fluorescent light. He was, she knew, prey to the same not-yet-well-founded sense as she: that they were looking at the 3.8-billion-year-old remnants of chlorophyll. She waited while he picked up the mass spec traces that corresponded to each of the four peaks and examined them with unnecessary care—they were, of course, identical.

"I don't suppose," he said, settling hard on his heels and folding his arms, "that you've done any of the kinetics for this reaction."

"Just an estimate," Tina said, unrolling the third chromatogram. "This is from a ninety-million-year-old sediment." She brushed her fingers across the section where the hydrocarbon stereoisomers appeared. The original, biological stereoisomer clearly dominated the group, its twin a narrow spike pushed out in front of it, the third sibling smaller still, riding the tail of the original like a baby clinging to its older sister's skirt, the fourth not even visible. Tina set the pad with her kinetics calculations on the lab bench and explained how she'd used the DSDP sediment and one heating experiment to estimate the reaction rates. She slipped the chromatogram of the Warrua sample out from under the pile. "If I use the maximum possible temperature and pressure from those papers you gave me," she said, "I get a *minimum* age for this hydrocarbon of 3.5 billion years. And if I use the most accepted, lower estimate for temperature, I get an age of 3.8 billion years. The same as they got for the rock."

"This is ridiculously rough," Garrett said, attempting the appropriate skepticism.

"I know. I need to do a proper kinetics study. I've got to do a million runs with real rock substrates, various temperatures, the whole shebang. It's going to take months. . . . But at least," she added, remembering what she was up to, "I have enough to write the ACS proposal." She glanced at Garrett, but he was looking over her calculations. "Garrett, I— Look, I'm sorry about—"

"You know," Garrett interrupted her, "I'm going to France in November. For the First International Earth's Earliest Biosphere Conference, which is a reincarnation of what we used to call the Origin of Life Conference." He set down the pad and turned toward Tina. "This would make a very provocative poster. All you'd need is the bare bones of the kinetics experiments. And a couple more Precambrian samples, some younger ones, say, from the Canadian series." Garrett laid his open hand on the chromatogram and pressed down, carefully, as if he were making a hand print. "I'm sure I can get you invited to present a poster. Maybe even funds for the trip."

"Orloff's cruise leaves November second," Tina said. "But you could present the poster for us. If you don't mind being a little speculative."

"Are you kidding?" Garrett laughed. "Speculation is the meat and bones of this conference. What we have here," he said, giving Tina's chromatogram a congratulatory slap, "is good empirical science in the context of this conference. If, that is, we resist the temptation to speculate about your speculative results." Garrett paused, and his expression grew more serious. He peered at Tina through the thick lenses of his glasses. "I'd forgotten about the cruise," he said. "You are including the paleoclimate work in the ACS proposal, aren't you?"

Tina nodded, though she hadn't started writing the proposal yet. "I'm going to try to buy some time off the director," she said. "Through the end of the year, I hope. This grant should come through by then. . . . If it even gets funded," she added morosely. She'd be back on the postdoc circuit if it didn't. Or vying for a state college job teaching undergraduate chemistry— a secure, well-salaried job that would no doubt make her father proud, a reasonable and successful culmination of all her years of study—a job with no lab, no research. Or maybe she'd wind up in industry after all, doing petroleum geochemistry that was even more narrowly focused than this ACS project.

"You'll get your funding," Garrett said. "The idea is too good. Though I wouldn't," he added with a grin, "put too much emphasis on the implications of your test run here."

Tina didn't need Garrett to tell her that. She wasn't about to mention the possibility that photosynthetic bacteria had been around for 3.8 billion years, not in this proposal. The ramifications of her Warrua rock analysis would have to go unnoted here. They were the flip side of the idea, the side no one would fund. The hydrocarbon's thumb-switching as a means for divining the history of heat, pressure and time in petroleum source rocks, that was the main act here. It was very clever, very useful if you were looking for oil—but not particularly enlightening. It was an overblown answer to a small question, Tina thought, a clever idea that ought be indulged briefly and then dismissed, a superficial flirtation, an idea with no depth. No soul. Not an idea to be married to, spend time with, stake hope on, a future.

And yet here she was. Thinking about it. Writing about it. Arguing its case. Day after day, two weeks, with the July fog pressing against her office window, rolling down the glass, dripping. Whoever was in charge of such things at BIO had turned off the heat for the summer, and Tina's office was cold and felt grimy and abandoned, with the janitor away on vacation and the insidious dampness permeating walls, clothes, skin, and muscle, chilling her marrow and innermost organs. She dressed in layers, nylon jacket, sweatshirt turtleneck, a tank top hidden hopefully next to her skin because it was *supposed* to be summer. . . but whenever the fog tried to lift or thin or drift out to sea, the land snatched it back, cleaving to a shroud of dull gray light that scorned the rise and progress of the sun, refusing to be roused. Tina glimpsed Chip's truck once on the main road into Brayton, noticed his bare elbow jutting out the window and realized that just inland, over a single ridge, it was sunny and hot. She felt a twinge of disappointment that he drove on without seeing her, that she hadn't run into him again since their dinner together, though there were signs that he had been around, attending to the duplex gardens.

She was cold and vaguely depressed and there was no joy, no pleasure whatsoever to be found in the writing of this proposal. She worked as quickly as she could, wrote like one dashing through a long narrow tunnel, eyes trained on the light at the end, afraid to stop or examine the dripping stone walls. She presented her method for separating the hydrocarbon stereoisomers, outlined the kinetics study and laid out the equations, gave her estimates of the rates. She found papers by the geologist whose seminar had inspired the idea and, citing them, showed how the temperature history of a rock could be fed into his model of sedimentary basins. Finally, she added a condensed version of her paleoclimate project and tried to ignore the awkward way it hung off the edge of the proposal— because no matter what she did, the main act of this proposal was too narrowly focused to accommodate such a big side show with any grace. When she lifted the final document and shuffled its pages with her thumb, it seemed a sorry, pitiful thing, like the dismembered corpse of her NSF proposal, stitched back together, covered over with make-up, and propped up in the casket. She slid it into an envelope, bid it good riddance and consigned it to its fate. Then she went to the director and found out about the "tide-you-over" fund Katharine had told her about. Submitted her plea. And got on with her work. Cold, still cold, the fog unrelenting—but she was a little less depressed.

She allowed herself some time in the library, where it was warm, and tried to catch up on the literature, get her arms around the growing girth of paleoclimate research. In the lab, she began the kinetics experiments for Garrett's poster session on the Warrua finding. It was a rudimentary study, still just a rough estimate, but with no technician to help her, the work was tedious and time-consuming. Hydrocarbon samples had to be sealed into glass tubes, heated at various temperatures for various lengths of time, and then run on the HPLC to check the progress of the thumb-switching reactions. Just preparing all the tubes was a chore. That was what she was doing when Katharine stopped by the Friday after Tina sent off her proposal, pulling tubes. It was not going well.

Ideally, you held the middle of a test tube over a flame and the glass glowed orange-red and stretched like taffy as you slowly pulled the two ends apart. Ideally, you lifted it out of the flame and it hardened into an hourglass shape that could be filled, broken off, and sealed into a neat little ampoule. But if you lifted the glass from the flame too soon the neck would be too thick and the ampoule hard to seal. If you left it too long, a thin thread of glass fell looping down where the neck should be. And if you were impatient and pulled too fast, then you found yourself standing like a fool with half a test tube clasped in a pair of tongs on either side of the torch, cursing and stomping your foot. Which was what had just happened to Tina when Katharine stuck her head into the lab and asked if she wanted to go to the TGIF down on the pier. Katharine heard the curse and retreated, but Tina tossed the ruined test tube into the glass bin and called her back. It was the third tube she'd ruined in ten minutes, and she figured she might as well give up and go to the TGIF with Katharine and Janice, a grad student from Orloff's lab, who was waiting in the hall.

The TGIFs were a graduate student tradition, the idea being that the lowliest first-year student might mix casually with the most revered of researchers, if they could just get together in neutral territory. Every Friday afternoon, from June through August, the students bought a keg of beer and set it up on the pier as a lure and democratizing agent. According to Katharine, the keg worked well as the former—and not so well as the latter. It was indeed an odd scene, Tina thought, as they turned onto the steep drive that led down from the bluff and the pier came into view. The fog had thinned to an uncertain sunlit mist that bathed the pier in white luminescent light, and the clusters of men standing about looked like so many bivouacked ghosts, plastic cups clutched like protective shields before their chests. One might be inclined to turn and run for cover, Tina thought, though BIO scientists at a purely social gathering should be harmless enough. A bit ludicrous, perhaps, but benign.

There was a table set up outside the shed at the entrance to the pier, and several of the ghosts were standing around it eating, each seemingly lost in his own private indulgence of crackers and cheese and chips, unaware of the others. They seemed eerily quiet, until Katharine arrived and they suddenly started talking, as if this great blonde fairy had released them from a spell with the touch of her wand: they talked to Katharine, and then they turned and spoke to each other, their voices rising above the crashing waves. Tina blinked and squinted in the glaring fog as Katharine coaxed a thin, pleasant-faced, white-haired man away from the food table and introduced him to Tina and Janice. Janice nodded shyly. Tina extended her hand, and he clasped it lightly and pulled back quickly, clearly unaccustomed to shaking hands with women. Tina knew the name. Conroy Decker's work with dissolved gases had been studied in every oceanography graduate program since the late sixties.

"Tina is working in Max Lindquist's lab," Katharine said by way of introduction.

"Oh really?" Decker said, warming a little. "And how is Max's work in Sweden going? When is he due back?"

"Not for a year and a half, at least," Tina said.

"Too bad. It would have been nice to have him on this winter's cruise."

"Tina will be on the cruise," Katharine interjected.

Conroy Decker nodded politely, but he didn't say anything.

Partly out of curiosity, and partly just to see if she could get him to talk to her, Tina asked him about the work he had planned for the cruise.

The question seemed to take him by surprise, but he answered readily enough. "PCO_2 measurements across the air-sea interface," he said. "See if we can't put an end to all the handwaving about the role of the oceans in CO_2 uptake."

Katharine turned aside to awaken another ghost. Janice faded into the fog, moving farther out the pier to join the graduate students gathered there. And Tina stayed where she was, listening to Conroy Decker. Whether it was the effect of the beer he was drinking or the subject raised, Tina didn't know, but he was loosening up, his bland face coming to life as he talked.

"Keeling has been waving this beautiful atmospheric CO_2 curve in our faces for years, and we still haven't figured out precisely, quantitatively, why it looks the way it does—besides pointing out the obvious, that the increase roughly mirrors increasing fossil fuel usage. Meanwhile, the climate modelers insist on ignoring this problem, making ever-more-sophisticated atmospheric circulation models to predict the effects of anthropogenic CO_2—based on numbers for future CO_2 levels that might as well be pulled out of a hat." He paused, directing his attention over Tina's head. "And not only that," he said loudly, "but they take their pet mathematicians much too seriously."

Tina looked over her shoulder to see Katharine's boyfriend, Fred, and his friend Alan approaching.

"What's this about pet mathematicians?" Alan said, reaching past her for a handful of crackers from the table.

"We were just talking about Sylvia Orloff's cruise. I was explaining that we'll be collecting ammunition for the never-ending battle to keep you and your climate modelers in line."

"Whoa," Alan said, holding his hands up. "Keep me out of this."

"I'd like to."

Tina tried to recall what he had told her about his work. Chaos mathematics. Random forces. Effect without cause. "You guys are working on a climate model?" she asked him, puzzled.

"I can assure you we have nothing to do with any battle," Alan said. "We know nothing about CO_2 uptake by the oceans."

"Traub has us working for these climatologists in Colorado," Fred explained. "He wants to see if we can introduce random, internal forces into an externally forced climate model—"

"God forbid," Conroy said. "They don't even understand the external—"

"What I would really like to know," Alan interrupted, "is how come no one has invited the pet mathematicians on this infamous cruise."

"It would be like taking a pet rat on board," Conroy said cheerfully. "They'd worry that it would escape and start breeding."

Tina wanted to know more about what Conroy Decker was doing, but they were interrupted by the arrival of a large, overweight middle-aged man in an untucked khaki shirt and huge dirty white deck shoes. This was no ghost. Tina could feel the slight give of the planks beneath her feet as the man approached, ploughing into their midst to stop in front of Conroy Decker as if Conroy were the only person on the pier and had just been standing there waiting for him. Which, indeed, he might have been.

"You seen the latest bullshit those biologists have come out with?" boomed Harper Gibson. Fred and Alan filled their cups at the keg and slipped away, but Tina stayed put. Even she knew Harper Gibson's reputation as a "brilliant son of a bitch," but she'd never met him and she was curious.

"They 'estimate' CO_2 emissions from deforestation at four to eight giga-tons per year," Harper Gibson was saying. "Add that to the fossil fuel emissions since 1958 and you *double* the total emissions." He laughed, a short, unpleasant bark. "Which means only a *quarter* of it has stayed in the atmosphere."

"I saw it," Conroy said. "Just where do they think it's all going?"

"Why, poof!" Harper Gibson brushed his hands against each other. "It's all sucked into the oceans, they say. Ignoring the fact that ocean uptake can't even account for all of the fossil fuel emissions. I guess they're too young to have read Revelle's paper in the fifties, but you'd think they'd have read yours." He shifted his weight as he gesticulated, and Tina had to back up against the table to avoid a collision.

"What gets me," Conroy said, "is the way these fools run to the popular press with such hogwash."

Tina suddenly recalled the frustrating dinner conversation she'd had the evening she'd spent at Chip's house. From the sound of it, things were even more unresolved than she'd suspected. She'd have to find that review she'd read, see what these guys were talking about, because it was clear that they weren't going to enlighten her now. Harper Gibson literally had his back to her, and Conroy hadn't seen fit to introduce them. She loaded up a napkin with chips and walked down toward the end of the pier.

The fog was so thin you could actually tell where the sun was. You could almost believe it would clear. It was almost too warm for a sweatshirt, Tina thought as she joined Katharine and her entourage at the end of the pier.

"Did you talk to Harper Gibson?" Katharine asked immediately.

Tina leaned over the railing to get a look at the seals that were making so much noise. She hadn't been out here in months. "I don't get the impression one exactly talks to Harper Gibson," she said over her shoulder. "Unless Harper Gibson sees fit to talk to one."

Katharine laughed. "He's such a jerk. He's going to be on the cruise, you know."

"Who's Harper Gibson?" Fred said.

"The big guy," Alan said. "The one that practically squashed Tina when she was talking to Conroy back there." He leaned against the railing next to Tina.

Tina turned around. "You know anything about what he's working on?" she asked Katharine.

"Harper Gibson was the one who started the whole thing with using chemical tracers to track deep sea current—"

"No, I mean now."

Katharine shook her head. "But what I hear, the wonder-boy shine is wearing off, and they're starting to hassle him about going through so many technicians and grad students." She turned to Janice and laid a sympathetic hand on her arm. "This guy makes Sylvia look like a saint. Every year there's some poor ego-crushed grad student floating around, homeless, looking for a new advisor. It's hard to believe that Harper Gibson is actually married. With kids! That he actually cohabits with other human beings! But there is, apparently, the proverbial little woman in the background, cooking the brilliant man's meals and washing the stains out of his underwear." Katharine interrupted herself to wave a greeting to two approaching scientists, who waved back and stopped next to the skiff on the other side of the pier.

"That's Eric Wright," Katharine whispered, though between the seals and the surf there was little chance of being overheard. "And his grad student. Lord, she's downright homely, isn't she? But they say she's got Wright wrapped around her little finger with that cute French accent and all. I heard she's been here for three years without even starting a dissertation project. He was going to take her on Orloff's cruise, but his wife found out and now all hell's broke loose—"

"Katharine," Tina said, laughing. "How do you know all these people?"

"It's this talent she has," Fred said, putting his arm around Katharine. "Loquacious? Is that the word? For people who can talk to anyone about anything?" He looked at Alan.

"Don't look at me. I'm just a dumb mathematician."

Katharine extricated herself from Fred's embrace and tossed her hair back self-consciously. "Come on," she said, starting back along the pier. "Let's go down to the beach. It's almost sunny."

Janice hung back when they got to the end of the pier, saying that her husband was supposed to be picking her up. And Tina said she was going home, but Katharine stopped her.

"No fair! Not everyone has a hovel by the sea to retire to. She lives in North Brayton," Katharine explained to Fred and Alan. "Though it's not exactly the usual North Brayton yuppie condo . . ." Katharine paused, remembering, perhaps, that Alan had seen Tina's place.

"Actually," Tina said, "It isn't such a hovel anymore. They've done a lot of work on it."

"They fixed up the hovel?" Katharine stared at Tina. "You didn't tell me that."

"Yeah. It was sold a few months ago, and the new owners have been fixing it up."

"Of course I've only been there a couple of times," Katharine said, lifting her chin and pursing her mouth in an expression that invariably belied its intended indifference. And Tina found herself trying to make amends by inviting everyone to see her upgraded hovel and take a walk on the North Brayton beach.

They drove over in Alan's Saab and spent a few minutes admiring Tina's new yard, then walked down to the beach, where they meandered along the sand throwing Alan's frisbee between them. Tina wished she could throw it like the men, in great arcing curves that stopped in midair to float down to the recipient, or slicing low and straight across a hundred meters of beach. Her own short, competent tosses bored her, and they all tired quickly of chasing Katharine's wild flings. Katharine finally tucked the frisbee under her arm and pulled Fred down to the water's edge to look for shells.

As Tina and Alan continued up the beach, Alan started talking about the collaboration Conroy had mentioned. He told Tina that the comment about pet mathematicians was misleading, that in actuality the atmospheric scientists couldn't fathom the new mathematics, that they seemed afraid of it somehow. He dropped his arm onto Tina's shoulder as he talked, and it was not unpleasant, the casual weight of his arm there, the pale graceful hand twisting into view as he gestured next to her face, the easy conversation, the fog still lingering uncertainly, but bright, promising to burn, shrivel, peel away and expose the blue plain of the sea. He had called her twice after that night they'd met, and she'd made excuses both times. But there was no reason, Tina thought now, no reason that she could think of why she shouldn't enjoy the attention of this tall, handsome, intelligent man. There was no reason why she should suddenly be more excited about the view he was blocking, the fog-shrouded Pacific horizon with nothing but an expectant luminescence to commend it, than she was about his arm around her shoulder. And there was certainly no reason to decline his invitation to dinner at an expensive seafood restaurant that she had never been to.

It was as if she were caught in the perverse and stubborn momentum of not wanting what she ought to want, Tina thought when they returned to the duplex and Alan asked her again if she wouldn't let him treat her to dinner, pausing with his hand on the open door to the Saab, Fred and Katharine already seated in the back, expecting, as Alan clearly expected and Tina herself expected, that she would finally say yes—which was the only reason Tina could think of that she said no, when all she had to look forward to was a lonely dinner of leftover chicken and string beans.

Chapter 9

It was warm, it was sunny, it was downright hot. It was a miracle day, clear since sunrise and impossible to imagine that just last week she had been sitting around depressed and shivering in three layers of cotton and a nylon jacket, all her hopeful red and yellow tank tops abandoned at the bottom of a drawer. Almost five in the afternoon and still hot. Tina was crouched down low, speeding down the hill with the wind wicking the sweat off her skin as fast as it formed. She was thinking about ice. About lots and lots of ice, why it came, why it went. She'd been free of the ACS proposal for over a week, reading and thinking and catching up on the literature, and now the fog had lifted and her mind was racing like a wild thing set loose. Brian Maitland had just published a hypothesis to explain the evidence in ice cores from the Greenland and Antarctic ice caps. Tina had only read the abstract, but she had the article in her knapsack, along with a review of Quaternary ice-age research. The oscillating glacial and interglacial climates of the past two million years were clearly linked to periodic variations in the earth's rotation and orbit, which produced small shifts in solar radiation. But whether these small shifts were enough to have initiated and terminated the ice ages was a hotly debated issue, and data from the ice cores had been adding new flame.

Tina cut over to the beach and slowed down to make her way between the walkers and skaters on the boardwalk. Air bubbles trapped in ice from the last ice age fifteen thousand years ago contained fifty percent less CO_2 than air from the warm interglacial, just five thousand years later—a radical change in an incredibly short time, a spectacular finding. But it was not clear whether the rise in CO_2 had been cause or effect of the glacial to interglacial climate shift, whether it had set things in motion, or was a result of warming due to orbital variations; and if it was a result then would the feedback effect—warming causing CO_2 to increase, and CO_2 more warming, and so on—have amplified the initial small warming enough to initiate the melting of the ice? And then there was feedback from the ice itself to consider: less ice to reflect the sun caused more warming which caused more ice to melt . . . All these interlinked feedbacks were the reason for the extreme zigs and zags in ice-age climates. They were also what made cause and effect almost impossible to untangle.

Tina turned off the boardwalk and headed up her street. She was hot and thirsty now, anticipating orange juice with ice, but she stood in the pedals to race up the slight incline, the sweat gathering on her face, trickling down between her breasts. She was thinking that she and Orloff were going to be studying a time without all those zigs and zags, with no ice to confuse the issue. She was thinking that fifty or a hundred million years ago the relationships between CO_2 and climate would be clearer. Except, of course, there was no way of knowing the CO_2 level back then, no hundred-million-year air bubbles to analyze. The Antarctic ice sheet was less than a million years old.

Chip's truck was parked in front of the duplex. He was sitting in a beach chair on the new deck reading a newspaper, which he lowered as Tina squealed to a halt behind the truck and edged her bike up the curb.

"Afternoon," he said cheerfully, squinting into the afternoon sun. "Gorgeous day, huh? Such a warm July, and now this."

Tina wiped the sweat out of her eyes and caught her breath. There was a small cooler next to him, an open beer bottle set on top. There was a smoking hibachi a few feet away. What was he doing? "That was a warm July?" she said.

"Sure. Fog wasn't as cold as it is sometimes, even down here." He folded the newspaper and set it down next to him, pushing himself upright in the low chair. "I was gonna go down to the beach," he said, gesturing at the hibachi. "But I figured, what the hell, might as well stay here and admire my handiwork. Enjoy this fancy new deck they built," he added, giving it a pat. "Since you apparently don't plan to."

"Oh. Well . . ." Tina shrugged, and when he didn't say anything more, she said, "Enjoy your picnic," and started up the path.

"There's another chair in the truck."

She stopped and looked back over her shoulder.

"Plenty of shishkebob too," he said, "though you might want to bring out some plates and silverware."

Tina nodded and continued around the building to park her bike. She didn't know what to think. Had he planned this? Or was this another spur-of-the-moment invitation, a non-date like that odd evening at his farm. She hadn't talked to him since then. His truck had been here on Friday when she stopped by with Katharine and Fred and Alan, but he'd been working out in back, and by the time they returned from the beach he was gone.

When she had gone inside and washed her face and exchanged her sweaty tank top for a clean one; when she had gathered together plates and silverware and napkins and his pie tin; when she had seen that there was only a stain of orange juice in the bottom of the bottle and found the three beers that had been pushed to the back of the refrigerator; when she balanced the beers and napkins and silverware on top of the plates and opened the door and saw the way he tilted his cap out of his face and watched her walk down the path and around the deck, Tina decided that he had, definitely, planned this. Though she still wasn't sure what to think about that.

He watched her as if she were some beautiful but alien animal that he wanted to touch but couldn't. Or shouldn't. Or maybe wasn't sure after all if he wanted to. Tina was puzzled, thrilled, embarrassed, and, again, puzzled. Puzzled because he'd seemed uninterested in having anything more to do with her after the night at his farm. Thrilled by the attention. Embarrassed because she was responding to his watching her as if he were touching her, sliding a large, rough hand up her calf and around her knee, running his fingers lightly up the inside of her thigh. And then again puzzled, because the look was so restrained, as if he might, at any moment, close it down and leave her to think she had imagined it. Which was what he did. By the time Tina sat down in the beach chair next to him, he'd dropped his eyes to the tray of marinade by his feet and the tiny purple potato he was impaling on a skewer.

"You see this latest in the *Brayton Bee*?" he asked her, christening the deck with drops of oil and soy sauce as he swung the skewer around to point at the newspaper.

"No," Tina said, unsure whether she was relieved or disappointed to have the intimacy of that look pass unacknowledged.

"The North Braytonites are trying to nix the transit project again," he said, handing her an empty skewer and nudging the tray with his foot until it was between them. "They're worried that their precious little town will get too built up, that people with jobs in the Bay Area will move up here and commute. But, Christ, that's what planning commissions are for." He paused, watching Tina slide a chunk of meat onto her skewer. "It works best if you put carrots or potatoes on the ends," he said, "and the squash flowers in the middle." He held up the skewer he'd just completed, the flower hanging from the middle like a wet mop, slick with olive oil and soy sauce.

Tina slid the meat off the skewer and fished a small round carrot out of the pan, while Chip went on about the transit system and the town politics. He was apparently involved with some sort of committee, working for rail systems throughout California. Tina knew absolutely nothing about any of it, but there was a calm conviction to his voice as he went on about what ought to be done, that she found herself almost envying.

"You can't even get a bus from Brayton to San Francisco without transferring three times," he told her. "Thirteen hours to go a hundred and thirty miles. Just about anywhere else in the world you go, they've got a better transit system than the States. And California has got to be the worst. You can't do anything without a car, can't work, can't—" He broke off suddenly and looked at Tina. "Though I guess a few people manage, don't they?"

"I have a car," Tina said, looking up from her skewer. "I just haven't gotten around to getting it fixed." He was smiling at her, and she had the feeling that he was paying her some sort of misplaced compliment. "I don't go anywhere but the Institute," she added.

"That's right, I forgot. You sleep in a chair at BIO." He set another shish-kebob on the grill. "You know, I've been thinking about this greenhouse effect you were telling me about. How we've hardly even heard anything about it, and yet you scientists have known for decades."

"We haven't exactly known—"

"Yeah, okay, but you've known we're probably changing the climate. That we should be letting up on the fossil fuels."

"That's a pretty complicated issue."

"Seems pretty obvious to me. But it always comes down to money, instant money. Like that's the only thing, the absolute only thing we should value. Blind, insatiable greed as the highest law of our land, that's what we have. You know the oil companies are gonna track down and suck out every drop of oil there is. No matter if the earth gets fried in the process. Like there's no such thing as other forms of energy out there. Clean, renewable forms. Just because they cost a little more. Solar, wind—who knows what else they could have developed, if the government weren't always pandering to the oil companies. And now Reagan comes along and cuts the few programs that did get started in the seventies. I can't believe that the fucker impounded the solar-energy funding."

He would certainly disapprove of the grant proposal she'd just written, Tina thought, as she set the last shishkebob on the grill. The man slipped in and out of rhetoric so unselfconsciously that she wanted to roll her eyes and laugh, or interrupt him rudely and argue, demand facts and statistics to back up the rhetoric. But she listened politely. She didn't actually disagree with most of what he was saying.

"It's amazing that one man can do so much damage. Less than two years in office and he's practically dismantled the EPA. Set back environmental laws to the dark ages. Christ, this is the eighties! Don't they get it that we don't have any room left to maneuver?" He noticed her trying to shake the bits of herb and garlic off her fingers and got up to turn on the hose at the corner of the deck, still talking. "You know, when I first heard that Reagan was shot last year, I actually found myself hoping he would die. Hoping for the death of a man—that's horrible! I think it's a little taste of what revolutionaries must feel, that desperation that leads to so much bloodshed."

"If you think about it," he said, holding the running hose while Tina rinsed her hands, "what's really scary isn't Reagan himself. He's just the mask of the monster. What's scary is that we elected him. If it weren't for the farm, I swear I would have left the country, gone back down to Mexico maybe. Not that it's any better. But it's like it's more honest—no one goes around pretending that it's a model of democracy and goodness." He handed her the hose and held out his hands. "And you don't feel so responsible for the mess when it's not your own country. It's the great expatriate cop-out."

Tina looked up from the water splashing over his hands, the blackened fingernail that looked as though it had been hit by a hammer. "You've traveled a lot?"

He had, it turned out, spent years wandering about South America, and he had lived for a little while in Mexico. When they sat down to eat he left off the politics and regaled her with stories of working on a farm in Chile and on ranches in southern Argentina, far removed from cities and politics. Uruguay? Tina asked him. Had he been to Uruguay?

"Never been there." Chip shook his head. "What's in Uruguay?"

"I don't know." She reached to break off a piece of the homely loaf of wheat bread he'd set on top of the cooler. "That's where my father is from."

"Oh yeah?" Chip looked up from his plate. "*¿Y tu madre?*"

"Also. But she died when I was four."

"*Así que hablas Español.*"

"Oh. Sure," Tina said. Though the only one she ever spoke Spanish to was the janitor at BIO. It was something that used to irritate her father, that he spoke to her in Spanish, only to be answered in English.

"I think Uruguay's a lot like Argentina," Chip said.

"I don't know," Tina said skeptically. She remembered her father telling sarcastic jokes about *los porteños*, the people from Buenos Aires. But, thinking about it now, she couldn't remember much of substance that he'd told her about Uruguay. "He doesn't talk that much about it. Well, sometimes he does, but it's just bits of trivia. You know—food. Nostalgia. Being awakened by the calls of the vendors in Montevideo or going to his grandfather's place in the country." She did remember asking him once why he'd left. She was a teenager, hoping he'd reveal some horrible and fascinating secret, some heroic political exile. But he'd told her that he and her mother had left long before all the trouble, two middle-class kids coming north for adventure. "He left when he was in his twenties," she said. "Only went back once, I think, when I was a baby."

"Maybe he had a fight with his father," Chip said, with a dry laugh. "I can relate to that."

"Oh?" Tina said, and he explained that he had left home at seventeen and never returned, never spoken to his father again. He didn't say what the fight was about, only that they had disagreed about absolutely everything.

Tina was glad when the subject veered away from fathers. She really needed to invite hers for a visit, buy him a ticket to San Francisco, get her car fixed and take him around. She pushed the uneaten squash flowers into a little pile on her plate and eyed the last shishkebob on the barbecue. Chip was making a point of telling her that he'd never finished college. He'd been lucky with the draft, he said, pins in his hip from an accident when he was a kid—but he'd dropped out and left the country anyway.

When he fell silent Tina asked him how he had come to be a farmer. She didn't really expect him to have an answer, any more than she did when people asked how she'd come to be a scientist. But he did. He had a whole story.

The farm, he told her, was a dream conceived when he was living in Mexico. He'd been penniless and stoned most of the time, living with his friend Jorge and Jorge's wife, Meche, and their first baby, all of them but the baby working on some big American estate in Guadalajara. He'd known Jorge since he was a kid, when Jorge had come up from Mexico to make his fortune and ended up working on Chip's father's "piece of agro-industrial wasteland" in the Central Valley. Jorge had been sixteen, Chip thirteen, and they'd been friends ever since. They all must have been stoned, Chip told her, when they decided to save their money and buy a farm together, except that Meche was in on it and she never smoked. They'd started a fund in a jar at the back of a cupboard in the three-room house they were renting outside Guadalajara. *Para la granja*, they'd say, like an incantation each time they stuffed a bill in. Chip laughed, telling the story. Jorge and Meche vowed not to make more babies for a while. Chip vowed to stop buying pot. There'd been a woman with him apparently, a girlfriend. Between the four of them, working at the estate, they managed to save about twenty pesos a week. Two or three dollars.

He broke off a chunk of bread, filled his mouth, chewed, and went on. A year later, he said, when they'd given up on the dream and he was back in California doing gardening and landscaping jobs, his father died and his mother sold the Central Valley farm, a place Chip apparently hated with a passion. Tina gathered that he had hated his father as fervently. There'd been a little left after the mortgage, he told her, shrugging, and he'd been raking in the dough with his landscaping business in Marin County. Jorge and Meche had come up from Mexico and bought in with their tiny bit of savings, a million ideas, and ten lifetimes worth of labor. He still had to subsidize the place with the landscaping, but some day he hoped he could quit and just farm.

Tina liked the funny, tender way he talked about his farm—proud, and a bit in thrall, it seemed, of his own conspiracy with nature. She liked the comforting, low cadence of his voice, liked his stories, and the ingenuous way he revealed himself, the bitter note that went unchecked when he mentioned the family farm, his father. She tried not to ask too many questions, didn't want to know too much. That might ruin it.

Ruin what? Her little adventure? The lust she was feeling? Was that what this was about—these sudden, powerful waves of whole-body desire that came over her whenever she sensed his blue eyes on her with their intoxicating mix of craving and restraint? She wasn't sure. But by the time they had eaten the last piece of bread and Chip had downed the last of the beers, and the delinquent fog had come floating in to smother the first pink hints of what would have been a spectacular sunset, she knew that she wanted him to stay.

She invited him in for coffee. Or cinnamon tea, which was what he opted for.

Chip looked around her apartment with undisguised curiosity, a bemused expression on his face, as if he were considering some new and exotic variety of tomato. That he was tempted to try. But that he suspected wouldn't do well. He stared at the spare furnishings and blank walls, the dirty orange carpet in the living room, the piles of books on the floor. He knelt down to read the titles of the books, mostly monographs of scientific conferences or collections of review papers. Tina turned the radio on and went into the kitchen to make the tea.

Her blue knapsack was sitting in the middle of the table, like a parcel waiting to be unwrapped, Maitland's paper waiting to be read, but she didn't feel impatient; in fact, it pleased her to let it wait, a treat for the morning. She took out cups and a tea bag and filled the kettle with water, put it on to boil. She wondered if she'd tell Katharine, *Hey, I slept with this farmer I met, the guy that was landscaping the hovel* . . . Tina smiled, imagining the look on her friend's face. Maybe not. Maybe she wouldn't even tell her. She went to the bathroom and put in her diaphragm.

When Tina came out of the bathroom, Chip was standing in front of the window, looking out through the porthole formed by the tree. She went over to stand next to him.

"You try the pears yet?" he said. "They look ripe."

"Pears?"

He glanced at her and then gestured impatiently at the brown baseball-sized fruits hanging on the tree.

"Oh I—I didn't think of eating them."

"You think they're decorations? That they're just gonna hang there all year round, never fall off and rot?"

Tina laughed, though he actually sounded irritated. She supposed she *had* been thinking of them as decorations. They didn't look like pears. They were round. And brown. Chip stepped behind her, and Tina ignored the screech of the kettle in the kitchen and turned to face him—but he was walking past her toward the door. For a moment she thought he was leaving, but then she realized he'd gone out to pick the fruit. She ran to take the kettle off the stove.

He walked into the kitchen carrying two of the baseballs. "Everything's early this year," he said, setting them on the counter and digging a pocket knife out of his jeans pocket.

"Shouldn't we be leaving them for the owners?"

"You really do think they last forever, don't you? Anyway, I put the tree on your side." He glanced at Tina, then turned his face up toward the ceiling and laughed abruptly. "In case you didn't notice."

"Oh. But are they ripe?" Tina touched one of the pears. "They seem kind of hard."

"They're supposed to be slightly crunchy. Some people call them 'apple pears,' but that's a misnomer. They're their own fruit." He picked up a pear and turned it slowly, ran his thumb across its surface. "You have to ripen most European pears in cold storage. But these," he said, slicing out a wedge, "you can eat right off the tree." He offered it to her on the tip of his knife, sliced another one, and popped it into his mouth.

Tina looked at the slice of fruit. It still didn't look like a pear. She put it into her mouth and chewed: it was crunchy, but not hard—not like an apple at all—juicy and refreshing with a subtle, exotic flavor, as strange to her as the texture.

"Another week and that rum flavor takes over," Chip said, watching her. "I kind of like them that way, but some people like them better like they are now, not too ripe." He was still watching Tina as she finished the piece of fruit. "So, what do you think?" he asked. "You like it?"

Only then did Tina understand. That the tree had been a gift.

She nodded. It did taste a little alcoholic, but the taste was more reminiscent of a smell, like the perfume of a flower, than any flavor she could think of. "Kind of strange," she said. "But good," she added quickly. "Delicious."

He laughed and relaxed. "That's what we're into here," he said. "Kind of strange but good. You got a plate?"

They sat across from each other on the living room floor with the plate of pear slices between them, sipping at their tea, and Chip talked about an orchard of similarly strange fruits he'd put in for some rich people down near the city the winter before. When they had finished the pear and he had stopped talking, Tina got up and started a tape on her little stereo. She sat down next to him then, leaning against the sofa with a narrow space between them, and they listened to Jean Pierre Rampal's flute wending romantically through Claude Bolling's sophisticated jazz piano, and even though Tina had heard the tape one too many times, she was enjoying sitting there with this little space of anticipatory tension between them, not talking or doing anything or even thinking about what would be said or done next. But then the tape ended and the silence was suddenly uncomfortable. Tina turned to him and smiled, but Chip was staring straight ahead, chewing on his mustache. She waited, but instead of turning to kiss her, he broke his eyes for the door.

"I guess I better be going," he said abruptly and stood up. He flashed her a quick, polite smile, and when she didn't say anything—not 'good night' or 'thanks for dinner'—he turned and started walking toward the door. He moved slowly, unwillingly, as if there were a large, invisible hand pressed into the small of his broad back pushing him along. Tina winced, watching him. Why was he leaving? She stood up, but she didn't say 'see you' or 'bye' or whatever she ought to say. Instead she said, or rather whispered, as if she hadn't quite decided to say it, she whispered to his back so he could pretend not to hear if he wanted, "You can stay if you want."

She supposed it was possible, just barely possible, that he hadn't figured out that she wanted him to stay.

He must have been listening very closely to have heard her. He stopped and dropped his arm where he'd reached for the door and said to the door before he turned back to her, "Ah shit," he mumbled. "Might as well."

Before Tina could decide what this meant—or wonder at the reticence or timidity or ambivalence or whatever it was, of a man who had conceived a pear tree as a flirtation before she'd even acknowledged his existence— before she could get angry or form a retort or withdraw her invitation he had taken the three strides across the room and was kissing her.

She would have made love to him right there standing in the middle of the living room, where he lifted her against him and she wrapped her legs around his middle, but after a while he set her down and laughed, and then she laughed, and he said, "I think I need a shower." And though Tina rather liked the way his farm lingered in his clothes, the musky smell of tomato plants and outdoor sweat and dirt, she showed him the shower, and that's where they made love the first time, too quickly, engulfed in soap lather and steam with the hot water running.

They went to bed then, and though Tina had never found hairy men or men with bellies attractive, she perched above the solid round barrel of his belly with her hands pressed into the graying blonde fur that covered his chest and made love to him with a passion that was wilder than she was accustomed to her passions being, that made him exclaim in surprise and pleasure, that he didn't quite manage to ride out . . . which was okay, which was enough, which was, for the moment, almost too much for Tina.

She fell asleep instantly, lying on top of him. After a while he groaned and lifted her hips away and nudged her off to his side, where he held her curled up against his chest. . . . But by the time Tina's alarm went off at four, she had tossed free and was stretched out on her stomach along the edge of the bed.

She turned off the alarm and slipped out of bed.

"What time is it?" He rose on one elbow and looked at the window for some sign of morning, but the only light shining through the slats of the blinds was the light from the street lamp across the way.

"Four."

He grunted and dropped back on the pillow. "Shit."

"You can go back to sleep," Tina said, pulling on the sweats she used in lieu of a robe.

"Why are you getting up so early?"

"I always get up this early." She felt around in a drawer for a pair of socks, and then she left the room, closing the door softly behind her. She did not want to deal with the man in her bed just yet.

Her knapsack was waiting on the kitchen table. She made coffee and toast and sat down to eat her breakfast and read the papers she'd brought home. Maitland's was provocative, as usual, peppered with exclamation points. It read more like a detective novel than a scientific paper. First, he proposed that the rapid increase in atmospheric CO_2 at the end of the last ice age was caused by a decrease in the amount of carbon stored as organic material in forests and soils or coastal sediments. But the data he gathered showed these organic reservoirs had *increased*, which meant *less* carbon in the ocean-atmosphere system and a *decrease* in atmospheric CO_2—the opposite of the ice-core evidence. We must probe further! Maitland wrote, as if he enjoyed outwitting himself. Next, he presented evidence that carbonate sediments had increased at the end of the glacial, which had the counterintuitive effect of releasing CO_2—just enough to make up for the decrease from removal of carbon to organic reservoirs. Which meant he was now back where he'd started! He'd explained why CO_2 wasn't *lower* during the interglacial, but not why it was *higher* by fifty percent.

Tina read on—the paper was over twenty pages long. She felt a thrill of recognition when Maitland postulated that phytoplankton had played a major role; even though most of the organic matter produced was quickly oxidized back to CO_2 by bacteria, this occurred after it sank out of the surface waters, effectively pumping CO_2 into the deep sea and out of contact with the atmosphere. Evidence from DSDP cores indicated that this "biological pump" had operated in high gear during the glacial period, and low during the interglacial, which would explain the increase in atmospheric CO_2. But why would phytoplankton productivity have decreased at the end of the ice age? As his final flourish, Maitland hypothesized that the slight warming from the earth's orbital variations melted glacial ice and flooded the continental shelves where organic matter accumulated so quickly that bacteria couldn't keep up and the precious organic phosphate and nitrate were buried in the sediments along with the carbon, which meant less in the ocean for the phytoplankton to eat—explaining both the decrease in productivity *and* the apparent increase in reservoirs of organic carbon!

The paper was riveting—a masterpiece of deductive reasoning, revolutionary in its attempt to include ocean ecology as a dynamic variable in the carbon cycle—and it was almost six by the time Tina got up from the table and went back into the bedroom to get dressed.

This time she switched on the lamp.

Chip groaned and threw his arm across his eyes.

"I thought you were an early riser," Tina said, not looking at him. She went to the window and peered through the blinds, trying to divine what the weather was going to do.

"Sometimes," he mumbled. "Sometimes I get up early. Depends."

Of course it was foggy. She didn't know why she bothered to look, just because they'd had one sunny day. You had to wear layers in Brayton, a layer for each contingency of weather. She took off her sweats and started rummaging through her drawers.

It was cold in the room. She felt the goosebumps rising on her back. She felt the man in the bed behind her raise his head to look at her. She found some panties and slipped them on. She couldn't find her yellow T-shirt.

"Why don't you come back in here for a minute," he said.

Tina didn't want to turn around. She was afraid she wasn't going to like what she saw lying in her bed. She was afraid she was going to be embarrassed in front of her own keen-eyed morning self. She was afraid she wouldn't know how to get rid of him. She peeked over her shoulder, not wanting to expose her cold little nipples to his scrutiny.

Chip was smiling. There were deep half-moon creases at the corners of his mouth, double parentheses enclosing the straight line of his mustache. He was lying on his back, his elbows jutting out from either side of his head, which he was holding up off the pillow. His thick hair was flattened on one side, sticking out in ridiculous clumps on the other. Tina laughed and turned around to get a better look.

She didn't mind. It was six in the morning, and she did not mind seeing this man in her bed. It was something of a relief. She needed to leave soon if she was to have a decent morning in the lab, but she climbed up on the bed and slipped under the covers he held open. She moved up against him, then moved closer. She laid an arm across his belly, a leg across his thighs. She let him stretch the panties up her hip and run his rough hand over her goosebumps, and then she fell asleep, clinging to his side like a starfish to a rock until almost seven, when the rock got up to go to the bathroom.

Chapter 10

By the time the summer fog lifted in earnest and the coast was blessed with entire days of warm September sun, Chip was spending almost every Saturday night at Tina's. Sometimes he would stay over during the week as well, when he had a job or errand to do in Brayton. His fresh farm produce filled her refrigerator. His pots and pans augmented the poor selection in her half-empty cupboards. An old guitar took up residence in her living room. His newspapers and magazines began to accumulate in the corner of the kitchen with the bottles, jars, and cans that he planned to take to the recycling center. Tina showed him the rock under the gas meter where she kept a key. Within weeks she was taking it all for granted: the dinners he cooked, the company, this relationship growing around her as if it were something she had nothing to do with. It was like going on a vacation, every time she went home and found him there, a little vacation from her life, a pleasant, even joyful thing apart from her life at BIO. It was not, however, anything she had intended to tell her father about . . . until, of course, he called one Sunday morning when Chip was there. Tina wasn't up to the overt subterfuge of not mentioning Chip when Chip was sitting on her living room floor with the newspaper spread out in front of him and a cup of coffee balanced on his knee, staring at her as if he expected to be introduced to her father over the telephone.

Tina carried the phone over to the sofa and sat down. Her father wanted to know if she was coming home for Christmas.

"It's only September, Dad," Tina said. "Anyway, I was thinking that you might want to come up here for a few days at Christmas." Of course he wanted to. She knew he'd only been waiting for her to suggest it. "I'll buy you a ticket to San Francisco," she told him.

"We can drive down in the truck and pick him up," Chip said.

Tina shook her head. She wanted to get rid of the Toyota and buy a new car before her father came.

"*¿Pero no estás lejos de San Francisco?*" her father was saying.

"See if he wants to stay up at the farm. I'll make Christmas dinner—"

Tina pressed her hand over the receiver. "Shush."

"Maybe I will drive," her father said. "I can stay the whole week. Leave on Christmas Eve, come back after New Year."

"It's okay. The ticket's not that expensive."

"But I want to drive. See the countryside."

"There's nothing to see until you get to San Francisco. You just go up the Central Valley like that time we went to Yosemite—Dad?" There was clumping and rustling on the other end of the line. "What are you doing? Dad?"

"Jorge finally shot one of those damn pigs last week," Chip said. "We cut a ham out of it, figured we'd have it for Christmas."

Tina covered the receiver and glared at him, but he went on.

"But Meche just announced that she wants to go to Mexico for Christmas, see her folks, take the kids and all. So it'd be just us, which might be nice if your father—"

"*Chip.*" She turned sideways on the sofa, so that she was facing away from him.

"*Aquí estoy.* I have the map. *No es tanto.*"

"What's not so much?"

"The drive. I take Highway 5, straight like an arrow. You have to give me directions. How is the weather there? I wonder if my coat is warm enough."

"Dad, you don't have to pack yet. It's only September."

"Well I know, honey, but maybe I won't talk to you. You're going away, no? On a ship?"

"I don't leave until November. And you talk to me almost every week."

"Three weeks. *Hace tres semanas que no te hablo.*"

"Oh. Well."

"I won't get there until late la *Nochebuena*. But we can do something special for Christmas."

"Uh . . . Dad?" Tina turned to look at Chip. "We might be having Christmas dinner at a friend's house."

"Ah . . . *Un amigo, pues.*"

"See if ham's okay. Does he like ham?"

"He's making a ham."

"*¿Y quién será? este amigo. ¿Cómo que no me contás?* Someone from your work? Is he nice? *¿Cómo se llama?*"

Tina closed her eyes and leaned back on the sofa. She could hear her father's expectations rising with each question, an exponential curve of hope caught in the timbre of his voice, her own annoyance rising as predictably, a choreographed dissonance. She opened her eyes and looked at Chip. "His name is Chip Stevenson," she said carefully. "For all that tells you. And yes, he's a very nice guy. Probably too nice," she added under her breath.

"*¿Cómo? No te oigo.*"

"I said he's nice. And no he doesn't work at BIO. He's owns a farm."

Chip was looking at her oddly. "You mean you haven't even told him—"

Tina shook her head, and he fell silent.

"That's wonderful, honey. A farm. Is it a big farm?"

"No. It's small but very pretty. He sells organic produce to health food stores and such. We'll go up there. He wants to make Christmas dinner there." Tina paused. "He likes to cook," she added.

"*Aii, mi 'jita.* I am so happy you met someone. *No sabés lo contento que me hace esto.* I am looking forward to meeting this Chip."

"Actually, he asked if you want to stay up there," Tina said. "At the farm. It's nicer than my apartment."

"*Por supuesto que sí.* This is going to be some vacation. A farm. Does it have animals? *¿Caballos? ¿Vacas? ¿Chanchos?*"

Tina laughed. "Just wild ones."

"*¿Cómo?*"

"The only animals are wild pigs, and they're something of a nuisance."

"I better bring some boots, no? And a present. What should I get as a present?"

"You don't have to bring anything. Look, I'm sure I'll talk to you before then, okay?"

"*Bueno, me hablás antes de irte en el* cruise, *no?*

"Sí, papá. I'll call you before I go."

"So he's coming?" Chip said when she hung up.

Tina nodded. "You know, it's kind of hard to talk on the phone with you talking in my other ear."

"Sorry." Chip leaned back on his hands examining her face. "I thought you said you were close to your father," he said.

"I am. Anyway, compared to you anyone's close to their father."

"My father's dead."

"Yeah, but from what you've told me you didn't even talk to him when he was alive."

Chip shook his head. "He wasn't a man worth talking to. But you love your father."

"Yeah," Tina said, sighing. "I do."

"I would think you'd at least want to tell him that I exist."

"I just told him." She got up to put the phone back on the table and laughed. "And you're probably going to wish I'd gone for the 'just a friend' scenario. Not that he would have fallen for it."

"Boy, I'd better brush up on my Spanish. *¿Por qué nunca hablas Español conmigo?*"

"He speaks perfect English, Chip. Well, almost perfect. Better than your Spanish, anyway."

"Sure, but I bet he likes speaking Spanish. You're sure ham will be okay? And a big salad. Does he like salad?"

"God, you're as bad as he is. Christmas is over three months away."

"So, is he going to fly or drive? What's your dad's name anyway?"

"Alberto. Alberto Arenas Rosenfeld."

"Alberto. You can use the truck if you want—"

"He's driving." Even so, Tina thought, she would have to do something about her car before he came. Hopefully, by Christmas her job would seem a little more stable and it would be safe to spend her savings.

BIO had granted her request for funds until the end of the year, a reprieve that the director said was a lien against her ACS grant—enough to cover a half-time salary, a pittance for supplies, and her travel for the cruise if need be. That this was a generous agreement from an institution famous for its callous disinheritance of unfunded researchers—particularly young, unknown ones—was not lost on Tina. Katharine made sure of that, alternately touting the director's vote of confidence and waxing indignant at the half-time salary. You're going to be the new darling, she told Tina, without malice or irony. Maybe someone will die and they'll offer you a permanent position. If they don't starve you to death first. For all their shortcomings, Katharine said, they do know brilliance when they see it. Tina would have liked to bask in the esteem, but usually she just felt embarrassed. Michael had come back from Europe the week before his classes started, and she'd had to tell him that her NSF proposal was turned down and she didn't have a job for him. To her surprise, he'd seemed almost relieved. He said that he was going through "culture shock," and he did seem changed—a little rougher around the edges, with a scraggly attempt at a beard, a new air of uncertainty—less perfect, and more likeable. Tina told him that she hoped he would still want to work for her if the ACS proposal got funded. She didn't mention her own ambivalence about the proposal, which, except for an occasional bout of worry that it wouldn't be funded, she hadn't thought about since mailing. She was busy finishing the experiments for Garrett's poster presentation, and Roy had sent her a draft of their paper with the *Rover* results.

Roy's cultures had given a satisfying explanation for the picoplankton's prevalence so deep in the photic zone: they thrived at exceptionally low light intensities and could utilize the wavelengths that penetrated most deeply in the water column. Roy postulated that their small size and proportionally large surface area made them more efficient absorbers of light; and that their blue-green and red pigments enabled them to utilize a wider spectrum than that used by green algae. Roy still wanted to study nutrient uptake and try to explain the high picoplankton productivity they'd found in areas where nutrients were so scarce it didn't seem possible. But he agreed with Tina and John Carr that it was time to publish the paper. They knew there would be a lot of skeptics. After all, the study called into question long-established ideas about marine primary productivity and, accordingly, all its attendant biological, chemical and geological cycles.

For her part, Tina was alternately excited and nervous about the picoplankton studies. Occasionally she would succumb to doubt about the validity of her Saturation Index and have to run through her own litany of evidence to convince herself that, despite how little they understood about the organisms that created her lipids, the Saturation Index was indeed a viable indicator of paleotemperatures; and even though the picoplankton could thrive at the bottom of the photic zone, they were always within the well-mixed surface layer where water and air temperatures were closely coupled; and there was every indication that she would find the lipids in some or all of the sediments from Orloff's cruise . . . And if occasionally she was unconvinced, if the doubt grew unreasonable and all-inclusive, and her project with Garrett seemed ethereal and insubstantial, and the tedious kinetics experiments offered no solace in the lab, and the HPLC took to pounding its threat of impending doom and demise—nowadays, Tina could escape to her vacation love affair. She could curl up in the warm haven of Chip's placid physique and it was as if he were a large sponge sopping up her anxiety and doubt in one quick swipe.

Tina imagined him up at his farm after his visits with her, squeezing himself clean, airing himself out in the sun. He tried to get her to spend some time up there with him, but a single Sunday afternoon in September was all she could manage. She didn't want *that* much of a vacation from her life, but just these evenings, these few moments in the shelter of his embrace, pretending she belonged there, small, protected, comforted. She loved it when he slipped his callused hands under her clothes and caressed her lightly, the silent turn of the caress from comfort to passion, the way he teased her then, gently pushing her away and leaving her to smolder while he finished cooking dinner and told her about his week. He always had a lot to tell, which was fine with Tina, who never had much to say about her own week. Occasionally, he'd recount some meeting of his transit committee, or the fledgling organization of organic farmers he was president of, and sometimes he would get going on politics or some environmental issue that had come up in the news—but she liked it best when he talked about the problems and triumphs of his small farm.

For all his joking about the economic hopelessness of the farm, he was intensely frustrated that after all these years he still needed the landscaping business to keep it going. Apparently it was essential to the dream he and Jorge and Meche had forged down in Mexico a decade ago that the farm be self-supporting. They were failing the land they had cultivated, he told Tina once, in a rare bout of melancholy and metaphysical self-loathing that took her by surprise. Usually when he talked about the farm, it was about the corporeal particulars, the day-to-day process, whether fruitful or futile. It was this that Tina found so charming and comforting, these stories of codling moths in apples and broken irrigation lines, of bumper crops of tomatoes and fancy lettuces with no market . . . the reports on the raucous pileated woodpecker in the woods, the honking pair of geese that flew over every night, and the silent wood ducks on the creek as if they were mutual friends whose health and family news he was relating. . . . And the pigs.

The first pig had ploughed through the deer fence in September and destroyed three rows of tomatoes in one night. Chip and Jorge patched the fence, but two days later the pig rooted beneath it. Jorge went out with a rifle at dusk the next night and ambushed the pig as it came under the fence—their Christmas ham. But apparently the pig had informed its friends of the bounty to be had. Soon there was a whole band of wild pigs descending on the farm and wreaking havoc almost every night. They had discovered the orchard, and not only were they eating all the fruit, they were demolishing fifty-year-old trees that Chip and Jorge had spent the last eight years restoring to production. Chip placed a trap at the hole under the fence. The pigs plowed through a new section of fence. Jorge suggested a pit trap in the orchard. The pigs went around it. They started taking turns then, sleeping out in the orchard with the shotgun. Chip got one. Jorge got two more.

Every time Chip came down to Brayton, throughout September and into October, there was some new story about the battle with the wild pigs. There was nothing funny about the damage done, but he told the stories with all the mortified humility of a man telling a joke on himself, and Tina found herself laughing, looking forward to the latest episode in the saga. She tried offering him HPLC stories in exchange, described its long vendetta against her, the pump's most recent bout of erratic behavior. Chip, however, was more puzzled than amused by these accounts. He kept asking what the thing looked like, and finally Tina had to admit that rampaging pigs were a little easier for the uninitiated to visualize than a rampaging HPLC. Chip even dared her to sleep out in the orchard with him, but she declined. He'd been filling her freezer with pork, and she wasn't sure she'd want to eat it if she had to watch him use the shotgun. By the second week of October, he and Jorge had shot five pigs and driven off the rest, but the leader of the band, an old male of mythical proportions and nightmare hideousness, eluded their nightly efforts. Finally, Jorge borrowed a second rifle and he and Chip set up an elaborate ambush, replete with blinding car lights: at two in the morning they finally got their last pig, which, it turned out, was too old and tough to even bother butchering.

Once the pig problem was resolved, Chip started spending more nights in Brayton. Tina had been staying late at BIO, tying up loose ends before she left on the cruise—getting her boxes of sterilized jars and materials shipped off to Guam, slapping together a paper about her hydrocarbon stereoisomer separation for the *Journal of Chromatography*. She'd finished with Roy's paper, and he'd submitted it to *Science*, but she and Garrett had yet to prepare their poster for the Earth's Earliest Biosphere conference. The days were short now, and it was dark when she rode to work in the morning, dark when she returned. She liked riding up and seeing the porch light on, stepping into an apartment filled with the smells of cooking, finding Chip sitting on her sofa strumming an old guitar and singing tonelessly to himself, or reading the paper or a magazine, sometimes a novel. One Saturday night she got home and found him sitting at her kitchen table, pecking at a mechanical typewriter. He greeted her without looking up, and Tina set her knapsack on a chair and went to the sink for a glass of water.

There were tomatoes, peppers, zucchinis, and onions sliced up in neat piles on the cutting board. There was a pot of water on the stove for pasta. She turned around and leaned against the counter, drinking her water. She'd never seen the typewriter, which was a tiny, ancient thing. With Chip hunkered over it, it looked more like some antique toy than an implement of business and communication.

"What are you doing?" she asked him. Considering that he only used his index fingers, he seemed to be making good progress.

"Typing a letter to the editor," he said, pausing to look over what he'd typed. "Damn." He glared at the page in the typewriter.

"What's wrong?"

"Oh, I screwed it up." He pushed back from the table and stood up, looking disgusted. "I'll have to start over," he said, moving to the stove and turning on the burner under the pot of water. "It's for the *Chronicle*, and I want it to be good. There was this long article yesterday about the traffic crunch on that stretch of highway north of San Francisco. Went on for half a page about possible solutions and 'planning for the future' when traffic is expected to double, what with all the development to the north and people driving longer distances to commute. Half a page, and all they could come up with was widening the fucking freeway." He took Tina's glass out of her hand, set it on the counter, and picked her up.

Tina closed her eyes and relaxed, let her weight hang from his shoulders.

"I brought my bike down," he said.

"Mmm."

"Weather's been so nice, I thought maybe we could go for a ride to-morrow. A long one, up the coast." He set Tina down, and she opened her eyes. "We could take a picnic," he said. "Stop at one of the beaches."

"Don't you have to go back to the farm?"

"No." He went to the stove and turned on the burner under the frying pan.

"I was planning to work tomorrow," Tina said.

"Yeah. I figured that." Chip turned to look at her. "I thought maybe you'd want to change your plan."

She had one of Garrett's samples extracted and ready to analyze, the second of two Precambrian samples with fossils that had been positively identified and dated. She had the last kinetics sample ready to run. There was half a day right there, HPLC willing. Then she needed to organize the results for her poster-designing meeting with Garrett next week. "I don't know," she said. "We're leaving for Guam in less than two weeks and I still—"

"Screw it," he said, turning back to the stove. "I'll go by myself."

Tina stared at his broad back. His disappointment was palpable. She wanted to snap her fingers and have it be gone, or lean up against his back, wrap her arms around his belly and make it disappear with a quick hug.

"You gonna take a shower before dinner, you better get on it," he said without turning.

Tina left the kitchen. She walked across the living room to the bathroom, pulled her T-shirt over her head, and stood there with her arms caught in the sleeves, staring at the floor. She went back to the kitchen.

"You could ride down to the lab with me," she said from the opening to the living room. "You could use my electric typewriter."

"Do what?" He turned, a slotted spoon held up in front of his chest.

"Type your letter on the typewriter in my office. It has a screen where you can see what you typed before it prints, like a little built-in computer."

"I've never used a computer." He lowered the spoon.

"It's not a computer, just a fancy typewriter. It'd be a lot easier than typing on that thing," she said, motioning with shirt-bound arms toward the antique on the table. "We could take a lunch and go down to the beach in the afternoon."

Chip nodded slowly. "Not exactly what I had in mind. But okay. We'll take a bike ride to BIO. I've never seen it from the inside."

"Not much to see," Tina said. "A bunch of labs and offices." She wriggled her arms out of her shirt and ran back to the bathroom to take her shower.

"Wow! Black-crowned night herons." Chip moved stealthily across Tina's office toward the window. "There must be a dozen of them," he whispered.

Tina laughed and walked past him. "I'm afraid they're sort of tame." She cranked open the creaky window. The herons didn't move. "I talk to them all the time. They ignore me."

"You mean to say they've been here all summer?" he said incredulously. "They nested here? Usually they're pretty shy."

"Come to think of it, I'm not sure where they nest. But they do seem to hang out here all year. Maybe these are just the bachelors. Or the senior citizens or something." Tina went to her desk and retrieved her lab coat from the back of the chair. "You want to see Cristina Arenas's famous laboratory?" she said, buttoning the front of the smock. "Before I get you started here?"

"Sure." He turned reluctantly away from the window.

"Don't worry, the herons will be there all day. By noon they'll probably be getting on your nerves— What?"

Chip was grinning. "It looks like you don't have anything on underneath."

"What?"

"Your little white coat. It's sexy."

Tina glanced down at her lab coat, her bare legs sticking out the bottom.

"Too bad it's contaminated," Chip added.

"Give me a break," Tina said, moving toward the door. "It's not contaminated."

She led him down the hall to the instrument lab. "These are actually Max Lindquist's labs," she said as she unlocked the door. "But he's in Sweden. Max Lindquist really is famous," she added, and smiled at the notion that Chip didn't have the slightest idea who Max Lindquist was. Or Harper Gibson or Conroy Decker or even Garrett Thomas, who was in everyone's biology textbook. She moved down to the end of the lab and started up the HPLC. Chip followed, but stopped halfway, as if he were afraid he was going to knock something over. He looked startlingly out of place, there in the middle of the instrument lab, like a redwood sculpture in a post-modern art exhibit. It was a good thing he wasn't a permanent fixture, Tina thought, because he took up an inordinate amount of space. She squeezed past him to retrieve a beaker from the sink.

"That's the Mass Spec," she said, gesturing at the instrument he was standing next to. "And this is the infamous HPLC. That instrument I'm always complaining about."

He moved a little closer to get a look. "This thing?" He sounded disappointed. He reached out and touched the instrument casing with his index finger.

"Actually," Tina said, listening to the pump, "it doesn't sound that bad now." She explained to Chip how the instrument worked, tracking the flow of solvent from injector to detectors, touching each of the components as she spoke . . . and laughed, when she realized she was talking it up, trying to get him to appreciate it. "Actually," she said, "it's an antiquated piece of junk, and as soon as I get some funding I'm going to trash it and get a new one."

Chip was much more impressed by the big wet lab down the hall than by anything in the instrument lab.

"Hey, now this is more like it," he said when she opened the door.

"More like what?"

"More like what I imagined your lab would look like." He gestured at the cumbersome floor-to-ceiling maze of glass bubbles, valves, and tubes that made up the vacuum line.

"Oh, that's just for drying." Tina peered through the plexiglass bubble at the samples she had left to dry. Carefully, she turned the valve on top, leaving it just a tiny bit open with the air hissing in, as she walked Chip through the lab. She explained the acid bath she used for sterilizing glassware, showed off the excellent scale and weighing station, even opened up the freezer and took out some frozen sediment samples to show him. Then they went back to her office and she showed him how to use the typewriter.

To Tina's surprise, she rather enjoyed having him there, pecking away across the hall while she worked. It was fun, vaguely illicit. They'd brought a picnic for lunch, and Chip had insisted they bring swimsuits, though it was too cold to swim. She scored the glass of her last ampoule from the kinetics experiment, gave it a whack with the file, and smiled as the tip fell away with the gratifying "pop" of a clean break. Small triumphs, she thought, glad to be done. For the time being, anyway. She deposited a measure of solvent into the ampoule and tapped at its side until the smudge of white powder dissolved. If the ACS grant got funded there would be dozens of kinetics experiments to do—and without Garrett's tales of unfathomably ancient life for inspiration. But then, if the grant got funded, she would have money to pay a technician. Michael, she hoped. She drew the sample into the pipette, deposited it in a clean vial, and looked around for the sheet of labels. Assuming Michael's lab habits hadn't changed while he was in Europe trying to grow a beard, he would do well with these experiments. She took the sample to the instrument lab and started the HPLC run, and then she went back to her office to see how Chip was doing.

It was obvious that he liked the typewriter, though he wouldn't admit it. Not only had he written his letter to the *San Francisco Chronicle* about mass transit, but he was writing letters to his congressmen and state assemblymen, and also to James Watt about what he thought of the Alaska pipeline and offshore drilling among other things. While he was at it, he'd decided to do an article for the op-ed page of the Brayton paper, something, Tina learned to her surprise, he did quite frequently.

"Check this out," he said, pulling her onto his lap and laying one of the typed pages over the typewriter keys. "This is for the *Brayton Bee*." He tapped the part he wanted her to read, the last paragraph.

"Man is changing the earth's climate," the article concluded. "If we continue burning fuel at the current rate, temperatures will rise six degrees by the year 2000 and the ice caps will melt, flooding coastal areas, including most of California. There are a hundred reasons to stop using fossil fuels, and it is now apparent that we can't just wait until we've used them all up to find better ways of doing things—such as transporting ourselves to and from work. So why are we still talking about widening freeways?"

"Where'd you hear that?" Tina said, pointing to "six degrees by the year 2000."

"It was in the *New York Times*. I've been reading this science section they have on Tuesdays. Why? It's not right?"

"I didn't think anyone had that good an understanding yet. To say how much, or when."

"Well, they did say that there are some scientists who disagree—who say it's only going to get marginally warmer, half a degree or something."

Tina twisted out of his lap and stood next to him, looking down at his letter. Hadn't she heard Conroy Decker complaining about the CO_2 levels the climatologists were using in their models? How could the climate predictions be any better than the information you fed into them? "This isn't my field," she said. "But I don't think you should be quoting these numbers like they're tomorrow's weather forecast. And this thing about the ice caps melting . . ." Tina gestured at the letter. "Maybe if you rephrased it," she said.

"But I'm just quoting what these scientists said."

"They were probably just speculating."

"I didn't think scientists were in the business of speculating."

"Sometimes it seems like that's all we do . . . though it is odd that anyone would speculate like that to the press." Tina moved toward the door. "Anyway," she said, "that part about too many cars and pollution and a generally deteriorating quality of life ought to be reason enough not to widen your freeway. Doesn't take much speculation to see that."

"But people don't see it. They don't think about it."

Tina stopped and turned around, folding her arms across her chest. "What, and you think they're going to see the planet warming up?"

"Maybe," Chip said, ignoring the sarcasm. "The point is, it's dramatic." As if to demonstrate, he rolled Tina's chair back from the desk and leaned toward her. "This isn't about something as mundane as sitting in a traffic jam," he said. "It's not just a bit of prime farmland being lost, or some obscure species of frog losing its habitat, the life and soul being drained out of the planet drip by drip. You tell people we're actually changing the climate, that in a mere twenty or thirty years whole cities will be flooded and crops fried, that we're actually making the planet uninhabitable—and they'll sit up and listen."

He was unnervingly absolute. He was immune to the kind of echoing, but then . . . but if . . . but we-don't-know-yet questions that habitually plagued Tina's thought patterns and inhibited her actions. She was almost jealous. It was a powerful, even attractive, sort of naiveté. He was leaning so far forward in her office chair that she feared it might shoot out from behind and dump his earnest ass on the hard linoleum floor. Why should she argue with him? So what if his phraseology bothered her? So what if he didn't make a distinction between *believing* something, and knowing it well enough to say it out loud, knowing it in a fully demonstrable way? She held her tongue and went back into the lab.

By the time Tina got Garrett's last rock sample running on the HPLC and returned to her office, Chip had changed into a pair of baggy blue swim trunks. She found him sprawled in the easy chair, his legs stretched out and crossed at the ankle, his hands folded quietly in his lap. He'd rearranged the chair so that he could watch the herons out the window. The herons were sitting there doing nothing.

"You finish all your letters?" Tina asked him, pushing the door closed behind her.

"Yup."

She picked up her knapsack and started rifling through it for her swimsuit. There was no way she was going in the water, but it was warm in the sun and it might feel good to sit on the beach.

"What are those pictures?" Chip said suddenly, gesturing toward the wall behind Tina's desk.

"Cyanobacteria. Aren't they cool?" Tina squinted at the picoplankton portraits across the room. They were beginning to look a little worn around the edges. "They're these tiny photosynthetic bacteria no one knows much about," she explained, toeing off her shoes. "So small no one ever detected them until recently. This guy in Illinois isolated them from some seawater samples. . . ."

Tina left off telling her picoplankton story when she realized that Chip had stopped listening. He was, rather, watching her undress, his mustache splayed with the hint of a smile, as if they were playing out some parody of a woman scientist's nightmare, her male colleague finding her rear end of more consequence than her pet theory. Tina laid her shorts on the desk next to her T-shirt and took off her socks. She had seen that happen once at the dissertation defense of a classmate, a pretty, pale-skinned blonde, growing pink-faced with rage and humiliation as she sensed her audience's lack of regard. Tina stepped into her bathing suit. Chip was not a colleague. And she wasn't angry that he didn't take her seriously. Indeed, she sometimes worried that he took her *too* seriously. She did not feel humiliated by the way he was watching her pull the swimsuit up her hips, his eyes moving over her skin as if it were made of polished gold—the curve of her buttock, the hill of her breast, the rounded corner of her shoulder all sparkling in the rays of sunlight that had made it past the trees—until she felt she would melt into a hot pool of precious ore if he looked a moment longer. She stuck her arm through the right strap and pulled it up. Chip reached out and casually peeled the whole thing back to her waist.

"This where you sleep when you stay overnight here?" he said. "This chair?"

She nodded.

She wondered if it was possible to come like that, just standing there with him admiring her. She took a step closer to the chair and he lifted his forearm and brushed the back of his hand lazily across her breasts. "I have this feeling," he said, raising his eyes to her face, "that I'm getting in way too deep here."

Getting in? Tina thought, moving around in front of him and sliding her knee onto the chair. He had it backward. This was getting out. This was escaping into a wide-open blue space like the one above the Pacific on a clear day, a space where nothing was known and nothing understood, where not a single mystery had ever been solved or would ever be solved and you weren't even tempted to try, an undeniably empty blue space that seemed to stretch to infinity. . . . Though you knew it didn't.

She hoped she hadn't screamed too loud. She stayed where he had pulled her in, reined her in at the last moment, and neither of them dared to move, in the musty old chair that had come with the office along with the windows and the chalkboard and the night herons looking on, all twisted up in the swimsuits they hadn't bothered to take off. It seemed like a long time but was really only a few minutes until Chip shifted under her and started talking, or rather continued talking, as if he had been carrying this thought with him through all that wild, thoughtless blue space.

He told her that he would probably still be trying to talk himself out of getting involved with her if he hadn't seen her with that man. Tina sat upright and slid back onto his knees, still dizzy. He was talking about Alan, that day back in August when they'd gone to the beach. Chip had come around the side of the duplex and seen them heading off down the sidewalk toward the beach, Katharine and Fred, Tina and Alan.

"What, the threat of a rival?" Tina said, laughing, and he admitted that that was part of it. Most of it. But there was something else. Something about the casual way the man laid his hand on her shoulder as they walked down the street talking. It made her seem less dangerous.

Tina stared at him, uncomprehending. Less dangerous? And then they both burst out laughing: it was hard to imagine a more unlikely source of danger than Tina at that moment, crouching in his lap, lightheaded and half-naked, her bony knees sticking up on either side of them.

As they dashed up the stairs, Chip still wet from his madman's swim around the pier, Tina greeted a postdoc from the lab next to hers and wondered how long it would be before Katharine heard about Chip. There was something satisfying about flaunting her secret lover—a lover that no one would know, or know of—in the halls of BIO. She felt like a child gleefully breaking the rules, though there weren't, of course, any rules against having a friend to one's lab, or taking an afternoon swim. According to Katharine, the technician for Geophysics kept a surfboard in his office. Making love in one's office might be going a little far, Tina thought, but then she wasn't flaunting that. She hoped. She pulled her towel tighter about her shoulders, and ran ahead of Chip, laughing as she turned the corner at the top of the stairs.

"What're you laughing at?" he said, coming around behind her.

But Tina had just opened the door to the instrument lab, and she had already stopped laughing and started cursing. She switched off the chart recorder, hurling expletives at the skewed chromatogram of Garrett's sample, moved to the microprocessor and punched at its keys, alternating questions with threats as the little screen maintained a series of flashing nines, no matter which keys she pushed. She went on at some length before it dawned on her that she was talking to a dead machine. The microprocessor had gone out. The pump was still thumping away stupidly, but the thing was braindead, in a permanent coma, and taunting her yet. She glanced at Chip, who was hovering in the doorway with a worried expression on his face.

"What's wrong?" he said cautiously.

Tina shook her head and turned back to the HPLC to do something she'd been wanting to do for a long time. She pulled her arm back and swung her open hand around to slap the side of the instrument casing.

Her palm came away bruised. And the pump didn't miss a beat.

Chapter 11

Garrett lived in a neat, unremarkable little tract house on the east side of Brayton. Tina smiled to find herself noticing the yard, which looked as though it sported the original low-maintenance landscaping: a lawn, some neatly trimmed shrubs along the house, and one large shade tree in the parkway. The inside was another matter altogether. The place was crowded with knickknacks from foreign countries, the walls covered with art work, mostly large black-and-white photographs, abstract renditions of plants and rocks and oddly skewed views of a European town. It was all too haphazard to be called cosmopolitan, more reminiscent of an old woman's fussy living room, except that the objects themselves weren't old womanish at all. There was an elaborate stereo system and half a wall lined with record albums in the living room, but when Tina asked Garrett about putting on some music while they worked, he shook his head and said he didn't like having music on unless he was really going to listen to it.

Working at a big table in the family room Garrett used for an office, they quickly chose the mass specs and chromatograms they wanted to photocopy and reduce for the poster. Then they leaned two large poster boards against the wall and used Post-its to indicate what was to go where. Garrett would mount the boards side by side on a panel in the conference hall. The left side would describe the kinetics of the chiral hydrocarbon. Here they would include a schematic of the thumb-switching reactions, a chromatogram of a standard with all the stereoisomers, a summary of the kinetics equations, and, finally, the chromatogram of the one Precambrian sample with known fossil material that Tina had run the day before the HPLC died. The right-hand poster board would be all about the Warrua sample, with four boxes arranged in a ring around the center of the space, each box outlined in a different color. The colors were Garrett's idea. An overview of the Warrua formation's geology and a summary of the controversy about the fossils would be encased in blue. Garrett's amino acid analysis, in green. Tina's analysis of the larger organic molecules, in orange. The chromatogram showing the four hydrocarbon stereoisomers and the corresponding age calculations would go in a red box. In the open square at the center of the ring, in bold black lettering against a yellow background, they would present a summary and conclusions.

The result of the study was straightforward: the 3.8-billion-year-old Warrua rock contained at least one 3.8-billion-year-old organic compound, and all evidence indicated it was the severed tail of the chlorophyll molecule. This, along with several other tell-tale organics found in the HPLC-Mass Spec analysis, was evidence that the marks in the rock were indeed fossils of carbon-dioxide-using, oxygen-producing photosynthetic bacteria and supported the hypothesis that they had been a type of cyanobacteria—with a chemical make-up not all that different from Tina's picoplankton, though the fossils lacked the picoplankton's special wardrobe of lipid jackets.

Garrett set down his pencil and leaned back in his chair. "Do you realize that this is the best hard evidence we've had in decades?"

"'Hard' evidence? I don't know, Garrett. That may be going a little far."

"Relatively speaking," he said, chuckling. "In terms of what is known about the events of 3.8 billion years ago, this is hard evidence. As far as we've taken it." He waved a hand at the square in the center of the poster. Tina had penciled in "SOLID YELLOW" in the corner, and their conclusions were outlined on Post-its stuck in the middle. "I don't think we've overstepped the data."

"It's not even about *events*," Tina said. "It's more a snapshot of the status quo 3.8 billion years ago. Here we are with these complete photosynthetic bacteria smack dab at the beginning of the geological record. And nothing but the usual conjectures about how they got there."

"Oh, I'm sure this will be bandied about as evidence for and against all sorts of existing theories. In fact, I'm expecting something of a feeding frenzy around this poster at the conference."

Tina leaned her elbows on the table and stared at their notes. "It's pretty damned incredible to think about photosynthesis being this old. The atmosphere only became oxygenated, what, about 2 billion years ago? Isn't the evidence for that pretty convincing? Those bands of iron oxide in the sediment?"

"Mmm. But that doesn't mean we know when the process started, how long it took. Despite claims to the contrary. We know nothing about the *rate* of oxygen production." Garrett tilted his chair back on two legs and contemplated the poster board with its overlapping yellow Post-its. "You know who's going to be the first to claim this," he said.

"Who?"

"The panspermia people. I can hear it now. They'll say that there wasn't enough time for life to begin and develop—that it couldn't, therefore, have originated on earth but must have come from some extraterrestrial source."

"How can they say that a few hundred million years isn't enough? Enough time for what? We don't even know what we're talking about when we talk about life beginning, what process. Enough time for something that's not been shown possible in *any* time span? And so what if life started somewhere else—*how* did it start? Talk about cop-outs. Why don't they just say 'God did it,' and stop wondering?"

Garrett was grinning. "You sure you don't want to go to the conference?"

Tina shook her head. She leaned back and stared at their poster. "To tell the truth," she said after a moment, "all of the origin-of-life theories seem pretty vague to me. I really don't see that our analysis of the Warrua rocks offers evidence for or against any of them because they're all too . . ." Tina flapped her hand in the air.

"Too chimerical?" Garrett offered. "But that's half the attraction. We're all closet fantasists, you know. Romantics. Religious fanatics. Science fiction aficionados." He flashed Tina a crazed smile. "It's true—some of these so-called theories are downright embarrassing. But it's always been that way."

"You've never been much of a romantic, Garrett, that I can make out. Haven't you always been the one 'let's have some evidence, folks' influence in the whole field of rampant hypothesizing? Even this project you brought me. Real rocks, real fossils, real organic chemicals."

"Real hard evidence," Garrett said.

Tina laughed. "Okay. Hard evidence. For something."

"You're right, of course, that a few hundred million years still gives us plenty of time to come up with cyanobacteria." Garrett picked up his pencil and poked at the air in the direction of the poster. "But what this does is force us to think about time as finite, limited, if not limiting. Time has always been the coveted wild card in our thinking. Lots and lots of time. In a way, it made us lazy. If you have enough time you can claim that the most improbable event becomes probable. You can start with a watery broth, turn it down to the barest simmer, and expect it to cook down to a thick stew. But even so, even *with* time as a wild card, we haven't been able to explain the presence on earth of anything but life's most basic building blocks. No one has come up with a way of putting the blocks together to form a wall, let alone an entire building, without making some giant leap of faith. Here we've been trying for decades, and we can't show that proteins and nucleotides—let alone RNA or DNA—could have been created under anything even remotely resembling early earth conditions. This 'RNA world' hypothesis that's become so popular really irritates me. Oh, as a hypothesis it's interesting, and the experiments were exciting, but now it's seeping into biochemistry textbooks as The Way Life Began: out of the prebiotic organic soup rose a world of replicating RNA, and out of RNA came the first organism. No matter that no one can show that RNA was even a possible ingredient in the early soup. We've shown that there could have been amino acids, simple sugars, urea, and that's it. More or less what I showed years ago, in the original experiments, with a few important changes in the particular amino acids we think were most prevalent. Any way you look at it, what you have is a meager broth, not a thick stew full of wish-list ingredients. A hypothesis based on that and some real chemistry and," he gestured at their poster, "the fossil evidence, is long overdue."

Tina had been leaning on the table, staring at their poster while she listened to Garrett. She sat up now and turned to look at him. He was going to put forth a new hypothesis?

Garrett had a quixotic smile on his face. "Not," he said, "that I have anything that you would consider 'hard evidence.'"

"That didn't stop your friend Jenner. What—?"

"Don't go getting all excited now. It's really just an update of the original organic soup theory. The problem is that it was too dilute. It needed a helping hand. Some stirring. Some spices. A thickening agent—"

"God, Garrett, you're starting to wax poetic."

"I know," he said, laughing. "I'm mellowing in my old age. Or getting soft in the head."

"Yeah, right, give me a break. What are you, fifty-seven, fifty-eight?"

"Old enough to be getting impatient. I'm tired of sitting on the sidelines of the debate like some sort of referee. I want to turn the fire up and watch the damn soup boil over." Garrett set his pencil down firmly and pushed his chair back. "Let's have some lunch."

"You mean you're not going to tell me what this new hypothesis is? What, I have to wait and read about it in the proceedings from the conference?"

"Oh, well, it's nothing so radical." He settled back into the chair and picked up the pencil. "You need a catalyst. You need something to hold all the building-block molecules in near proximity, a container or a template of sorts. And, the part that everyone ignores, you need some primitive way to harness energy from the outset, because the broth just isn't rich enough to keep anything alive. You probably don't remember, but you were onto this when you spouted off at Jenner's seminar. Here we have our earliest evidence of life pointing to these cyanobacteria-like photosynthetic organisms, with no signs of the more primitive, biochemically simpler sulfur-consuming organisms we assumed came first. Like Jenner, I started running through what exactly was likely to have been around in quantity. And instead of what I *wanted* to have in the soup, I focused on the humic material that was actually the main product in all of my prebiotic syntheses. The stuff we all ignored, like good organic chemists looking for the desired product and trying to minimize the sludge, the resins that coated the flask when we finished. This humic material would have collected on the water surface, formed a scum. And small organic molecules would be adsorbed on the water side of the scum—"

"The way humic acids accumulate in present-day oceans, attracting organics out of solution."

"Exactly. So you have a template of sorts, or I should say a plethora of templates, with a profusion of possible patterns. And you have this rich source of UV-light-absorbing chemistry—all the aromatics and conjugated double bonds in the scum—so there is the possibility of reactions in thermodynamically unfavorable directions. As in life. What I'm working on in the lab is the photochemistry of the humics, and the possibility of energy transfer to the small water-soluble organics. . . ."

It was an organic chemist's theory, rigorously, even tediously thought out: the organic soup, replete with cooking instructions this time. There was no central miraculous factor shining with the enlightened glow of THE MISSING PIECE, nothing wild or heroic or exceptionally intriguing, like Jenner's clay organisms, or self-replicating RNA. It was a classical sort of theory, an aggregate of small, chemically reasonable processes leading to the large, unreasonable one called life. Some of the processes could, in theory, be simulated in the lab, which was the approach Garrett was known for. It certainly wasn't an eloquent theory—no theory that revolved around humic acids was ever going to be eloquent. They were too messy and poorly understood, organic chemistry's latrine, its black box. Which, Tina thought, was probably as good a place as any for life to begin.

It was after two by the time they sat down to the lunch Garrett had prepared. He set out a plate of dainty open-face sandwiches, announcing that they were from a recipe in *Bon Appetit*.

"You like to cook?" Tina asked dubiously.

"Of course," he said, handing her a dish of sliced lemons that he indicated were for the shrimp salad. "All organic chemists like to cook."

"What about farmers?" she mumbled.

"What about what?"

"Nothing," Tina said. She squeezed lemon onto her salad. "I don't like to cook."

"You don't?" Garrett sounded surprised. He studied Tina's face for a moment. "Must be your mixed blood. The geochemist in you. Geologists don't cook. Do you like pancakes?"

"Pancakes?" Tina shrugged. "They're okay."

"Geologists are all nuts about pancakes."

"Orloff?" Tina said, incredulous. "Sylvia Orloff eats pancakes?"

"Well." Garrett bit into a sandwich. "There are exceptions. I think Sylvia's husband cooks for her. He was a chemist, you know."

"I've never seen Katharine eat pancakes."

"Who's Katharine?"

"My geologist friend—one of Orloff's postdocs. You might have seen her around. Big Amazon woman with blonde hair."

"Oh, yes." Garrett nodded. "I think I met her in your office once. But as I recall, you were busy blaming me for the bad judgement of the director of earth sciences at NSF and the lowly status of basic research in the eighties, among other things. I don't think we were ever introduced."

Tina swallowed. "That was Katharine," she said. She picked a sandwich off the plate and tried to think of something to say about that day that would make sense. She peeled the leaf off the top of the sandwich and nibbled on it.

"You like that?" Garrett said. "It's arugula. That gourmet foods store downtown has started carrying some produce. I got it there." He forked up a shrimp and slipped it into his mouth, and Tina realized that he wasn't asking her for an explanation.

"It's delicious," she said gratefully. She didn't mention that arugula grew like a weed, that it got spicy instead of bitter when it went to flower in the summer, or that she knew the man who had convinced the gourmet foods store to try carrying produce. She looked up from her sandwich and caught Garrett's eye. "I am sorry," she said, "for lighting into you that day." He shook his head once and made a little back-handed motion with his fork, as if swatting the whole matter away.

"By the way," he said, "I've been meaning to ask you if you want to use the Mercury while I'm gone." Garrett suddenly adjusted his glasses and looked closely at Tina. "You do know how to drive, don't you?"

"Get off it, of course I know how to drive. And thank you very much, but I don't think I'd want to drive that boat of yours."

"Just thought I'd offer," he said, feigning insult. "I'm taking a vacation after the conference, visiting an old friend in Paris. I'll be gone for over a month."

"I'm leaving the week after you, anyway. Won't be back till just before Christmas," Tina added, with a surge of excitement about the cruise.

They finished their lunch and made a few more additions to their poster, and then Tina fended off Garrett's offer to drive her back to BIO and rode her bike back, leaving him to finish the poster. She was surprised at the relief she felt at being done with the project. She spent a good part of the following week reading Deep Sea Drilling Project reports, learning more about the paleontology, geology, and geochemistry they'd be doing on the *Explorer*. Indeed, she went all week without thinking about the Warrua sample, so that when Garrett stopped by her office to show her the finished poster, it was something of a surprise, as if it were someone else's work entirely, someone else's radical idea. The two boards were taped together along the black line to make a sort of hinge in back, and Garrett unfolded it and propped it up on the easy chair.

The glaringly bright shade of yellow that he'd chosen for the center box did exactly what it was supposed to do: Tina's eyes went straight to the conclusions, then made their way around the surrounding boxes in search of justification. "I think it's a good thing it's got Garrett Thomas as co-author," she said when he asked her what she thought. But they agreed to do a paper together when they returned, and then they wished each other bon voyage.

"Have fun," Tina called after him as he stepped out of her office with the poster tucked under his arm. Garrett stopped in the middle of the hall and did a little twirl on his toe, making Tina think of the Nowhere Man spinning round and round on the hill in the old Beatles movie—except that this Nowhere Man stopped spinning to continue energetically down the hall, like a man intent on having some fun.

Chapter 12

She was ready to leave. Excited. Her duffel bag packed. She'd been in the library all day, gathering up books that the *Explorer's* library wouldn't have, making photocopies, trying to anticipate what she would want. They were allowed to take one small box in addition to what they'd already shipped off, and she added the papers and books to the few last minute things from the lab that she'd packed. Katharine said they'd swing by on their way to the airport in the morning, get the boxes. It was late, almost ten, when Tina left BIO. Dark on the bluff road, moonless. Gangs of kids still roaming the streets of Brayton, getting into trouble. When she got home she was thinking about leaving, going, being gone.

Chip was in the living room, sitting on the couch listening to a program of international guitar music on the radio. He didn't greet her, and Tina wondered if he was still upset about his new landscaping job in Marin County. He'd complained about the long drive and the pretentious clients, with their perfect "estate." He turned the radio off and went into the kitchen.

"You didn't eat yet?" Tina asked, following him.

He shook his head and turned on the stove under the wok, then stood there waiting for the oil to heat. Tina deposited her knapsack in a chair and moved up behind him. She wrapped her arms around his belly and hugged his back. "Watch out," he said, unwrapping her arms. "You're gonna get burned." He dumped a bowl of chopped pork and garlic and ginger into the sizzling oil, and Tina stepped back. She moved to set the table, but it was already set with chopsticks and the cloth napkins he insisted on.

She thought he was just in a hurry to get dinner on the table, so she went to the bathroom and washed up. When she returned he was frying the rice, dribbling soy sauce around the edges, tossing in the scrambled eggs and green onions. It wasn't until he walked past her with two bowls full of rice and slammed them down on the table that Tina realized he was mad.

"What's wrong?" She sat down across from him.

Chip had picked up his chopsticks to eat, but now he looked up from his bowl incredulously. "You're asking me what's wrong? You come coasting in here at eleven o'clock at night, no phone call, no nothing, and you're asking me what's wrong?" He stabbed at his rice and scooped up a bite.

"Chip?"

"What. Eat your rice. It's gonna get cold."

"You should eat without me when I'm late. I'll just throw something together when I get home."

"What's the point of that? Why would I want to come all the way down here to this little suburban shithole just so I can eat alone and worry about why the hell you're not home yet?"

"Sorry. I guess I should have called you. . . . I just thought you'd figure it out that I was working late—"

"Fuck!" He threw his chopsticks down on the table and stood up, walked a few steps toward the living room, and then turned around to glare at Tina, who was looking confused and a little scared.

She hadn't seen it coming. But then she hadn't been looking. She had been walking without watching where, without anticipation or direction— walking right into this fight and not even knowing that's what it was until she found herself dazed and bewildered in its midst, as if it had dropped down from the sky with no warning or prelude.

"Of course you're fucking working late! Of course! Working early, working late, whatever the hell it is you do down there. Of course I should figure this out. Why should you have to stop for two minutes to call me up, after all? And God forbid you should ask me to come get you, instead of riding that bike home in the dark in the middle of the fucking night." He went into the living room and stood staring out the porthole window at the yard he had created. He stood there for a full minute and then he closed the blinds and returned to the kitchen, where Tina was sitting up straight in her chair with her hands in her lap, looking at her bowl of rice. "Eat, it's getting cold." He sat down and took a bite. "Shit." He grabbed Tina's bowl out from under her, picked up his own, and took the rice back to reheat in the wok.

"I thought you didn't believe in unnecessary driving," Tina said weakly. He spun around to look at her.

"Come on, Tina, shall I define unnecessary? Do you read the paper?" He snorted. "Of course not. Did it even cross your mind that it's Halloween? When every weirdo and his mother's uncle is out roaming the streets? No. In spite of what you may want to think, you are still one small, no, tiny, little half-pint woman, and for someone with more brains than anyone I've ever met you are awfully stupid. Maybe you'll get lucky and just get run over by a speeding car. Or a not-speeding car who doesn't expect some fool to be riding around on her bicycle in the middle of the night." He turned back to the rice, cursing because it had started to stick.

"Brayton's not exactly New York City," Tina said softly.

"It's not exactly a village in the sticks either. Christ."

"I have a light—"

"Oh yes, a veritable spotlight. It will stop the rapist in his tracks. Blinded by the light. Rape? Murder? You ever heard of that? You might try reading the paper now and then. Broaden your horizons. At least to the city limits of Brayton."

Tina started to cry. All of the sudden there were tears flooding her eyes and running silently down her face. She wasn't sure why she was crying, if it was because he would have her acquiesce to such a hateful, limiting fear, whatever he'd read in the paper that she didn't want to know about. Or because he was chastising her for not reading the paper and she knew he was right. Or if she was crying simply because this source of solid comfort was yelling at her, or because she thought her tears might stem his anger and turn it back to comfort. She'd never had a lover yell at her before. They just left. Or she left, or the relationship floated without comment into non-being. Certainly none of them had ever been foolish enough to worry about her. The only person who'd ever done that was her father. And she felt, oddly, a little like she remembered feeling as a child when her father got mad enough to yell—crying because he was mad and at the same time pitying him, even before she knew the meaning of the word, crying because he seemed so pathetic and doomed, worrying about her doing what she was bound and determined to do regardless of his anger or grief. Of course, her father would never have said "fuck."

Chip set the bowl of rice firmly down in front of her. He didn't notice her tears until he sat down and looked across the table. When he spoke his tone was gentler. "Come on, Tina. Eat your rice."

She picked up her chopsticks and lifted a few grains to her mouth. He was watching her.

She sat there trying to chew the rice in her mouth with her nose running, sniffling, trying not to cry. She shouldn't be crying. She ought to yell back at him, cut him loose. It was only fair.

He started eating and tried to change the subject. "I was in town with Jorge today," he said, "and we stopped by here to see if we could get your Toyota running. Jorge's a real whiz with cars." He shoveled rice into his mouth, more furiously with each bite, emptying his bowl while Tina pushed the contents of hers into a neat mound in the middle. "But your fucking engine's froze up from sitting so long."

Tina didn't say anything.

"I suppose you don't care," he said. "Seeing as how you're leaving."

She pressed her lips together. Her eyes filled. She felt as if she were reading the script for someone else's part, a charade, a manipulative cliché: cry. Toy with your food.

"Hey. I didn't mean to yell at you. I suppose you can't help it if you're hopelessly impractical." He looked down at his empty bowl and laid his chopsticks on the table. "And inconsiderate and self-absorbed."

When he looked up he was smiling, but Tina's tears were flowing again anyway. He'd suckered right into the tears, and she could see that it wasn't fair, but she couldn't make herself stop.

"That was a joke," he said, reaching across the table to touch her wrist. "I'm teasing you."

"I know, but . . ." She laughed weakly. "It's probably true."

He took his hand away. "Of course it's true. But then, it's not going to matter, is it? On a ship in the middle of the Pacific Ocean." He got up and carried his bowl to the stove for seconds.

Tina wiped her eyes with the back of her hand. That was true too. She had been thinking about leaving, preparing to go, but she hadn't even considered what it meant to leave Chip for six weeks. She hadn't considered what it meant to *be* with Chip for the past three months. And she had no desire to consider it now, so close to the other side of leaving where, Chip was right, it wasn't going to matter. He sat back down and she worked at finishing the rice in her bowl, and the silence she left between them was so absolute that when the doorbell rang, she jumped and knocked her chopsticks across the table.

TRICK OR TREAT! A group of teenagers stood expectantly on the steps. They were all dressed in black with the barest effort at costumes—a pair of Groucho glasses, dracula teeth, a glow-in-the dark skeleton on a T-shirt. Tina was apologizing, telling them that she didn't have anything, when Chip handed her a half-empty bag of miniature chocolate bars.

"You missed the cute ones," he said, when the teenagers had sauntered off with their treats. He turned off the porch light and the living room light, and Tina moved up to him in the dark for an apologetic hug, which he accepted briefly, uncertainly. He didn't yell again, nor did he leave, and in the early hours of the morning he woke her to make love. But the goodbye he said a few hours later was cool and cursory, and as Tina tucked a few last-minute items into her duffel bag and waited for Katharine to pick her up, she found herself wondering sadly if the whole fanciful edifice of their relationship would simply collapse in her absence, disappear as readily as it had appeared—unheralded, neglected, unexamined.

Perhaps that was why she told Katharine about Chip that morning, on the way to the airport. Or perhaps it was just to see if she could shock Katharine into a few minutes of silence. They were on the highway just north of San Francisco, Katharine driving, and rambling on about the paleontologist she'd picked out for Tina.

"To tell the truth," Tina said, interrupting a description of Nigel Martinelli's many virtues, "I kind of like this guy I met a while back."

"Oh?" Katharine perked up. "Who's this? He's going to be on the cruise?"

"No, no." Tina laughed. "He is, I think, extremely land-bound."

"A geologist? Do I know him?"

"I doubt it." If Katharine had heard anything about a strange man in Tina's lab, she wasn't letting on. "He's the gardener for the couple who bought the hovel."

"The *gardener*?"

"Or landscaper, really, is more what you'd call him. He's also a farmer."

"A farmer?" Katharine shot Tina a skeptical glance and turned back to the road, shaking her head. "You're pulling my leg."

For a moment Tina felt triumphant, revealing her secret, seeing Katharine's unguarded surprise—but the feeling was short-lived. Chip just wouldn't show well in Katharine's world. Tina tried to describe his farm. She started to tell Katharine about the pigs but cut the story short, as if the enchantment might burst into a righteous cloud of dust at the telling—her vacation love exposed as her own construct, the flesh and blood man she described too flimsy a support.

"How long have you been seeing this guy?" Katharine said when Tina faltered.

Since August, Tina thought, feeling foolish and exposed. A few months. But to tell Katharine that was to invite more serious inquiry, not to mention hurt feelings. "A few weeks," she said.

"Well, I still think you'll like this geologist," Katharine said.

"Maybe." Tina shifted restlessly in the scratchy seat, the musty vestiges of morning sex seeping out between her legs like a taunt. They were on the bridge now, and she turned and pressed her nose to the window, looking out. The sky was overcast with a high fog, but she could see the water in the bay, sprinkled with whitecaps, roughed up by the wind. "Aren't you excited?" she asked, turning back to Katharine. "I mean, about the cores? Just think of it . . . we'll be the first ones to see them. . . ."

"I *am* excited . . ." Katharine paused as she pulled up to the toll booth and paid. "But Sylvia's been driving me crazy," she said when they were back in the flow of traffic. "I might as well be back in grad school, the way she treats me—like my education was meaningless, since she didn't have anything to do with it. She's always implying that I don't work hard enough, just because I'm not in the lab at all hours like her students. She never notices how efficient I am when I *am* there. She firmly believes that no woman with a decent social life could possibly do good or serious work. I don't think she realizes how unoriginal that concept is. Just because she had such a hard time of it when she was our age. . . . You know what people say, don't you? That she got set up by marrying Ben Chesfield? He was a big shot back then, you know, her graduate advisor. God he's almost eighty now, twenty-five years older than her. Ugly little guy, looks like a dwarf, and flirts with all her students. It's totally archetypal—"

"Come on, Katharine, you don't have to believe everything you hear,"

Tina interrupted her. "I mean, Sylvia Orloff has done important work. Some of her papers are classics."

"Yeah. She's done important work. Still does. Can't argue with that. I don't know . . . I can't tell if it's just that she wants to be sure of leaving her mark on me, the way she does with her students, you know, mold us all in her image . . . or if it's that she really doesn't respect me as a scientist. She's always doubting 'the depth of my insight,' ridiculing me at our group meetings." Katharine's tone had gone suddenly slack, devoid of all its bravado and self-confidence.

"Oh, Katharine. You know full well that she thinks you are a perfectly competent geologist."

"That's just it," Katharine said dejectedly. "'Perfectly competent' doesn't rate. Not in Orloff's lab. Not for a woman at BIO."

Tina looked at her in surprise. What had inspired this? Normally Katharine would rail in the face of such an attitude.

"Lord," Katharine groaned, laying her head on the back of the seat and stretching her arms out taut to the steering wheel as she accelerated onto the freeway. "Six weeks."

"What's with you? I thought you were looking forward to this cruise. I thought you were happy that Orloff invited you."

Katharine glanced at Tina's face and pulled herself up in her seat. "Okay," she said, brushing her hair back from her face. "So that's not the real problem."

"The real problem?"

"I guess the real problem is Fred," Katharine went on. "I'm going to miss Fred terribly."

"Oh. Well, it's only six weeks. . . . What are you guys going to do when your postdocs run out, anyway? If you can't find jobs in the same place?"

"We made a deal. Whoever gets the best job takes it, and the other one follows, job or not. The way it looks," Katharine added, grimacing, "I'm going to be the one following. Which is probably for the best, much as I hate the *idea* of it, tagging along after your man and all that. But it makes sense, because I can probably find something decent in industry, wherever we end up, and who knows what Fred would do if he's not at a university . . . maybe teach algebra to sixteen-year-olds or something." She let out a loud sigh.

"Oh, Katharine," Tina said, and she couldn't help laughing. "From what I've heard about cruises, you're going to be too busy to miss Fred."

For her part, Tina was growing more excited by the minute. Only now, as the signs for the airport turn-off started appearing, did it dawn on her to be excited about the voyage itself—not just the work she was going to be doing, but the adventure of a new place. She'd never been out of the United States, and now here she was headed to the South Pacific. No matter that people said Guam was boring, or that she would only be there one night and the rest of the time they would be making their way south on a floating island of laboratories and scientists, never setting foot on any real islands. The very idea that the sky would be different—the air, the horizon, her view of the sea, not to mention what they would be bringing up from its depths—the very concept of all this impending newness was exciting.

Chapter 13

The veterans of other research vessels sang the *Explorer's* praises as they cruised southeast from Guam toward their first drill site. Originally an oil exploration vessel, the ship's raison d'etre was still the derrick that rose some two hundred feet above its midsection and the rig deck and drill floor at its base where drilling operations took place. The drilling equipment had been upgraded, however, and the four-hundred-foot ship reoutfitted for research. It now sported six levels of laboratories and offices, refrigerated core storage rooms, a photography darkroom, a library, conference room, lounge, and even a small gym.

The sea was calm those first few days and the *Explorer* was an exceptionally stable ship, but even so, a few members of the scientific crew were sick. One young geologist spent the whole time vomiting over the side of the main deck, comforted by a good-humored Dutch sedimentologist who was likewise engaged. The sedimentologist was a veteran of the DSDP ship, however, and he assured everyone who inquired that he would feel better in precisely five days. Tina was relieved to find that she wasn't prone to seasickness. She felt only a mild queasiness that seemed to have as much to do with the constant smell of diesel and the claustrophobia of tiny windowless quarters and labs as it did with the movement of the ship. Tina's biggest problem, those first few days, was that she kept getting lost in the ship's maze of passages and small rooms, and she could hardly open the heavy bulkhead doors onto the decks. The doors irritated her, made her feel self-conscious, as if she were a bumbling foreign visitor, a guest in a world made for larger, stronger people—a feeling that was only aggravated by the succession of inevitably male arms reaching out to rescue her. She became adept at hanging her weight on the door handles and kicking off the sill, but it wasn't something she could do with any finesse, and it was only natural that anyone who saw her would feel compelled to offer help. She shared a cabin with Katharine, Orloff's student, Janice, and a middle-aged French paleontologist who seemed unfazed by his coed quarters, but the bulkhead doors made her conscious, in a way she never was on shore, of the essential maleness of the world she worked in.

They spent a morning with the first mate, going over the rules of the ship and walking through an emergency drill. The rest of the time in transit was taken up by training sessions and meetings with Sylvia Orloff, who was surprisingly keyed up and nervous, like a potentate readying her vassals for a foray into new territory. For the scientists who had never been on a drill ship, there was a lot to learn. Everyone was assigned a daily two-hour shift at the core-sampling table, cutting out plugs according to the sampling plan Orloff had assembled from their various requests. The rest of the tasks during their twelve-hour watches varied. From noon to five Tina would be in the chemistry lab doing various organic chemical analyses. She had the six to eight slot at the sampling table, and then from eight until midnight she was in charge of monitoring the cores for hydrocarbons to insure that drilling didn't pose a safety or pollution hazard. Orloff made it clear that whether they were on watch or off, they had to keep up with the cores coming in. She wanted each core processed and materials for the site report in her office before they began drilling the following site. When they disembarked in New Zealand, core descriptions and analytic data had to be ready for publication in the "Initial Reports," which, if the cores were any good, would be used by the wider scientific community for years to come.

At three o'clock in the morning on their fourth day at sea, the crew dropped the sonar beacon that would maintain the ship's position over the first drill site. Tina and Katharine both had the noon-to-midnight watch and if they'd had any sense they would have been sleeping at that hour, but they were too excited. They found a spot on the drawworks behind the drill floor where they could watch the drill pipe being fed through the moonhole in the bottom of the ship. They weren't really supposed to be down there during drilling unless they had some reason, which they didn't, but then Tina didn't suppose any of the other half-dozen members of the scientific crew on the drawworks had reason to be there either. Except Orloff, of course, who seemed to be everywhere at once, looking regal and tyrannical even in steel-toed safety shoes and a ridiculous orange hard hat. She had been down on the drill floor trying to oversee assembly of the pipe, but the drilling crew were apparently unimpressed and had banished her to the drawworks to watch.

Tina leaned out over the railing and looked up at the derrick. They were using a corer for soft sediments that wasn't a drill at all but rather a hydraulic piston device that forced a tube into the sediment, like a giant apple corer powered by jets of water. The corer was already attached to the end of the drill pipe and being lowered through a funnel-like guide into the water. As the pipe was lowered, more sections were added from the top, lifted off a rack next to the derrick and swung into place by a crane. Tina tried to imagine the pipe trailing down beneath them. It had thirty-eight hundred meters to go before it reached the sea floor, over two miles of water, of absolute darkness. And this was one of the shallower sites, above the Ontong Java Plateau, a few degrees north of the equator. Their huge ship suddenly seemed tiny when she pictured it floating on the skin of such a great mass of water with this narrow cord swinging down from its midsection like an umbilical cord growing backward toward the womb, resuming a prenatal role . . .

"Tina!"

Tina turned to Katharine, who had taken hold of her arm, her voice lost in the rumble of the thruster engines that held the ship on site.

"Come on," Katharine yelled. "They said it'll be eleven hours before they even get to the bottom. And then another hour before the first section comes up. We'd better get some sleep before our watch."

Tina followed her. Katharine was right, they should sleep while they could. Eleven hours? As they started up the steps, Tina glanced back at the moonhole, and the image returned, of the drill string dangling beneath their puny ship, the corer nosing into the sediments—spudding in, was that what they called it? And then pressing downward, inching back through time, their ship attached to the earth like a newborn baby, nourished by knowledge from two hundred million years of prehistory.

≋ ≋ ≋

By the evening of their fifth day at the first site, they had drilled over a thousand meters below the sea floor. They had almost nine hundred meters of sediment core in storage. No mere conceptual construct, this, but a timeline incarnate, extending back through forty-five million years—and they were still coring! Finished with her shift at the sampling table, Tina stepped over to the description table where the Dutch sedimentologist was busy describing the archive half of a beautiful core from the end of the Paleocene and beginning of the Eocene. Tina had seen it when it was first split open—pink and pale blue with narrow bands of gray and purple and bright glistening green, a few nodules of red chert—but some of the colors were already beginning to fade from exposure to the air, the blue turning white, the purple losing its bewildered brilliance, the green mellowing to a dusty pastel. Tina peered at the Dutchman's clipboard: "Foraminifer Nannofossil Ooze and Foraminifer Nannofossil Chalk." The cores weren't fractured, and there was little bioturbation, promising a good continuous record for her temperature analyses.

"I'm going to go find something to eat," Katharine mumbled, stepping up next to Tina. Katharine had spent the last four hours sitting at the microscope on the other side of the core lab looking at smear slides of sediments.

"Don't you want to see this next core?" Tina asked, gesturing toward the core-splitting table. "They dated the core catcher sediments as late Cretaceous."

"I'm too tired to see anything. And I've got another four hours to do at the microscope in the paleontology lab."

Katharine's eyes were red, her face pale.

"I'd tell you to make yourself a *mate*," Tina said, "but it's in the cabin. I suppose you could sneak in . . ."

But the ship's rule against entering quarters when off-watch cabinmates were sleeping was an unusually well-respected one, and Katharine didn't want to break it. She trudged off toward the stairs, and Tina stepped out onto the catwalk to get some fresh air.

It was dark out, but there was a warm breeze, a tropical breath cutting through the smells of oil and diesel from the thruster engines. Her sampling partner was out there taking a break as well, juggling the three little balls he carried around in his pockets. How Katharine had influenced Orloff's scheduling to get Tina paired with Nigel Martinelli for her sampling table shift, Tina didn't know and didn't intend to ask. She couldn't say she minded. She could have done worse for a sampling partner than this friendly, witty young geologist-juggler—she could have been paired with Harper Gibson, god forbid. As it was, she had to spend a good part of her watch in the chemistry lab with him. Rumor had it that he had tried to get out of being assigned a regular twelve-hour watch. He and Conroy Decker were the only ones whose research didn't involve the cores; they were using a contraption they'd set up on the *Explorer's* bow to collect water samples during the ship's transits, a project that challenged the norms of operation for a drill ship. No one knew how Orloff had been convinced to approve it, but one thing was certain: she wasn't about to let Harper Gibson take up ship space without putting in a full shift of core processing and analysis. Rumor had it that she'd threatened to turn the ship around and take him back to Guam, and that Conroy Decker had to intervene to calm the two of them down.

Harper aside, it was amazing how well this interdisciplinary melange of scientists was working together. Of course, they'd only been out a week, but so far it was truly a group production, with everyone eagerly exchanging samples and raw data and equally raw ideas, as if their egos had all gone off on sabbatical at the same time. Whether this was Orloff's doing, or simply the result of throwing them all together on a ship and handing them sediment cores to study, Tina didn't know, though she suspected it was mostly the latter. The cores held them in thrall, drew the most intransigent loners out of their cocoons. The resource they constituted, working in such close quarters and thus united, was phenomenal: a paleontologist who wanted to know if a sediment was volcanic in origin had only to find the jovial, no-longer-seasick Dutchman; a geologist who wanted to know the chemical composition of a sediment need only find the Chinese geochemist from Woods Hole who everyone called Zhang because they couldn't say his first name; the sedimentologist who wanted to know the organic carbon content of an unusually thick dark band had only to carry a sample downstairs to Tina in the chemistry lab; and one could always hunt down the French paleontologist or the young American, Nigel, and within a few hours have a sample roughly dated.

Nigel had pocketed his juggling balls and gone back into the lab to work on the core being split, and Tina was about to follow when the cry came from the rig floor, "CORE ON DECK!"

"Core on deck!" Tina took up the cry as she hurried down the stairs to help carry the new core. The drill team had just pulled the plastic liner from the pipe, and crew members and scientists were lining up along its nine-meter length. Tina slipped in to support a sagging middle section, and they carried it up to the rack on the catwalk outside the core lab. While the technicians began cutting it into more manageable segments, Tina went through the precautionary routine of checking for dangerous gas or hydrocarbon accumulations. Then she went into the lab to get a sample for gas analysis from the core they were splitting. There was a geologist and a paleontologist on duty at the sampling table, and Orloff was hovering about, choosing a sample for pore water analysis. Nigel had already taken some material down to the paleontology lab to see if he could distinguish the KT boundary.

Tina sealed her sample vial and moved to the description table. If she could have, she would have worked in the core lab for the entire twelve hours of her watch. She wanted to leap for joy, clap her hands in anticipation every time the two halves of a segment were parted and the sediments exposed. This was a rather homely section compared to the last, mostly white chalk with an occasional band of chert or ash—but while Tina was standing there looking at it, Nigel returned with the news that he'd identified the KT boundary. Tina looked at the two-centimeter section he indicated. There was a distinct band of dark ash there, and though Tina knew that a layer of ash was not necessarily indicative of the KT boundary, the dark band *looked* like a boundary should look, like an end, a holocaust, a hiatus—like she'd always imagined the KT boundary would look. She compared the sediments on either side of it: the Cretaceous sediments extending down core appeared, to the naked eye, exactly like the sediments in the Paleocene above the boundary, an unremarkable mass of white nannofossil chalk. She tried to imagine the individual forams and coccoliths that had created this mass: a single microscopic plankton living and dying and decaying within its calcite armor, floating ever-so-slowly downward from the surface waters . . . or eaten by some zooplankton to reemerge as a fecal pellet, heavier now, falling, perhaps adhering to other particles along the way to form a larger clump and picking up speed . . . until it finally dropped into place on the ocean floor to form these sediments— shell by shell, clump by clump, layer by layer. Tina thought of her tiny picoplankton with no shells to attest their presence, no calcareous ooze or chalk or limestone, no legacy but a few distinctive organic molecules left undigested by sediment bacteria. Standing before this core, imagining the picoplankton's legacy of lipids, she had the strange feeling that it was *she* who was standing in *their* future, rather than they who had been dug up from her past. She felt an urge to touch the core, press her fingertip into the band of dark ash, lay her cheek on the smooth surface of the chalk and inhale its ancient musty odor, extend her tongue to taste a nodule of red chert. . . .

"This is excellent," Orloff was saying repeatedly from the other side of the table. "Excellent." The core lab was getting crowded, scientists pressing in around the table to get a look, as word spread that they were into the Cretaceous and that the KT boundary looked good, intact, that there was actually something to analyze—a foreshortening in the sediment column, yes, a hiatus perhaps, but not a total disappearance of the record as was so often the case.

Tina glanced back at the sampling table. A couple of people were tagging new requests for KT boundary samples, and she was glad that hers was already in the plan, because samples were going to be limited. What was it, she wondered, this quickening of interest, this fascination with the holocaust, the cataclysmic end? It was one of several in the geologic record, and not the most extreme, but it was the most recent, more pronounced than anything that had happened since. Even with mounting evidence for Alvarez's asteroid theory, some paleontologists insisted that the die-outs hadn't been cataclysmic at all, but rather gradual, over the last twenty million years of the Cretaceous. She glanced around for a paleontologist to ask about this, but Nigel had disappeared. Her cabinmate, Maurice, was probably still asleep. And she had work to do downstairs in the chemistry lab.

Harper was down there working at the GC. "Good evening!" Tina exclaimed loudly and cheerfully. She stood there staring at him, waiting for a reply. Usually she just ignored him, as he ignored her, but she was feeling mischievous. He lifted his head and turned slightly in her direction, as if he were trying to locate an insect he'd heard buzzing about his head.

"Did you hear," Tina said, "that we got a good KT boundary?"

He gave a quick nod, still not looking at her. Tina smiled and shook her head, turning her attention to the routine of sample preparation. She supposed there were worse things than working in a ten-by-twenty-foot lab with someone who didn't see fit to acknowledge her existence. It wasn't that Harper didn't talk—she herself didn't like to talk while she worked—but he acted as if she weren't there at all, as if he could neither see nor hear her. Indeed, Tina was beginning to think it wasn't an act. It was as if his line of sight were too high to include her, as if he were deaf to the particular frequency of her voice, his lack of civility the byproduct of an arrogance so deep and immutable it was built into his physique. It was impersonal, Tina thought, unintentional.

It was almost midnight when Nigel stuck his head in the door and announced that they were abandoning the hole. They'd hit basement, he said, drilled into the basalt of the plateau, even managed to retrieve a good sample. It was a textbook-perfect site, Tina thought, as Nigel hurried off, nearly a hundred and twenty million years, twelve hundred meters of sediment in evidence.

Tina was supposed to be off watch at midnight, but it was almost two by the time she'd worked through her backlog of analyses and left the lab. There were less than two days of transit time to the next site, and everyone was scrambling to finish analyses and write up results, hoping to get a little extra sleep before cores started coming in again. Tina went down to the cabin to retrieve her *mate*, stopped off in the mess hall to fill her thermos, and headed up to the library to work on her write-up for the site report.

Sylvia Orloff was the only one in the library when Tina went in. The chief scientist had her own office, but she apparently preferred the library, either because it contained the big volumes of DSDP reports, or, as Katharine maintained, because she could snare any off-watch scientists who wandered in to read, get them to put in a little extra time in the paleontology lab. She had one of the two tables completely covered with computer print-outs, core photographs, and open DSDP volumes. "How's it going?" Tina asked, stepping over to the other table. She set down her folder of results, opened her thermos, poured water into her *mate* gourd and, still awaiting the reply to her greeting, turned back to Orloff.

Sylvia Orloff was sitting with her elbow resting on the arm of the chair and a coffee mug suspended in midair. Her face was tilted back slightly, her lips parted, and her eyes closed. It looked as though she'd just leaned back to take a sip of coffee and think for a moment, but she was snoring. Softly. Tina stared, waiting for the coffee cup to fall, wondering how full it was— but neither cup nor bearer moved. She had been wondering when the woman slept. They were all tired, but rumor had it that Orloff had been overseeing the sampling for every single core, and the cores had been coming in steadily, one every hour or two, twenty-four hours a day for the past five days.

Quietly, Tina slipped into a chair at the other table, sucked her *mate* dry, and set to work, trying not to rustle papers. But when she glanced over a few minutes later, Sylvia had set down the coffee mug and was busily examining the data strewn out about her, taking notes in a green notebook.

With sleep at such a premium, Tina could not believe that she was being roused for an emergency drill, what seemed like minutes after she'd crawled into her bunk. The alarm was loud and unrelenting, a long blast alternating with two quick ones, but she couldn't remember which kind of drill it was supposed to signal. She reached for the light switch and glanced at her watch. It was almost 7:00 A.M., which meant she had actually slept two and a half hours. She looked over at Katharine's bunk, but it was still neatly made up, the stuffed skunk Katharine had appointed cabin mascot sitting on the pillow. Orloff must really be driving her hard, Tina thought as she rolled out of bed, for Katharine to go more than a day without sleep.

The one-two blast pattern turned out to be the abandon ship signal, and to Tina's amazement they actually seemed to be carrying through with it. She found herself herded onto one of the inflatable life rafts with Katharine, Janice, an English paleomagnetics expert whose name was Richard something, a graduate student Tina didn't know, and a young Brazilian who was part of the kitchen crew. Everyone else was standing on deck watching. Tina squinted in the bright morning light and rubbed the sleep from her eyes, confused by the whole operation. Why weren't the others getting into lifeboats? Several people seemed to have been in such haste to attend to the alarm that they'd wrapped themselves in the sheets off their beds. They looked like characters out of a high school English class rendition of a Greek play. Looking up at the crew members who were lowering the raft, Tina realized that they were, actually, wearing costumes. The sheets were carefully draped togas, and they had crowns made of twisted steel cable on their heads. One of them, an older man with a big white beard and wizened face, looked rather regal in what looked to be a real crown, with jewels sticking up around it, glistening in the sun—what were those, thin layer slides, glued to the cable? He had a bucket in his free hand and he was leaning out over them chanting something—

"What the hell?" Tina shouted as the bucket tipped, dousing her with water so cold it felt like it had just come out of the freezer. When she looked up again she saw that there was now a whole line of people above them with buckets—scientists, technicians, and crew members. And just as she was about to inquire again what was going on, she saw the amiable Dutchman tip his bucket and let a slimy yellow mass slide out. Thankfully, the yellow stuff landed between Katharine and Janice, but it was soon followed by something more serious—what appeared to be a bucketful of dirty vegetable oil.

Katharine let out a scream as the whole viscous mess landed in her lap. "Damn it all to hell, this is going too far. That was *oil*! If you guys got this stuff in my hair, I'm going to kill you!" she shouted up at the rowdy mob on deck.

"What are they *doing*?" Tina finally got out, looking around at her fellow victims, just as a suspiciously green liquid landed square on the bald head of the Englishman.

"I always fancied myself with a malachite-green head," he said, referring to the green dye that was used to stain samples in the paleontology lab. "I hope they know for a fact that it's not toxic," he added, extracting a handkerchief from his pocket.

"I believe we are being initiated," Katharine said as their boat touched the water. The young man from the kitchen, no more than a boy actually, quickly grabbed the oars and rowed them out of range of the buckets above, and Katharine explained to Tina—who seemed to be the only one who didn't know—that a centuries-old ritual required that anyone who had never crossed the equator at sea go through a rite of passage.

"Row south!" the old crew member commanded them through a bullhorn.

"¡Puxa vida!" said the kitchen boy, who seemed to be bleeding from a head wound. "They want we row across."

"What happened to your head?" Janice asked him.

"Ketchup," he said. "They—" He set down an oar to mime a squirting motion directed at his face. "I was in my bunk, asleep."

"I can't believe Sylvia is actually going along with this," Katharine said. "Oh lord, I think they fried fish in this oil."

"Neptune don't listen to Dr. Orloff," said the boy.

"Neptune?" Tina said, realizing that she was suspiciously sticky from the water she'd been doused with, as if it had been . . . saturated with sugar?

"God of the sea," said the Englishman.

"We're being initiated as sons and daughters of Neptune," Katharine explained. "Which I guess is why they dump water on you. But oil? Ketchup?" She dipped a finger in the yellow blob in the bottom of the skiff and held it up to her nose.

"Mustard and mayonnaise," the kitchen boy told her. "I heard worse things," he added.

"I wonder what they'd do if we didn't cooperate," Katharine said. "If we just sat here." But the ship had already moved past them to the south.

Suddenly, the boy, who had been dutifully rowing after the ship, stopped and looked around at the little group in the raft. He brought the oars up, lifted his arms in the air, and grinned broadly. "We have all the womans!" he exclaimed, looking from the student to the Englishman.

The student shrugged, and the Englishman, a squat middle-aged fellow who had always seemed rather reserved and prudish to Tina, laughed and glanced lasciviously at Janice, who, to Tina's amazement, blushed. "Wait until I tell Maurice," he said.

The young cook had decided to concentrate on Tina. "We swim?" he said, pulling off his shirt and untying his shoes.

Tina looked at Katharine, who laughed, and then back at the boy, who made a great display of slipping off his pants and jumping into the water in his undershorts. Ketchup bled into the water around his head, and Tina caught herself looking about for sharks. Not likely, she thought. They had seen sharks once, en route to the first site, but just because the ketchup *looked* like blood . . .

The sun was well above the horizon, the morning bright, the air balmy, but not yet too hot. The surface of the sea was so calm they might have walked across its smooth, polished surface to the equator, might have skated or slid across in stockinged feet. It would have been rather pleasant out there in the raft, if not for the rogues on the ship watching them through binoculars and using the bullhorn to call out taunts and exhortations to hurry. Eventually, they all jumped into the water with their clothes on, trying, with limited success, to wash off the various substances they had been doused with. Tina's sugar came off easily enough, but then she had to sit there in her wet T-shirt and clinging shorts putting up with the amorous attentions of young Joao, who chivalrously relieved her of the oars when she tried to take her turn at rowing and proved impossibly inept. It took them almost half an hour to make their way to where the ship had stalled its engines to wait—more than had been anticipated, apparently, but even so, when the raft was hauled up and they climbed back on deck, they were doused anew. This time, mercifully, it was only cold—ice cold—water. Tina smiled wanly at her tormenters and was rewarded with a second bucketful in the face before she made it out of the line of fire. She found herself standing next to Sylvia Orloff, who had a little camera and was recording the whole spectacle as if it were data for one of her reports. Tina reached up to squeeze the water out of her hair, and Sylvia lowered the camera and leaned toward her.

"I was on the *Albatross IV* the first time I crossed," she confided. "Working along the coast from Panama to Ecuador. They blindfolded us and took us down to the cold room, wrapped us up in the biologists' net with its slimy haul, and made us drink a liter erlenmeyer flask full of ethanol punch before they'd let us out. There was a lot of debate about whether or not to strip us before they put us in the nets. That was almost twenty years ago and they didn't know what to make of a woman on board."

Tina turned to look at her, but before she could ask what they had decided, Sylvia stepped away, raising her camera to get a picture of the old guy with the beard—the designated Neptune—dousing Katharine and Janice.

Chapter 14

It was as though the ship were a land and culture all its own with different rules and mores than real life. They were like kids off at summer camp or youths at a rock concert, giddy with the freedom, full of wisecracking, hormone-charged adolescent energy—in spite of, or perhaps because of, the grueling schedules. It was as if nothing they said or did had anything at all to do with their lives back on shore. Men who never went to parties gave parties, brief five or six person affairs squeezed in at odd hours of the day and night, usually involving the consumption of some illicit substance. Stimulants were big. One MIT student had a good supply of both speed and pot—speed when you went on watch, pot when you wanted to sleep—and his cabin was one of the more popular off-watch hangouts. Tina's *mate* was a big hit, as was the espresso machine someone set up in the X-ray lab. And then, of course, there were the private stashes of booze, the drug of choice for the older scientists. There were rules about alcohol—that it be drunk only in the mess hall, that it be limited to the beer and wine occasionally served with dinner—but within the scientists' quarters the rules were broken almost daily, and no one seemed to care. They scrounged snacks from the mess hall, and they even had a little music at their cabin parties. A stratigrapher from the University of Washington had brought his mandolin, and there were several tape players with music ranging from Brahms to The Police. Drugs, food, music—all they lacked was a bit of sex, though one wouldn't know it from listening to all the banal innuendo. There were moments when the ship seemed like a giant floating male locker room with a few stray women in its midst. As far as Tina could tell it was mostly just talk, but then there were only three women on board, besides Orloff. She supposed there could be other sorts of affairs, but she wouldn't know. She hadn't even known that quiet, shy, recently married Janice and their French cabinmate were an item, right there under her nose, until Katharine let it drop their third week at sea.

Tina did know that the most unlikely men seemed to think it appropriate to flirt with her—from the teenage kitchen boy, Joao, to the distinguished geophysicist from New York, who was at least thirty years her senior. She ignored most of it, and laughed off what she couldn't ignore. The only one she might actually have considered was Katharine's pick for her, Nigel. He was everything Katharine had billed him as: interesting, clever, successful, tall, black hair, small dark eyes, direct gaze, etc. A nice tan to go with the black hair, because he spent as much time as he could in the field. He liked to ski and climb mountains. He liked pancakes. And, as it turned out, he liked tall women.

The coring went remarkably well, the scientific crew working together like one big happy, if slightly incestuous, family. Despite Orloff's grumpiness about gaps in the foram record, the second site was a huge success. There was no record of the KT boundary to speak of, but the core was continuous back to the early Cretaceous, surprising them with periodic narrow bands of black organic-rich shales between 90 and 130 million years ago. Similar bands had been found in Atlantic deep sea cores, but never in the Pacific. Spirits were high as they analyzed the shale layers and argued over theories for their formation. Had productivity increased? Or had the water of the deep sea become so depleted in oxygen that decay was retarded and the organics accumulated without an increase in supply? Warm water held less oxygen than cold—had the deep sea been so warm it was always on the edge, just waiting to swing over into this anoxic state . . . ? They had four days in transit, and Orloff asked them to prepare presentations for a seminar, which she scheduled for the last watch change before coring started up again.

Tina was in the computer room working on her presentation, when Katharine came in, sat down at the other computer, worked for a half-hour and then suggested they take a break and go for a walk. It was the last night of the transit.

"You have your write-up done for the site report?" Tina asked dubiously.

She had finished her own earlier that day, but it looked as if Katharine had just started. "Sylvia said she wanted them by tomorrow morning, at the latest."

"This morning," Katharine said, looking at her watch. "It's twelve-twenty." She looked back at the computer screen, then shrugged and logged off. "It won't take me long. And Sylvia will find some reason to complain," she added, lowering her voice, "no matter what I do."

"Oh Katharine," Tina said, though she was beginning to see that it was true. Sylvia seemed to pick on Katharine even more than she picked on her students. Tina tucked her files in between the two monitors and followed Katharine out of the tiny computer room and down the passage to the nearest bulkhead door.

It was a sultry night, the swells just large enough to be felt in the movement of the ship, as they walked along the edge of the main deck, heading aft. When they came to the steps that led to the poopdeck, Katharine started up.

"Where are we going?" Tina called after her, hanging back. The poopdeck was crowded with geophysics instrumentation and quite likely to be occupied by a certain distinguished geophysicist who Tina would just as soon avoid.

"Up to the helipad," Katharine said over her shoulder, continuing up the steps.

Tina had never had reason to go up to the helipad, which was a big octagonal platform suspended above the poopdeck. There were some large wooden storage containers in the middle of it, but not much else up there, no labs or anything of use, which, Tina quickly realized, was the charm of the place. The moon was up and almost full, but otherwise the helipad was unlit, out of range of the spotlights that lit up every other corner of the decks. It was a large, mercifully unoccupied space, away from the looming derrick and the cranes and the myriad apparatus and machinery of the decks, as peaceful as a deserted beach even with the engines rumbling in the background . . . or perhaps not so deserted. When they stepped free of the containers Tina noticed two men standing near the stern, one of them obviously Harper Gibson, because there was no one else that big on the ship, which meant the other must be Conroy Decker, because who else would be hanging out with Harper? Unless it was the Dutchman? But no, it was Decker. Tina could just make out their voices over the drone of the engines as she and Katharine neared.

"Let's see if we can blackmail them for a couple of beers," Katharine said cheerfully, apparently unsurprised by their presence there.

"Huh?" Tina said, but then she saw that they were indeed drinking beer—and having what appeared to be a heated argument.

"I didn't say that the model is misguided! But *something* is off."

"Sure. Like your interpretation of your carbon-13 data." Harper Gibson glanced up as Tina and Katharine approached.

"Are you two still arguing?" Katharine said. "Every time I see these two they're arguing," she told Tina.

"We're not arguing," Conroy said. "Our results are arguing."

"They are not. Our *interpretations* are arguing. We have this problem with disappearing CO_2, and Conroy wants to make it worse."

To Tina's amazement, Harper Gibson was actually talking to her. Or, rather, to Katharine. Sort of. He had directed his comment into the dark in their general direction anyway. "Anthropogenic CO_2?" she tried, curious, for she had only a vague idea of what their work was about. "Is that what you guys are talking about?"

"That's it," Harper said. "The stuff we've been spewing into the air for the last century. The Great Experiment, to paraphrase Revelle. Except it's not working." He picked up a paper cup from the top of the little ice chest at their feet and downed its contents.

"Don't listen to him," Conroy said. "Of course it's working. We just don't have enough data yet."

"Looks like you've got plenty of brew, though," Katharine interjected, eyeing the ice chest.

"It's not much of an experiment," Harper said, "when you dump CO_2 into the system and it just disappears. Vanishes."

"What do you mean?" Tina said quickly. "'It disappears.'"

"Exactly that," Conroy said. "We can't balance the carbon budget— there's less CO_2 in the atmosphere than we would expect, given what man has produced, taking into consideration all the known sources and sinks. As usual, everyone waves their hands at the ocean to be taking it up, but the calculations can't account for it."

"The tracer data can account for even less of it," Harper yelled, and

Tina suddenly realized that it was because of the engines that they were shouting.

"But I thought Revelle did those calculations thirty years ago," she said. "Isn't that why Keeling started measuring the CO_2 in the atmosphere to begin with?"

"Revelle's calculations were based purely on the chemistry of the CO_2-carbonate equilibrium," Conroy explained. "They considered what would happen if the ocean had a giant mixer on the bottom, stirring it up so that all of the water was in contact with the atmosphere. He couldn't take into account the layering of the ocean, and he didn't know what we now know about deep sea circulation, how slow it is. Nor did he have the modeling capability the computers have given us or, for that matter, this past decade's worth of seawater carbon measurements."

"So this 'missing' CO_2—is it a lot, I mean, a significant proportion of the emissions?"

"Depends on who you talk to," Conroy said, extracting cans of beer from the cooler. He offered one to Tina and one to Katharine. "Harper's got some scotch to chase that with if you want."

They accepted the beers and declined the scotch, which Harper made no move to offer to them, anyway.

"If you ask me," Conroy went on, "the missing carbon is about thirty percent of the total emissions. But Harper only comes up with five percent."

"Not to say it's not an important five percent," Harper injected.

They were both quite drunk, Tina realized suddenly, which probably explained why they were answering her questions so candidly, when for the past two weeks they had hardly even acknowledged her existence. Katharine slipped away quietly with her unopened can of beer, but Tina opened hers and stayed put. "If the disappearing CO_2 isn't going into the ocean," she said, "where's it going?"

"Million dollar question," Harper said sarcastically.

"We just don't know," Conroy said. "We have to assume it's going into the terrestrial biosphere, but no one's found a way of determining exactly how much carbon is being taken up globally by land plants. One theory has it that the northern forests growing back after being leveled in the last century might be taking it up."

"Then, just to keep things thoroughly confused," Harper said, "there's a few demented biologists who have suddenly decided that the destruction of rain forest is spewing out *another* four gigatons of CO_2, if you take their lowest estimates. All of which they blithely claim disappears into the great mysterious ocean here." He took a sip of scotch and chased it with beer. "Maybe we should redefine Madame Orloff's cruise for her. We can call it the Search for the Great Vacuum Cleaner in the Sea."

"The Great Carbon Syphon."

"The Pacific Black Hole."

Tina laughed. "Who else is working on this?"

"Just us," Conroy said.

Just two of the most well-known geochemists in the world, Tina thought. "So you're doing total carbon analyses in those water samples you're collecting?" she asked them. "Trying to measure the change directly?"

"No, no. The carbon pool in the ocean is so huge, relative to the increase from the fossil fuel CO_2, that those measurements would have to be unbelievably precise to be of much use. And there's so much seasonal variability, that it would require constant monitoring, at a dense network of stations. . . . Though there is some talk of setting up something of the sort."

How ironic, Tina thought, that they should have as much trouble understanding the carbon cycle of the here and now, with all the evidence at hand, as she would have deciphering its ancient history from the sediments. "What are you doing then?"

"Drinking beer and scotch," Harper said and sucked the last drops of beer out of the can he was holding.

"The isotopes of the dissolved inorganic carbon," Conroy told her. "Carbon-14 to calibrate the computer model. And carbon-13, which I'm using to trace the fossil fuel CO_2."

Tina knew about using the radioactive carbon-14 that had been released into the atmosphere by hydrogen bomb tests back in the sixties to trace the rate at which CO_2 moved from the atmosphere into the ocean. And Conroy's study depended on the fact that fossil fuels—and the CO_2 from burning them—contained the two naturally occurring isotopes, carbon-13 and the predominant carbon-12, in the low ratio characteristic of plant material. Conroy could, in principle, track anthropogenic CO_2 by measuring this ratio in the atmosphere, ocean, and biosphere. She sipped at her beer and watched Harper open another can for himself. "How do you handle marine primary productivity in your budgets and models?" she asked after a moment. "Uptake of CO_2 by phytoplankton . . . For that matter, how do you handle organic carbon fluxes in general, to the sediments, or into the deep sea in the form of dissolved organic carbon? None of that's very well documented."

"We ignore them," Harper said.

"You what?"

"We assume a steady state," Conroy explained. "CO_2 taken up by the phytoplankton is compensated by the same amount produced by remineralization. There's no evidence that atmospheric CO_2 varied significantly in the two thousand years before the industrial revolution. So we assume that the entire cycle was in steady state, and we treat the anthropogenic CO_2 as a perturbation. For land plants, higher atmospheric CO_2 can stimulate more growth, so the forests can, theoretically, absorb some of the excess fossil fuel CO_2 . . . unless, of course, we are destroying the forests at the same time. Marine productivity, on the other hand, is maxed out, limited by the nutrients available in surface waters. It can't respond to the increase in CO_2. So it remains constant and we can ignore it."

"Okay," Tina said, though she wasn't entirely convinced. "But just for the sake of argument . . . What if we know less than we think we know? What if marine primary productivity has been underestimated?" She paused and peered up at the men's faces, to see if they were going to engage her argument. They didn't say anything, and she couldn't quite make out their expressions. She took a breath. "What if," she said, "there's a group of marine phytoplankton that are so tiny they pass through the usual filters—a group of picoplankton that we didn't even know existed? And what if these picoplankton aren't limited by the low surface water phosphorus and nitrogen concentrations we've been measuring? What if they thrive at the bottom of the photic zone where there's less competition from other phytoplankton and nutrients aren't as depleted . . . ? Or what if they're linked to nutrient release by bacteria or they utilize small dissolved organic molecules—"

"And what if Santa Claus lived in a hydrothermal vent," Conroy said, laughing.

Harper raised both hands, beer can in one, scotch in the other, in a toast. "To Santa Claus, riding on a cloud of sulfur," he said, drinking first from the left, then from the right hand. He suddenly started singing in a surprisingly pleasant baritone voice. "Jingle bells, jingle bells, jingle all the way. Rising from the vent. On a one-worm open sleigh. O'er the ridge we go. Laughing all the way . . . "

"But I'm serious," Tina protested, laughing anyway, and drinking to the toast. The beer, her fatigue, and the giddy rush of new ideas had conspired to make her almost as drunk as they. When Harper had worn out his song, she saw that she'd lost their attention completely. They were gazing out at the water, watching the wake of the ship spread out behind them, Conroy sitting on the ice chest, Harper standing, leaning against one of the wooden boxes. Tina moved into their line of vision, next to the two thick cables that served as railing around the edge of the helipad. Using a stanchion and the bottom cable for support, she hoisted herself up to sit on the top cable. She then proceeded to recount the entire story of the picoplankton, culminating theatrically with the unanticipated abundance she and John Carr had found in the productivity study from the *Rover* cruise. She had their full attention now, if only because of her precarious perch above the water. Clinging to the top cable with both hands, one foot hooked under the bottom cable and one leg wrapped around the stanchion, she continued her monologue, speculating wildly, like some sea-going spider entangling them in an unlikely but seductive web of "what ifs." What if, she wondered aloud, there really were a vacuum cleaner in the sea sucking up all that unexplained CO_2 man had been spewing out—or rather billions of tiny little microscopic vacuum cleaners down in the penumbra of the photic zone . . . ?

They heard her out, and they were amused by her antics, but when she finished talking and they started questioning her, it became clear that the only one entangled in any web of speculation was Tina. They didn't believe a word she'd said about the productivity study.

"But it's true," she said finally, annoyed. She unwound her leg and climbed down from the cable. "No matter what you think of my lipid biomarkers, you can't argue with the productivity results. We just did standard primary productivity measurements on a smaller size fraction. *Science* has already accepted the paper we wrote with Roy Shimohata," she said, when they didn't react. "You can ask Gerald Steinberg about it. He saw a preprint."

"Might," Harper said.

"Might what?"

"Ask Gerald Steinberg. Where is he?"

"Probably asleep," Conroy said. "I think he works the noon to midnight watch."

"Well, let's go see what he says." Harper set out across the helipad.

"Oh god, he wouldn't, would he?" Tina looked from Harper's receding back, to Conroy. She hardly knew Gerald Steinberg. He did paleoproductivity studies, and he'd heard about the picoplankton work from John Carr and asked to see the paper.

"Of course he would," Conroy said cheerfully. "After all, we don't know you from Adam. Eve. You could be some deluded half-baked graduate student, for all we know."

"Shit," Tina said, under her breath. "Assholes." Where the hell was Katharine, anyway? Maybe she'd gone back to work on her site report. It must be two or three o'clock. They'd be arriving at the new site soon. Tina walked over to one of the piles of containers. They were stacked like a pyramid, easy to climb. She pushed herself up from box to box, to the topmost box, where she stood and looked around as if she could tell where they were from looking at the undulating water—as if the water in the New Hebrides Basin would look different from the water in the Tasmin Sea, their drill site marked with a white X that glowed in the moonlight like the whitecaps flickering and glowing on some of the swells. She turned around and looked out over the ship, noting that there was some activity around the derrick, a sign that they were indeed nearing the site.

It must have been the movement that drew Tina's eye downward then, made her focus on that one little space between the crates. She certainly couldn't have heard anything from where she was, not over the engines. The moon was still high, angling down between the crates like a spotlight. Tina started to turn away, and then she paused, unwillingly, transfixed for one second, two—just long enough to see the tangle of naked limbs, a brown back, the flash of a lean white ass, a familiar blaze of golden hair— and then she continued, turning away and scrambling down from the pyramid so quickly that she scraped her knees.

Why hadn't Katharine just told her? For God's sake, Tina thought, they could have used the cabin, when Tina was working. It wasn't as if she would care, Katharine must know that. She went and sat down near Conroy, leaned back against a container.

"Anything going on yet?" he asked, and Tina gaped at him, thinking for a moment that he was referring to the two lovers going at it just a stone's throw away.

"Oh," she said, when she realized he was asking about the rig floor activity. "It looks like they're going to start maneuvering onto the site pretty soon." She picked up the empty beer can she'd left by the cooler, set it down.

Conroy lifted himself off the cooler and reached in. "Last one," he said, handing her a can.

"Thanks." She popped it open and gulped the beer as if it were water, her throat dry. "So tell me what if," she said.

"What if what?" Conroy glanced down at her.

"How do you think it would affect your carbon cycle models if these picoplankton are as widespread as it looks like they are?"

"Well," Conroy said, "the fluxes and reservoirs of carbon in the models would look different. But even setting aside nutrient limitations, the only way your picoplankton would make a difference in the budget of anthropogenic CO_2 is if their growth were somehow stimulated by a higher CO_2 concentration. And there is quite a bit of evidence that phytoplankton in general don't respond to excess CO_2 the way land plants do."

"I don't know," Tina said, considering. "The picoplankton respond differently to nutrients and light than other phytoplankton . . . " They were interrupted by Harper clomping across the helipad toward them.

"What did Steinberg say?" Conroy asked as Harper came to a halt in front of them.

"He said 'Go fuck yourself.'"

Conroy chuckled. "I take it he was asleep. What else did he say?"

"He said to ask Cristina Arenas, because it was her project. He said he didn't even know these plankton existed until she came along." Harper set his hands on his knees and bent down to peer at Tina, as if he didn't work with her in the chemistry lab every day and hadn't just spent the last few hours talking with her. "I take it you're Cristina Arenas?"

"Right. Tina." She turned to Conroy. "We met last summer at one of the TGIFs," she said. "I've got Max Lindquist's labs . . . "

Conroy shrugged. He obviously had no recollection of having met her before the cruise.

Harper eased himself down on the deck next to Conroy and Tina. They asked about her work with the picoplankton lipids, and though they were still a little dubious, they now listened carefully to what she had to say. Tina admitted that she actually had no idea what the geochemical implications of the picoplankton might be, if any.

"Life is so awfully messy," Harper quipped. "We'd just as soon have as little to do with it as possible, thank you very much."

Tina laughed. He was right, of course. Trying to include the marine biota in a geochemical model would be a daunting task. And if you had to reevaluate notions of nutrient limitation, it would be more daunting still.

Tina leaned her head back against the side of the container and stretched out her legs. Her companions had fallen silent, Conroy sitting on the cooler, staring at his feet, Harper leaning against the box next to her. She thought about going down to the dining hall to see if she could find something to eat. What a fool she was, missing dinner, the best meal. There was always a bowl of fruit sitting out, though lately all it had in it was bananas. Someone had convinced the kitchen crew to leave out a jar of peanut butter and a loaf of bread, but they'd forgotten to tell them about the jam. Uninspired, Tina stayed where she was. The moon was shining in her face, bright enough to make her squint. The sound of the engines had changed, and the ship had slowed down. They would be looking for the site now, the seismic system scanning the sea floor, Orloff with the geophysicist in the lab below directing the captain up on the bridge. Tina closed her eyes. She should probably be somewhere. Doing something. She should go print out her handout for the seminar, retrieve her notes from the computer room. How was Katharine ever going to get her site write-up done? Was she still over there, between the boxes? Tina opened her eyes, banishing the image of Katharine and Nigel making love. She didn't care—why should she care? Still . . . after all Katharine's moaning about missing Fred, and about Sylvia pushing her so hard, never getting enough sleep. And why hadn't Katharine told her? She was intensely embarrassed to have seen them like that, though she was sure they hadn't noticed. They probably thought they'd found the most private spot on the ship, wedged in between the crates, protected by the dark and the noise of the engines. Who would ever think someone would be climbing one of those piles to admire the view in the middle of the night? She closed her eyes again. What she should be doing, she thought, was sleeping. The meeting wasn't until eleven. As long as she got her report to Sylvia by eight . . .

She thought they were going to a meeting, but it looks more like a party than a meeting, and now Katharine has gone off and left her and she's hungry and she doesn't know anyone and the only thing to eat is carbon dioxide. At least they have more than one flavor: there's carbon-13 dioxide and a little carbon-14 dioxide and tons of C-12 dioxide, though that's going fast, by far the most popular. What kind of meeting is this? *she asks a stranger standing next to her at the food table.* Meeting? *he says, daintily impaling a C-14 dioxide with a toothpick.* This is Harper Gibson's Annual Isotope Party. *Tina surveys the array on the table.* Isotope party? How come there are only carbon isotopes? *she says.* They could at least spice up the CO_2 with a little O-18, instead of all this boring old O-16, *but the stranger just shrugs and stabs another C-14 dioxide. He slips it into his mouth and turns his back to Tina, who is slightly annoyed, though she figures he doesn't have long to live anyway, imbibing radiocarbon like that, clearly an addict, she supposes he can't help it—*

She was startled awake by a loud roar that sent her leaping to her feet with visions of eighteenth-century sea monsters—until she realized that the noise had come from Harper, who had fallen asleep next to her and was snoring in an oddly intermittent fashion, punctuating the night with arrhythmic blasts. Conroy was nowhere to be seen, and the ice chest was gone. The moon was still skipping across the water from the west, casting so much light that Tina couldn't tell what was happening on the eastern horizon, but dawn couldn't be far off. She stumbled across the helipad toward the stairs. The ship had stopped moving, and it sounded like the thruster engines were on, so they must be on the site.

By all standards, the first month of the cruise was a roaring success. They'd had a minimum of equipment failures, good luck with the site selections, and perfect Tasmin Sea summer weather. They drilled two holes on the Lord Howe Rise northwest of New Zealand, one back to ninety million years, the other abandoned in the Miocene when sediments changed from consolidated ooze to a brittle, loosely cemented material that wouldn't stay in the core liners. Even the hole they abandoned was a success, because the fine-grained ooze in the Quaternary afforded an almost perfect record of the ice-age cycles. As they began their fifth week at sea spirits were running high in the scientific crew. Indeed, spirits had been running high for the past month, or so it seemed to Tina as she sat in the dining hall one afternoon before her watch, trying to eat lunch. Relentlessly high. She was tired of high spirits. Her own, and everyone else's. She dipped the tip of her fork into the black beans on her plate, but she couldn't bring herself to taste them. She tried a few grains of rice. The cooks seemed to be getting more and more uninspired as their choices of ingredients narrowed—or perhaps she was just tired. Tired of their food, tired of high spirits, tired of the movement of the ship, which today seemed more pronounced than ever. Tired of all these people, Tina thought, as she looked up and saw George Walker, the sixty-year-old geophysicist from New York, in his lime-green nylon running shorts, scanning the room for someplace to sit. She looked away quickly, staring intently at her plate. All these scientists masquerading as people, trying on eccentric personalities like children playing dress-up. She was feeling acutely lonely, as if she were not really part of this bustling shipboard community, this family that worked played ate slept together, but simply suspended in its midst, like the ship floating in the sea, separate and alien from its water and life. Tina dredged her fork through the beans, suddenly, unexpectedly, missing Chip: his beckoning, bear-like specter eclipsed the flesh-and-bones colleagues at the surrounding tables and filled her with an obtuse, mindless, profound and physical yearning, like the need to yawn or blink, like the craving for sleep, the longing for fresh food, for the nutlike bite of arugula or the alcoholic essence of a pear she didn't know the name of. . . .

"Almost time to hit the Dramamine!" Katharine slid a tray onto Tina's table, bursting into her thoughts with the annoying brashness of a mockingbird singing in the dead of night. "This is supposed to be one whopper of a storm! They're even talking about pulling the drill string, but Sylvia's pressuring them to keep at it." Katharine lifted the top of her sandwich and examined the contents. "This is definitely going to make me puke," she said, though it was just a chunk of french bread with some ham and a slice of tomato so thin it almost didn't exist. She dropped the bread back into place and looked across the table at Tina. "Aren't you sick?"

Tina pushed aside the beans she had yet to taste. "Now that you mention it . . . " She took a deep breath and tried to concentrate on the rice. "You just had to mention it, didn't you?"

"Sorry. Quick, talk about something else. . . . Oh, this is great—did you hear what Sylvia pulled last night? She's working on the computer, right, typing away, and she pauses a moment and then looks up to see that her whole file has disappeared. She panics and dashes off to wake up the technician, ranting about how the system must have crashed and she's lost six hours worth of work and she doesn't know what happened. So the technician goes down there, and it turns out that the only thing that had crashed was Sylvia. She apparently fell asleep with her hand on the space bar and inserted a couple hundred empty pages at the end of her document, so she couldn't find her text!" Katharine laughed and picked up her sandwich. "To tell the truth, I don't know how she does it," she said. "I swear she *never* goes to bed. I'm so tired I could sleep for a week surrounded by pounding jackhammers and not wake up once. In fact, I kind of hope they stop coring during the storm, because if I have to take Dramamine it's going to be a lost cause."

Tina toyed with her rice. She knew Katharine was exhausted. She knew it wasn't just from overwork. "It might help if you used your bed," she heard herself saying. They had never discussed Katharine's affair with Nigel.

Katharine slowly lowered her sandwich, set it down on the plate.

"I'm not particularly thrilled about the idea of trading cabins with Nigel," Tina went on, keeping her eyes on the rice she was arranging grain by grain in a ring along the edge of her plate. "But you know I always work until three or so. You've got the cabin to yourself for a few hours anyway." She looked up.

Katharine was staring at her, caught off-guard and, for a rare moment, speechless. "You don't care?" she said finally.

"If you screw Nigel in the cabin? No."

"Shhh." Katharine glanced around. "You don't have to advertise it."

"You really think there's anyone on board who doesn't know?"

"Orloff?" Katharine said after a moment. "I don't think Sylvia knows. And I'd kind of like to keep it that way."

"I doubt she'd care," Tina said.

Katharine combed her hand through her hair and held it back. "Maybe not. But I would." She dropped her hand so that the hair fell back loose around her face. "I didn't plan this, you know. It just happened. He came on to me and . . . It doesn't mean anything. He lives on the other side of the country. With his girlfriend."

"I see. So you were trying to set me up with a married man, eh?"

"I said girlfriend, not wife. And if you hadn't acted so indifferent . . . " Katharine picked up her sandwich, looked at it, and set it back down again. "It's just a cruise affair," she said, on the verge of tears. "It has nothing to do with anything. With Fred."

"Oh Katharine," Tina said. "I'm sorry. I didn't mean to tease you. Look, the guy is charming—I probably would have done the same thing if he'd come on to me."

"But you're not engaged," Katharine said, sniffling. "He was *supposed* to come on to you."

"Right. But he didn't—" Tina grabbed her plate as they were jolted by a wave that sent it sliding toward her lap.

Katharine made no move to retrieve her sandwich, which had toppled onto the table. "I suppose I should be suspicious," she said, wiping her nose with her napkin. "That he brought along such a good supply of condoms." She saw the look on Tina's face and giggled, the teariness suddenly gone. "Hey, they got me through high school."

"I hope they get you through this cruise."

"Oh lord, can you imagine? Getting pregnant from a cruise affair?"

"Getting pregnant from any—" The ship jolted again, and Tina paused and took a deep breath. "Uh, Katharine?"

"What?"

"Did you say you had some Dramamine on you?" But Tina was up and dashing for the door before Katharine could answer.

By noon virtually everyone was sick. Gut-wrenchingly sick, stumbling about the labs and quarters, employing every available toilet and sink. Even most of the ship's crew was sick, the drill team nevertheless working, struggling in the driving horizontal rain to secure the drill string and corer. But despite their best efforts, by the time the storm passed them by just before dawn the next day they had a broken drill string, a corer stuck down in the hole and, worst of all, the computer system that positioned the ship during drilling was malfunctioning.

Temperatures soared to a horrendously humid ninety in the wake of the storm, the air so heavy and still it seemed to bind one's every move. Delayed on site with no cores coming in while the drill crew and engineers worked at repairs, it should have been a chance for the scientists to catch up on reports, check the literature in the library, discuss their results, a chance to sleep . . . but instead they spent two days pacing and worrying and fretting. Even in the air-conditioned labs and quarters the humidity made for damp, clammy skin and clinging clothes, a cold sweat like that from fever or nerves. Sylvia Orloff terrorized the drill crew, who were surly and short-tempered from the heat, until the captain actually had to order her away from the rig floor. She called a meeting of the scientific crew then, where she submitted anyone whose reports didn't live up to her standards to public ridicule and abuse, singling out Janice and Katharine for the worst of the attack.

Operations had been stalled for two days when the captain announced that they would have to forgo drilling at their three southern sites and head for port, cutting through the strait to Wellington, instead of circling around New Zealand to their sites as planned. The drilling apparatus was repaired, but the engineers couldn't figure out what was wrong with the positioning system. The scientific crew protested to Orloff, badmouthing the two frazzled engineers, who continued to work even as the *Explorer* set course to the east. They were tired of the ship and tired of each other, but they chafed at having to disembark without coring the last three sites, as if all the successes of the past month had only made them greedy for more. To be stopped by basalt, or chert, to find sediments so jumbled by bioturbation as to be useless—these things they could put up with. But to be thwarted by something as mundane as the ship's computer system seemed unbearable. As they entered the passage between New Zealand's north and south islands, the spectacular scenery went unremarked, as did the cold, invigorating wind and the pleasant spring weather.

When the engineers finally located the problem, they were just six hours out of Wellington. Orloff and the captain announced that they would continue through the Cook Strait and head down the east side of the island to their southern sites, omitting only one of the three. There was a brief celebration, the lush green mountains and picturesque fluffs of fog were extolled, and the scientists went back to work with a vengeance. But though the weather remained pleasant, the sea calm, and the cores obtained in those last ten days were among the most fruitful of the cruise, they could not reclaim the good humor and camaraderie of their first month at sea. The Dutchman maintained that this happened on every cruise, even if drilling proceeded without mishap (which it never did), that it was an incontrovertible fact of the fifth week at sea—of no more fruit or lettuce, no more *mate* or good coffee, of rehashed gossip and worn out music, of jumping out of a bunk to be on watch in five minutes and finding the bathroom occupied by the perennially constipated senior scientist in the next cabin, of missing families and wives and boyfriends that one had never expected to miss. Even the lovers seemed to draw apart, the ship no longer the libertine haven that had given rise to their affairs. Despite the good cores, the group brilliance and cooperation that had graced work at the earlier sites was absent: they collected data, hoarded samples, and guarded their ideas, retreating into the isolation of their singular minds and projects.

Chapter 15

The apartment smelled of—mint? Tina set her duffel bag down in the bedroom and looked around as if she were in someone else's home. A fern hung in her bedroom window. A strangely twisted begonia-like thing with red leathery leaves graced the living room. There was a small potted plant in the middle of the kitchen table. The plant responsible for the smell was hanging over the kitchen sink. Tina peered out the window at the backyard, but it was too dark to see much. She opened the refrigerator, expecting to be greeted by moldy cheese and rotten tomatoes, but it was stocked with fresh milk and butter, ham, lettuce, spinach, and the biggest cabbage she had ever seen.

She had been expecting the stale air of an unused, closed-up apartment. She had, she realized now, been prepared for her abode in its pre-Chip state: the flowers in the yard withered from lack of attention, the trees yanked up and carted off, pink and green gravel sprawled anew over the flower beds. His pots and newspapers and magazines gone. The extra key sitting forlorn in the middle of an empty table. She had, without actually thinking that it would be so, been prepared for the man and all signs of his existence to have disappeared, like a dream leaving only the confused, disjointed vestiges of its passage. She had been prepared to feel lonely, depressed, tired, sad.

Instead she just felt comfortably, deliciously alone. And tired. And hungry—though, curiously, she also felt slightly seasick. She paused in the middle of the kitchen with her feet planted apart and looked at the walls and floor in amazement: it was as though the continent were shifting and sliding under her feet, her body yearning for the stability of water. She took a deep breath, gave her head a shake, and went about making herself a ham sandwich.

Sitting at the kitchen table, chewing her sandwich slowly, Tina stared at the plant on the table and tried to imagine Chip anticipating her arrival, stocking her refrigerator . . . missing her? The image both pleased and distressed her. She glanced at the newspaper he'd left lying on the table, something he wanted her to read, no doubt, but she didn't pick it up. She felt so content sitting alone, eating the food he'd left her, that she made no move to call him. It was, she reasoned, too late. He would be asleep. She toyed with the leaves of the plant on the table and they released a lemony smell to mingle with the mint above the sink—as though he had anticipated this strange inverted seasickness and arranged the smells of her kitchen accordingly, lemon and mint. Tina set her sandwich down and gulped at the freshly scented air. She was simultaneously relishing both the man's absence and his presence.

She fell asleep with the land rolling and rocking under her, but when she climbed out of bed in the morning everything was just as steady and solid as could be. She called Chip at the farm, but it was after six and he was already gone. Tina made herself some good coffee and ate four pieces of toast from the bread he had left her. Then she got on her bike and rode through a monotonous winter gray dawn to BIO.

There, in the carton of catalogues and advertisements for labware that had accumulated while she was gone, was the letter that she had been waiting without waiting for, wanting without wanting. Tina read it as though she had never doubted what it would say, never doubted that the proposal would, or even should, be funded; as if she'd never doubted that she would be able to stay at BIO and hire a technician and buy a new HPLC to analyze the boxes of samples that were due to arrive in a few days. She spent the rest of the morning looking through instrument catalogues and making phone inquiries about HPLC systems, confirming that the one she'd coveted for the past year was indeed the best choice. By midday it was ordered, the paperwork done. She would teach Michael to use it. Maybe she would even give him responsibility for the hydrocarbon kinetics project.

It was funny, she thought, as she dialed Michael's number, that a problem could seem so important and insurmountable one moment, and the next you wondered what the big deal had been. The phone rang four times and then stopped. Strange, rowdy punk music came over the line, and then faded out to Michael's serious, businesslike voice with instructions to leave a message after the beep. Tina listened until the beep came and then hung up. This was new. She thought for a moment, composing a message, and then she called back. "I have a job for you," she said this time. "And a new HPLC arriving in three weeks, just after New Year's— Uh, for Michael," she added, in case his roommate listened to the message. She hung up, only to realize that she hadn't identified herself. Well. He would figure it out.

Tina spent most of the afternoon making phone calls. She returned a call from a Petron Corporation geologist who said he'd heard that she was doing some interesting biomarker kinetics work and wanted to visit her lab. He was going to be in San Francisco for a meeting in January, he said, and he'd be driving up to Brayton to meet with someone at the university. Tina told him that she was just beginning the kinetics study, but he was certainly welcome to visit her lab. Only after they'd set a date and she'd hung up did it occur to her to wonder where he'd heard about the project. Not that it was a secret. He might have talked to someone who had reviewed one of her proposals. For that matter, Garrett had presented the basics of the kinetics at his conference in France, though in another context. . . . She picked up the phone again and dialed Garrett's number, but his student answered and told her that Garrett was holed up at home working on a paper. Tina tried calling him there, but he didn't answer. She wondered how the poster had been received, how people had responded to Garrett's new theory—she'd laughed to see his name on the list of upcoming BIO seminars with the title "Life from Humic Scum." She called his office back and left a message with the student for him to call her. She tried Chip again at the farm, but there was no answer.

It was only four, but almost dark when Tina left BIO, the pale gray sky turned to charcoal. She could just make out the night herons huddled quietly in the middle of their grove of pines, and the scent of impending rain was in the air.

When she turned up her street, Tina saw Chip's truck parked at the curb, but he was nowhere in sight when she got to the duplex. She rode up the path to the drainpipe and parked her bike. She was kneeling, threading the chain through the wheel and frame, when she looked up from the lock and saw him standing at the back corner of the duplex, watching her.

Tina gasped. He was just standing there, this burly, faintly familiar stranger with the stupid red cap, wiping his hands on his jeans, staring at her. Even after she noticed him, he didn't say anything, as if he were waiting for some kind of sign from her.

Tina snapped the lock closed and stood up. She was still breathing hard from her ride.

"Thanks," she said. "For the food. And the plants. It was nice." But apparently that wasn't the sign he was waiting for, because he just kept staring at her. "I tried to call you at the farm earlier, but I guess you were down here."

He nodded then, still not taking his eyes off her.

"Finishing up the belgian fence," he said after a moment. "You want to see it?" He finally looked away, turned, and started toward the backyard without waiting for her answer.

Tina followed him around back to see the fence that he'd created by overlapping the branches of young fruit trees that had been trained into a Y shape. "It's beautiful," she said, and it was, this graceful symmetry he'd achieved with the bare young branches.

He nodded, and then he started describing how the belgian fence would look when it was grown, how the branches would grow up and cross again forming a second row of diamond-shaped windows, how he'd included apple trees of various varieties . . . as if Tina were one of his landscaping clients.

She went over to stand in the passage to the alley and was looking up at the arch he'd fashioned from the trees on either side when a huge drop of rain landed in the middle of her forehead. She wiped it away and looked over her shoulder at Chip, who had stopped talking and was standing with his hat in his hand and his head tilted back, gaping up at the dripping sky. A giant comic-book drop splattered on his nose, and then another in his eye, and then the sky suddenly went from dripping to pouring and they were both running for the door, Tina digging through her knapsack pocket for her keys. By the time she got the door open, they were both soaking wet and laughing.

Tina peeled off her clothes and dropped them in a puddle by the door.

They had yet to touch, or even greet each other properly, but the man she left tugging at his boots as she ran laughing to the shower no longer seemed a stranger: he was her lover, and he had not burst into a righteous cloud of dust, or packed up his Garden of Eden and faded like a dream into a blue or even a gray winter sky. Not yet, anyway.

"Did you see any neat birds?" Chip was padding about the kitchen barefoot, a towel wrapped around his waist. He took the cabbage out of the refrigerator and set it on the cutting board in front of Tina.

"Birds?" Tina said, still giddy from their shower, still thinking about the surprised, desperate look on his face when he'd stepped under the scalding hot water and touched her. "No," she said. "I don't think so. There were gulls, I guess, or something like them flying around the ship. We saw some sharks. And dolphins."

"Really? Sharks?"

"Mm-hmm." She was thinking about the frantic sex they'd just had, the strange, alien feel of it . . . and yet with her period just begun and the intimacy of knowing that neither of them minded.

"God, did I miss your vegetables," she said. She tore off a piece of cabbage and stuck it into her mouth. "It's sweet, literally sweet. How do you do that? Grow sweet cabbage?" She picked up the cabbage in both hands and examined it.

Chip grinned. "It's a secret," he said. "The sweet-cabbage magic charm. Farmers have been using it for centuries to lure beautiful women into their beds."

Tina rolled her eyes and laughed. "Come on, seriously. How come it's sweeter than cabbage you buy at the store? Is it just fresher? Do the sugars oxidize or something when it sits around?"

"It's the timing. You get it going at the right time in the early fall, and then the cold weather comes just as it's maturing and makes it sweet. Same thing with carrots. Even brussels sprouts."

"The cold makes it sweet? That's almost counter-intuitive. Though I guess if you think about it . . . Maybe it starts making sugar for storage, because it's not growing as fast?"

"I don't know. That sounds reasonable."

"Makes sense for carrots. But cabbage? Storing sugar in the leaves . . . ?" Tina paused and looked at the array of vegetables on the cutting board. "What are we making?"

"I'm making spinach pie, and you're shredding cabbage for a salad." He went back to the sink and dumped the spinach in. "So what else?"

"That's not enough? There might be some chicken or something in the freezer, but—"

"No, the cruise. Tell me about the cruise. What's it like living on a boat for six weeks?"

"Oh. I don't know what to tell. All I did was work."

"Well that's nothing new."

Tina glanced over her shoulder, but he had his back to her. "More," she said. "You work even more. Everyone does. You hardly get to sleep." She started shredding the cabbage. "And there's this weird social structure. Something about being stuck together on this boat out in the middle of nowhere. People do things they would never do back on shore."

"Such as?"

"Like they drink and party and talk more, and there were even a couple of slightly sleazy affairs. In spite of the fact that there's so much work. It's like everyone's drugged from lack of sleep or something."

"I thought you said there were only a few women."

"Four, counting the chief scientist. A record number, or so they say." She paused, then burst out laughing. "That's what makes it so funny! There was this one grad student all the men had the hots for—I swear, that's how people were talking. But she ended up with the dumpy middle-aged French guy who was our cabinmate. Even my friend Katharine—"

"And you?"

"Did I have a sleazy affair? No."

"After all, I'm sure you had your choice. All those brilliant scientists."

"Right." Tina held her knife still against the cutting board. "All those brilliant, inconsiderate, self-absorbed scientists to choose from." Chip didn't respond, and she started the knife moving again, concentrating on making the slices paper-thin. He set the pot of spinach on the stove and turned the burner on. Then he came up behind her and leaned over her shoulder. He wrapped one thick hairy arm across her chest and the other around her stomach and Tina let go of the knife as he lifted her up off her feet, folding her into the curve of his body.

"You don't," he whispered into her ear, "have to use the whole thing." He pressed her into him so hard it took her breath away, and then released his hold and let her slide back to the ground.

Tina stared at the mountain of cabbage she'd shredded. It completely covered the cutting board. She smiled sheepishly and tried to push it into a more compact pile. "It'll still be good tomorrow, won't it?"

He laughed. "Probably. But I don't know about next week. Now tell me more. Tell me about the work, if that's all there is to tell."

By the time Chip had put his pie in the oven and they had sipped their way through half a bottle of wine, Tina had told him as much as she could think to tell about the cruise: about becoming a daughter of Neptune and the Brazilians' food and getting drunk with Harper and Conroy and the storm that made everyone sick. She told him how the cores were brought up and split, and a little about how they were processed. Chip asked her about the picoplankton, remembering the pictures on her office wall, and she told him that she hadn't been able to do her analyses in the ship's labs and wouldn't know anything until she got her new HPLC.

The rain had picked up while Tina was talking, and now it was pounding the roof with such vehemence that it almost drowned out their conversation.

"Will you listen to that," Chip said. "I bet we're getting an inch an hour!" He went over to the kitchen window and rubbed it free of fog with the back of his sleeve. The buzzer on the oven went off, and Tina got up to set the table. She was about to toss the newspaper Chip had left there onto the pile in the corner when he brought the spinach pie to the table.

"You read that yet?" he said, nodding toward the paper in her hand.

"No," Tina said guiltily, and set it back down on the table. It was the *New York Times* folded open to the science section.

"That was in the paper a couple weeks ago, and I saved it for you. About the greenhouse effect."

She went to the cupboard for plates. "You're really getting into this, aren't you?"

"Of course I am. Everyone should be. We're changing the climate. Completely upsetting the balance of nature on the entire planet."

"Life has been changing the composition of the atmosphere and the climate for the past 3.8 billion years," Tina said, just to bait him. She set the plates on the table and sat down. If you were a geoscientist, she thought, you could say that, wave your hand and say, Ah, a climatic shift, another catastrophe—how exciting! And you wouldn't bother to point out what made this change so different from the ones that came before, because it was so obvious. That time made it different. Scale. The very fact that you got to watch it, as if you were living in geologic time, and yet you weren't. Continents would not have slid across the globe, nor life evolved perceptibly in the time it took for this catastrophe. She waited for Chip's reply.

"But *we* didn't change it."

She watched him slide a piece of the pie onto her plate. "I'm not so sure about that," she said. "Certainly man has changed regional climates in the past. The desertification of the Sahara, in fact, from overgrazing."

"But . . . " He hesitated, and Tina thought she had him stumped. "But not consciously," he said finally. "We didn't know what we were doing. And now we do."

She shook her head. "The point is," she said, reaching for the bowl of cabbage, "that when life has affected climate, it has done so either gradually or regionally. It has never, that we know of, created global changes as rapid as the change in atmospheric CO_2 that we have created. We're talking about a timescale of decades, here, a century."

"They say there that they can already detect the warming," Chip said, waving his fork at the newspaper.

"They do? Who's saying that?" Tina pulled the paper toward her.

"Why don't you read it?" He started eating, and Tina skimmed the article. "You know those guys?" he asked when she set the paper aside.

"No. Why would I know them? It's some group of atmospheric scientists at NASA."

"Well, so, what do you think?"

"The article's too vague to say. It's not even clear what they used for their temperature data. Historical records? Do we even have records with that good a coverage? Too short a timescale to use sediments. . . . And even if they had a good temperature record, how did they separate out the natural fluctuations? And then there's these predictions again. Six to nine degrees Fahrenheit warming in the next fifty years? How did they come up with these numbers?"

"It says they use computer models, like simulations or something."

"Of course. But what went into the models? And there's someone—" She pulled the paper back into view. "They mention this other guy. A plant physiologist? He supposedly comes up with less than one degree change by the end of the next century. So he must have used some other technique, or another sort of model or something. But what?" She paused, squinting across the table at Chip.

"Shit, Tina, why are you cross-examining *me*? *I* don't know. You're the one who's supposed to know."

Tina blinked. "I'm not cross-examining you. I was just wondering why this guy's prediction is so different from the other group's." She laughed. "Though it's not surprising. You know those two guys I told you about, that I got drunk with on the cruise? They couldn't even agree on how much CO_2 the ocean is taking up. And they were working together." She looked at the article again. "Those two were saying that they can't account for all of the anthropogenic CO_2 that supposedly would have had to go into the ocean for the atmospheric CO_2 curve to look the way it does. Which means they certainly can't predict what that curve will look like in the future . . . which makes one wonder what these climate models are basing their predictions on. No?" Tina tossed the newspaper onto a chair and turned her attention to the food on her plate. The article was only the more frustrating for her interest. Six to nine degrees Fahrenheit by the year 2020? The earth had never been that warm during the Holocene, had it? In man's time? One of these days she wanted to get down to the library and look up some of Harper Gibson's and Conroy Decker's carbon cycle papers, and maybe she'd see if she could find this NASA group's paper . . . not that she was likely to understand much of a paper about atmospheric circulation computer models.

The rain was still pounding on the roof when they finished their dinner, still coming down in inches per hour when Tina finished doing the dishes and went into the living room to join Chip. He was standing at the window, staring out at the rain, which was just visible in the light of the street-light across the way. Tina walked over and stood next to him. She glanced at his face, amused that he could be so thoroughly entertained by this steady movement of water from sky to earth, as if the rain were a grand and varied spectacle, a show of fireworks, an opera or ballet.

"We should be up at the farm," he said wistfully. He slipped an arm around Tina, and leaned down to kiss the side of her neck softly. "We could sleep up in the loft," he said, sliding his hand under her T-shirt and moving it up the side of her breast. "Listen to it come down. Just stay up there until the storm's over."

"God, I hope it's not raining when my father drives up."

"Storm should be past by then." Chip dropped his arm back to his side. "I've been thinking about your father's visit," he said.

"Oh, don't worry about it," Tina said. "I'll just do something for him down here." She turned and glanced around the tiny living room. "Get a Christmas tree or something."

"Oh no, come on, I've got it all planned. I was thinking we could give him the bedroom and we'll sleep in the loft. Or is he old-fashioned? You think he'll mind us sleeping together?"

"No."

"I could always sleep on the cou—"

"He's not going to care, Chip."

"The only thing is, I don't know what to get him for a Christmas present. I thought of giving him a bareroot apple or pear tree, but I don't have anything low-chill enough for southern California. How 'bout a bottle of homemade cider?"

"Fine. You don't need to give him anything, for that matter. Though I'd better get on it myself. When I lived in San Diego it was easy because there was a Spanish bookstore and I used to buy him books. He always liked that."

"We'd have to go down to the city."

Tina shook her head. "There's too much to do this week. I'll just get him a shirt or something at the Penney's." There would be the samples to deal with at the lab . . . and then there was the problem of the car. "I've got to—"

"I know," Chip interrupted her. "You've got to go to the lab." He laughed and pressed his nose to the window. "At least she's predictable," he said to the rain outside, as if it were the audience, he and Tina the show.

"Well, I do," Tina said, "have to go to the lab. And I also have to buy a car."

"You have to what?" He pulled his face back from the window to look at her.

"I have to buy a car before my dad gets here. And get rid of the Toyota."

Chip moved to the sofa and sat down. "You don't just go out and buy a car in an hour, Tina. We can start shopping around, doing a little research, but that takes time, and you just said you have a lot to do."

"I'll just go to one of those used car lots and trade in the Toyota," Tina said. "Pay the rest on time."

"Oh yeah, and get royally ripped off. And I hate to break it to you, but they don't take trade-ins with frozen engines. Christ, you don't even know what kind of car to buy."

"Another Toyota?"

"Jorge and I could find you a good car for half the price you'll pay at a dealer. It might take a while—"

"But there isn't a while."

"And why, may I ask, do you have to do this before Christmas? Your dad is driving up. You'll have his car."

Tina was shaking her head. "It's not that. It's just that my father expects me to own a decent car. It doesn't have to be fancy, but it has to run. And look 'nice.' The idea of me driving a car that's all rusty and broke-down would depress him no end."

"Hell, I can relate to that—"

"No, it's different. You just can't stand it because it seems so wasteful and ridiculous that I didn't get it fixed. But to my father it means more than that. It's sort of like his shoe fetish."

"Shoe fetish?" Chip was staring at her now, a seriously puzzled expression on his face.

Tina sighed. "My father has this thing about good, as in 'nice,' shoes—like they're indicative of a person's well-being and self-worth. And it's the same thing with the car. . . . I'm supposed to be this successful scientist, right? A professional. He's inordinately proud of that." Tina shrugged, embarrassed to be admitting this. "Not that he has the foggiest idea what I do for him to be proud of. But it doesn't matter. The point is, it makes him happy. And if I don't have a car it'll blow the whole thing. . . . Look," Tina said, "it's just one of those things you do to make your father happy, okay? A filial duty." She glanced at Chip, who was still looking puzzled, chewing on his mustache. "So who said interactions with one's father are supposed to be rational?" she said finally, exasperated—and then she recalled that Chip had washed his hands of his own father as soon as he'd reached adulthood. How could she expect him to understand?

He got up and went back to the window to look at the rain.

"I lied," he said after a moment, shaking his head.

"What?"

"You're not predictable."

Chapter 16

The storm lasted two days, and the rest of that week before Christmas was cold, clear, and windy. On Thursday, Garrett wandered into Tina's office unannounced and said that he had a yen to take a walk on the beach. It was too windy for a walk on the beach, but Tina wanted to talk to Garrett, and he was oddly intent on taking a walk, so she went along. She would have laughed at him, out there on the beach—leaning into the wind at an awkward angle, the thin nylon of his jacket flapping about his arms, his black shoes forlorn and out of place on the wet sand—if he didn't look so serious, so distracted. Between the wind and the surf, it was so noisy that she had to stay close by his side to hear as he told her about the conference, where their poster had made less of a stir than he'd predicted.

"'Hard evidence' was not the happening thing this year," Garrett said.

"And your Humic Scum theory?" Tina asked. "I see you're giving a seminar next month."

"Oh, that was well received, I suppose. But the hot items on the agenda were two new theories based on computer simulations—pure mathematics, no chemistry at all. If you ask me, they're just post-modern reincarnations of the spontaneous generation theories for the origin of life, theories we got rid of a hundred years ago, but people couldn't see past the glitz of the mathematics to recognize that. It's just a fad," Garrett said, attempting a dismissive flutter of his hand that the wind made impossible. "But the problem with fads is that they receive an inordinate amount of uncritical attention." They had come to the end of the beach, and Tina paused, thinking they would start back, but Garrett continued onto the rocks. "Unfortunately, I had agreed to edit the conference monograph," he said, crawling awkwardly up the side of a huge boulder. He paused at the top, while Tina scrambled up after him, and then he eased himself down the other side.

Tina leaped off the boulder and landed next to him. They were on a large, open expanse of sandstone, riddled with tide pools.

"We should publish those Warrua results soon," Garrett said, setting off across the sandstone platform. "What's happening with your grant?"

"It's been funded. I already ordered my new HPLC!"

"Congratulations."

"Thanks. And thank you for telling me about it. . . . You were right."

"Maybe." They had come to a narrow fissure in the sandstone where the water rushed in, and Garrett stopped to peer over the edge at the churning white froth. "I'm not always right, you know."

Tina waited for him to look up, expecting to see the familiar half-mocking spark in his eye, but instead he turned and walked along the fissure toward its mouth, where the waves were breaking on a jumble of rocks. He stopped just at the edge of the spray and sat down on a small rock.

"I'm trying to get Michael back," Tina said, coming up next to him and yelling to be heard over the waves. "I'm thinking about turning the kinetics experiments over to him—let him get a paper or two out of it. In fact, we should probably wait and publish some of that with the Warrua study, don't you think?"

Tina couldn't hear Garrett's reply. She cupped her hand to her ear, and he glanced up and nodded once, then turned back to stare out at the horizon, the sun glinting off his glasses, his expression dark, unreadable. Tina herself was feeling ambivalent about the Warrua project, her mind on the boxes of samples that had just arrived, but she had expected Garrett to be more enthusiastic. He seemed uncharacteristically gloomy and untalkative, sitting on a rock that was clearly too small to be comfortable, his bit of hair whipping about with such ferocity it looked as though the last few strands might blow off his head and leave him completely bald. She couldn't imagine that he was upset because his theory was out of style. Maybe he himself was unhappy with his theory? But if that were the case, he'd be talking about it, she was sure. Maybe, Tina thought, he liked it in France and hadn't wanted to come back. For all she knew, he had a sweetheart there. . . . But it was easier to imagine Garrett brooding over a problematic theory than a sweetheart.

She squatted down by a tide pool a couple of feet away from Garrett's rock and watched the crabs skitter into hiding as she moved her hand to cast shadows. She was cold and restless. She had been looking forward to talking with Garrett about the cores from the cruise, and about all these half-formed new ideas about the carbon cycle that were churning around in her head. But Garrett wasn't talking. He hadn't even asked her about the cruise.

She picked up a fragment of rock and dropped it into the center of a pink anemone, watching the creature close around it, then open again, betrayed. Cruel as a child burning ants, Tina picked up another bit of stone—but tossed it aside when she realized that Garrett was also watching the anemone. A large wave crashed on the rocks and spilled onto their sandstone flat, filling the tide pools at its edge. Tina stood up and took a few steps back, remembering the stories she'd heard about people being swept off these rocks by sleeper waves. "Is the tide coming in or going out?" she shouted.

"Looks like it might be coming in," Garrett said, but he made no move to get up from his rock.

Tina looked around. There was a big mass of basalt rising above the sandstone a few yards away, and she went over and climbed up its side. She was high above the spray there, with a better view of the waves. She sat down and looked over at Garrett, perched on his too-small rock, oblivious of the cold wind and spray. He had turned to watch her climb the rock, and he gave her a reassuring wave and even a bit of a smile—as if this were all something they were in the habit of doing, climbing around on rocks and silently communing with nature together.

Tina hugged her knees to keep warm and scanned the water for seals, but there weren't any around. She watched the kelp bubbles floating on the swells beyond the froth like heads bobbing in and out of view. What was it she'd read about kelp—that it was anchored to the rocks below by a sort of hand or claw, but took its nutrients from the water? Tina rested her chin on her knees and watched two of the bubble heads rise up on a swell, tilting toward each other and bending suddenly into a brief kiss, then dipping out of sight. A tangle of dusky green ropes billowed up in their place, looking warm and content as snakes in the afternoon sun, and it seemed an amazing thing, such sensuous peace at the edge of so much churning froth. It was restful, watching them, calming. . . .

The kelp heads are strung out single-file across the water, rising and ducking, kissing and separating—now connected like a string of beads, now bobbing about separately, not beads but charms, strange and fanciful charms such as a child might collect. There's a miniature tube of sediment that crumbles if you touch it; there's a single lonely dinosaur waving goodbye; a little green and blue globe; a dirt-stained human hand; a large bubble of CO_2 caught in a beer bottle . . . a gelatinous cluster of picoplankton clinging together in bewilderment, surprised to be part of this chain at all—for each of the charms is tied to the next by a sinuous length of glistening green lipid, strung together in a grand and unlikely necklace. Tina would like to drape it over her head, but it's hopelessly tangled. She tries to be patient, setting herself down on a rock to untangle it, but the slimy tendons of the thread elude her every grasp. She can't even find the end or the beginning of the silly thing, and she doesn't have much time because she wants to wrap it for Christmas but she doesn't have any wrapping paper. She finds a piece of newspaper and wraps it around the whole slimy mess, ties it up with a red bow, writes a note saying that she will untangle it later, and puts it in the campus mail, but it's already Christmas Eve and she has to get home because her father is coming—

"We'd better head back."

Tina jerked her head up. Garrett was standing next to the rock, looking up at her.

She scrambled down. The sun had turned orange and was sinking on the horizon in a simple, no-thrills sunset. The wind had died down a little, and the tide was definitely coming in. The dream left Tina feeling optimistic. She bounded along beside Garrett, who seemed to cheer up a little, as if infected by her mood. He finally asked her about the cruise and listened sympathetically—though he was suspiciously uncritical—while she babbled about her plans for the core samples.

It was too easy, Tina warned herself, to feel optimistic when you didn't have any data yet to screw things up. She thought of the unlikely chain of iconized ideas in her dream, and was reminded of how she'd felt after each of her three adolescent experiments with psychedelic drugs: elated, as if she'd had some great revelation, and yet unable to recall exactly what it was that was revealed, to grasp the source of her joy. Garrett took his leave in the parking lot, and she wished him Merry Christmas. As they went their separate ways, she realized that she didn't have the faintest idea how Garrett felt about Christmas, or what he would be doing. For all she knew, that was why he seemed so quiet, so subdued—maybe he had the Christmas blues.

In spite of his skepticism, Chip went with Tina to look at the car, a white Mazda with no rust, no dents. It started right up when Tina turned the key. It idled smoothly. It wasn't, according to Chip, a total rip-off—it wasn't a good deal either, but Tina didn't care. She wrote out a check. She paid thirty dollars to have the Toyota towed away and parked the Mazda in its place.

Her father was due to arrive on Christmas Eve, which Chip was spending with Jorge and Meche and their three kids, who would be taking the midnight flight to Mexico. Tina and her father would spend the night at the duplex, then move up to the farm on Christmas day.

Tina got up early, as usual, but she didn't go to the lab. She cleaned her apartment. She went to the laundromat. Then she went Christmas shopping. She went to Penney's and bought a shirt for her father and wrapping paper and a string of twinkling Christmas lights. She spent a half-hour in the bookstore trying to decide what to get Chip and ended up buying two books, unable to choose between them: *The Gardener's All-Season Cookbook*, and a book by a local author about the birds of Brayton County. Then she went to the store and bought meat and potatoes and squash for a *puchero*, an Uruguayan dish that her father liked and that was easy to make—she just had to throw everything into a pot of water and boil it for a long time. She wrapped the presents and decorated the pear tree with the string of Christmas lights. She baked the chocolate chip cookies she'd learned to make as a child, cookies her father always raved about, even though they were just the recipe on the package. It grew dark out, and Tina kept dashing into the living room to look out through the twinkling red-and-green halo of the pear tree, thinking she'd heard him drive up. When he did finally arrive, a little before seven, she didn't hear him until he knocked at the door.

Ever since the pizza franchise failed and he lost the house—when, in the space of a few months, he'd seemed to age, to visibly sag—Tina worried with each visit that she would suddenly find herself opening the door on an old man. She lifted her cheek to her father's now, pressed against the familiar scratch of his evening stubble, and felt the rush of relief as he crushed her to him—that he looked fit, unaged, that he was so pleased to see her. If anything, he seemed younger, seemed to be thriving in his low-income, semi-retired life as suburban apartment house manager. He spoke of it with good cheer, as if he enjoyed it, the tinkering and fixing, the people, the swimming pool. Tina couldn't remember him ever talking about his job at the restaurant.

The dinner she'd made pleased him, as did the plate of homely chocolate chip cookies she set in front of him, as did the very idea of this week with his daughter. And her "amigo."

She could tell he didn't quite approve of the apartment, though he didn't say so. He just pointed out things she should get the landlord to do—replace the worn carpet, paint. But she knew that what bothered him was that it was so obviously the apartment of someone who lived alone, and more like a bachelor's pad than a single woman's. Not a home. Not a place where he could imagine his grandchildren frolicking. She began to feel irritated and told herself to stop, that he was simply concerned, worried about her living alone, worried she wasn't happy . . . and instead she ended up worrying about him worrying about her, a worry as old and familiar as the chafe of his stubble against her cheek. She supposed she should have fixed the place up a little more. Hung something on the walls, bought some flowers. Got some bookshelves. There were Chip's plants. . . . She thought about taking him out on the porch and showing off the yard, but that would be hard to do without mentioning that it was all Chip's doing. And he was already way too excited about Chip. He insisted on unwrapping the present he'd bought and showing it to Tina, wanting to make sure it was appropriate. Tina laughed when her father opened the little box: he'd bought Chip a Swiss Army knife.

"It has a screwdriver and a wood file and, you see here? It even has a little saw." He unfolded the tools to demonstrate. "The clerk at the hardware store said it was the best one."

"He'll love it," Tina said, amazed, and even a little jealous that her father had chosen such a perfect present.

"What time are we going to the farm tomorrow? In the morning?"

"No. Early afternoon, I guess."

"I brought some nice clothes. Some people like to get dressed up for Christmas."

"Chip's a farmer, Dad. He wears jeans."

"Well, I know honey, that's what I thought. But I brought a sports coat and a good shirt, you know, just in case."

"What you have on is fine," she told him. He was wearing cotton slacks and a nice sweater.

She was glad that he was so happy to be with her, that he was looking forward to their week together. But by the time they went to bed—early, her father tired from the long drive—she was feeling a guilty desire to have it over with, even while she yearned to give him more, to make this happiness his norm. Tina sighed, settling into the bed she'd made herself on the couch. He was so pitifully easy to please.

As planned, Tina drove her father up to the farm in her new used Mazda. And, also as planned, her father thought the car was "very nice." When they got to the farm, Chip was standing out in the drive, waiting to greet them. He was wearing a pair of dark brown corduroy slacks and a chamois shirt, neither of which Tina had ever seen before. She was tempted to just drop her father off and let them have a blind date. But she parked the car and got out with her father and introduced them, and then she stood back and watched while they shook hands and her father clasped Chip's shoulder with his other hand and gazed into his eyes as if he were a long lost brother—or son.

For all their fretting, they took to each other immediately. Chip had been practicing his Spanish all week, convinced that speaking the man's native tongue was the way to win his heart. Maybe he was right, Tina thought, watching the two of them talk their way through Christmas dinner. Her father loved the farm, loved it that the carrots and salad and steamed kale he was eating had all been grown by his host. He was clearly charmed by the history of their Christmas ham, the tale of marauding pigs told in Chip's winningly clumsy Spanish.

The two men talked on and on, their words not a flood, but a slow, plodding leisurely flow that made the afternoon supper drag on for hours. Tina sat there looking on, stuffing herself with ham and feeling alternately bored and jealous. It was disconcerting, listening to her father regale her lover in the gentle cadences of her childhood, their father-daughter language—secret because none of her friends had understood it and she'd been a bit ashamed, but a well-guarded and cherished secret, because it was her father's and hers alone. They rambled on about Brayton and the weather, about Chip's landscaping business and Alberto's failed franchise business that she'd never heard him talk about, and about how he'd landed in Los Angeles, a young man and his bride on an adventure in North America. Chip seemed as content as her father with this prosaic mix of the mundane and significant, genuinely deferential to the older man—even as her father launched into a tedious series of stories from Tina's childhood.

"She got into everything when she was little, this one," her father said, still speaking Spanish. Chip eyed Tina curiously. "One time she stepped out of the tree—she was only six and climbing the tree already. She was pretending to be a bird and she just stepped into the air in front of my eyes. She was a very expensive child. I was always at the hospital. I thought I would die of a heart attack before she was grown. Three times she fell out of trees. I said no more trees, but she was spoiled. She didn't listen. And she used to drive me crazy with her questions. Papá, how far is distance? That was a good one. I still remember. Once she learned how to say 'why,' I was lost. I never should have taught her that word. I tried to answer, but how can you answer questions like that? And then if I did answer, she didn't believe me. She just asked another question about the answer."

Chip was laughing. "She hasn't changed," he said, looking at Tina, whose mouth was full of ham.

"I'm sure that was just a sign of her scientific mind, but what did I know?"

Tina rolled her eyes and swallowed. "Dad," she said in English. "All kids ask those kinds of questions. I think there's even a phase called the 'why' phase."

"I know that," he said indignantly, also in English. "I read all those books. The ones they had then, that Dr. Spock. I learned to read English with those books. But you were worse. And you didn't grow out of it." He turned back to Chip and went on in Spanish, waving his fork at Tina as if she were just a child again, looking on. She served herself a third helping of ham. "You see how she always speaks English? That's one thing they didn't talk about in the books. She goes to Kindergarten and comes home refusing to speak Spanish. I swear. One day. She learned English in one day. 'Dad'—I hate that, she calls me 'Dad.' Papá, I said, you call me papá. She ignored me. No respect, you know, even then. I wanted her to speak Spanish to me, I don't know, I guess because of her mother. Me, I grew up speaking German and Spanish. But her mother's family was from Spain.

Nowadays they say it's good for the children to speak two languages, but back then they said it was bad. They told me I should only speak English with her, to help her 'assimilate.' Assimilate to what? She was born assimilated. I ignored them. I didn't speak English very well back then—so what am I going to do, speak English to my daughter and have her grow up thinking her father has the vocabulary of a five year-old?"

Tina couldn't believe he was going on like this. She looked at Chip. He was soaking it up. He was clearly amused. She looked at his plate. He was just finishing his first serving of ham.

"I know I spoiled her. I let her do anything."

"You did not." Tina got up and carried the ham platter into the kitchen for replenishing.

"I didn't make you do your homework," he called after her.

She stopped and turned to look at him. "I didn't do my homework?"

"Well, I guess you did it," her father conceded. "The teachers never complained, anyway. "When she was in high school," he said to Chip, switching back to Spanish, "she used to say she was doing it while we watched T.V. Now they say how bad it is, to let the children watch too much T.V., but we used to watch it together every night. She would sit there with a book in her lap and the T.V. on, somehow reading and watching at the same time. She used to like those fantasy books, and science fiction." He laughed. "And then I remember when she was about sixteen she started reading those Russian novels and for a while that's all she did, sit around reading those long books."

Chip turned to Tina. "You read novels?" he said incredulously, speaking English for the first time all evening. "Dostoyevsky, Tolstoy? I've never seen you read anything but those journals you bring home."

"I like novels," Tina said. She set the full platter in front of her father and sat down. "I just don't have time now. I can't even keep up with the scientific literature."

Chip turned back to her father. "Well, you must have done something right," he said in Spanish. "She seems to have turned out okay."

Tina glared at him. "Since when do you think that?" she said, suddenly conscious of the bilingual cadence of their conversation.

Chip ignored her.

"I never imagined in a million years that she would become a scientist," her father said. "With a Ph.D. When she was in school she was never interested in taking the science classes. And math, she said math was boring." Tina nudged the platter of ham closer to her father, hoping he'd stop talking and eat. He picked it up and passed it to Chip. "I thought she would maybe be a poet. She wrote such nice poems when she was in high school."

"You did?"

Tina shrugged.

"I used to take her to the beach every chance I got. I'm sure that's where her love for oceanography comes from. Her favorite place didn't even have a beach, just rocks. She liked to collect things from the tide pools. Sometimes she would just sit there watching the creatures in the pool for hours."

"I'm afraid my brand of oceanography doesn't have anything to do with tide pools," Tina said.

"She works with stuff dug up from the bottom of the ocean," Chip said. He turned to Tina and switched to English. "You should take your father down to BIO to see your lab."

"Oh, I'd love that. I don't suppose we could go on the ship, could we, Tina?"

"The ship isn't there. But we'll go down tomorrow, if you want, and I'll show you my lab. There's a visitor's center you might like, if it's open. And we can go out on the pier, or maybe go for a walk on the beach." Tina smiled. "There are some good tide pools down there," she said.

"To tell you the truth," her father said, turning to Chip, "I've never completely understood exactly what it is she does."

"She's studying the climate," Chip said, and proceeded to explain Tina's work to her father, encountering the limits of his Spanish and switching to English in the process. He explained what a sediment core was and described how Tina used "stuff that algae had left behind in the sediments" to figure out what the climate had been in the distant past. Her father's head bobbed in understanding. When Chip asked if Alberto had heard about the greenhouse effect, Tina got up and started clearing the table, though they were still picking at the ham.

"This is very interesting, sweetheart," her father said when she returned to the table for another load of dishes. "You know, Chip, I think I saw something in the paper a while back. Are you going to study this too Tina? This greenhouse effect?"

Tina shook her head. "The people doing that research need to know the climate history of the past hundred years. What I do is on a scale of millions of years. A thousand years between data points is about the best I can do with deep sea sediments. We're talking about a layer as thin as this material—" She lifted the corner of a napkin for him to see. She told him a little about the cores from the cruise, and then, because he'd seemed interested when Chip was explaining it, she told him about the pico-plankton lipids and her Saturation Index. She had started talking about the climate of the Cretaceous and what they were hoping to find out from the cruise sediments, when she noticed that her father's head no longer bobbed encouragingly. He was smiling at her with an expression of awe and incomprehension on his face.

"You lost me," he said. "Never could keep up with her," he said to Chip, who gave a sympathetic shrug.

Tina felt her face grow hot. She picked up the empty salad bowl and the platter of ham, and looked at Chip. "Why don't we take a tour of the farm before it gets too late," she said, and was relieved when he jumped up from the table and went off to look for his sweater. She took the dishes into the kitchen. She would get him talking about his lettuce crop. His five kinds of kale. His arugula.

Her father came over and leaned across the counter to talk to her while she put away the food and scraped the plates into the compost bucket.

"¿Te vas a casar, m'ija?"

"Dad. He speaks Spanish, in case you haven't noticed. And no, I'm not going to get married." Chip was probably in the next room, she thought, pretending not to hear this.

"Pero es buena persona," her father whispered. "And it's obvious how much he loves you."

"Oh, por dios. Why don't you marry him yourself, if you like him so much." It wasn't fair. No one had ever pressured him to remarry. She had never nagged him for a mother. She looked up just in time to see the hurt register on her father's face, and was immediately sorry.

He turned away from her and went to sit on the bench in the dining room, where he busied himself with his boot laces. Tina moved to the counter. "Papá," she said. "Disculpáme . . . Pero, ya sabés que—"

"No importa," he said, cutting off her apology.

She watched him unlace and relace his boots. They were obviously new. He must have bought them for the trip, Tina thought. He'd always had this thing about shoes. They had to look nice. Always. They couldn't be scuffed up—old was okay, as long as they didn't look old—or ugly. Running shoes and Birkenstocks were an affront to civilization as far as her father was concerned. It used to drive her crazy. She'd always had to wear nice shoes, even for play, even in summer, when the rest of the world was running around in brightly-colored twenty-nine-cent thongs. She turned her attention back to the dishes.

"Let's go!" Chip said, sweeping into the kitchen. "*Ven, mi amor*, leave those for later." He dropped an arm around her and reached for the plate in her hand.

"Wait a minute." Tina held onto the plate and tried to duck out from under his arm. "I'm just getting the food off of them."

"Okay," Chip said, stepping aside. "One minute."

Tina glanced at his face, but he was busy adjusting the bill of his cap. She repressed an urge to grab the stupid old thing off his head and add it to the garbage she was scraping into the compost bucket. He'd just get a new one, and a new one might be worse. Bright red. She set the lid on the bucket and rinsed her hands. She knew perfectly well that he would not think it funny if she threw his hat into the compost bucket. Was that what she wanted? To make him mad, ruin his good mood? She didn't know why she was so annoyed with them both, why she found their good cheer so insufferable. She felt like they were ganging up on her somehow, she felt—trapped.

By the time they were halfway down the hill, her father was once again enjoying himself immensely, as he would continue to do for the rest of his stay at the farm . . . while Tina collected up regrets enough to last the year—for all the times she snapped at him, for not doing more, for never ever doing enough to make him truly happy.

Chapter 17

No one could remember the last time Garrett Thomas had given a talk at BIO. The room was filling quickly, and Tina hurried down the aisle to where Katharine was sitting with Orloff and one of her graduate students. She made her way along the row to stand in front of a vacant seat at the edge of the group, and was surprised to find herself standing next to Alan. "How come you're here?" she said without thinking.

"Excuse *me*," he said, rising as if to go.

"No, I didn't mean that," Tina said, laughing.

Alan settled back into his seat. "A friend talked me into coming. There's this new theory using chaos mathematics that was presented at the early biosphere conference where Dr. Thomas was the keynote speaker, and we thought he might—"

"Tina Arenas—" Orloff leaned forward in her seat, talking past Katharine and Alan. "I've been wanting to talk to you. Have you worked through any of the cruise sediments yet?"

Tina shook her head. They'd only been back for three weeks, and there'd been Christmas to deal with. She started to explain about her dead HPLC and her grant that had just been funded and the new instrument that had been late in arriving because of the holidays.

"Here, why don't you sit down," Alan said, sliding over and placing a hand on Tina's waist to guide her into the seat next to Katharine.

Tina sat on the edge of the chair, looking past Katharine at Orloff.

"We're not sure how reliable the O-18 is going to be," Orloff said. "There are some Cretaceous segments where the foram record is inadequate." She glanced at Katharine, as if the poor state of preservation of seventy-million-year-old foraminifera shells were her fault. "I'm eager to see the temperatures from your Saturation Index."

"The forams don't look *that* bad," Katharine said. "Except for—" She fell silent as the director of BIO moved up to the podium to introduce Garrett, and everyone's attention shifted to the front of the auditorium.

When Garrett opened his talk with slides of the Warrua rocks and their controversial fossils, there was an almost visible skepticism in the room, people settling back in their seats, cocking their heads to the side, folding their arms. Tina's hydrocarbon evidence of the age and photosynthetic nature of the fossils roused a surprised murmur, and there was some head-swiveling, but once Garrett launched into the main body of his talk—a description of his new theory—he seemed to lose his audience. Tina recalled the last talk she'd heard Garrett give, at a conference she'd gone to as a grad student with Jake. The content of that talk couldn't have been as exciting as what he was presenting now—a whole new theory—and yet the audience had been rapt, held spellbound by Garrett's sheer exuberance for his subject. Tina glanced around the assembly room. This audience was definitely bored. Alan, sitting next to her with his arm draped casually over the back of her seat, actually seemed to doze off. Well, but he was a mathematician. She tried to concentrate on what Garrett was saying. The experiments he was describing and the details of his humic template idea were new to her, but even she found her mind wandering.

The problem was that Garrett himself sounded indifferent. He was up there talking about his favorite subject, his life's work, the object of all his considerable intelligence and creativity—and he just sounded tired. Disenchanted. Like a man falling out of love, a man realizing for the first time that he was all alone, his voice flat and uninspired and easily ignored. He was droning. *You've got a room full of people here!* Tina wanted to yell at him. She watched his face as he slipped another transparency onto the projector. Was he sick? He had seemed out of sorts when she'd seen him before Christmas, that strange walk they'd gone on . . . He didn't *look* sick. A little more disheveled than usual, perhaps, a little distracted, but not sick.

When Garrett finally started fielding questions, Alan moved so smoothly out of his nap that Tina wondered if she'd only imagined that his eyes had been closed, mouth parted, breathing slowed. He lifted his arm off the back of her seat and raised it to be acknowledged. "Rumor has it," he said, "that there's a new computer simulation which uses nonlinear process mathematics—"

"Yes," Garrett said shortly, as if he too had just awakened. "It was all the rage at the Earth's Early Biosphere conference in Paris last month. It was billed as a simulation of the spontaneous formation of life in a prebiotic world, but I'm afraid that's more than a little misleading. It begins with a set of random interactions and lets it run long enough to generate a simple, structured, self-perpetuating component within the larger chaos— a flashy but superficial exercise in theoretical mathematics that makes no attempt to emulate chemical systems that might have existed on the early earth. All the experiment does is reinforce the now conventional wisdom that given enough time, the unlikely event is possible. The computer does effectively speed up time and concentrate events, something we can't manage in the lab. Curiously enough, in the four runs of the simulation, the self-perpetuating component never formed in less than the equivalent of a billion years of earth time." Garrett's gaze shifted from Alan to Tina, then back to Alan. "And we've just seen evidence—not from one of our own two-bit confabulations, but from rocks and organic chemicals—that life came to exist in a fraction of that time."

Before Alan could respond, Garrett turned away to answer the next question, from a chemist wanting to know what pre-analysis treatment he used on the tar-like material that was the "humic scum" in his experiments.

"I guess he doesn't like the new theories," Alan whispered.

Tina shrugged, listening to Garrett's explanation to the chemist. At least he had stopped sounding like a talking corpse—though he still didn't sound quite like himself. He seemed to lack his usual sense of humor with regard to the new theories, these "two-bit confabulations."

"He's still milking his one fluke of an experiment, isn't he," Katharine said, standing and stretching as Garrett moved away from the podium.

It wasn't true—the experiments on humic acid photochemistry were new, and the idea of humic scum serving as a template for macromolecules to form, not to mention the work Tina had done—and Tina was about to say as much, when Orloff addressed her.

"It's amazing what can be done with these biomarker techniques of yours, Tina."

"It really is," Tina said. "And it's still wide open. We're just beginning. I've even been thinking that there must be some way to get a direct measure of paleo-CO_2 out of them."

"You can do that?" Orloff said quickly, her green eyes suddenly fixing on Tina's face. They were all standing now, Tina and Orloff on either side of Katharine, talking past her.

"No," Tina said. "No . . . I just keep thinking there must be a way," she added lamely, wondering why she'd even said anything. Alan touched her shoulder to say goodbye and she smiled and waved in a careless, distracted manner.

"I must say I'm a little surprised," Orloff said, with a flick of her wrist toward the podium, "that you've been wasting your time with this sort of thing."

"Oh, well, I was working on this hydrocarbon kinetics technique anyway, and he offered me the samples—"

"In any event, I'm hoping to see some of those temperature results soon," Orloff said, and with a perfunctory nod, she squeezed past Katharine and Tina and hurried toward the door.

"You guys have already done the O-18?" Tina asked Katharine.

Katharine let out a short bark of a laugh. "She wishes. I just got back from Dallas yesterday." She moved toward the aisle, and Tina followed her out of the building.

What an off-the-cuff thing to mention to Orloff, Tina thought as they headed down the hill, about doing paleo-CO_2 from biomarkers. When all she had was this vague notion that organic molecules made by photosynthetic organisms should, in *some* way, reflect atmospheric CO_2 concentration. Like it was their duty to do so, she thought, laughing at herself. And not only that, but they had to make the mark indelible, preserve it in the sediments. . . .

"She's even got you doing it," Katharine said suddenly.

"Huh?" They were on the bluff path, nearing Tina's building, and she suddenly realized that her loquacious friend hadn't said a word during their entire walk from the Geophysics building. "Who's got me doing what?"

"Sylvia," Katharine said. "She's got the great, stubborn, idealistic Cristina

Arenas kissing her ass." She spoke solemnly, as if she were eulogizing a fallen hero—in jest, but with an edge to her tone that caught Tina's attention.

"What are you talking about?" She stopped walking and stood in the path a few steps behind Katharine.

"Nothing," Katharine said, turning to look at Tina. "I suppose I should be glad that you're joining the real world. Showing a little ambition. Of course you shouldn't be wasting your time with projects like that one." Katharine flicked her wrist in a perfect imitation of Orloff's gesture of a few minutes ago.

Tina stared at her friend's face, but the hurt or disappointment or whatever it was she thought she'd heard was so carefully camouflaged in Katharine's familiar affectation—uptilted chin, pursed mouth, studied indifference—that Tina wondered if she hadn't just imagined it. Why should Katharine, of all people, be upset that in one inconsequential conversation with Sylvia Orloff Tina had tried to distance herself from Garrett, denied her interest in his work . . . ? Was that what she'd done? Tina thought, cringing.

"You know what it is, don't you?" Katharine turned and continued along the path, taking long defensive strides, so that Tina had to jog to catch up.

"What?"

"She sees that she can use you. She knows you're onto something and she wants first dibs."

"Orloff? On what, my temperature curves?"

"Maybe. Or maybe something else that you haven't even thought of yet. She has a great nose for hot data—her own and everybody else's. Right now she's onto yours, though it's a little tough because it's an organic chemist's data, and she's going to need the chemist to interpret it."

"Oh Katharine, that's ridiculous."

"Of course, you could do worse. You could do a lot worse than to be in possession of something that Sylvia Orloff wants." Tina glanced up, wondering at Katharine's injured, acrimonious tone. "You really should be careful," she went on. "She's power hungry. And getting weirder by the minute." Katharine paused, considering. Then she laughed. "She's acting like a *man*," she said. "That's what it is! Like a goddamn man. Only worse, because it's all so exaggerated. . . . I guess that's what you do to make up for not *being* one. You do what they do, only more so."

Tina was relieved when they arrived at her building. Katharine continued on to the parking lot, and she headed for her bike, glad that she'd already locked up the labs. Power hungry? What was that supposed to mean? She didn't even want to know. Nor did she want to think that she had endorsed Sylvia Orloff's contempt for Garrett—a man whose work, whose very field of study, embodied an ideal of science that Tina, in fact, respected and identified with. What she did want to know about, as she headed for home with the frigid wind at her back on this first Friday of the new year, was "hot data." She laughed out loud at Katharine's hyperbole. Because the truth of the matter was, the new HPLC hadn't arrived and she didn't have any data yet—hot, cold, or lukewarm.

Chapter 18

Michael and the new HPLC both showed up in Tina's lab the Monday after Garrett's seminar. "Need some help?" Michael inquired by way of greeting when he found Tina in the instrument lab, standing knee-deep in packing materials. For the first time since she'd hired him, Tina was completely happy to see him. He seemed genuinely interested in the hydrocarbon kinetics and was visibly pleased to be given responsibility for the project. Tina gave him reading material—her grant proposal, a text on organic reaction kinetics, a monograph on petroleum biomarkers—and within a week he was back in her office with questions, eager to get started. Tina helped him design the experiments, ordered the necessary materials, and arranged to borrow Jenner's heating block. On the day the Petron geologist visited the lab, Michael was setting up his first set of experiments, the new HPLC was up and running, and Tina had turned her attention to the hundreds of sediment samples awaiting extraction.

If she had checked her calendar the day before, she might have brought something to wear besides her jeans with the acid holes; and if he had not arrived forty-five minutes early, she might have been a little more decorous about receiving him, because she had seen the appointment on her calendar in the morning and knew he was coming, a Dr. Gilderslee from Petron Corporation. But as it was, Tina had just hung up the phone from talking to Roy about his latest picoplankton experiment and was making notes and muttering to herself when the stranger—dressed in a dark blue suit and tie and obviously not from BIO or the university—appeared abruptly in the doorway of her office, and she did her usual gasp and jump routine.

"I'm looking for Dr. Arenas," the man said, as if there were no possibility that this startled young woman, sitting like a contortionist with one leg draped over the arm of her office chair, could be the Cristina T. Arenas advertised on the nameplate by the door.

Tina untangled herself from the chair and stood up. "Dr. Gilderslee?" she said, stepping toward him and extending her hand. "Please come in." The man hesitated, literally looking her up and down before shaking it. He appeared to be in his early forties—young enough to know better, Tina thought, suddenly conscious of the holes in her jeans and her nipples against the thin pink cloth of her turtleneck. She invited him to sit down and tried to make some polite conversation, commenting on how lucky he was to have hit a break in the rain, asking about the drive from San Francisco, if he'd been up to the university . . . but she was relieved when the conversation moved to her work.

"I just got back from a cruise in the South Central Pacific," she told him, "and we have a wonderful collection of new core material. Some of it is coherent across the KT boundary, and three of the cores go well into the Cretaceous, one of them back to a hundred and twenty million years. We're using a new biomarker technique to look at paleoclimate—"

"I'm actually more interested in your method for determining the thermal history of a sedimentary basin," Gilderslee interrupted her.

"Yes, of course. That's one of the applications for the hydrocarbon kinetics we're studying. We've also been using it to assess the age and nature of Precambrian organic material." She went over to the bookshelf and took a couple of chromatograms out of a binder, including one of the ones where she'd drawn in the conformations of the hydrocarbon molecule. "This is work I've been doing with Garrett Thomas, validating some fossil-like markings in the Warrua formation." She handed him the chromatograms, but he just glanced at them and handed them back.

"Yes, I've seen these," he said.

"You have?" Tina set the chromatograms down and sat down behind her desk.

"I was a reviewer for your ACS proposal." Gilderslee paused, casually unbuttoning his jacket. "There's a basin that Petron is just starting to investigate," he said then, and without telling Tina where the basin was, he went on at some length about its geology. "With your method and the oil formation and migration model I've been working on we might be able to determine its potential without drilling," he said finally. "How long do you think it will be before you have the kinetics figured out?"

"I don't know," Tina said, unnerved by the man's self-assurance—his air of importance, the way he sat with his legs crossed in the expensive-looking blue suit, his eyes darting over her at disconcerting intervals—and by his tacit assumption that she would be interested in collaborating with him. "My technician is just beginning an in-depth study," she said. "And we've got our hands full with these cruise samples right now and the paleoclimate work. . . . I don't think we can take on the sort of project you're talking about. But, uh, why don't you let me show you the lab," she said, standing. "You might be interested in seeing our set-up."

She led him into the main lab and introduced him to Michael.

"Michael is a senior at U.C. Brayton," Tina said as the two men shook hands. "He's just starting on the kinetic experiments."

"If I can tear you away from your new HPLC long enough to run my samples," Michael quipped cheerfully. "The kinetics project is something of a second-class citizen around here," he said to Gilderslee.

"Why Michael," Tina said, glad for the relief from her humorless visitor. "You'll be able to use the HPLC any time between midnight and four A.M.—perfect hours for a student." He laughed, and she asked him to explain the experiment he was setting up to Gilderslee. Then the three of them walked down to the instrument lab, and Tina showed off her jerry-rigged HPLC-Mass Spec.

She explained how the system worked and started to tell the story of tracking down the picoplankton lipids, but Gilderslee turned the conversation back to his sedimentary basin, speaking to Michael now and repeating much of what he'd told Tina in her office. The three of them were lined up in the narrow aisle of the instrument lab, with Michael in the middle.

"Once you've done the kinetics," Gilderslee said, directing himself to Michael, "I can give you some samples from this basin to work with."

Michael turned to Tina, looking confused. She laid a hand on his arm and moved a half-step closer, looking at Gilderslee. "As I mentioned earlier," she said, "we're really not prepared to commit to a project like this."

She squeezed past the two men and stepped out into the hall, holding the door open for them to follow.

"Yes, of course," Gilderslee said smoothly. "You have a lot of work to do yet. But do keep me posted." He extracted two business cards from his jacket pocket, and then he shook hands with Michael and nodded to Tina, taking his leave there in the hall.

"Damn," Tina said, walking down the hall to the main lab with Michael. "What a creep." She was suddenly angry and embarrassed, disgusted with herself for having been intimidated.

"He was kind of a nerd," Michael said. "But what do you expect? He's a businessman, right? Guy probably rakes in eighty thousand a year."

"I guess." Michael, she supposed, felt perfectly at home with blue suits, the scraggly growth on his chin notwithstanding. Well, she had no intention of working with the man, would probably never see him again . . . and yet, when she drove up to the farm later that afternoon, she was still trying to shake off the ugly, diminished feeling he'd left her with, which, she decided, had as much to do with his attitude toward her work—that it was some sort of commodity created just for him and Petron—as it did with his sexist bullying.

Chip was down in the salad-bowl field, still working in the waning light. He was walking around with a big white bucket, depositing cupfuls of its contents in little piles around the field.

"What are you doing?" Tina asked, joining him.

"Feeding slugs. God-damned slugs are driving us crazy." He moved down the row with his bucket. "Crop looks like shit. Here we just convinced these restaurants that it's worth paying a little more for our fancy varieties of organic lettuce—and this customer finds a slug in her salad. They ought to wash it better, but still . . . It's these damn little ones that are so hard to get rid of."

"What is that stuff?"

"Bran. I don't know. I can't tell if we're just feeding the suckers or if this really works. The idea is they're supposed to eat themselves to death—blow up or shit their innards out or something. Far as I can tell, it just attracts them. We put some out last night, and when I came down to check there must have been a billion slugs and snails just gorging themselves—"

"It attracts them? How's that? How do slugs sense things, anyway? Don't they have like anten—"

"Tina. I don't know. I don't care. I'm sick of thinking about slugs. Let's go have dinner." They'd come to the end of the row, and he started back along the side of the field, then paused and glanced down at the bucket in his hand. "Jorge thinks we oughta come out in the middle of the night, scoop 'em all up, and dump 'em in salt. Talk about labor intensive . . . " He looked at his field, but it was too dark to see the bran he'd set out. "Maybe we can get some kind of low containers. Mix the bran with salt and see if they'll just crawl in and die . . . 'till it rains, and we end up with a field full of salt. Shit." He continued along the edge of the field toward the creek, dropping his arm around Tina as she came alongside him. "Do me a favor, will you, and tell me something to stop me from thinking about slugs. How was your day? Better than mine, I hope."

"Actually, it was kind of strange. This weird guy visited my lab, this geologist. He was interested in this project we just got funded. . . . "

Tina found herself talking about the hydrocarbon project to Chip for the first time. She launched into a long explanation of chiral molecules and the four interconvertible versions of the hydrocarbon, pausing on the hill to demonstrate . . . until she realized that it was too dark for Chip to see the hands she was holding up as models. He hadn't said a word since she started her monologue. He had stopped halfway up the hill when she had, and was waiting patiently for her to finish. Poor man, Tina thought, he was probably still fretting about his slugs. Why on earth was she trying to explain chiral molecules to him? In the dark. Without benefit of real models, or even pencil and paper. She took his hand and continued up to the house in silence, and not until they had cooked the rice and warmed up the leftover curry and sat down to eat was it apparent that she had indeed succeeded in distracting him from his slugs.

"I take it," he said, "that there's some connection between the weird guy who visited your lab and the molecules with the removable thumbs?"

Tina nodded. She swallowed a bite of the curry and grabbed for her glass of water. "He works for the Petron Corporation," she said. "It was this project he was interested in." She pushed some of the curry off her rice and glanced at Chip. Suddenly she knew why she had been explaining chiral molecules to him: if she was going to tell him about the hydro-carbon project, then she wanted him to be able to appreciate the beauty of the science. She wanted him to see it as she had originally conceived it— as an innocent and alluring mental puzzle.

She told him that she had been studying a very slow set of thumb-swapping reactions in a certain chiral organic molecule found in rocks. She told him about the work with Garrett, how they had used the reaction to tell the age of organic material found in rocks that were older than the first known life, and yet appeared to contain fossils. She told him that the progress of the reactions—the swapping of thumbs in the molecule with four versions—also bore witness to the heat and pressure that the molecule, and the rock that contained it, had endured; and this, she told him, was information that geologists used to determine if conditions had been right for the formation of petroleum.

As soon as she said the word "petroleum," Tina knew it would eclipse everything she'd just told him.

He set down his fork and looked at her with a perplexed expression on his face. Beads of sweat stood out on his forehead from the spicy curry. "Christ, Tina. You never mentioned you were doing anything like this. 'Petroleum exploration'?"

Tina sighed. He was never going to see the hydrocarbon project outside of its technological context. She wasn't even sure he appreciated the difference between science and technology, between the compulsion to *know* the universe and technology's compulsion to *use* it. What would he make, she suddenly wondered, of Garrett's lifelong attempt to understand how life had come to exist, an unarguably benign quest? "It's something that I wrote into my grant last year," she said. "When my NSF proposal was turned down."

She explained about the original paleoclimate proposal, about using this clever hydrocarbon idea in the conclusion as an advertisement for her new brand of geochemistry. "I was pretty upset," Tina said, "when they shot down my paleoclimate proposal and had the gall to suggest that this hydrocarbon project was more promising. It wasn't something I wanted to pursue. But I had to get funding from somewhere, and ACS has this Petroleum Geochemistry Research Award for basic res—"

"What's ACS?"

"American Chemical Society. What I did was develop this hydrocarbon project for their research award, and let my paleoclimate work tag along for the ride. And as it turns out, I've used the hydrocarbon kinetics in the work I've been doing with Garrett—"

"It's like what the politicians in Congress are always doing," Chip said.

"Tacking together completely unrelated bills, good with bad, popular with unpopular, so that they can get what they want."

"Well, yeah, I guess so. The proposal did get funded. I got the new HPLC and enough money to keep my job and the lab going for a year. And I've turned the hydrocarbon project over to Michael, who should get a good first paper out of it. . . . "

Tina fell silent and scooped rice into her mouth, avoiding his gaze. He was still not eating, still looking at her with that perplexed expression—eyes narrowed, brow furrowed, concentrating on her face as if it were a diseased leaf on his favorite tree, something that eluded diagnosis.

"Sometimes," he said, speaking slowly, "I wonder if I even know who the hell you are. You're off all day—shit, all day and half the night sometimes, and you come home and you might as well have been off on Mars, for all I know about what you're doing. . . . " He shook his head and lowered his gaze, picked up his fork, set it down again.

Tina didn't say anything. What could she say? It was true . . . but she resented him for saying it, felt a sudden panic that he should want more of her, that her vacation love might intrude itself into her real life where it didn't belong, didn't fit.

"So this guy who came to your lab. He was from the oil company that's been funding you. Petron, you said?"

"I'm not funded by an oil company, Chip. I'm funded by ACS—"

"The 'Petroleum Research Award'? Who the fuck do you think puts up the money?" He shoved the half-empty plate away from him.

"I don't know. ACS is a non-profit organization. So the oil industry endows a fund? It doesn't mean they have any direct input into how it's used—"

"Come on, Tina, get real. Obviously, if they're forking out money for your research, they want to see some results they can use. Why else would they do it?"

"First of all, I don't even know that they are forking out money, and—"

"And what you don't know can't hurt, is that the deal?"

She stared at him. He didn't even know what he was talking about. "And second of all," she continued, "those big companies contribute money to all sorts of causes, for the tax deduction and the good public relations, whatever. The ACS grant is for basic research—"

"Basic research? Is that what petroleum exploration is?"

"Oh god, will you give me a break? We're talking about hydrocarbon kinetics, not the atom bomb."

"And this guy who came to your lab. He was just trying to encourage 'good public relations,' right?"

"He wasn't from ACS. He was just some jerk of a sexist asshole, if you want to know the truth. Trying to score on my work, okay? And if it makes you feel any better, I have no intention of collaborating with him. Neither he nor his company have anything to do with my work or my funding—"

"There's no denying that I'm just a dumb farmer," Chip interrupted her. "I do have a hard time appreciating the finer things in life, like the singular beauty of a molecule swapping thumbs with its three twins. Hell, I'm not even sure I have a proper idea of what a molecule is. But you know what I think? I think there are a few things, yes it's amazing folks, but there are actually a few things that Dr. Cristina Teresa Arenas does not want to know. Mundane stuff, you know, like where her funding comes from? That's what I prefer to think, anyway. Because I must admit I'm just a tiny bit shocked to learn after seven, no eight, months of intimate involvement that she works for the petroleum industry, when all along—"

"God damn it, I do not work for the petroleum industry!" She was yelling now. "Shit." She tossed her napkin onto the table and stood up, took a few steps toward the door, then turned back to face him. "You want everything in black and white, don't you, in your simple little good-guy bad-guy scheme—"

"You're damned right I do. And I don't think it's too much to ask, to want to know that the woman I sleep with is in the good-guy category."

"Well then maybe you should go find yourself a politician or something to screw, just so you can be sure. There must be a few pretty ones in your good-guy category, don't you think? A few sweet, cliché-minded blondes perhaps?"

"Go to hell."

She slammed the door with such force the glass in its window shook. It was cold, and so foggy that even when her eyes adjusted to the dark she couldn't make out the Mazda a few yards away. Her throat hurt from yelling or from not yelling enough, it wasn't clear which, and she felt like opening the door and slamming it again, slamming it harder so that the glass would shatter. She stepped carefully off the porch into the dark.

"Tina."

She ignored him, making her way across the gravel.

"TINA!" His bellow hung in the night, then disappeared.

She felt for the handle on the car door, located it, and got into the car—but when she reached to pull the door closed, she found that he'd followed her and had his hand on the door, holding it open. "What are you doing?" she said. "Leave me alone."

"That's what I plan to do, believe me. But you can't drive down to Brayton now. It's too late. Too foggy."

"I'll drive home when I want to drive home, thank you."

"Unh-uh." To her amazement, he reached in with one arm and lifted her out of the car.

"Goddamn you! What does it matter to you—"

"I don't fucking know the answer to that, so don't ask."

She couldn't move in the grip he had her in, couldn't jam an elbow into his gut or even pound ineffectually on his chest, couldn't budge.

He carried her into the house and deposited her on the couch, threw a blanket at her, and went into his room. She sat there for a half-hour, then slipped outside and got into her car. The keys were still in the ignition. She revved it up and made as much noise as she could backing down the hill.

When she got home the phone was ringing. She considered taking it off the hook, but she didn't want him to have the satisfaction of knowing she was home. She tucked it under the cushions on the couch and went to bed.

Chapter 19

She would not think about him. She stayed at the lab long hours, ridiculous hours, unnecessary hours. She spent the week buried in the monotony of sediment extractions, hovering about the new HPLC like a mother with a newborn, though it was indifferent to her attention. It did what it was supposed to do, without her constant coaxing and tinkering, without being cursed or praised or talked at. She taught Michael to use it in an afternoon. She explained how she had developed the stereoisomer separation, talked about various other techniques she could have tried. Most of his heating experiments needed to go for another few weeks, but he ran a standard and a couple of samples from the high temperature series.

She made her sediment extractions and dried, redissolved, and injected them, hour after hour, sample after sample. She kept her mind tuned to the dull, soothing rhythm of the lab work and Bach or Mozart or Haydn on the radio, and nothing else. It was the nature of vacations that they had to end, and hers had ended and she was back in her life and working. Working well and not unhappy, delighting in the precise beauty of the chromatograms that tumbled off the chart recorder, the sharp peaks, the flat baselines. The rows of numbers from her first core segment accumulated on her charts: sediment depth in the first column, then saturated lipid concentration, unsaturated lipid, then the quotient of the two—the Saturation Index—and the temperature from her calibration graph. And then the two columns of numbers she'd decided to add after talking to Roy the last time.

It was clear now that the picoplankton responded differently to light and nutrient availability than did most other phytoplankton, and the last two columns on Tina's data charts were an attempt to detect this idiosyncratic response to changing environmental factors in the geological record. It was a long shot, but the data was, essentially, bonus data, requiring only a few extra calculations and a change in the computer's data collection program. In the early stages of her research, before she found the picoplankton lipids, Tina had identified many common lipids from all the major groups of phytoplankton. These common lipids eluted from the column well before the picoplankton lipids, in a separate clump of peaks: the bonus data was simply the ratio between her picoplankton lipids—saturated and unsaturated together—and this clump of common lipids, the idea being that this gave a measure of picoplankton abundance relative to the overall phytoplankton population. If the picoplankton had responded differently to environmental changes, then the ratios should vary over time in Tina's sediment cores, registering changes in nutrients or solar radiation, in deep ocean circulation or volcanic activity, or the impact of a giant asteroid at the KT boundary. . . . And then again, the ratios might not vary in any significant or intelligible way at all.

Normally, Tina would have been eyeing her numbers, anticipating trends that were not yet apparent, looking for ways to speed things up. Normally, she would not have been so patient with the tedium of lab work, her charts so neat, her lab bench so organized. But that week when her vacation life came to an end, and the week after, and on into the first week of February, she was content to watch dumbly as the data for the first core segment accrued, extraction by extraction, number by number . . . centimeter by centimeter, through ten meters and forty million years of plodding geologic time.

He must have slipped past while she was in the instrument lab. Tina walked into her office and found him sitting in the chair behind her desk. He had it angled so that he could see out the window, pushed back from the desk, and he was sitting very still, with his elbows on the arms of the chair, hands folded quietly in front of him, suspended above his lap. It was late afternoon. His hair was damp and he wasn't wearing his cap—he must have showered, changed his clothes. When he started talking, which he did as soon as he turned his head and saw her standing in the doorway, Tina felt as if she had interrupted all the peace and quiet in the world: a bunch of herons suddenly screamed and flapped outside the window and the man's hands that had been hanging so perfectly balanced and still in the air above his lap flew apart to grip the arms of the chair so hard that Tina could see the muscles in his fingers from where she stood, and it made her want to cry, but she didn't.

"I don't know what the fuck I'm doing here, any more than I know why the fuck I got involved with you to begin with instead of listening to my basic dumb farmer instincts, which are usually pretty good about most things."

She pulled the door shut. Then she reached back and locked it.

"That's what I thought when I met you. I said to myself, Chip, old buddy, you're just a dumb farmer, now, you stay away from that *chemist*." He pushed out of the chair and paced about in the little space between her desk and the wall. "I said, you don't have any business looking at this woman. You and she are living in different worlds, and you better keep it that way. No way in hell you want to have anything to do with this woman who sleeps in a chair in her office, no way." He picked up a reprint that was sitting out on the desk, one of Tina's early papers on the picoplankton, and held it aloft. "'HPLC-Mass Spectrometer Separation and Identification of a Novel Class of Lipids in Marine Cyanobacterial Picoplankton and their Potential as a Paleoclimate Proxy.'" He let the reprint drop back on the desk. "How can you talk to a person who writes stuff like that? Shit, we don't even speak the same language. I thought, Jesus Christ what am I getting into, this woman might as well be from Mars. But then I went and got into it anyway, just like I didn't see any of it, I had to go and get involved with a woman who doesn't even know the meaning of the word 'involved.'"

Tina bit her lip and shook her head, though it was true, she knew it was true, and for the first time she wished it weren't. Her arms hung stiff by her sides, lost in the sleeves of her lab coat.

"Some kind of blind dumb-ass love, that's what we have here." He shook his head, staring at her, squinting as if she were hard to see, the creases running hard and deep across his forehead, in the corners by his eyes.

Tina hadn't moved since closing the door. She wanted him to touch her so badly she thought her bones would fly apart, explode with the wanting.

Touch me. Just touch me, god damn you, but she didn't say a word. Two renegade tears escaped, one from each eye.

"Ah! The Martian cries. Amazing." A grin began to form in his mustache. "Maybe she can be educated in the ways of humans after all. There's no denying she's a smart Martian."

She wanted to punch him in the mouth.

He turned away, turned toward the wall as if he'd had a sudden urge to examine the picoplankton portraits taped up there. He reached up and touched one of the micrographs carefully with his fingertips. "I don't really think she's a bad guy," he said after a moment, speaking softly now, to the wall, to the picoplankton, to himself. "So I guess it's okay to sleep with her, right?" He turned around to face her, the grin gone. "*Un tonto* and a clever Martian. Both blind as bats."

Tina shook her head.

"Come home with me."

She shook her head again. Then she nodded. "*Vos no sos tonto,*" she whispered, surprised to hear her own voice.

"'*Vos*'? You even speak Martian Spanish."

"Uruguayan."

He laughed. "I know, Tina. And Argentinean, and I think maybe Nicaraguan . . . " He stepped around the desk, and Tina finally moved toward him, but he stopped her, gingerly unbuttoning her lab coat and pushing it off her shoulders until her arms were tangled in the sleeves, and then she had to struggle out of them before he would kiss her, so that the kiss and the embrace were marred, not quite what her bones were aching for, whatever that was.

There was no treaty signed, no agreement reached, no sudden peace between sparring world views—nothing but an awkward truce, a bivouac in emotional territory that was beyond the reach of their war. Tina didn't think of their relationship as something that grew, not like a body of data that accumulated and took on meaning so that eventually you became impatient and wanted to make sense of it. Not like that at all. More like an environmental change, a shift in the light, in the length and pattern of her days. And yet, if she still saw her love affair with Chip as a thing apart, incidental and peripheral to her life—an overly long, not-quite-idyllic vacation that she did not want to end—she was not entirely unaware of its effect. She knew she was a little more conscious of her place in the world as "not a bad guy." There was no avoiding the news he brought to her table along with his vegetables and fruit. She couldn't help but feel the special stress of February with its preparations for spring planting and fickle weather, nor could she deny a certain new impatience with her own long hours in the lab.

She was a month into the core analyses now and tired of the repetitive lab work, eager for results. Orloff had suggested that they begin with two segments, one from the northernmost site and one from the southernmost so that they would detect latitudinal temperature differences, but after a month of hard work, with entire nights spent at the lab running samples, Tina wasn't even through the first segment. And now Michael needed the HPLC in the afternoons for his kinetics study, and Tina didn't want to spend her nights in the lab.

She found an automatic HPLC injector that could purportedly inject six samples, one after the other, without the help of a human being. It was new on the market, definitely not cheap, and Tina used funds she'd allocated for column replacements to purchase it. She spent three days watching it do its thing and monitoring her chromatograms before she would trust it, and the first time she left it running unattended she woke in a panic at two in the morning and drove back to the lab. But the instrument ran smoothly with its new contraption, and now she could spend the night at home in her bed, or, occasionally, up at the farm in Chip's bed, and still have six new rows of numbers when she arrived in the morning.

Chapter 20

The ice was a surprise—not at all what Tina and Sylvia Orloff were expecting to see when they compared the first of their sea-surface temperature graphs. Not in the Cretaceous and early Cenozoic sediments they'd been working on. The formation of permanent ice sheets at the poles was believed to have started late in the Cenozoic, initializing the modern ocean-atmosphere system in the mid-Miocene, some fifteen million years ago. But there it was, one of the few things that was clear—beautifully, undeniably, crystal clear—in the incomplete data that lay on the table before them: ice in the late Eocene, over forty million years ago, long before any evidence of an ice age. The other thing that was clear, though not such a surprise, was that the Cretaceous was every bit as warm, latitudinally homogeneous, and ice-free as earlier studies had indicated.

They were in Orloff's office, what Katharine always referred to as the "inner sanctum" because it could be entered through a second office, the one she shared with the lab's computer and plotter. Tina was bouncing on her toes, her fingers against the edge of the table where they had the graphs laid out. Orloff was standing like a monolith in front of it, a yellow wooden pencil turning slowly between her fingers.

"This is incredible," Tina said, looking from her painstakingly hand-plotted graph of Saturation Index temperatures, to the computer-generated O-18 curve from Orloff's lab, both plotted against depth in core, with estimates of sediment age from the shipboard work noted alongside. The curves began during the latter years of the dinosaurs' reign in the mid-Cretaceous, a hundred and ten million years ago, and spanned seventy million years to the end of the Eocene. There was a level of detail in Tina's temperature curves that didn't show in the O-18, but the general trends in the two data sets corresponded well until the advent of the ice. Throughout the Cretaceous, from the bottom of the cores up to the KT boundary holocaust sixty-five million years ago, Tina's Saturation Index had created a level but gently undulating curve—consistently warm, but with small, repetitive variations of a degree or two, variations that were too small to show up in the O-18 data. There was a dip in temperature, a tiny notch where the Cretaceous ended at the KT boundary, a slight cooling at the beginning of the Paleocene, interrupted by a dramatic spike in temperature, a heat wave, at the beginning of the Eocene. The spike was followed by continued cooling, steeper and more pronounced than before, and then, near the end of the Eocene, Tina's temperature curves and the O-18 curves began to diverge, gradually, but steadily, dramatically. Ice had begun to accumulate—ice made of snow formed from water that had evaporated from the ocean—leaving the ocean, and the forams growing there, enriched in O-18, because water made of O-16 evaporated more readily. The onset of ice was even more apparent, more irrefutable, than Tina had imagined it would be, which was a good thing, because it was also more than twenty million years earlier than she or anyone else had expected.

Orloff balanced the eraser end of her pencil on the O-18 graph, at the point where the data sets diverged. "We'll have better dates from the biostratigraphers within the week," she said. "But this is definitely late Eocene, in both cores."

"This is going to blow away every hypothesis of Cenozoic climate there is," Tina said. "They're all linked to the changing geography and ocean circulation of the Miocene. Even Brian Maitland's latest, that burial of organic carbon in continental shelf sediments lowered atmospheric CO_2 and initiated accumulation of ice on Antarctica. Such an elegantly constructed hypothesis, and here we are blowing it all to shreds. Though I don't doubt that Maitland will pick up the pieces and build a new one that accounts for our news."

"Maitland's off on something else now," Orloff said. "But you're absolutely right that ice in the Eocene puts a kink in all of these theories."

"We'll have to re-examine the whole body of Cenozoic data," Tina said. "Not that it's a particularly big body. Maybe we should do some upcore samples, through the Miocene . . . "

But Orloff was already tapping her eraser on the Cretaceous portion of their graphs, shifting her attention to the other irrefutable result in their data, the warm and homogeneous nature of the Cretaceous climate. "Katharine is still working on the strontium for this second core," she said. "But it's clear that hydrothermal activity was exceptionally high throughout the mid and late Cretaceous, much higher than at present. A greenhouse effect from the CO_2 emitted could well account for these temperatures."

"Can you quantify that? The CO_2 emitted? And what that means in terms of actual atmospheric CO_2?"

"We can get a rough estimate by plugging the strontium data into a box model that accounts for fluxes in CO_2 from the various sources and sinks."

"What about organic carbon? Weathering and burial of organic material in sediments, changes in primary productivity?"

"No. The assumption," Orloff said impatiently, "is that on a greater-than-million-year timescale fluxes in organic carbon are insignificant compared to hydrothermal activity, seafloor spreading, and weathering—the tectonic effects."

"On what timescale? We have temperature data that's showing change down to a five thousand year interval in some of these sections." Tina glanced over at a graph she'd set on the edge of the table when she came in, the data from the last column on her charts, the lipid ratios that had been something of an afterthought. She didn't know what to make of it yet and was a little nervous about showing it to Orloff. "Have you heard from Zhang at Woods Hole? He's doing the carbon isotopes, carbon-13 in benthic forams, right? Using it to estimate the amount of carbon stored as organic material . . . ?"

"Last I heard," Orloff said, turning to look at Tina. "Zhang was having reservations about how to interpret that data."

"I guess what I'm wondering," Tina said, reaching for her graph of the lipid ratios, "is if we're going to be able to make any sense of this." She lined the graph up with her temperature curve.

"What am I looking at?"

"This is the ratio of picoplankton lipids to total other phytoplankton lipids." Orloff's phone started to ring, and Tina paused, waiting for her to answer it. But Orloff ignored the phone. "It's a measure of picoplankton productivity," Tina continued, "relative to the rest of the phytoplankton." She slowly traced the wavy line that made up the first part of the curve. "Look at how it's almost the exact inverse of my temperature curve, even these undulations. And the correlation continues with just a few deviations, throughout these segments, all the way up through the Eocene."

"So, it looks like your picoplankton thrive in cool water," Orloff said. "I don't know why this would be," she added dismissively, "but then I'm no biologist."

"I know that's how it looks, like they're just responding to the temperature changes," Tina said. "But the thing is, they don't. They don't thrive in cold water any better than they do in warm. Neither the results from the *Rover* nor the studies Roy's done with cultures show anything of the sort."

"Sylvia?" Katharine was leaning into the office through the open door.

"Come in, Katharine," Orloff said without looking up. "You should see this."

"The phone's for you," Katharine said, coming into the office, and Orloff went over to her desk to answer the phone. "I'm almost done with the strontium for one of these cores," Katharine said as she looked at the graphs.

"Be interesting to see it," Tina said, but she was still looking at her picoplankton productivity curve. There was a very slight offset to the correlation with temperature, the picoplankton rise coming just before the temperature drops. If the picoplankton were reacting to temperature, then any offset should be in the other direction.

"Let's put a paper together on this," Orloff said as she hung up the phone. "By the end of March, I'd say. Katharine should be able to finish the strontium by then, if she doesn't go on any more vacations. Let's have it through the Eocene, Katharine, on all the cores."

"You want to look at what we have so far?" Katharine asked. "It'll only take me a minute—"

"Not now." Orloff glanced at her watch. "I have to be at a meeting in ten minutes. But you can print out a copy of the O-18 data for Tina."

Tina would have liked to continue discussing the picoplankton curve, which had her thoroughly befuddled, but Orloff obviously didn't think it important. Tina picked up her graphs and reluctantly followed Katharine into the adjoining office. She supposed it was inefficient to speculate until they had the rest of the data.

"Jesus," Katharine said under her breath. "She even treats *you* like one of her grad students."

Tina glanced back at the open door to Orloff's office.

"Don't worry," Katharine said, reaching past her to pull it closed. "She's oblivious." She went over to the computer, on a table in the middle of the room, and started typing in directions while she talked. "So, I haven't seen you in ages. What have you been up to? How's your love life—hey, whatever happened with your gardener?"

"Farmer," Tina said. "He's a farmer. I still see him. . . . But I've been in the lab a lot lately," she added, suddenly conscious of how little time she actually spent at Chip's farm.

"Oh lord, me too. I went home for a couple weeks at Christmas, and damned if she hasn't been making me pay for it ever since. Acts like the whole world is waiting on the edge of its seat for this strontium data. And I've had to take on the O-18 analyses too, since she lost her third-year slave. Did you hear that Janice quit?"

"She *quit*? You mean she dropped out?" Tina lowered her voice. "Sylvia must be livid. Losing a student after three years."

"You don't have to whisper," Katharine said. "She's already gone. Went out the other door. For reasons I've never been able to figure out, she always enters through my office and goes out the hall door. It's part of some Inner Sanctum ritual. Anyway, it's her own fault that Janice quit. Janice told her she was pregnant—"

"Oh my god, you're kidding. Not from—"

"No, no. That ended as soon as they got off the ship. Janice is married, you know. She says this was planned. They had been trying for a while, but apparently the time apart while she was on the cruise did the trick. Maybe her husband's sperm count was up," Katharine said, giggling. "I don't think *he'd* been fooling around. Personally, I would have waited a little longer to tell Sylvia. But Janice didn't see the point in that. . . . All she wanted was to take a year's leave of absence when the baby was born, then come back and finish her thesis. But Sylvia wouldn't hear of it, told Janice that if she left, she would not be welcome back. Janice says that she walked right out of Sylvia's office, went down the hall, and packed up her stuff. I thought it was kind of gutsy, though I guess it's kind of strange to think of quitting grad school as a gutsy thing to do."

"It's too bad," Tina said. "Though, really, you'd think she would wait until she finished her doctorate to have a baby."

"Men don't wait, unless they're strapped for money."

"But they don't usually ask for a leave of absence, do they?"

"That wasn't really the issue. Not for Sylvia. It was the *idea* of it that bugged her. Of split loyalties."

"Oh Katharine . . . " Tina shook her head. "Maybe you should have been a shrink." She gestured impatiently at the printer. "Are you going to turn that on?" She wanted to go back to her office and look at the data again.

Katharine switched on the printer and adjusted the paper. She let out a short, bitter grunt. "Here she's got me rushing to get all these Cretaceous sections finished and write it up, and then she'll probably sit on it for six months. Do you realize that she hasn't even submitted the first paper we did together? After pushing me to finish it all in a hurry last year. It's just a minor paper," she said as the printer started running. "If you happen to be Sylvia Orloff."

Tina watched the columns of numbers as they appeared. "I don't know that this one is going to be minor," she said.

"I would like to see this work published. . . . I developed this technique, you know. Of course it was Orloff's idea, using the strontium isotopes to gauge hydrothermal activity. Pretty clever, I must admit." She tore off Tina's printout and handed it to her. "I can give you what I've got of the strontium, if you want, but—"

"I'll wait," Tina said, moving toward the door.

Maybe Orloff was right, she thought, when she got back to her office and spread the graphs out on her desk. Maybe these changes in pico-plankton productivity were just a physiological response to temperature. Maybe Roy's culture studies were wrong, or maybe the picoplankton had changed, evolved. But it just didn't make sense. The picoplankton had all those different lipid jackets to insulate them from temperature change— why would they be more sensitive than other phytoplankton?

She picked up a pencil and started a scale for the oxygen isotope data along the right side of her temperature graph. But she wasn't paying much attention to what she was doing, and she kept making mistakes. She put the pencil down. She got up, cranked open all the windows, and returned to her desk.

Of course, the temperature didn't have to affect the picoplankton directly. Tina picked up a pad of paper with a list she'd made of factors that might link temperature and picoplankton productivity. Ecology was one. Maybe some predator that was wild about the picoplankton thrived in warm waters—no way of assessing that. Nutrients were another possibility. Warmer sea surface temperatures would make deep sea circulation sluggish, which would slow the upwelling that resupplied nutrients to surface waters. That would mean a decrease in overall primary productivity, which might appear as an increase in the relative productivity of the picoplankton . . . and a positive correlation between temperature and picoplankton productivity—the opposite of what was on her graph. Tina let the pad drop back to her desk.

Maybe the picoplankton hadn't been responding to temperature, but rather acting in parallel with it, both responding to some other environmental change—such as CO_2. She leaned her elbows on the desk and rested her chin between her hands. Roy was doing culture experiments to check the picoplankton's response to CO_2 concentration, but she hadn't heard from him yet. The thing was, if the picoplankton were sensitive to CO_2—and Roy had been skeptical—then certainly it would be in a positive way, with higher CO_2 causing an *increase* in picoplankton productivity. And any correlation between temperature and CO_2 would certainly be positive, which meant the associated temperature-picoplankton correlation would be—wrong again.

Tina closed her eyes and laid her face in her hands, and there they were, the two curves, picoplankton and temperature, imprinted on the backs of her eyelids. Maybe the correlation wasn't even parallel, but the other way around, with the picoplankton regulating the rises and dips in CO_2, and thus the temperature? She pressed her palms into her eyelids until blue-and-purple starbursts appeared against the black. She was thinking like a deluded parent, imagining her diminutive plankton in such exalted roles . . . as if they really could have caused those undulations in the Cretaceous temperature, made the dinosaurs sweat and shiver in their scales— Did dinosaurs sweat and shiver? Or was that a mammalian trait?

Tina jerked her head up. The air coming through the open windows was making her shiver, but it certainly wasn't keeping her awake. She closed all the windows and pulled on the heavy wool sweater she'd worn that morning. Then she headed for the easy chair, something she'd been doing a lot lately.

Why should she be cold when she has a whole room full of jackets to choose from? Let the dinosaurs shiver if they want, Cristina Arenas has this nice highly saturated lipid jacket with the ten double bonds. She'd better hurry because she's running late, and she has an appointment with the Queen in the inner sanctum. She rushes out without thinking about what she's wearing, but when she steps into the room and looks around she realizes that her oversaturated jacket is entirely inappropriate to the occasion. The Queen herself is wearing a linen suit jacket with hardly a double bond in its weave, and it's extremely hot in the room, which is packed full of strangers. They all seem to be looking for something, ignoring Tina and each other. Tina would like to speak to the Queen, who invited her here, and she thinks maybe if she goes out the side door and changes her jacket and comes back she'll be given an audience—but the door is locked. So she tries the door she came in, but that too is locked, as are the windows, all closed and locked, and the air is so heavy and warm that she is sweating profusely in her jacket, which is a little too small for her. Nothing is ever too small for Tina, but this jacket is definitely too tight and she's dying to take it off, but she can't because she's naked underneath and probably smelly now from sweating so much. The air is stifling, positively oppressive, and it seems to be getting worse by the minute. There are no windows, just the air pumped in through the floor, and the people in the crowd seem oblivious, but Tina is having a hard time breathing. There's too much CO_2 in the mix of gases the Queen ordered, and Tina's jacket is soaking it up, the good and the bad, C-12 and C-13, getting heavier and heavier and heavier until finally there is nothing to do but tear the jacket off and stand there naked and dripping with sweat and relief in the midst of the crowd. A hush descends on the room, which is suddenly empty but for Tina and the Queen, who is staring down at her in disgust and amazement.

She woke up sweating. The heater had come on and her head was next to the baffles along the wall. She was wearing her wool sweater and a long-sleeved cotton T-shirt and a turtleneck under that. It was very quiet. She got up and went to the window and cranked open the wrong pane, the one that only opened an inch. She pushed her face up next to it anyway and stood there with cold fresh air cooling her left cheek.

She was close. She could feel it in the air on her cheek, within reach, at her fingertips, at the tip of her nose pressed against the window glass, so close she could taste it. If she stood very still. If she thought without thinking. If she stayed as unmoving and unseeing as the solitary night heron sitting beak to nose on the other side of the glass . . .

If the concentration of CO_2 had been exceptionally high, the air thick, oppressive, with CO_2 . . . Oppressive? To whom? Plants would love it. It was their ice cream. Their chocolate, their drug of choice, their *mate* . . . They'd wolf it down, suck it up—become satiated? But the more there was, the easier it was to get. And if it was easy to get, then wouldn't they be more discriminating, imbibing only the best brand of chocolate, favorite flavor of ice cream—favorite isotope of carbon . . . ?

She had it. Her mind reached out like a tentacle, curling around the idea, scooping it up and clutching it to her chest—she laughed out loud, a whoop of joy, and the heron startled and resettled on a branch a few feet back from the window. It wasn't what she thought she'd been looking for. It wasn't an explanation of the curves on her graphs, or of Orloff's hydrothermal activity. It was, rather, the thread that tied them all together, an end to the second-guessing, the crucial missing variable itself: it was a way to analyze for paleo-CO_2.

Who knew if it would work, Tina thought. On closer examination the idea might prove itself so flawed that she would be embarrassed to have thought it. Indeed, with a freezer overflowing with samples to be analyzed and several papers in the works, including the one with Garrett, she might be better off if that were the case, if she found out right away that it wasn't going to fly. She peered at the little clock on her desk. It was only four o'clock. She could go to the library right now. But she didn't want to. Why not indulge the idea for a day or two, savor the sweet promise of it, before she had to go shoot it down? Why not take the joy of it and run, carry it home—share it with Chip? Or better yet, go up to the farm.

She could ride home and get her car, drive up there. She picked up the phone. Chip was coming down to Brayton tonight, but if he hadn't left yet maybe she could get him to change plans. She let it ring ten times and was about to hang up when he answered, out of breath. He'd just come up the hill from digging and loading the trees for his job the next day, but he said the trees didn't care if they sat in the truck at the farm or at her place. He was pleased that she wanted to come up to the farm, and he laughed at her mood, said she sounded like she was high on something and cautioned her to be careful on her bike.

Tina was in no mood for careful. She had been feeling a little tired and out of sorts for the last few days, but now she was shot through with adrenaline. She pedaled as hard as she could in the highest gear with the wind at her back, winding down from the bluffs and into the rush hour traffic without so much as touching the brakes, going faster than she had any right to be going and just barely in control of the bike, the wind-chill freezing her fingers on the handlebars and slicing through layers of wool and cotton, the cold alive and sexy against her skin as she raced off to see her lover with her bundle of joy . . . and when she finally got up to the farm and saw him sitting on the porch rail drinking a beer, she climbed up on the rail next to him, and when he asked what she was so psyched up about she told him, or started to tell him. In intricate detail.

"Remember I told you about the picoplankton? How they leave a molecular record of sea surface temperature in the sediment? Well, I might be able to use that same record, the ratio of carbon isotopes in those same molecules, to tell how much CO_2 was in the atmosphere. In the surface water, actually, but we should be able to calculate atmospheric CO_2 from that."

"What's an isotope?"

"Oh. Isotopes. Well, isotopes are different kinds of the same atoms that have the same chemical properties, but different masses. In nature, one kind is usually dominant and the others occur in very small proportions, if at all. The common kind of carbon is C-12. But there's a heavy isotope, C-13, which also occurs naturally and makes up about one percent of all the carbon on earth. So this idea I had is based on the fact that plants prefer C-12 and they discriminate against C-13 in photosynthesis—and how *much* they discriminate depends on how much CO_2 is available!" Tina paused as if she expected Chip to applaud. "It's sort of like how in a rich country," she went on when he didn't respond, "in a land of plenty, people can be pickier about the food they eat, whereas in a poor country they'll eat anything and everything, just to survive. Sort of. Anyway, the idea is that you should be able to tell how CO_2 rich or poor the surface water was by looking at how much of the C-13 isotope the algae were taking up. Algae that lived in water with a lot of CO_2 could afford to be pickier and would have less C13 in their tissues than algae that lived in water with low CO_2. In theory, it could be very complicated because different kinds of algae might have different preferences for the isotopes. And biochemical processes after the initial uptake of the CO_2 could cause problems. But I'm going to get around all that by only looking at one class of compounds in one group of algae: the lipids in the picoplankton. . . . The only problem," she said slowly, thinking the idea through now, Chip giving her an excuse to think it out loud, though he hadn't said a word since asking about isotopes. "The amount of C-13 in the lipids depends not only on the CO_2 concentration, but also on the background level of C-13 in the oceanic CO_2. So we need to know what that was. If it had been constant over time, it would be easy." She looked around the porch, wanting a chalkboard or a pencil and paper. There was a roll of green plastic ribbon lying next to Chip's clippers on the banister; she picked it up and cut off a generous length.

"Hey! Tie tape's not cheap, you know."

"Oh. Sorry." Tina looked from the ribbon in her hand to Chip's face, but when she saw that he was more amused than annoyed, she hopped off the banister and started arranging the tie tape in a circle on the porch.

"Say this is the surface layer of the ocean," she said. She reached into the kitchen to turn the porch light on. Then she leaned over the banister and stripped some leaves off a branch of the bay tree. "The bay leaves are the C-12," she said, dropping them into the circle on the porch. She ran down the drive a little ways and scooped up a handful of dry brown oak leaves from the ground. "Okay," she said, returning to the porch and squatting down at the edge of the tie-tape circle. "The green leaves are the C-12, the brown ones are the C-13." She dropped a few of the oak leaves in with the bay leaves. "And you have a certain ratio of brown to green . . . " Tina paused, considering her ocean. "Actually, there should be a lot more green leaves than that." She stood up and pulled more leaves off the bay tree and dropped them into the ocean. "There. Now if the algae prefer green leaves over brown—"

"Who wouldn't?"

Tina looked up. She'd almost forgotten about her audience. He was leaning forward off the banister, peering down at her ocean. "Right," she said. "So if algae prefer the green leaves over the brown, then they're going to use up more of the green ones." She picked up four bay leaves and one oak leaf. "Leaving the surface water enriched in brown leaves. And the real clincher is that if there are a lot of algae, than it's going to be more enriched than if there are just a few." Tina scooped up a handful of green leaves.

"Which means that the background level of C-13 in the CO_2 in surface water depends on primary productivity, which has varied. And then, who knows what effect a change in mixing or deep sea circulation would have. God. If we had to figure all that out, it would be hopeless. . . . But we don't!" She jumped up triumphantly and tossed the leaves in her hand over the banister. "Of course we don't. We have a direct record of the background level of C-13. In the sediment carbonate. Zhang is doing something similar at Woods Hole. Except he's using fossil shells from benthic forams, bugs that lived on the seafloor, because he wants to know the C-13 enrichment in the deep ocean water, which reflects a sort of global average. What I need is for someone to pick out the *surface* forams and do the C-13 in those. Orloff's lab can do that, I think, Katharine already—"

"Tina?"

"Huh?"

"This is all very interesting, and I'm glad you're happy and everything, but aren't you getting hungry?"

"Oh, yeah, actually. I don't know why we're sitting out here. It's freezing. How can you be drinking beer?"

"I've got more insulation than you." He grinned. "Lots of lipids," he said, clearly pleased with himself. "But if you'll stop talking long enough we can go inside and I'll build you a fire."

She followed him in. She was hungry. And happy. She drank a half-bottle of wine with dinner, which they ate sitting on the floor in the living room next to the wood stove, and she didn't say another word about her idea, because she didn't want to think of all the other not-so-easy-to-solve problems. Like if she could even adapt her Mass Spec to measure the isotope ratios in the lipids. Among other things.

Chapter 21

Unlike Tina's, Chip's work flowed and ebbed with the seasons and, within the seasons, with the weather. February ended and March began with torrential El Niño rains. Chip complained about spending so much time in the barn with Jorge—fixing the tractor, tuning their trucks, building some sort of contraption for planting potatoes—that they were getting on each other's nerves, bickering like an old married couple about how early to start their tomatoes in the hothouse and how to treat the potatoes, which they would be growing for the first time. Tina supposed the rain afforded him more time to read, or think, or perhaps things in the world were getting worse, because their dinner conversations had been comprised of one political rant after another, usually followed by one of his letter campaigns or attendance at some meeting. The election of George Deukmejian as governor of California had initiated a whole ream of new complaints, and the news that the CIA had been training Salvadoran generals in the art of torture had him so riled up he had been threatening to go down there and enlist with the guerrillas. Tina didn't know how he could stand the frustration of caring so deeply about things he had no control over. Even locally, where he had some stature and influence, his victories were few and tenuous. He and his group of farmers had obtained a court injunction to stop gravel mining on the Brayton River, which was causing erosion and a drop in the water table—only to watch the mining company ignore the injunction and the county supervisors ignore the violation. Still, he kept on.

Tina didn't know what had him so riled up today that he had to meet her at the door with it. It had been raining in the morning and she had driven instead of riding her bike, and now she regretted it. She was tired and preoccupied, and the bike ride would have helped. She'd forced herself to leave the lab early because Chip was coming over, and she wouldn't have minded being greeted at the door with his usual warm hug or a kiss, or not being greeted at all, for that matter, but she was not ready to deal with the newspaper he was holding up in front of her like a protest sign in small print.

"Can I just get something to drink first?" She moved past him toward the kitchen. She'd spent the day extracting sediments, running samples, and poring over her data, with the growing sensation that there was something important, something intrinsic that neither she nor Orloff was getting. It was as though they were holding bits of string that were too short and flimsy to tie together and every time Tina tried to tuck the end of one through the loop of another, her fingers went thick and spastic and the string slipped from her grasp. She sighed and took the carton of orange juice out of the refrigerator. She was hoping the paleo-CO_2 method would clarify things, if she could make it work. She'd talked to the analytical chemist who'd built her HPLC-Mass Spec interface and he thought the instrument could be adapted—

"Don't tell me you don't know about this," Chip said, waving the paper at her.

Tina turned to look at him. She had arrived home too suddenly, with no bike ride for buffer, and she felt as if she'd just stepped from a dark movie theater into bright sunlight where everything that was presumably real seemed acutely less real than what was in the movie. "About what?" she asked, blinking.

"About this article."

Tina shook her head. She picked up her glass of orange juice and glanced around for signs of dinner in the making—and felt immediately ashamed. Where did she get off expecting Chip to make her dinner every time he came over? "Okay," she said, trying not to be the inconsiderate self-absorbed Martian she had more than once been accused of being. "Let's go sit down, and I'll read it." She drank from her glass of orange juice, went into the living room, and sat down on the couch. Chip followed her, but when she held out her hand for the paper he made no move to give it to her. He'd stopped on the other side of the room, near the opening to the dining room, and he was looking at her with a puzzled, skeptical expression, eyes narrowed. He shook his head, lowered his eyes to the newspaper in his hand, and started to read the article aloud.

"You know I hate being read to," Tina interrupted. But he ignored her and kept reading.

It was one of the Tuesday science section articles he'd taken to reading and asking her about. Anything to do with the weather or climate was of interest to him, the El Niño being his latest fascination. Tina supposed it made sense considering that his livelihood depended on weather, but he seemed to think that she, as a scientist studying paleoclimates, would know all about everything even remotely connected to weather or climate—he made no distinction—from storm patterns and El Niños, to the regional effects of the Mt. St. Helens and El Chichón eruptions, not to mention the greenhouse effect of fossil fuel CO_2. Tina found it particularly annoying when he asked her about the latter, because she still hadn't gotten around to catching up on the relevant literature and it really was something she should know about. Why Chip found this particular article—which was as vague and frustrating as most of the articles he showed her—so compelling that he had to discuss it with her the second she walked in the door, Tina didn't know. Simultaneously exhausted and wired from too much *mate* in the afternoon, her eyes seemed to be glued open, as if she were stuck in the "on" position, burning out. And to make things worse, her period must be about to start, because her back hurt and her breasts were sore. Now that she was completely, mind and body, away from the lab and her preoccupation with the core data, she was having a hard time thinking about anything but a hot shower and a glass of wine. And dinner. They could go out, for a change. Mexican food sounded good. A beer, maybe.

Chip paused and looked up to see if she was listening.

Tina sighed. "Are you going to read me the whole thing?" she said, with a weak smile.

He looked at her oddly, and read on. "'Furthermore, says Cox, the recent findings of Dr. Cristina Arenas of the Brayton Institute of Oceanography invalidate the models—'"

"What?! You're making that up."

"'—used by scientists to predict future levels of atmospheric carbon dioxide. Cox maintains that, not only has the climate's response to a rise in carbon dioxide been exaggerated tenfold, but that it will, in fact, never rise to the levels predicted—' I can't believe you didn't know about this."

"Give me that!" Tina jumped up and snatched the paper out of his hand. She scanned the article until she came to her name, there in the science section of the *New York Times*, as mentioned by a scientist she'd never heard of, attributed to "findings" that weren't even described, let alone referenced.

Tina glanced up at Chip, an incredulous smile beginning to form around her mouth. She shook her head, then looked back at the newspaper.

"What, it's not right?"

"Wait." But there was nothing else about Tina or her work. Just the one line. Tina reread the beginning of the article. The only thing she could think of was that this guy Cox had seen her and Roy's paper about the pico-plankton, which had just come out in *Science*, not that they'd said anything to warrant these remarks. The article said that he was a plant physiologist, so it made sense that he would have noticed a paper about the picoplankton. . . . And started speculating? Much as she herself had done when, with those results fresh in her mind, she'd heard Harper Gibson and Conroy Decker discussing the problem of the missing sink for anthropogenic CO_2. An intoxicated moment of speculative abandon out in the middle of the Pacific was one thing, Tina thought, but she would never have gone on the record with such nebulous ideas. How could she possibly "invalidate" climate models she knew nothing about? For a moment she wondered if Harper and Conroy had mentioned their discussion to someone . . . but that was ridiculous. They had dismissed her idea that the picoplankton results might make a difference in the CO_2 budget. Tina tossed the newspaper onto the floor in disgust. "I can't believe they print this stuff without investigating it."

"You mean that's not what you said?"

"*I* didn't say anything. All I can think of is that this guy Cox, whoever he is, has decided to construe this study we did last April as support for his theory about CO_2 build-up. Whatever that theory is. It's not exactly clear in this article."

"But it says that your research shows that predictions of global warming have been exaggerated."

"That's not quite what it says. And no, my research doesn't show anything of the kind." Tina leaned over to set her juice glass on the table next to the phone. She settled back on the couch and turned toward Chip with an impish smile. "And if it did? Then that would be good news, right?"

"Of course," Chip said, looking confused. "If it was true. But it's not."

"And how would you know that? How would you know if it were true or not? If my research shows one thing, or I interpret it to show one thing, and someone else's shows the opposite, which do you believe? Isn't that the problem here?"

"But the majority of scientists are saying that global warming is inevitable. Oh, sure, they use words like 'probably' and 'maybe,' but a few are starting to concede that we should do something. This Cox is a dissenting opinion."

"Sometimes the dissenting opinions are the important ones."

"So you know this guy?"

"No, no. I've never even heard of him. But without seeing his papers I really can't say if there's anything to his dissension." Tina shrugged, a little exasperated. They never followed the same line of reasoning. "Look, Chip, the paper that this guy must have seen was about the picoplankton—remember, I told you about the tiny cyanobacteria that provide my paleoclimate markers? Well, all our study showed was that they're prevalent in the open ocean, and that past estimates of marine primary productivity may be way too low. The paper was meant to make waves, stir people up, make them think in new ways about old problems—but we certainly didn't say anything about the picoplankton's effect on these climate models. Those are atmospheric circulation models, about which I know absolutely nothing." Tina shook her head. The more she thought about it, the less amused and more irritated she became. If the guy was referring to the *Science* paper why didn't he say so? And why would he use her name and not Roy's? Or John Carr's, for that matter? "It's pretty irresponsible of this Cox to misrepresent my work. In fact, it's hard to believe anyone would say something off-the-cuff like that to the press. Maybe it was the reporter who got it wrong?"

Chip picked the paper up off the floor. "What you have to do," he said, dropping it into Tina's lap, "is write a letter to the editor. Tell them about your research yourself."

"Chip. I am not going to write a letter to the editor about my research. It's a newspaper, not a scientific journal."

"That's right, mi amor, a newspaper. One of those dull, pointless publications that millions of literate people read every day—unlike the illustrious Dr. Arenas, who simply doesn't have time. Who probably doesn't even know that Congress just voted to give millions of dollars to the Salvadoran military so they can better torture and exploit their people, or that the EPA and all that it stood for is fast becoming history—"

"But that research doesn't belong in the news, Chip. God, our paper in *Science* was just a report on work in progress, not even a full-fledged article—"

"It's already *in* the news, Tina, like it or not. Christ, you just said they misquoted you. How can you let that stand?"

"They didn't misquote me. They didn't even talk to me. They misquoted Cox. Or he misquoted me, though why in the world anyone would do such a thing, I don't know. . . . I can't believe anyone could be that desperate to garner support for a theory, if that's what he thought he was doing. And in the newspaper, of all places?"

"He's probably been bribed by the petroleum industry."

"Oh, come on—" Tina looked at the article. "He's a professor in the Agriculture Department at the University of Arizona." She laughed. "I didn't know there was such a thing as agriculture in Arizona."

"I'm serious. They have a whole campaign going, you know, to discredit the theories of global warming."

"'They'?" Tina said in the most mocking tone she could muster.

Chip glared at her. He turned and took a couple of steps away from the couch, then stopped and turned back. "I'll never understand you. You question everything. You question the taste in your mouth, the rain on your head, the fucking slugs liking bran—the most solid and observable of facts. But you don't question people's motives. You wouldn't think to question money and power."

"Money and power?" Tina mimicked his tone. "I think you've got things a little mixed up. That's what economists and politicians do. I'm a scientist, in case you haven't noticed."

"So, what, money and power don't have anything to do with you? What exactly do you call a grant from Petron if not money and power influencing your results—"

"Oh, for God's sake. Nobody has influenced my results. Nobody has even tried to influence my results."

"No? But they've nudged you into doing a certain type of research, haven't they? You think it's such a big step—"

"Yes! Of course! It's a huge step, it's not even—" The phone rang, and Tina moved to answer it. Money and power, what did that mean? A cliché, rhetoric. Why didn't he just blame things on the devil, Tina thought, picking up the phone. "Hello?"

"Hola, sweetheart," her father's voice came over the line, a little breathless. "I know it's not the cheap time, but I just had to call. The neighbor just showed me the article about you in the paper. I didn't even know myself, but Jackie from Number 9 came up with the paper and said, Alfredo, isn't this your daughter they are talking about here, and there you were. Dr. Cristina Arenas of the Brayton Institute of Oceanography. The expert."

"In the *L.A. Times*?"

"No, no. The neighbor doesn't like our paper, you know, she gets the *New York Times*. Did you see it yet, *hija*? This article all about the global warming. *¿Te lo mando?* Here, I'll read it to you, the part about you—"

"No, that's okay. I saw it." She glanced at Chip, who was watching her, arms folded, chewing on his mustache.

"I was so proud, *tan orgulloso. Y en un gran diario como el de New York. La vecina dice que—*"

"Dad, I'm afraid that's nothing to be proud of. It's a mistake."

"A mistake?"

He sounded so disappointed when she explained about the reference to her work being misguided that Tina wondered if maybe she should have just played along and let him be proud.

"So it was in the L.A. paper too," Chip said when she hung up, as if it proved some point.

"No it wasn't. He has a neighbor who reads the *New York Times*."

"See? Millions of people are going to be misled because they think that Dr. Arenas has done research showing that global warming is nothing to worry about. You think that's not your responsibility? You think because you're a scientist, Tina, you don't need to be engaged in the world? Or do you think we're all too dumb to understand this? Well, I've got news for you. If that's the case we're into the big-time shit. Because it ain't scientists making the rules, and if you can't make the people who are—those economists and politicians you like to dismiss, not to mention us ordinary voting types—"

"OKAY! I'll write a goddamn letter to your goddamn *New York Times*! Jesus."

Chip stared at her.

"I'll write a letter," Tina said more quietly. "If it'll make you happy." She hadn't meant to yell. He was right, of course. She should set the record straight. The problem, the thing that made her yell . . . She wasn't about to tell him that for all his flawed reasoning and vacuous idealism, he made her feel guilty. About not keeping up with the news, about having forgotten to vote in the 1980 election—as if her vote might have blocked the landslide victory of Reagan, the torture of Salvadorans, the imposition of war on the Sandinistas . . . as if her attention might stop the warming of the planet, the melting of the icecaps, depletion of the ozone, the loss of wild places he so mourned, as if . . .

Chip smiled, suddenly, victoriously. "It doesn't have to be very long." He sat down on the couch and leaned back, clasping his hands behind his head. Tina was still standing by the phone. "In fact, it shouldn't be more than a couple of paragraphs or they'll butcher it to make it fit. What you just told me about your research being misrepresented should be enough. You want me to write it for you?"

"Oh no," Tina said, shaking her head adamantly—until she noticed the grin in his mustache. She let out a long sigh that ended in a short bewildered laugh and glanced up at the ceiling. How was it possible to feel such a horrendous tenderness for a man you had been mocking not two minutes before? You had to respect someone who acted on their beliefs and ideas the way he did, Tina thought. That the ideas were sometimes unsupported, and the beliefs unquestioned, almost like religious beliefs . . . well, so what? Why did that irritate her so? He wasn't a scientist. He wasn't obligated to support his beliefs with data—was he?

He heaved himself up from the couch, and before she knew what he was doing, he'd walked over and picked her up, raised her up high so that her head was above his. He leaned his torso back to see her face, but Tina slithered down and buried it against his shoulder, clinging to his neck. *He* might not be obligated, but she certainly was. Speculation was one thing, an entirely different matter, but she had no right to profess a belief that she couldn't eventually support—with data, with deductive reasoning, with all available knowledge. No reason to feel guilty about that, damn him.

But she did. She felt guilty for not knowing enough.

Chapter 22

Thursday mornings were not a busy time at the BIO library. It was as quiet as a funeral home, the air still, the heat turned up too high. Tina paused a few steps inside, fighting down a wave of nausea and claustrophobia. She took a deep breath and set her knapsack on the floor so that she could pull off her sweater, which was damp from her dash through the rain, and then she headed for the Chem Abstracts.

She had finally finished her portion of the Warrua paper, and Garrett was supposed to meet with her to discuss it later that afternoon. She'd left him a message to look for her at the library, where she planned to spend the day, reading and copying articles, finding out what sort of work this fellow William Cox had done, among other things. True to her promise to Chip, she had written a letter to the editor of the *New York Times*, three lines to the effect that her work had been misrepresented in the article, and she had no connection with the climate models referred to and had not "proved" anything whatsoever about their validity. Chip wasn't entirely satisfied—rather than being too long, he said, the letter was too short and wouldn't command enough attention. But she didn't have anything else to say, Tina told him, exasperated, and he'd retreated, not wanting, he told her pointedly, to argue.

There was an abstract of a paper by Cox in the most recent volume of the Chemical Abstracts, the work he'd discussed with the reporter: "a reassessment of the global climate sensitivity to the doubling in atmospheric CO_2 predicted for the next century," according to the abstract. Tina went upstairs to the stacks. She stood in the dimly lit aisle between shelves of bound journals and tried to skim quickly through Cox's article, but it wasn't easy to understand. It was not the sort of article she would have expected from a plant physiologist in an agriculture department. She sank down on a stool to read more carefully.

The underlying premise of the greenhouse effect was that as the concentration of CO_2 in the atmosphere increased, outgoing radiation in the form of heat decreased, and things got hot. How much the outgoing radiation would decrease for a given amount of CO_2, and just how hot things got as a result, were still up for debate. In the first half of his paper Cox calculated the net change in radiation at the earth's surface that would result if the CO_2 in the atmosphere were to double. This was the domain of atmospheric scientists and physicists, and Tina couldn't follow the calculation. She hunched over the heavy volume of *Science* in her lap and read on.

Cox had determined a quantity he called the "Global Temperature Sensitivity" by measuring how much air temperature changed when some natural phenomena such as clouds or haze changed the amount of radiation at the earth's surface. Then he multiplied this Temperature Sensitivity by the change in radiation he had calculated for a doubling of CO_2 and claimed that the result, a mere two-tenths of a degree, was the maximum change in average global temperature to be expected in the next century. This was an order of magnitude smaller than the two-to-four degree change that global climate models were predicting and, citing a similar result based on another "empirical" study published by a different lab earlier that year, Cox called for a "complete reconsideration of the CO_2-climate problem." An increase of two-tenths of a degree Celsius over a century was certainly no cause for alarm, he concluded, and there was strong evidence that the higher CO_2 content in the atmosphere would be beneficial to agriculture. He referenced several of his own papers in support of this latter.

Thinking she must have missed something, Tina read through the article again; but the experiments Cox had used to determine his "Temperature Sensitivity" were not described, and the reference given was for a paper listed as "in preparation." Well, that was annoying, Tina thought, since as far as she could see this whole paper depended on those experiments. She stood up and set aside the volume she was reading. She was scanning the tables of contents of the most recent issues of *Science*, hoping to find the paper that had been in preparation, when Harper Gibson turned up her aisle. He walked over and reached up to pluck a volume off the shelf above Tina's head.

"Hi," Tina said, moving out from under his arm.

He nodded a greeting and looked at the journal he'd pulled off the shelf. Then he looked back at Tina as if he'd just remembered who she was. "How are your picoplankton faring?"

"They're holding their own," Tina said, smiling. She paused, and then she retrieved the journal she'd left lying open on an empty section of shelf. "You know this guy's work?" she said, holding it out for him to see.

He cocked his head around to read the heading, and when he saw who it was he let out an alarmingly loud snort. Tina took a step backward, stumbling over the stool and almost dropping the heavy journal. "That guy's work," Harper boomed, "is a crock of shit, is what it is. I'd give anything to know who the hell funds that jackass."

His voice echoed in the cement building, and Tina winced, hoping he wouldn't ask why she was interested. But he'd already opened the volume of *Science* he'd come for and was scanning an article, even as he turned and started back down the aisle. He must have lost his last graduate student, Tina thought, if he was coming to the library himself, doing his own fetching and photocopying. She almost laughed out loud when she realized she was pitying him. Katharine liked to tell a story about how Harper Gibson once tried to convince the department secretary, who had worked at BIO for over twenty years, that going to the library for him was part of her job. Ruth was an old hand with arrogance, but the story went that Harper had looked so helplessly bewildered by her refusal that she almost felt sorry for him and relented.

Tina couldn't find the paper Cox had cited as "in preparation," but she did find two letters criticizing the paper she'd just read. A group of atmospheric scientists in Colorado took *Science* editors to task for having published his paper at all. It was inappropriate, they said, for a high-caliber refereed journal to publish an article with a provocative main conclusion based on a reference still in preparation. Both letters, the second from a NASA research group, said that the simplifications made in calculating the radiation change from CO_2 doubling were invalid. They pointed out that similar errors in the paper Cox cited as independent verification had already been acknowledged in the literature by that paper's author, leaving no excuse for their repetition. The Colorado group sounded angry: Cox's calculations contributed nothing to the understanding of climate change, did nothing to narrow or resolve the well-recognized inadequacies in global climate models, and certainly did not justify his call for a "complete reconsideration" of the problem.

Tina found Cox's rebuttal in the December issue. His tone was studiedly collegiate. He apologized for the crucial paper not being available yet and blamed this on the "vagaries of the publication process." Tina looked back at the reference in the original paper. The work was listed as "in preparation," not "in press"; how could it be victim to the vagaries of publication if it hadn't been accepted for publication yet? She read on. To alleviate readers' concerns about the unpublished work, he listed the "natural phenomena" used to determine his Global Temperature Sensitivity: dust storms in Arizona, the summer monsoon in the southwestern U.S., and monthly variations in solar radiation at stations off the coast of California. Tina paused and reread the paragraph. This was supposed to alleviate concerns? How could he derive a "global temperature sensitivity" representing changes over decades and centuries, from such local, short-term fluctuations? In defense of the *Science* editors, Cox noted that they had requested this material for review by the referees when considering his paper. He went on as if the objections to his paper were purely philosophical, ignoring the assertions that his calculations were in error. The modelers' approach, Cox said, was to calculate how the climate *ought* to respond to a given perturbation. He, however, was taking an experimentalist's approach, looking at what actually happened in the atmosphere, using the real earth as a model. Sounded good, Tina thought, sounded like what she was trying to do for paleoclimate research—but as far as she could tell from the scant information in Cox's letter, his so-called "experiments" were just bad analogies.

Tina stretched. Her eyes burned from reading in the dimly lit aisle. Her back ached. The stool she was sitting on seemed to float unsteadily on its spring every time she shifted her weight. . . . Seasick—that was how she was beginning to feel. The stuffy library air was oppressive, and though her stomach was growling, she felt queasy. It must be after noon, and the only thing she'd learned was that Harper had not been exaggerating when he called William Cox's work a "crock of shit." She still didn't understand how Cox had construed the report on picoplankton productivity as either friend or foe to his analysis. She supposed she could call and confront him, but after reading his paper and letter she really didn't want anything to do with him. She stood up, and the stool popped up behind her with an indignant little click, as if she had been abusing it by sitting there so long. She slid the journals back into their slots. Why would anyone try to defend such an obviously flawed study? And then talk to the press about it? And why, for that matter, were the newspapers quoting a scientist whose work had already been repudiated in the scientific literature? That was a question for Chip, she thought, as she headed for the stairs, though she wasn't sure she wanted to hear his answer. She did want to learn more about these climate models Cox claimed to discredit, but first she needed to get some air and eat something.

The library was in the midst of its post-lunch rush, the photocopy machines humming, the tables near the current journals occupied, a line at the check-out desk. . . . Tina pulled on her sweater and went outside. There was a wide cement bench under the overhang of the library entrance, out of the rain, and she was tempted to stretch out and take a nap, but she sat down and took out her lunch bag instead. She really was hungry, but the only thing in the bag that appealed to her were some carrots from the farm. Like everything Chip and Jorge grew, they didn't look like the ones from the supermarket. They were shorter and fatter, a brighter shade of orange. Sweeter, even a little juicy. Carrots, Tina thought, gnawing on the end of one, would be a good thing to have on a cruise for seasickness. She swallowed and looked down at the half-eaten carrot in her hand. She was seasick from sitting on a stool in the library? She was almost tired enough to lie down and take a nap on this bench right here next to the entrance? Her breasts hurt and her period seemed to have been pending for weeks? She glanced at the brown lunch bag on the bench, as if this fearful intimation were to be found lurking in its dark interior with her uneaten sandwich, the unopened bag of nuts and raisins. It was, she decided, impossible. She had never been pregnant. She used the diaphragm, or nowadays the sponges that had replaced it, carefully, religiously. Her period had never been very regular anyway. Only in the past few years had it settled into a monthly cycle, and the cruise had thrown that off. Perhaps it was reverting to its old trick of random disappearances, ambushing her with hormones at unpredictable intervals. She hated this horrid, dragged-out premenstrual state, though if the thing would just get started, she knew she would feel fine—not like poor Katharine, who spent three very regular days of every month doped up on painkillers. Better to have an occasional late period, Tina thought, than that. She finished the carrots and forced herself to eat half her cheese sandwich. Then she took a few deep breaths of fresh rain-scented air and went back into the library.

This time she dragged the journals out to a table near a window where there was plenty of light and a comfortable chair with cushions, and where Garrett could find her easily. She started with the two references in Cox's paper, but soon she had the table covered.

Tina hunted down paper after paper on the computer climate models that atmospheric scientists had been developing, complex mathematical interpretations of the physical laws governing air movements, solar radiation and reflectivity . . . and she didn't understand a word. The papers built one upon the other, and she kept moving backward in the literature, searching for an early one where the models would be fully described, terms defined. She built a fortress of unfamiliar journals on the table around her—*Journal of Atmospheric Science, Applied Meteorology, Geophysical Research*—and she still couldn't understand. She found a 1967 paper where what appeared to be one of the first "general circulation models" was described. She found a review article, a basic text on atmospheric physics, a monograph on computer modeling techniques. She sought out a text on multi-degree differential equations . . . and gave up trying to make sense of the mathematics. All she wanted, after all, was a qualitative understanding of how the models were put together, what assumptions were made, what the boundary conditions were—what they could and could not do. It took her all afternoon.

The simplest of the models calculated an average global temperature based on the energy balance between the earth's reflectivity and the greenhouse properties of the atmosphere. The most complex computer models, called general circulation models, or GCMs, could calculate the variation of temperature in four dimensions—latitude, longitude, altitude, and time, and included the effects of humidity, wind, soil moisture, sea ice, etc. The models *were* fraught with problems, Tina thought, as she gained some understanding of how they worked. They were just beginning to couple ocean circulation to the atmospheric circulation, so large effects such as heat transport from low to high latitudes in surface currents, or the slow exchange between the surface layer and the cold deep water hadn't been accounted for. And there were important small-scale effects such as cloud cover, that couldn't be resolved by even the most sophisticated model. Cox's criticism was redundant because the modelers conceded the myriad problems with their creations in their own papers, readily pointing out that their predictions were only good to within a factor of two or three. Cox's prediction, however, differed by a factor of ten, well beyond the uncertainty in the models. And, despite his claims to the contrary, even his low estimate of two-tenths of a degree global warming might well be something to worry about, given the regional variation that the GCMs indicated: an average global increase of two-tenths of a degree might include a five-degree change at the equator and no change in Antarctica, and since regional differences in temperature were responsible for winds and currents and storm systems, this would wreak total havoc with the climate system.

Tina contemplated her fortress of books. Despite the uncertainties, the models were clearly a useful method for understanding the effects of increasing atmospheric CO_2 concentration. They were not, as Cox had implied, entirely divorced from the "real world," but were checked and calibrated with meteorological data, and attempts were made to predict backward and duplicate temperature averages of the past century. Of course, the meteorological data was geographically spotty and temperature records for the past century were incomplete and inaccurate. . . . Speaking of which, hadn't Chip shown her some newspaper article that said a warming trend had, in fact, already been detected? She pushed herself out of the chair and headed back into the stacks.

The paper the news story was based on was in the December issue of *Nature*. It was refreshingly easy to follow and included the background and context for the study, which Tina found helpful. Taken at face value, the temperature record from 1940 to 1970 actually showed a cooling trend. When this was first reported in the seventies, it had caused a lot of skepticism about the youthful field of climate modeling, because according to the models, the rise in atmospheric CO_2 that Keeling had been measuring since the fifties should have produced a warming trend during that same period. In this recent paper the NASA group—the same one that responded to Cox's paper in *Science*—claimed that the seventies study had been incomplete. They reassessed the temperature record, extended through 1981, and this time they factored out several effects that the models couldn't take into account: the cooling effects of sunspots, and of dust and sulfates from volcanoes, which were extremely active during the seventies. This revealed a warming component that they claimed was associated with the increase in CO_2. The NASA group predicted that in another decade, certainly by the early nineties, the warming would be in evidence, too severe to be compensated by natural fluctuations.

There was a flurry of letters and reports on the heels of the NASA group's paper, generally supporting their assertion that volcanism and sunspots accounted for the cooling from 1940 to 1970. But the consensus was that their model still contained too many unsupportable assumptions, that their conclusions and their dire predictions, though not necessarily wrong, were premature. The letters censured the NASA group for its overconfidence, and several subsequent reports by other researchers concluded that warming caused by greenhouse gases could not yet be positively identified.

Tina closed the journal she'd been reading and pushed it aside. Garrett should be arriving any time now. She leaned her head in her hand and closed her burning eyes for a moment. What was it Harper Gibson had called this whole anthropogenic CO_2 dilemma? The "Great Experiment"? He said it wasn't working, and it did seem to Tina that the only clear data they had was Keeling's curve showing the rise in atmospheric CO_2 since the fifties.

She pulled her feet up in the chair and turned to face the window, hugging her legs. There were no trees blocking this view from the second story of the BIO library, no herons staring back at her—just gray sky and gray ocean, gray rain, and her own reflection. She rested her chin on her knees. The problem, Tina thought, was that there was no blank run. What they needed was a duplicate earth. Someplace where they could run a control experiment. An earlier earth, perhaps? Use the sediment record? After all, they had a 180 million years of climate changes recorded in the deep sea sediments—and maybe, just maybe, if she could pull it off, they could have an equally long record of CO_2. Roy was enthusiastic, though the only thing they'd found to guide them was a study of isotope fractionation during the CO_2 uptake by corn plants. Tina looked away from the window. Garrett was standing quietly on the other side of her mountain of books, flipping through one of the climate journals on top. She stared blankly at the desolate strands of hair on his head. Wouldn't be much of a duplicate, her earlier earth. The timescales were all wrong, millenniums instead of centuries, geological time instead of historical. Continents in different places. Different plants, animals. Different currents, deep sea circulation, different everything.

"Garrett," she said, "do you know anything about carbon isotope fractionation during photosynthesis and biosynthesis?"

He closed the journal he'd been leafing through, pushed a pile of books to the other end of the table, and sat down. "Not much," he said.

She was dying to talk about her paleo-CO_2 idea, but he immediately opened the folder he'd brought with him. Tina took her part of the paper out of her knapsack, and they traded. Then they sat in silence while Garrett skimmed what Tina had written and Tina skimmed what he had written, only half-concentrating. She had begun to see this paper as a sort of last fling before she got down to business—a lovely and profound, but eminently unserious and decidedly unpromising bit of research. The search for an answer to an unanswerable question. Garrett's search. Garrett's question. Not hers. Tina was beginning to suspect that *her* questions might have answers, that her tangles of inquiry might stretch into an ordered net where the answers hung like weights, ballast for her soul.

There wasn't much to discuss. Garrett had written the introduction, discussion, and conclusion, and Tina had done the experimental procedure and presentation of the data. This included the hydrocarbon kinetics, so she had acknowledged support from her grant, as well as some of Michael's work, and now she asked Garrett how he felt about adding him as third author.

"Of course," Garrett said. "We can put him down as first author if you want."

"No. I don't think it's appropriate. I'll put him as first author when we publish the results of the petroleum project."

"How's that going?"

"Fine," Tina said shrugging. "Michael's doing some good chemistry. He's studying the effects of different types of rock matrices on the kinetics. And I got him some samples from a geologist at UCLA, from a basin they know the thermal history of." Tina laughed. "Speaking of which, I never did tell you about this geologist from Petron that came to visit the lab a couple months ago."

"From where?"

"Petron. The oil company. This guy was one of the people that reviewed the ACS proposal. He wanted to collaborate, give us samples from some new basin they were studying."

"I take it you told him you weren't interested."

"Yeah. The guy was a real jerk. I wouldn't want to work with him, even if it was something interesting."

"How about a sample from the Murchison meteorite?" Garrett said, slipping Tina's manuscript pages into his folder. "I don't suppose you'd be interested in checking out the organics."

"I think I've got my hands full," Tina said. "Not to mention my freezer."

Garrett nodded. She handed him back his part of the manuscript and watched him add it to the folder. He looked sad—even his eyebrows seemed plucked and pitiful, and uncharacteristically immobile. She hadn't seen him in a couple of months, since his seminar, and she remembered now that he'd seemed sad then too; she'd thought it was just his disillusionment with the conference, but now she wasn't sure. Maybe he really did miss his friends in France. Maybe he was lonely. She thought of him in his house full of exotic knickknacks and photographs, his fancy stereo. Did he fill it with music to drown out the silence? With mementos to occupy the emptiness? He liked to cook, but who was there to cook for? She should know, Tina thought, she should ask . . . but it wasn't part of their repertoire.

Garrett stood up and tucked the folder under his arm. When would she ever see him, if they weren't collaborating? What excuse would they have to get together for one of their rambling debates? She had never thought of Garrett as a lonely man, a man to be pitied, someone whose happiness might be dependent on other human beings. The thought suddenly filled Tina with despair. What did any of it matter, the things they filled their lives with? If Garrett was lonely? She thought of her argument with Chip the other night, the way he chafed and rubbed at her like an irritating piece of clothing she wanted to shake free of. She thought of her father's phone call, his misplaced pride, his disappointment, and she felt her own mood plummeting, like a boat dropping down the side of a swell, an almost physical sensation—excessive, unreasonable, and entirely out of her control.

"Tina?" Garrett was examining her face, looking concerned. He started to come around the table to her, but she shook her head and stood up, busied herself stuffing her pad and papers into her knapsack. Why in the world was she crying? Jesus. Because Garrett's eyebrows looked sad? She didn't want to pity Garrett. She wanted to talk to him about carbon isotope fractionation in cyanobacteria.

"Come on," he said, touching her shoulder. "Let's get out of here. We'll go for a drive."

"But it's raining."

"No it's not. Look there might even be a bit of a sunset. Come on."

Tina glanced out the window. It had stopped raining, and the sun was peeking through a crack in the clouds just over the water, getting ready to drop out of sight. She picked up her knapsack and sweater and followed Garrett down the stairs.

Once they were in the Mercury, winding north along the coast at breakneck speed, Garrett seemed to cheer up a little. Tina wondered how she had ever agreed to go for a drive with him.

She stared straight ahead, trying to keep her mind off the nausea rising in her throat. "Why don't we stop and watch the sunset," she suggested, pointing to a turn-out up ahead.

Garrett pulled in, maneuvering so that the sunset was perfectly centered in the windshield.

"Now," he said, when he'd turned off the engine. "Tell me what the tears are all about. I thought you were riding high and happy on the hog of success. You've got so many projects in the kettle that you aren't even tempted by my nuggets of meteorite. You've got funding, a good instrument, a good technician . . . " He glanced at her with a hint of his old twinkle and added, "I was even suspecting that you might have found yourself a good man."

Tina had been too busy trying not to throw up to do anything but stare straight ahead, but now she turned to look at Garrett. He was facing her, his shoulder leaning into the back of the seat. She was relieved to see that his eyebrows had moved; they now soared expectantly above his glasses. "*You*," she said. "You looked so sad. I think you reminded me of my father or something, though I can't think of a more unlikely comparison. . . . " Tina laughed, embarrassed. "God, Garrett, I'm sorry. To tell you the truth, I think my goddamn hormones are acting up—though I'm not supposed to admit that, am I?" She shook her head and looked away. The sun had dropped from sight, but the narrow fissure in the clouds just above the horizon was still glowing.

"No reason to be sorry," Garrett said. "I *am* sad." He shifted around so that he too was facing forward. "It's probably a good thing to cry like that. Too bad I don't have the right kind of hormones."

Tina turned her head. He was sitting upright on the seat, his hands folded over the top of the steering wheel. It was getting dark in the car, but she could make out his expression and it was serious. He glanced at her staring at him, and then he unfolded his hands and reached across the car to brush a wisp of hair back from her temple, as if it were the most natural thing in the world for him to do. He refolded his hands on the steering wheel. "You can cry all you want here in the Mercury," he said. "It's a far better place for crying than the library. Feel free to use it any time. You don't even have to ask. Just find the car, let yourself in. It's never locked."

"Garrett," Tina said finally, and then didn't know what it was she wanted to say. That he'd stepped out of character, was changing roles before her very eyes? She'd started that, hadn't she? "Garrett," she said, "aren't you ever lonely?"

He sighed and slid down in the seat enough to lean his head back on its top. "Ah, lonely. I thought I'd forgotten what lonely means. You're talking about family, I suppose. Or, in my case, lovers." He grasped the bottom of the steering wheel and leaned forward to peer out at the darkening sky. "I really just sort of gave up on all that, years ago. Not worth the trouble." He laughed, and glanced quickly at Tina, who was still sitting there staring at him, her mouth half-agape. "It's funny," he said. "I used to think being a woman would be harder than being gay. At least being gay was something one could hide. Women, though, women didn't have a chance. Not back in the fifties or sixties. And I suppose that even now, when you stand up to give a talk or present a paper, you must feel it: all those male eyes looking at you, curious about the woman they're seeing, instead of listening to what you're saying. Is she married? Is she a prude? Will she fall apart when we attack? It's been a long time since I've thought much about this. One likes to think that women scientists have come into their own. That it's no longer a problem. But then I see that Tina Arenas is humiliated just because she feels like shedding a few tears, and I realize that she still has to maintain, even with her closest friends and colleagues—even with *herself*—this unnatural façade of emotional and physical neutrality. A male façade is what it is. Fine to be a woman as long as you hide everything that might make that different from being a man—no, not hide, *deny*—everything that boys, even gay boys, are taught to hide from birth. In a way, it's about the same thing, you see, stumbling through life in a suit that doesn't fit because they only make the one size in the style you want. Don't you think?"

Tina stared at Garrett, parting her lips to speak, then closing them several times before she finally started to laugh. She faced forward and leaned back in the seat, drawing her legs up to sit cross-legged. "What a trade," she said. "I give you premenstrual stress, and you give me a lifetime of closet homosexuality."

"Not exactly an equal trade, is it? I don't think anyone's ever been blackmailed by revelations of premenstrual stress. Though I wouldn't exactly say I'm in the closet, you know. It's just that by the time it seemed safe to come out—not that long ago, actually, maybe the late seventies wouldn't have been too devastating—well, by then it was sort of anticlimactic. A closet celibate? Doesn't exactly make news, does it?"

Tina wanted to tell him about Chip, about wondering if it was worth the trouble, but instead they fell into an uneasy silence that she didn't know how to break, sitting at either end of the wide seat, watching the crack in the clouds close and cease to glow, staring at the windshield as if they could see into the dark on the other side, neither of them moving. Then it began to rain, and with the first few random, arrhythmic splats on the car roof, Tina felt her heartbeat quicken with the urge to flee, to run for shelter—though they were, in fact, quite dry and safe in Garrett's boat of a car. She rolled down the window a crack. She uncrossed her legs and let them hang over the edge of the seat. She heard Garrett shifting in the seat next to her, and she wondered if there might be some biochemical response to the onset of rain, the sound of those first drops. She wondered exactly what instinct was. The random splats on the roof picked up, gained rhythm, became a regular patter. Tina rolled the window up. Garrett took the keys out of the ignition and jiggled them in his palm.

"It seems," he said out of the dark, "that the preference for C-12 over C-13 must be in that first step, when CO_2 binds to the receptor. There must be a slightly lower energy barrier."

Tina leaned back in the seat and relaxed, though the rain was pounding more insistently on the roof. She felt the smile spreading slowly across her face. All the while they'd been reading their paper and driving and talking about loneliness and watching the sun set through a crack in the clouds and sitting in uneasy silence listening to the rain begin, Garrett had been mulling over her question. She didn't respond right away. A diagram of all the reactions involved in photosynthesis and the Calvin cycle appeared in front of her, as if projected on the dark windshield, something recalled from a college textbook. For a moment she felt as though she and Garrett were watching an old movie together at a drive-in theater like the one her father used to take her to in L.A., and she was content to be warm and dry, their silence easy now, companionable. Garrett had taught this stuff for years. His movie would include the energy differences and chemical structures for each step of the cycle.

As she told him about the paleo-CO_2 idea, Tina realized that she wanted him to like it—not think it clever, or even necessarily think it feasible, but just like it for it's own self, now, in its embryo state—and he did. He questioned her energetically. His spirits seemed to lift, and he wondered if they might adapt the method to work on older rocks, investigate the atmosphere of the early earth. What method? Tina said, and Garrett laughed. He shoved the keys into the ignition and started the car.

"You'll be fine," he mumbled, talking more to himself than to Tina as he turned on the headlights and launched them onto a nearly invisible road.

"What?" Tina shouted, not knowing if she'd heard him correctly, between the engine turning over and the rain.

"Oh, the way that grant of yours turned out," Garrett said. "I was a little worried that I'd steered you wrong. The whole funding scene nowadays . . . it's easy to lose sight of what you're about. But I think you're going to be okay. Though, I don't know, anyone who would turn down a chance at the Murchison meteorite . . . "

Why wouldn't she be okay? Tina thought, pressing her knuckles against the dashboard as he whipped around a curve. If he just got her back to Brayton alive, she'd be fine. He was the one who'd been sad, she thought, though he had definitely cheered up now. "You never told me why you were so sad," she said.

"Ah. That is what precipitated all this, isn't it. Me looking sad." He didn't say anything for a moment, but Tina didn't dare turn to look at him, because she was already getting sick again. He accelerated on a curve, slowed down coming out of it, accelerated again. "I went to see an old friend in Paris," he said then. "Hadn't seen him in ten years. We spent two weeks alternately having a great time and carrying on a ten-year-old argument. And then one day while we were walking down the street he had a heart attack. Just keeled over and died," Garrett said bitterly, as if he were angry at his friend for dying. "He wasn't even sick. He just had to make sure he had the last word."

"I'm sorry," Tina said. She didn't know what else to say. "Was he a scientist?" she asked stupidly.

"No, thank god." Garrett chuckled, and his voice loosened up a little. "He was an artist. A photographer. In France that's a real thing to be. His work sold well, and he had government support, fellowships, endowments. They are beautiful, Serge's photographs, beautiful and disturbing." He fell silent, and stayed silent as they sped along the coast back to BIO.

By the time Garrett pulled into the parking lot next to Tina's building, it was all she could do to keep from vomiting. She sat there breathing deeply and trying to calm her stomach. She wanted to comfort him. Wanted to let him follow his own advice and cry, now that they were stopped and safe in the dark parking lot. But Garrett left the engine running, the lights on. Tina reached for her knapsack on the floor.

"I'll send down the final version of the paper next week," Garrett said.

"Okay. Fine." Tina opened the door but didn't get out.

"Let me know if you change your mind about the Murchison sample."

"Right."

If he hadn't been behind the wheel of the car . . . If she hadn't been struggling with the urge to vomit . . . If it hadn't been so dark and they could have seen the expressions on each other's faces . . . If she hadn't looked up and seen Sylvia Orloff hurrying across the parking lot just then, shielding her eyes from the rude glare of the Mercury's brights . . . Tina probably would have given him a hug. But as it was, there was just an awkward pause while she sat there with the door open, and then they bid each other good night and she got out.

Chapter 23

Tina checked the vial, and then the chart, and then the vial again. She did this four times. Accustomed as she was to using small, subtle chemical variations to establish large, significant concepts, this particular not-so-subtle color change evaded comprehension. The test was merely a precaution; scientific intuition had not prepared her for a positive result, and she was naked and vulnerable before it—deeply, genuinely incredulous, and literally naked. It had not occurred to her that her intuition wouldn't apply to the body standing hunched over at the bathroom counter.

It was a cold morning. Tina's bare feet recoiled from the linoleum, her toes curled under. Her legs were pressed together, her arms crossed tightly under her breasts, and her shoulders hunched up around her ears as if one might garner warmth from such a measly compilation of skin and bones. She was too skinny to be pregnant. All Chip's fine farm produce and lovingly prepared dinners hadn't changed that.

He was still asleep down the hall. She had been careful not to wake him when she got up to pee into the plastic cup, careful again when she climbed back into bed to wait the requisite half-hour. She had almost fallen asleep again, waiting, so sure was she that the test would be negative, a waste of nine dollars on a passing paranoia. She picked up the vial now, in its little plastic stand, and set it in the waste basket. She crumpled up the box it had come in and the insert with the instructions and tossed them in on top of it. She tore off a piece of toilet paper and dropped it in on top of the rest so she wouldn't have to look at the evidence. Careful not to look in the mirror over the sink, she washed her hands in scalding hot water. Then she walked the few steps down the hall to her bedroom.

He was on his back with his hands folded on top of his chest and his elbows sticking out on either side, snoring softly. Shivering, Tina crawled under the blankets. She wormed up under his arm, and he stopped snoring and moved it around her shoulders, his hand resting on her hip. She pressed her cheek against his rib cage and clung tightly to his warm, solid, substantial side.

She told his ribs that she was pregnant.

"You're what?" Chip burst from half-sleep and lifted his head and shoulders off the pillow. Tina peeled herself away from his side and turned onto her back.

"I'm pregnant."

"Pregnant? From me?" He propped himself up on his elbow and looked at her. A cold draft rushed in under the blankets.

"No, stupid, from the gardener." Tina tried to laugh. She started to cry instead.

Now that he was fully awake, Chip didn't act shocked. He held her while she cried, stroking her hair patiently and telling her not to worry, that everything would be okay. He did this until Tina was tired of crying and tired of being held and tired of the gentle, monotonous caress of his voice. She threw back the covers and got out of bed.

She noticed Chip eyeing her body as she emerged from the blankets, and suddenly she wanted it covered. It was as though her body were no longer hers at all, but some sort of duplicitous machine that had ducked out of her control, and she did not want him looking it over, searching for signs of this betrayal. She grabbed a pair of sweat pants from the top of the dresser, the first shirt she found when she opened the drawer. Chip got out of bed, and she immediately straightened the blankets and pulled the comforter over the pillows, as if the bed itself were party to the betrayal and needed to be covered up as well. By the time Chip came back from the bathroom, Tina was perched on the edge of a neatly made bed, facing the window with her hands clenched in her lap like a pianist about to give a recital.

He pulled open the blinds on a gray morning and sat down next to her.

She thought of the red-tailed hawks he had pointed out to her above the farm, the way they floated effortlessly upward on an updraft of air. She imagined how it must feel when they lost the updraft and were left to fly unsupported, and that's how she felt now, as if she had been rising toward the sun and the warm pocket of air that carried her had suddenly cooled and left her to fall—except that the hawk with its strong wings would have control of its descent, and Tina was just falling, more like a helicopter with no engine than a soaring bird. She did not even have control of her own goddamn body. "Why now," she said, thinking of the day that had been awaiting her. That would be awaiting her still, if she hadn't gone into the bathroom and done this nine-dollar test. She thought of all there was to do, of the outline she had started for the paper with Orloff, and the story that was still hidden in their cores, awaiting data from a method she had only just begun to develop. Even now, she could feel it, the familiar ripping sensation of separating herself from the work she most wanted to be doing, this absurd and childish rage that she contained, even knowing— the worse for knowing—that the work was a small and unessential thing out here in this world where she was pregnant. She glanced at Chip, who was sitting quietly next to her, looking out the window and waiting.

"I don't want a baby," she said, but it sounded more like a plea than the declaration she meant it to be, as if she were making an announcement to some disapproving audience. As if she were telling her father. "I just don't want one," she said more firmly, shaking her head, as if her unequivocal not wanting should be enough to make it not be. Chip didn't say anything, and after a moment Tina turned to face him, still shaking her head with conviction . . . and in disbelief, that looking at him she should feel compelled to add, "Not now. Not yet."

Chip only nodded, in what might have been agreement or might have been resignation, and Tina was left to ask. "You don't— You wouldn't want— You don't want a baby, right?" she finally got out, laughing a little nervously because it sounded funny, asking him that, and she was suddenly reminded of the first time he'd made love to her, how he'd made her ask him to stay. They had never talked about babies.

He didn't answer immediately, but sat there considering, as if he were only now thinking about what it seemed to Tina she had known all her life: that she did not want to be a mother. To hold an infant to milk-soaked breasts. To spend her hours in a repetitive cycle of nurturing loving caring for cleaning, chasing, and educating a human being. But Chip was not thinking about "having a baby" and all that entailed. Chip, Tina realized with a sudden, dreadful sense of wonder, was thinking about *this* baby— the specific unwanted thing inside of her at that very moment, which, if left unchecked, would grow into a particular unwanted creature, and then into an individual unloved child. . . . Though it was unimaginable that Chip would fail to love anything so helpless.

"It's too soon," he said finally. "You're just getting your career off the ground. It won't always be that way," he said, turning toward her. "Famous scientists have kids too, right?"

Not the women, Tina thought, though, in fact, the only famous woman scientist she knew was Orloff. It was, however, irrelevant, like worrying about whether you could keep a zebra in a suburban backyard, when you had no desire whatsoever to own a zebra.

"Hell, I don't know that I'm ready myself," Chip went on, "but if you'd wanted it . . . " He shrugged. "After all," he said wistfully, "farm's big enough for a kid or two."

Tears started rolling down Tina's cheeks. She was confused and amazed at the relief she felt: she had not wanted to hear that his aversion—to what was, after all, a joining of the two of them—might be as great as her own. She stared at Chip's face, at the rough skin of his cheeks, the fine wrinkles around his eyes, the thick brush of his mustache, the camouflaged mouth. She reached up and ran the flat of her finger down the bridge of his nose, combed the mustache hairs into place. Was it lying, she wondered, to say "not yet," when what she meant was "not ever"? Was it possible that there could be a love that made you change the person that you were, that made you want a thing that you had so vehemently not wanted for your entire life—not now, no not now, oh god, not now, but someday? Was that the right word—love? Surely she had used it and heard it used, and yet it had never meant *this* before, such a puny, inadequate word, like naming all the men in the world Joe—but what other name was there? *Amor? El enamoramiento, el querer?* She had never expected this of *el amor,* this inexplicable wrenching of the soul just from gazing on a man's face, the pink of his hidden lips, the awkward grace of his hands, the god-damned dirt carved into his cuticles. She could almost understand how it could happen, how a baby might be connected to this, the product of it. She did not want to be a mother, not now, not ever, but the image of Chip as a father, those big hands cradling a tiny infant, making amends for the nurture its mother withheld . . . was almost irresistible.

"It's okay," he said, reaching over and gathering her up against him. He laid his cheek against the top of her head. "It's no big deal nowadays. You'll go to a doctor."

It took her three calls to find the right place. It was Monday morning. They gave her an appointment for Thursday afternoon. Chip said that he would take her. He told her not to worry about the three hundred dollars they said she had to pay in advance. He told her not to worry about anything, but he himself looked worried when Tina got on her bike and rode off to BIO without drinking her morning coffee.

She couldn't quite focus her mind, those days before Thursday. She worked in silence, the radio off, feeling dazed and dreamy, suspended in the space between thoughts. It was as though she were outside her own life, traversing the curved surface of a soap bubble, peering in at a miniature Tina. She had to move carefully not to burst the bubble's fragile skin or overstep its foreshortened arc and gravitational field, and she could see herself inside—measuring out solvent, labeling a vial, talking to colleagues in this eerie, blue-filmed fairy world.

She was unusually, perversely, popular during those three days. She didn't want to talk to anyone, but people kept calling or stopping by the lab. Michael came in to tell her that he'd just been accepted to graduate school at MIT and would be leaving in the middle of June, just a month away. Katharine came like a spy from the next building to report that they'd just completed the strontium analyses and Orloff was pushing to get a paper written. Roy Shimohata called to tell her that the culture experiments she'd asked him to do showed that picoplankton growth rate was not affected by CO_2 concentration. Finally, Orloff herself stopped by Tina's lab to drop off the strontium data, and they set a date the following week to discuss their paper. Tina wanted to talk to her about the paleo-CO_2 method, ask about doing C-13 analyses in the surface forams, but Orloff was in a hurry, and Tina was in no mood to waylay her. She tried to look at the strontium data, but she couldn't concentrate, couldn't make sense of it.

It was impossible, now that she knew, not to be sensitive to what was happening in her body. Impossible not to notice the exhaustion, the finicky appetite, this delicate, precarious, absurdly feminine sensation that her body knew something she didn't know, that it was leading her into a world she had never before been privy to. She could almost, not quite but almost, imagine how it might be to want this. Momentarily, the way you might want an ice cream cone or a shower, the way you might want sex. The fact that she could cancel Thursday—and the fact that she didn't— gave her a certain freedom. Freedom to take a peek at what she had wanted so desperately to hide from that first morning. To let Chip have a glimpse.

He was so funny, so attentive. He insisted on taking her up to the farm every night. He baked huge quantities of sweetmeat squash for her because it was the only thing she felt like eating. Carefully, almost surreptitiously, he assessed her body, uncovering the clues she had so frantically covered: he weighed her tender, slightly swollen breasts in his palms, lingered uncertainly on the ever-so-subtle curve of her girlish belly. I love you, he told her; *te quiero, te amo*, she answered, all those corny old words they were unaccustomed to saying, it was impossible not to say them out loud, every day of those three days before Thursday, as if the words had the power to make everything okay, as if they were absolute.

Maybe that was all there was to it, Tina thought. Perhaps even an unwanted creature like the one inside of her could harness a mother with love, rein her in to its tiny, circumscribed world. Maybe it happened at the birth—the helpless interloper became the focus, the reason for existence, the thing that mattered. No more flying down the hill with a tail wind, contemplating the convolutions of the carbon cycle. No more arriving at your door and not remembering how you got there: with a baby seat balanced on the back of your bike you would be acutely aware of every pebble, every pothole, every passing car, your mind captive to the millions of tedious little details of keeping this helpless, soft-boned little thing alive—clean, healthy, happy. Probably, Tina thought, you wouldn't even risk riding around with the baby back there.

He picked her up at BIO on Thursday afternoon, and they went straight to the clinic. Just a woman's clinic, no big deal. Like going to get a check-up, buying birth control, taking the car in for repair.

Tina was nervous, though the clinic was clean and modern. She left Chip in the waiting room, and a nurse took her blood and her urine. The nurse sat down with a clipboard and asked what she'd been using for birth control. Tina said she used the sponge, had been using it since it first came out earlier that year. The problem, she added, was during her period, when she couldn't use the sponge; she thought it didn't matter, thought she was infertile then. She probably was, the nurse told her, she probably got pregnant with the sponge. There was a twelve-percent chance, the nurse said, and went on to talk about "other options."

Tina knew about all the options. She had not thought about the twelve chances in a hundred to get pregnant. She had, rather, compared the 88% effectiveness of the sponges with the 88% effectiveness of the diaphragm, which was cumbersome and uncomfortable; she knew all about the IUD, which caused dangerous infections, and the pill, which might cause cancer and which she had gone off of when she was in college. She did not believe now, there was no reason to believe, that she was part of the twelve percent—nor was there good reason to think that she wasn't, except that she preferred not to. She would use the sponges every time. She would not have sex when she was bleeding. She would be more careful than careful, if they would just make her unpregnant this time, this one time. Please.

They left her to wait again, left her sitting there, remembering the first time she had heard about the options. They had not changed much since she was fifteen, when her father had taken her to a doctor to be counseled on sex and birth control. She'd had a boyfriend, and her father had worried that with no mamá to counsel her she would get pregnant, which, she supposed, she might have soon enough. She did not remember any counseling, but they had come away with a prescription for the pill. *Pobre papá,* she thought morosely. He had not known then that he was signing away his only chance for a grandchild.

By the time Tina's turn came, she had almost gotten over being nervous. The nurse told her that she could have an anesthetic if she wanted one, but she didn't really need it. The shot probably hurt almost as much as the procedure, which, the nurse assured her, would be over before she knew it. So Tina said okay, who wanted a shot she didn't need? She undressed and got up on the table and put her feet in the stirrups as directed—and was immediately nervous again.

The doctor came in, but he didn't greet Tina or acknowledge her presence there on the table, with her knees sticking up. He stayed down at the end of the room, and she craned her neck around to the side to see what he was doing. He was a large, unsmiling man, dressed in a loose-fitting brown shirt instead of doctor's white, and he was fooling with a machine. Tina dropped her head back, waiting for him to come around to the head of the table and talk to her. But he stepped up to the stirrups instead, and she could only see him if she lifted her head and shoulders. He didn't say anything. Her knees had fallen together in a more natural and modest position, and he pushed them apart. With no more warning than that, she felt cold hard metal shoved roughly into her—she closed her eyes. She felt him tightening a screw, prying her apart, without a word, without a single word, and then she opened her eyes because it hurt as he shoved something else into her, something from the machine, she could hear a motor, and this time he just kept pushing deeper and deeper, and oh god it hurt, it *hurt*, as if he had crammed his fist, his whole arm up into her and was grabbing handfuls of flesh and pulling it slowly away from her bones, yanking out her soul piece by piece and scraping at the raw spots with his claws—it hurt, but they said it would be fast, and so she held the pain and waited for it to end, to be fast, but it didn't end and the pain kept growing and growing, *What was he doing?* If she only knew, if she only knew what and when and why she could hold the pain, and she lifted her head and said quickly the words in a rush please, please, how much longer, please, oh please, just tell me tell me tell me what you're doing. But no one answered, no one said a thing, and all she could see was this large brown monster looming between her legs, and she held the pain, she thought she was holding the pain and she didn't realize that she was fighting, that she was pushing him away, off, out of her—so that when finally it eased, when the pain let up and the pressure eased, she thought it was over, finally over. But then the nurse was pressing her knees apart, and Tina lifted her head and said, "Isn't it over?" and the nurse broke the code of silence to tell her that no, she had forced the speculum out. Relax, the nurse admonished, holding her legs open. Just relax.

He shoved the speculum back in. Rougher. Tightened the screw. Tighter. Shoved in the cold arm, and kept on shoving, the claw having at it, taking its time, scooping out her womb as if it were a pumpkin to spook the children with, a rotten pumpkin to be carved out scraped out destroyed, and this time she could not hold onto this pain that was not fast, that was not one minute or two minutes, not three, four, five, not a thing to be got through, not a cure, a remedy, not a shot to be endured a medicine to be taken, six seven eight minutes of scraping and scouring pain that she could not, no she could not hold on to. She started to scream.

They ignored her.

When he finally yanked everything out of her, she could feel the metal dragging at the sides of her vagina as if he would yank that out as well. She had stopped screaming. She was whimpering, she could hear herself whimpering, and then she was crying with such a deep, physical shame and remorse she couldn't separate it from the pain in her womb, and she wanted her mother, wanted to tell her, Mamá . . . What mother? There was only papá, and there was Chip, and they were hovering like two disfigured birds about her head, and all she could think to say to them was that she was sorry, so sorry, she hadn't meant to deny them, to be so horribly selfish, and now she had let them down, let everyone down including the doctor who was so disgusted he had disappeared without ever having uttered a single word, and the kind, sensitive nurse giving her the pads for the blood and helping her dress and leading her to a room where she could rest and she was so very very sorry she had caused them so much trouble.

Chip was pacing up and down the balcony outside the waiting room, where they'd sent him because he was making the other patients nervous. She let him help her walk, though she thought she didn't need his help. Shouldn't. When they got to the stairs he simply picked her up without asking and she knew by the ease with which he carried her that she was almost weightless, just an empty scraped-out, vacuumed-out shell of a thing, a weak, empty, unstoical, less-than-woman woman. Useless.

"Are you okay?" he asked her, because she was crying again, saying I'm sorry, I'm sorry, I'm sorry, and though neither of them knew what they were talking about he set her down on the seat of the truck and held her, saying it's okay it's okay it's okay.

He worried over her, and she let him. She let him worry that night, when she curled up with the pain washing through her abdomen, and she didn't tell him that it wasn't such a terrible pain, that it was the huge brown lump of doctor lurking between her legs, the *memory* of pain that made her cower so with each brown clot of blood she passed. It couldn't possibly have been that bad, she told herself. Could it? Longer than fast, but not long after all. She'd been on that table—what, a half-hour? Forty minutes? Or less even—she realized she had no idea. She thought about women screaming in childbirth and men pacing for hours and hours, a much greater pain, certainly, a pain that deserved those screams, a clean, shameless, useful pain. It's okay, she said, the next morning. I'm okay. And she went to work, against Chip's protests, took her blood and her cramps and her edgy tears to the lab where there was a pretty good chance she wouldn't have to talk to anyone if she didn't answer her phone. She said it was okay, and she kept saying it was okay, no big deal, it was okay, because she couldn't believe, was ashamed to think, that it wasn't.

Chapter 24

She was still bleeding the day she met with Orloff to discuss their paper. She had been bleeding for over a week. Tired, no matter how much she slept, racked by a deep limb-numbing exhaustion. Fighting it. It was like having her period, she told herself. Same blood, same cramps, same emotional fragility, same hormone-weakened condition . . . Not a particularly good time to be meeting with Sylvia Orloff.

They couldn't agree.

Perhaps her explanation of the paleo-CO_2 method was uninspired, Tina thought. Orloff was noncommittal. She heard Tina out, seemed interested, but not enthusiastic, as Tina had hoped. Orloff was not convinced that it was worth delaying publication of their Cretaceous core results, which was what Tina wanted to do.

They were sitting in Orloff's office, Sylvia behind her desk, Tina opposite, the graphs spread out between them. They were looking at the exact same set of data—same graphs, same numbers, same correlations and lack of—but what they saw was not the same.

As far as Tina could see the only things that were clear in that data were the same things that had been clear when they'd looked at the results from the first two sites: a warm Cretaceous and the advent of permanent ice sheets in the late Eocene. The strontium data did indicate elevated hydrothermal activity during the Cretaceous and show a general decrease at its end, but as far as Tina was concerned that was the extent of what they could say about it. She wanted to do a paper on just the ice results, the

Eocene O-18 and Saturation Index temperatures. This discovery, she argued, should stand alone in any case. But Orloff wanted to publish their complete span of temperature and strontium data with a big sprawling discussion of the climatic effects of hydrothermal activity, weathering, continental drift, and deep sea circulation.

"But there's so much here we can't explain," Tina protested. "It's just not enough—"

"Proof of a greenhouse Cretaceous isn't enough?"

"But even that isn't totally clear in this data." Tina set her forearms on the edge of the desk and leaned forward, trying to summon energy for this argument. "All we know for sure is that there was a bit more CO_2 being spewed out of the mantle than there was in the Tertiary. And then there's Zhang's C-13 record of organic carbon storage, which is showing a surprising correlation with my temperature curve—"

"—and isn't supported by any other geologic indicators of organic matter in the sediment or rock record, including your own shipboard analyses of the organic content of the cores. Or the published data for other DSDP cores. Nor does it jive with what we know about terrestrial organic matter storage."

"But that's my point! There's too much we can't explain. But if we had actual values for the atmospheric CO_2, we could see directly how it was related to these changes in climate. And with *that* crucial variable constrained we really *could* evaluate the relative importance of various inputs."

"But this new method you described—you say you haven't even adapted the instrument to do the measurements. We have no idea if it's going to work, or how long it will take. But we can account for some of the gross features of these temperature curves right now, and I think we ought to do it." Orloff started folding up the data printouts in front of her.

"I just think we need to dig a little deeper before we publish this," Tina said. She paused, squeezing her eyes shut in a protracted blink. "Why don't we just publish the Eocene data now? The advent of the ice is such a clear result. Why can't we just wait on the rest of it, give the paleo-CO_2 a chance?" She could hear the tears threatening at the edge of her voice. Untimely, traitorous tears. It sounded like she was pleading.

"*If* you get the paleo-CO_2."

Could Sylvia sense her weakness? she wondered suddenly. Could she smell the blood that was like the blood of a period but not, did it inspire contempt . . . ? Tina stood up. She had to get out of there. "I want to split this into two papers," she forced herself to say. The ice was hers, after all, her idea, her Saturation Index, her paper, with Sylvia Orloff as second author. She could insist. "If you want to publish the strontium results without me, that's up to you. But the evidence for the formation of ice in the Eocene is so solid that I don't want to mix it up with—"

"Fine," Orloff said, to Tina's surprise. "You have everything you need here?"

Tina nodded, not daring to make a sound. Had she just imagined that Sylvia Orloff was being uncooperative? She took the file Orloff was offering. Gathered up her notes and graphs. Maybe Sylvia just wanted to make sure the paleo-CO_2 project was going to fly before she committed to it.

The study was straightforward and eloquent, the paper Tina produced short and to the point. It practically wrote itself. Tina was proud of it. It took her a week, during which she stopped bleeding.

She was supposed to go for a checkup, but she could not bring herself to crawl up on a table and put her feet in the stirrups, even at the university clinic, where there was a female gynecologist. She could not, did not, would not go. With the willfulness of an only child, she reclaimed her body, and there was only one thing she knew now that she hadn't known before: she would never do it again. And though she knew that couldn't be right, to have a baby you didn't want just so you wouldn't have to go through the abortion, it was, finally, what made it okay. What enabled her to force the pain, shame, and remorse out of her thoughts not three weeks after the fact; to inhale the Narcissus-scented air of spring and feel lust for the man who'd had the foresight to set the bulbs in the ground in the middle of winter; and to utter the corny new words—I love you, *te quiero, te amo*—that she'd learned to say without irony.

She gave the ice paper to Orloff for review on Monday, and she found the revised version in her box in the department office on Friday afternoon. She had expected her draft back, with Orloff's notes and comments attached, but what she found was a fully revised manuscript, ready for submission. It was stapled together and there was a yellow Post-it stuck to the front: "*Sent 4/2/83, Geochim. Cosmochim.*"

Tina stood in front of the row of staff boxes, staring at the three-word note. No explanation, not even "I took the liberty of . . . " As if that had been their agreement. April second—that was yesterday. Tina glanced over her shoulder at Ruth, who was typing at her desk across the office. A grad student was hanging around waiting for something. She looked back at the Post-it. Sylvia hadn't even signed it. Tina tried to remember the note she'd penned on the draft, something to the effect that Sylvia should add whatever was needed about the O-18 and anything else she thought was missing. A geologist's insight was what Tina expected, perhaps a reinterpretation of the hard rock record to account for ice in the Eocene. It was probably fine, Tina thought, starting to skim the paper. She had just assumed that she'd see the paper again before it went out—indeed, she had assumed she would be the one to send it.

It was not fine. Tina hardly recognized her own paper. Orloff had added the strontium data and a discussion of the Cretaceous results, precisely what they had agreed not to include. She'd presented the strontium as evidence of a Cretaceous greenhouse effect induced by CO_2 emissions from hydrothermal activity. A series of linked equations was used to estimate the atmospheric CO_2, and there was a long discussion of the various geochemical processes they represented.

Tina left the office, reading the manuscript as she walked. There was nothing in the paper that she categorically disagreed with. Six months ago she might even have been pleased with such a wide-reaching, speculative work. Six months ago it wouldn't have bothered her so much to produce a work that used a limited description of the carbon cycle to guess at paleo-CO_2, or claimed CO_2 was responsible for the high temperatures of the Cretaceous when they could only guess at how much CO_2 it would take to produce such temperatures. Tina stopped at the top of the stairs to finish looking over the manuscript, then flipped the pages back into place and started down. Arguments about CO_2 and paleoclimate had always been suspiciously circular. Indeed, Tina thought, recalling her foray into global warming research, arguments about CO_2 and climate in general— paleo, historic, and future—were circular, because that had been the best they could do, the only way they could approach it. But now she was in the process, on the verge, of doing better, and such a discussion only muddied the water for what was to come.

Sylvia couldn't possibly have misunderstood her intentions for the paper. But why would she do this? It didn't make sense. The simple, eloquent beauty of the ice discovery was lost and obscured in this longer work full of conjecture and uncertainty—why hadn't Sylvia seen that? Tina pushed the door open and stepped outside. An April storm had broken up that morning, and a north wind was still blowing. The sky was alive with dark, theatrical displays of clouds, moving overhead with such grandeur that Tina felt her dilemma belittled. She had no idea what she was going to say to Sylvia Orloff.

She followed the path through the trees to the geology building and rounded the corner in front of its west entrance. She was about to enter the building, when she saw Orloff down below on the drive that led to the parking lot, talking to Katharine. Tina couldn't hear their voices, but they appeared to be having an animated conversation, a small dark figure gesticulating with the briefcase in her hand, and Katharine, standing tall and regal in a brightly colored sweater and bluejeans, tossing her blaze of blonde hair defiantly into the wind. Tina stared in astonishment: the sea was glistening in the sunlight behind them, a small black cloud was cruising over their heads, and Katharine was towering like the Statue of Liberty above her boss. Sylvia Orloff, whom Tina had always seen as a tall, stately woman, was in fact not much larger than Tina herself. And Katharine, who tended to slouch when she talked to Tina, straining to hear and be heard, seemed content to stand erect and let her words fly loose in the air above Orloff's head, where she could catch them if she would—though it appeared that she wasn't inclined to try. Orloff gestured impatiently toward the parking lot with her briefcase, and then the two women parted, Katharine turning up the walkway toward Tina, just as Tina decided to start down it.

Tina sighed and stopped walking, not relishing the idea of running after Orloff, waving their paper at her. She watched Katharine striding up the path in all her big-boned pink-cheeked glory, her thin lips curving into a smile when she saw Tina.

"She's in a fury," Katharine said cheerfully, as soon as she was in earshot.

"Sylvia's in a fury?" Tina said, thinking that she was the one who ought to be angry.

"Affirmative. Professor Orloff is pissed off. I told her about my new job."

"You got a job?"

"Yes. Come on, I'll tell you about it. Where are you headed?"

"Actually, I was headed up to your office. To talk to Sylvia," Tina said, looking toward the parking lot, where Orloff had disappeared.

"Oh, she's gone for the weekend now," Katharine said. "But let's go up to the office. It's freezing out here. I can't wait to move—San Diego, here we come!" She grasped Tina's arm. "Can you believe it? We're getting married! Fred actually took me out to dinner and proposed, gave me a ring, the whole bit." She stuck her hand out in front of them so Tina could see the gold band with its tiny diamond. "Not bad, is it? For a mathematician."

"It's nice," Tina said, pulling open the heavy door of the geology building and holding it for Katharine, who sailed past her like a Nordic goddess. She looked positively beautiful, Tina thought, literally aglow.

"The wedding is set for July twelfth, and then we're going to Europe for a month for our honeymoon. My mother is beside herself that we're not giving her more time to plan the wedding of the century, but I'm glad. I don't want my wedding to be one of her big show-off affairs. I wish you could be there, Tina. I don't suppose there's a chance . . . ?"

Tina shook her head. "I don't think so. Where do they live—Texas?"

"Dallas. What if— What if I gave you a ticket? I could ask my parents, for a wedding present—"

"Oh Katharine, I couldn't do that."

"I guess not."

"Tell me about your job," Tina said as they entered Katharine's office.

"It's on the Navy base." Katharine plopped into the chair behind her desk, and Tina set down the manuscript she'd been clutching in her hand and hoisted herself up on the table next to the computer.

"In their environmental lab," Katharine went on. "There's a whole research team dedicated to cleaning up their messes. Trace metals, mostly. And oil. They're trying to figure out what to do about all the oil they spilt on the floor of the bay down there. I know it doesn't sound that exciting to someone like you, Tina, but you wouldn't believe what they're paying me. I guess they have a hard time attracting research scientists."

"Well, it will be a change from what you've been doing here. Why is Sylvia mad? Isn't your postdoc up pretty soon?"

"Are you kidding? The Navy? I might as well tell her I took a job as a garbage collector. Sylvia sees herself as the creator of superwoman scientists—meaning tenure-track academic scientists publishing in *Nature* and *Science* and *Geochimica* several times a year. It adds to her power, having us scattered throughout the country's finest research labs. Whenever we publish important work people are supposed to look at the name and think, 'Oh, of course, she was one of Sylvia Orloff's students.' But now we're betraying her right and left. First Janice decides that having a baby is more important than a Ph.D. from BIO, and now I'm going off to work for the Navy and publish who knows what kind of drivel, if I even publish at all. She probably wouldn't have cared a year ago, but now we're going to have this major paper with our names linked so that it looks like I'm one of her protégés. If I disappear into oblivion now, it looks like she's failed."

Tina had picked up the manuscript she'd laid on the table. She tilted her head to the side and looked at her friend, feeling more perplexed by the minute. "So . . . you knew she did this?"

"Did what?"

"Rewrote our paper to include your strontium data without my consent?"

"What do you mean without your consent?" Katharine righted herself in her chair. "She said you'd agreed, that you'd decided to include the— No?" Tina was shaking her head. "You didn't talk about this? You still want to do the ice and the strontium in separate papers?"

"Wanted."

"Oh, I don't think she's—"

Tina held up the manuscript with its Post-it note for Katharine to see.

"Oh no." Katharine got up and took the manuscript out of Tina's hand. She looked at the note, paged through the text, and started striding about her office at random angles. "The bitch. The damn bitch. The royal bitch to end all bitches. She's done it. She's gone off the deep end, gone completely banana-bonkers. She really has."

"Maybe we're overreacting, Katharine. I mean, she's so arrogant, maybe she really *did* think I wouldn't mind—"

"No. She did it on purpose. I should have known. I should have suspected. Look at this. Janice did most of these O-18 measurements, but is Janice's name on the paper? No. Janice has up and died and gone to hell in a hand basket, never to return."

"I don't understand any of this. Why would Orloff deny authorship to her own grad student? Even if she did quit—"

"Spite," Katharine said. "Pure spite. Oh lord almighty, Tina, did you see this? Did you agree to this?"

"What?"

"She put the star next to her name. Tina, the way she has this it looks like we're *both* Orloff's Women."

Tina reached for the paper.

Her name was listed first, then Katharine's, and then Orloff's. But the star that indicated the author to whom correspondence and questions should be sent was next to Orloff's name, a common practice for principal investigators publishing with their students and postdocs. "Shit, what does she have against *me*?" Tina tossed the manuscript aside in disgust. "*I didn't quit to have a baby.*"

Her own words caught her by surprise, slammed into her like cold metal twisting, scraping, sucking at the softest of tissues, bringing to mind what she had so carefully banned. The muscles in her thighs and buttocks tightened, and she gripped the edge of the table, forcing herself to focus on what Katharine was saying. She had not told Katharine about the abortion, and she had no intention of telling her now.

"She doesn't have anything against you," Katharine said. She had started pacing again. "She wants your data. Your good ideas. You. She wants you. She's a shark in a feeding frenzy, wants to sink her teeth into everything that's fresh and new. If you ask me, she still has plenty of good ideas of her own, but it's not enough for her. Never enough. It's a kind of greed." Katharine walked back to her desk and sank dejectedly into her chair. "I'm sorry, Tina," she said contritely. "I had no idea she would do anything this perverse. I should have known, I should have warned you, I should—"

"Katharine," Tina said, relaxing her grip on the table. "Give me a break, will you? You can't know everything. Anyway, you *have* warned me about Sylvia. I just ignored you." She glanced at the manuscript lying next to her leg where she'd tossed it, and she was filled with regret. The paper she had written had been so clean, so solid and self-contained, the clear-cut beauty of the ice discovery standing out like a jewel, not obscured by fuzzy speculations. "I'm just going to have to ask her to withdraw it," she said.

"Good luck. She'll never agree to that. Not unless you force her hand, tell her you're contacting the editor. And that would be a mess—I mean, what would you say? 'Sylvia Orloff submitted a paper without my consent. The star is by the wrong name.' Like they're going to believe you." Katharine paused, then pushed herself upright in her chair. "The thing to do," she said, picking up a pen and tapping the tip of it on her desk, "is make up some innocent excuse, send a note to the editor and withdraw the paper without telling Sylvia. You'd risk her wrath, of course—no, you'd be assured of it. She'd never agree to resubmit the paper. If you do that . . . Well, if you do that, we'll have to sit on this finding." Katharine dropped the pen and slumped back in her chair. "Lord. You're damned if you do and damned if you don't."

Tina looked at her. She had no desire to "sit on" the ice finding. And Katharine hadn't mentioned that she herself would be disappointed if the paper wasn't published, but Tina knew it must be true. She glanced down at the manuscript again. It wasn't as if it misrepresented their findings. It just *confused* them. And so what? The advent of ice in the Eocene was clear enough. And if her paleo-CO_2 work made things any clearer for the Cretaceous then she would write another, better, paper. And if it didn't, then Sylvia's discussion wasn't all that bad anyway. She picked up the manuscript and flipped it over, laid her hand on top of it. "You know what, Katharine?" she said. "This whole thing is extremely weird. And depressing. And intensely frustrating. But in the long run, it probably doesn't matter that much."

"Of course it matters. Don't you see what she's done? Any work you do now that's even remotely related to this, and people are going to look at your name, Cristina T. Arenas, and think 'Sylvia Orloff.' Don't you see? It's Sylvia's way of linking herself to whatever you do."

Of linking herself to the paleo-CO_2 work? Tina couldn't help but wonder. She shook her head. It didn't make sense. Orloff had been skeptical of the method, reticent about collaborating on it.

"This is an important paper, the first you've published on this stuff, right? And Orloff has manipulated it so that it looks like she was the driving force behind it."

It had not occurred to Tina, when she'd been arguing for two separate papers, that a paper containing the strontium results would be more Orloff's than hers; and, as a matter of fact, the placement of the star by Orloff's name in the paper as it stood now was not entirely without justification. She blinked, trying to clear her head. "I can't believe that she actually planned it that way," she said. It was too ludicrous, like a millionaire planning the burglary of a convenience store . . . and with such elaborate scheming. "It's hard to imagine Sylvia Orloff spending her precious time thinking about this sort of thing."

"Oh, she didn't, I assure you. She doesn't have to think about it. It's second nature. That's what happens when you work in a certain environment long enough."

"God, Katharine, for someone who's about to get married you sure are sounding cynical." She should probably be angrier, Tina thought, but she was mostly just confused and depressed by the whole affair—a quagmire of duplicity and ambition, it seemed, which she would do best to give a wide berth. Let Sylvia Orloff wade through the mud if she wanted . . . though try as she might, Tina could not picture the dignified, principled scientist she was acquainted with slogging through the mud. Of course, until a half-hour ago she'd also thought the woman was tall and physically imposing. "I don't think anyone is going to divorce my name from this work," she said, trying to reassure Katharine, who actually seemed angrier than she was. "The method is already published, for one thing. And I really think we're onto something with this paleo-CO_2 method. Though, without Orloff's collaboration . . . I don't suppose C-13 analyses in surface forams is something one could do in a Navy environmental lab, is it?" She smiled, meaning it as a joke on herself, but as soon as the words were out of her mouth, she wondered if it didn't sound like a put-down. Katharine, however, just shrugged.

"Not likely," she said lightly. Then her face lit up and she sat forward in her chair. "But I've still got a few months here," she said. "I can do them before I go. Or when we get back from Europe in August. We're not moving until the end of September, and I told Sylvia I'd work until then. She doesn't have to know anything about it—"

"Oh no," Tina said.

"Why not? We've already got samples sorted, all I have to do is change the—"

"Katharine. Forget it."

Katharine sighed and slumped back in her chair. "It would be such sweet revenge," she said, and Tina couldn't help but laugh.

Chapter 25

The Brayton summer blues didn't stand a chance with Tina this year. The summer fog was as unrelenting as ever, descending on the coast in late May and staying glued in place through most of August, but Tina hardly noticed it. She put together an NSF proposal that was so solid and original there was no need for sideshows, no call for buzzwords. This year not even a biased program director could say that Brian Maitland or Sylvia Orloff or anyone else had the field covered: Cristina T. Arenas had ploughed it up and reseeded with her own unmistakable breed of grass.

Once she'd sent off the proposal, Tina started spending more weekends at the farm. She became accustomed to the scratch of the bay tree on the roof all night, to the songbirds singing her awake at dawn, to an extra hour or two of sleep. She noticed that she rarely needed an afternoon nap anymore, though whether it was the extra sleep, or a change in the nature of her work she wasn't sure. Sometimes it seemed as though the naps were tied to a need for something more than sleep, to some groping, wandering state of mind, and for now, as she analyzed cruise sediments and developed her new method, she seemed to know where she was going. Michael finished the kinetics experiments, and Tina helped him write up the results and submit a paper; in June he left for Boston, eager to start in the lab at MIT.

At the beginning of July, Tina's landlords finally came from New Mexico to enjoy their 'edible landscape.' They stayed through August, and Tina found she rather liked having them next door. Though Brayton was at its foggiest, they didn't seem to mind, even seemed to relish the cloying damp and chill. The cool coastal summer was the reason they'd bought the property, they told Tina, and fog or no fog, they always seemed to be outside puttering about in their yard or sitting on their deck. They were retired, in their early sixties, and once they'd figured out the relationship between their tenant and their gardener—and that Tina was the only reason Chip continued to work for them—they were friendly and solicitous almost to a fault. When Chip told them that he had extricated himself completely from the landscaping business, they carried on about their yard as if they were the owners of a famous newly dead painter's art.

Chip was oblivious to the praise his clients lavished on his landscaping work. It pleased him no end to be free of it, to be able to say, that summer of '83, that the farm was finally standing on its own two feet. He was intensely, fiercely, proud of this fact, proud of the produce he and Jorge were harvesting, of the wooded hills they had resisted clearing, the pasture they had reseeded in native grasses, of the healthy, mature orchard by the creek, and of the growing demand for organic vegetables in northern California—a demand that Chip had played a large part in fostering. The produce market in San Francisco was now buying the entire crop of tomatoes, and two North Brayton restaurants had arrangements for year round biweekly deliveries of salad greens. The potatoes they'd planted in what had once been the espalier field were such a huge success that Chip and Jorge spent the first couple weeks of August arguing about whose idea they had been, until Meche reminded them that it had been her idea to plant potatoes in the new field—though the five gourmet varieties that accounted for their marketing success had been Chip's idea, and Jorge's insistence on an extra load of compost probably explained the bumper crop. With the landscaping business out of the way, Chip thought he would be able to take a vacation that summer, and he talked about taking Tina backpacking in the Sierras. But the trip was delayed by slow-germinating tomato starts, and then by Tina's grant proposal, and after that a bad case of poison oak she got from picking wild blackberries along the creek, and then there was a shortage of workers for the tomato harvest and a new band of rampaging pigs . . . until finally Chip stopped talking about going backpacking and satisfied himself instead with hikes and picnics in the hills around the farm.

Sometimes they walked for miles, up the creek to the north, or over the hills to the ridge where they could see the ocean, and once they went all the way to the beach. But mostly they climbed the same hill, not far from the house, less than an hour's walk to where they had a view out to the river. There was a single oak tree at the top of the hill, and they would spread out their blanket in the grass at the edge of its shade and eat their picnic dinner. Sometimes they made love up there, and once they stayed late and hiked back looking for owls by the light of the full moon.

Spending more time at the farm, Tina was beginning to understand Chip's pride in it, his feeling for the place and what it represented, how all his passions, his earnestness—about the environment, the local politics, the precarious global climate, even his love for her—had rooted themselves in its California clay. Whether it was this understanding, this deepening respect, that loosened her tongue, or the simple fact of no one else to talk to, Tina didn't know, but she regularly talked to Chip about her work now, her vacation love life and her real life beginning to dovetail, the moods and thoughts from the one slipping in and out of the other as if they were part and parcel of a single package, if not quite one and the same.

On this particular mid-August Friday afternoon they were walking up the hill to their oak tree and talking, or rather Tina was walking and talking, and Chip was just walking, climbing up the deer path in front of her. She had just started the paleo-CO_2 analyses on the cruise cores, and she was excited by the result.

"I'm giving a talk at the big AGU conference this fall, and you know what I'm calling it? 'Midget Plankton Tell it Like it Was: Climate and CO_2 of the Mid-Cretaceous and Early Cenozoic.'" Tina giggled, though Chip didn't say anything. "The thing is, they make you register so far in advance, I had to write the abstract for the talk before I even started the CO_2 analyses. It's an act of blind faith, you know, promising to present data you don't have yet—and then hoping you can make some sense of it." She'd called Garrett the other day, because she'd wanted to tell him about her talk—Garrett, she figured, would get a kick out of her title—but he wasn't around. She hadn't seen him all summer, though they'd spoken briefly on the phone once or twice, and he'd just sent her reprints of their paper. He'd enclosed a funny note about his work on the meteorite, said he planned to present it at the AGU conference and asked if Tina wanted to drive down there with him. When the schedule came out, Tina thought, grabbing the branch Chip was holding so it wouldn't whip back into her face, she'd call and offer him a ride down in *her* car. Though that was months away. Maybe she'd call sooner, see if he wanted to get together for lunch.

"So," she said to Chip's back, "you might ask, What is it that the midget plankton have to say?" She jogged a few steps to get up alongside him, taking hold of his arm to slow him down.

"I might ask," Chip said, glancing down at her. He pushed her gently back onto the path. "If you think you can stay on the trail while you tell me. The poison oak is fierce in here."

They were on the steepest part of the hill, climbing up the barest hint of a path, through a tangle of oak and bay, madrone and horse chestnut. She fell back into line behind him and kept talking. "Actually, I don't know the whole story yet. Remember I told you about this method for determining CO_2 from the picoplankton lipids? Well I've finally got all the kinks worked out. I just started running sediments today. Hopefully I'll have them done before the conference. And hopefully they'll shed some light on what the midgets have told us about the climate. We've shown irrefutably that the Cretaceous was warm, right? An average of five degrees warmer than now, to give you some idea, nine degrees Fahrenheit. And we've shown that it was an all-tropical world, without any temperate or polar climates like now."

"Tina." Chip had stopped and turned around, and Tina thought he was going to ask her a question.

"What?"

"Are you watching out for the poison oak? It's smaller in here, hard to see."

Tina glanced around. They were up where the brush wasn't as thick, which made walking easier, but he was right about the poison oak. It was tucked down in the detritus where you couldn't see it, almost worse than down below where the vines rose up in front of your face. "I'm being careful," Tina said, but Chip had already turned and was continuing up the hill. She hurried after him, trying to watch for poison oak while she talked.

"So, our work puts an end to doubts about the Cretaceous climate," she said, raising her voice to be heard above the afternoon cacophony of jays and screaming hawks. "But as for *why* it was so warm for so long and what caused the little fluctuations in my temperature data and then why it cooled . . . One possibility was that atmospheric CO_2 was high, creating a greenhouse effect—you know how that works. The sample I ran today was mid-Cretaceous, about a hundred and twenty million years old. And it looks like atmospheric CO_2 would have been seven to eight hundred parts per million! That's three times what it is now!

"Sylvia Orloff's lab found that hydrothermal activity was higher during the Cretaceous than it has been in the last few million years. Orloff thought that alone was strong evidence for a greenhouse Cretaceous, which it is. But there's very little correlation between my temperature curves and her estimates of CO_2 from hydrothermal activity . . . which might mean that CO_2 was not actually the dominant feature in the climate changes. Or it might mean that atmospheric CO_2 was regulated by other aspects of the carbon cycle. And then there are these other inexplicable bits of the puzzle. Like Zhang's estimates of organic carbon reservoirs. And my picoplankton productivity curve . . . Unfortunately, Orloff didn't agree with me that the study was too ambiguous to publish. I think I told you about this. She's the one who burned me by submitting our paper without my approval?"

Chip didn't respond, and Tina wondered if he was even listening to her. They were nearing the place near the top of the hill where the woods gave way to pasture, and she stepped up on a rotting log and paused to catch her breath, letting him go on ahead. She had never confronted Sylvia, but their interaction was now limited to the occasional brisk greeting when their paths happened to cross at BIO. Zhi-Jiang Zhang at Wood's Hole was collaborating on Tina's paleo-CO_2 project, doing the C-13 in surface forams. The paper that Tina still thought of as the ice paper, despite Orloff's additions, was scheduled for publication in November or December. Tina supposed that it could make things awkward at the conference, though, of course, that depended on what she came up with in the next couple of months—she couldn't wait to see the CO_2 curves!

She took a jubilant leap off the log she was standing on, but it failed to be much of a leap, the hill rising to meet her, the detritus causing her to stumble. She laughed and did a little curtsey when she noticed that Chip had stopped and was watching her from above. He turned and headed off across the pasture. He probably hadn't heard a word she'd said, Tina thought, squinting as she stepped out from under the trees into the glare of the afternoon sun. He had a way of filtering her monologues for what he considered to be the point of the matter, inevitably a different point from the one Tina thought she was making.

"I'm really excited about this method," she said when she caught up with him. He was standing near their oak tree at the top of the hill, gazing out at the view.

"I can see that. When is this conference?"

"Not until December. The American Geophysical Union sponsors it every year in San Francisco, a whole week of talks and poster presentations. I've gone to it a couple of times, but I've never given a paper. It used to be mostly geology, but they've been expanding the focus to include atmospheric and ocean sciences—which means just about everything. God knows what people are going to think when they see my abstract. I said I was going to talk about CO_2, hydrothermal activity and picoplankton productivity with respect to the sea surface temperature record. I figured that ought to make people curious enough to come to my talk . . . though I suppose I'll be sorry if I can't make sense of it all."

"You gonna stay down there?"

"I think so—a few days at least. I don't know. I was going to see if Garrett wants to drive down with me, so I guess it'll depend a little on what he's doing."

"Who's Garrett?" Chip turned away from the view to look at her.

"This guy from the university who I was collaborating with. In fact, our paper was just published. You've heard me talk about him, I'm sure."

"I don't remember you mentioning any Garrett."

Tina looked up at Chip's face and started to laugh. "You're jealous! I don't believe it, he's jealous of Garrett!"

"I am not." He looked away.

"If you saw Garrett . . . He's an old guy, my graduate advisor's advisor." It occurred to Tina that she'd once been sort of attracted to Garrett. "I've known him forever," she said more gently. "And he's gay, if that makes you feel any better."

"I am not jealous. I'm just wondering why I've never met any of your friends from BIO."

"I don't have any friends at BIO except Katharine. And Garrett."

"Well, if he's such an old friend, you should ask him up for dinner some time." He slipped the knapsack off his back and knelt to pull out the blanket.

Maybe she would, Tina thought, looking out at the wide river valley in the distance, the fields of Chip's farm nestling in the hills at its edge. Garrett might get a kick out of the farm . . . though what he and Chip would make of each other, she had absolutely no idea.

They positioned the blanket in the shade of the oak tree and set out the dinner Chip had packed for them. There was cheese, bread, a bottle of wine, tri-colored potato salad, and green bean salad with chunks of the giant orange-and-yellow striped tomatoes Chip was fond of but couldn't sell. Tina pealed the lid off the container of potato salad and eyed its contents—a mix of solid red, blue, and butter-yellow potatoes dressed with olive oil and garlic chives. Maybe, if she invited Garrett to dinner, he and Chip could talk about cooking. Maybe they would even like each other. She picked up the bottle of wine and the opener, smiling at the thought.

"What would that mean for us?" Chip said, lifting the bottle out of her hands. "That there was a greenhouse effect back then, during the dinosaurs' time."

"*If*," Tina said relinquishing the bottle opener, a little two-pronged affair that she had yet to use successfully. At least he'd been listening to her. Sort of. "I told you I just started this," she said. "I've only got one data point." She held out the camp mugs for him to fill. "What, you think it might be a lesson?" She set down the cups and picked up her fork. "A precautionary tale? Like maybe the dinosaurs had their own oil industry? Maybe they burned fossil fuel from the Carbonaceous period and got the world all heated up. Of course, the dinosaurs *liked* those hot days, those sauna-like marshes in North America. As did most of the other flora and fauna of the time. To tell the truth," Tina said, warming to her tale, waving her fork about for emphasis, "it appears that it might actually have been the cold that put an end to them all. My temperature curve shows a sudden dip at the KT boundary, about the time the dinosaurs disappeared, along with hundreds of other species. The current theory is that a giant asteroid smashed into the earth and raised so much dust it caused a sudden cooling. Not much of a cautionary tale in that, I suppose. But maybe," Tina exclaimed spearing a morsel of blue potato and holding it up in the air, "that's not what happened at all! Maybe they did it to themselves, after all—used up their fossil fuel and when there was none left to burn the CO_2 level dropped, and they had the opposite of our problem—"

"Makes it easy, doesn't it?" Chip interrupted her casually. "Living with your head buried in those sediments." Tina lowered her fork. He had stopped eating and was studying her face, the hint of a smile around his eyes, teasing, and yet somehow sympathetic.

Tina looked away and tried to shrug. She broke off a piece of bread and stuffed it into her mouth.

"You gonna answer my question?"

"What a greenhouse Cretaceous would imply for the contemporary greenhouse situation? I don't know. It was a different earth." Tina paused, chewing on more bread and watching the first stray wisps of fog float into view down by the river. "Eventually," she said, "with a good record of both CO_2 and temperature for the Cretaceous and Cenozoic, we may be able to understand the mechanisms and relative importance of internal feedbacks in the carbon cycle—ocean circulation and chemistry, primary productivity, sedimentation rates—compared to outside forcing from volcanism or hydrothermal activity . . . or the anthropogenic input." She turned to look at Chip, squinting, her head cocked to the side. "You know," she said, "it's a shame that they can't just turn off the anthropogenic CO_2, cut it off. Then you'd have this big spike of CO_2 into the atmosphere, sort of like the spikes of radioactive gases from atomic bomb testing that oceanographers use as water-movement tracers. The CO_2 spike would be an actual perturbation of the carbon cycle, and we could see clearly how various aspects of the cycle respond and how they affect the climate system. . . . But if we just keep injecting CO_2 it's not a perturbation at all. It's more like we've created a whole new component in the cycle—"

"Tina."

"Huh?"

"You talk like this is all just some experiment you scientists drummed up."

"No . . . I was just pointing out what a dumb experiment it is, actually." She glanced at his face. "I'm sure we could have done better," she added, grinning. But he didn't rise to the bait.

"I've been doing some reading about this," he said seriously. He was eating again, talking around mouthfuls of salad and bread. "I found a whole book about the greenhouse effect. You know, Tina, it's scary, all these scientists calmly arguing about whether temperatures are going to increase three or five or nine degrees when—not if, but when—the atmospheric CO_2 doubles. The politicians act like this is all off in some distant science fiction future, like the world ends with the millennium. But hell, fifty, a hundred years isn't very long. And that's what they're—" He interrupted himself and pointed at an osprey flying toward them from the river, weighed down by a huge fish hanging from its talons like a bomb.

"Incredible," Chip said softly when the bird had passed over their heads and out of sight. "They're really starting to make a comeback." He glanced at Tina, then reached for the wine and filled both their cups. "Now, there's an example," he said. "A scientist spoke up, loud and clear. Rachel Carson wrote a book that everyone could understand, and we did something. But no one is going to do anything about CO_2 emissions until you scientists come out and say, loudly and unequivocally, that burning fossil fuels is causing global warming. Unfortunately, that's a word most scientists don't seem to know—'unequivocal.'"

"I read the paper by those NASA scientists," Tina offered. "The ones who thought they'd detected the warming component in their averages last year. There were a lot of objections to their work, but everyone agreed that volcanic activity had obliterated the greenhouse warming we should have seen in the seventies—and now I guess El Chichón and that Indonesian volcano erupting last year will probably confuse the issue further. Anyway, the consensus was that we still can't see a definitive warming signal caused by anthropogenic CO_2, but by the mid-nineties—"

"Oh great," Chip said, making a vehement stab at the pile of bean salad on his plate. "Of course. We have to *be* in the future before we decide what to do about it. Another decade down this path of no return. Another decade for the developing countries to become as dependent on fossil fuel as we are, instead of looking for alternative ways to develop. What the hell are we thinking? It's not like everyone can suddenly stop driving their cars and using their washing machines and refrigerators, turn off the lights, just go cold turkey the second the scientists blow the whistle and say, 'Okay folks, we agree, we can detect the warming, you should stop now.'"

He paused to bite into the sandwich he'd assembled of bread and cheese, then went on, still chewing. "It's not really like DDT, where you could just ban a single chemical from use. We're talking about the whole base of industrial society here. It's going to take some time to change that.

We should have started twenty years ago—but, no, we're going to wait another ten years at least. In that book I read they had these predictions, based on various scenarios of fossil fuel use. The scenarios didn't even include cutting back use. No one is talking about that. Whatever little progress we made in the seventies to decrease our dependence has already been reversed. Do you realize that they just changed the rules for automobile manufacturers?" He turned to look at Tina, who was contemplating the container of potato salad, trying to decide if she could possibly eat more without making herself sick. She reached over with her fork and scooped out one last bite. "No," Chip answered himself. "Of course you don't. Well, for your information, our government has once again given its blessing to the building of bigger-than-ever gas-guzzling cars. The best-case scenario they gave in this book had us freezing fossil fuel use at the 1983 level—obviously an unrealistic pipedream—and even then they predicted that by the year 2050, the amount of CO_2 in the atmosphere will be double the natural level. And that when it doubles there'll be a three-to-nine-degree increase in temperature. That's Fahrenheit," he added, with a glance at Tina. "So much for the *best* case scenario. The worst, and most likely case, given the political climate in the most influential industrial nation in the world, was for an unrestricted increase in fossil fuel use. Then they expect CO_2 to double by the year 2020. They don't talk about what happens after that, but it doesn't stop there, of course, unless we stop. They talked about other things that are making it worse, too, like cutting down the rain forests." Chip paused to concentrate on his dinner. He finished his sandwich and emptied what was left of the potato salad onto his plate.

"I saw something else recently," Tina said, setting her empty plate aside and leaning back on her hands. "I think it was in *Science*. There's some indication that trace industrial gases might contribute as much to the greenhouse effect as CO_2 does. I don't think they've even tried to work that into the climate models yet."

"Christ. What a mess we've made." Chip shook his head, talking with his mouth full. "They didn't mention that in this book. And the predictions about the exact effects of this 'average' global warming were pretty confusing. But one thing they seemed pretty sure of is that a warming of seven degrees would be enough to melt the icecaps. The North Brayton boardwalk might well be underwater by the year 2050. They said that the climate could shift so drastically that northern California would be in a desert belt, like northern Mexico." He made an odd, bewildered little gesture that managed to take in the fields below, the hills and the river, even the ocean, off in the distance. "Just think," he said, "what our grandchildren . . . Hell, what our kids will have to deal with."

Tina turned to look at Chip, following his odd gesture, watching his face now. But he went on, apparently oblivious of the assumption in his words. He meant the "our" in a general way, she realized, what society's children would have to deal with. She reached for the last chunk of cheese and popped it into her mouth.

"We've just got to stop," he said. "All this . . . meddling. Not for us. Not even for our children, all our generations to come. But for everything else . . . "

"Everything else?"

"For— For the earth. For its own self," he said.

Tina rolled her eyes. "And how, pray tell, do you know what 'the earth' wants?"

He set his plate on top of Tina's and waved his hand impatiently. At a loss for words. "It's like . . . It's like we're fucking with God."

"God?" She laughed. "Since when have you believed in 'God'?"

He turned and glowered at her. "You know perfectly well what I mean," he said, holding her gaze.

A chill ran down Tina's spine, and the smile on her lips faded. She shifted her position on the blanket, sat up and hunched forward, examined her hands in her lap. Of course she knew. This reason that was no reason at all, that made so much and so little sense that she couldn't bring herself to think, let alone voice it. She glanced back at Chip, and suddenly his gaze softened and he smiled, abruptly, victoriously, as if he'd just understood the truth of his accusation.

"What you were saying about the carbon cycle," he said, "that we're creating a new component. You don't particularly like that idea, do you? That what you're studying is all man's doing. It's not as . . . What? Glorious? As studying nature's cycles. That's it, isn't it?"

Tina shrugged. Then she nodded.

"Of course, it all depends on who you believe," Chip said. "There are a couple of scientists out there who say the others are completely off, and we're not having any effect on the carbon cycle or the climate or anything. That guy Cox who quoted you says that global warming will never amount to more than half a degree—he's in all of the articles."

"William Cox is? What, in the newspaper?"

"Everywhere. He was even mentioned in that book. He and this one other guy, whose name I forget, represent the 'dissenting opinion.' But they seem to get more press than the majority opinion."

"I looked up some of Cox's papers a while back," Tina said. "And the only one that had to do with the global temperature sensitivity to CO_2 was entirely discredited a month after it was published. In fact, the consensus in the scientific community seems to be that the guy's work is a crock of shit—as one of BIO's most esteemed oceanographers so eloquently phrased it."

"Well, the press seems to have the impression that he's a perfectly legitimate voice in the scientific debate."

Tina considered this for a moment. "I don't know," she said. "Sometimes a paper is published and then later shown to be wrong—but in the meantime someone has referenced it, and then someone else sees *that* paper and references it, and so on, until pretty soon you have these totally wrong assumptions entrenched in the literature, and no one bothers to go back and assess the original paper." She paused, remembering the rebuttals to Cox's work. "But that's not what happened with William Cox's paper. It was so obviously flawed, it was discredited right away, the work dismissed. I doubt it's even been referenced since then. To tell the truth, it seems kind of irresponsible of the press not to have figured out that he doesn't know what he's talking about."

"Maybe it's irresponsible of the press," Chip said. "Or maybe they have a slanted take on this issue. But it's also irresponsible of all you scientists who won't talk to the press and enlighten them."

"We do talk to the press," Tina said. "When we have something to say."

Chip made a doubtful noise in his throat.

"Hey, I wrote a letter to the editor of your *New York Times* about this guy Cox," she said. "Remember?"

"Only because I bugged you." He picked up the bottle of wine and emptied it into their cups. "And you didn't really say anything."

"I didn't have anything to say." Tina drank the bit of wine he'd poured her and set her cup on top of their plates. "It's really strange," she said, "that Cox would keep mouthing off and making a fool of himself, when everyone knows he's wrong."

"'Everyone' doesn't know he's wrong, Tina. Only the few people who read your scientific journals know he's wrong. And from what you've told me about funding for research, it's easy enough to imagine why he's so outspoken. Imagine if everyone in your academic world thinks your work is a crock of shit. Or maybe they don't even think that, maybe your work is great," he said, turning to look at her, "but you simply can't get funding. Think about the compromise you made when you decided to write that proposal for the petroleum fund—"

"I'm never going to live that down, am I?"

"So one day," Chip went on, ignoring her, "these industrial scientists show up and start praising and applauding you and your work, like that thug from Petron, say, who visited your lab. Imagine that they arrange press conferences for you and you gain a certain amount of respect and fame from it all. Hell, maybe you even believe that you are doing good work and you close your ears to the criticism from your colleagues. You repeat the wrong thing so loudly and so often that it begins to seem like a real possibility."

Tina picked up an acorn from the ground at the edge of the blanket and rolled it between her fingers, pressing the pointed end into the flesh of her thumb.

"That guy called me again last week," she said.

"He did? And what did he say?"

"Fuel for your argument." She laughed uneasily. She hadn't wanted to tell Chip about the call, but there it was. "He's still trying to get me to collaborate. He saw a paper we did with Garrett that included some of the hydrocarbon kinetics, the work the ACS grant was for. He was really pushy this time. He went on and on about how promising the method is, how he's sure we could get project funding from NSF. I guess he knows that my ACS grant was only for a year. He told me about this experimental program NSF is initiating to encourage liaisons between industry and academic science. A company puts up half the funds and NSF matches them, or some such." Tina shook her head. "I don't know if it's just because I'm not used to the corporate world or what, but this guy made everything sound so sleazy. Like he was offering me a personal bribe or something, rather than just suggesting a collaboration on a grant proposal."

"Of course it was a bribe," Chip said, lifting his cup to his mouth and tilting his head back to drain it of the last few drops. "He was just using an appropriate currency. Guy must know he's dealing with someone who considers research funding more important than the roof over her head or the food in her mouth. Or the man in her bed." He slid his eyes toward Tina, then quickly away. "NSF is a federal agency, isn't it?"

Tina nodded, ignoring his gibes. "I'd heard about something like this," she said. "Collaborations between NSF and industry—I think Katharine mentioned it last year." She paused, thinking of Katharine, who would be back from Europe any day now, working in Orloff's lab until her move to San Diego. BIO seemed so quiet with her gone. "How Katharine always knows about these things, I'll never know," Tina said. "But the whole idea seems sort of suspect to me. Like it goes against what NSF is all about."

"Well, I'm glad to hear that your suspicious nature is, at last, beginning to apply itself to mundane events like the intrusion of for-profit interests in the allocation of taxpayers' money. So, what did you tell this guy?"

"I told him I wasn't interested," Tina said. "Then he has the gall to ask about Michael, but I told him that Michael had gone off to bigger and better things at MIT. God, I must have repeated myself five times. He said he was going to send me a pamphlet about the grants, just in case I changed my mind." Tina laughed. "The guy was like some sort of door to door salesman, or no, worse than that—what are those religious people who come on Sundays and try to convert you?"

"Jehovah's Witness. You have to tell them you're Jewish."

"Really? How about a Jewish grandmother? Dad says his mom was a German Jew—think that would work?" Tina was laughing, but when she looked at Chip, he was chewing on his mustache, his forearms resting on his bent knees, his hands dangling between them, the empty cup suspended loosely in one. He was gazing intensely at the valley, the dark band of river winding lazily down its green belly, a pale swath of fog crawling slowly up, the hills rolling off to the horizon on the other side. . . . As if whatever he was planning to say next—as if everything he might ever want to say about anything—could be read from within that horizon, in this small arc of the planet where he lived.

"What are you going to do?" he said finally, not turning away from the view.

"Do? I don't know that there's anything to be done."

"What about funding for next year?"

"I told you, I sent in an NSF proposal over a month ago. It includes this new paleo-CO_2 work. I'm sure they'll fund it now," Tina said, her good humor returning as she thought about the proposal. "Who knows, maybe BIO will even offer me a real job."

"And if they don't?"

"I think they'll let me stay as a researcher as long as I have money," she said. "Though I'll have to share the lab, because Max Lindquist is—"

"No, I mean if NSF doesn't fund your grant."

"They will."

"Why?"

"Because it's good." Tina turned to look at him. She reached over and took the cup out of his hand, put it next to hers on top of their dirty plates. She lifted his right boot off the blanket and extended one leg, then the other, and then she climbed on top of him and sat straddling his hips, blocking his view. "Because," she said, pressing on his chest until he lay back, "it's *exceptionally* good. Because it asks, and hopefully will provide answers to, worthy questions—questions a lot of scientists want answers too." She stretched out flat on top of him and laid her head on his chest. "And because," she whispered so that he couldn't hear her, "I want to stay in Brayton."

Chapter 26

Tina hadn't called Garrett. She hadn't called Garrett, and now it was September and she was going to call Garrett last week but she hadn't gotten around to it, and she was going to call yesterday, or today, or maybe she would call tomorrow . . . She lowered the syringe in her hand very, very slowly, listening to Katharine's news.

Katharine had been back for almost a month. She would be gone in a few days, off to San Diego. Maybe Tina would miss her then, but right now all she wanted was for Katharine to take her news and her contented newly-wed face and get out of the instrument lab.

She was vaguely aware that she was choking.

"I'm sorry," Katharine said. "I know you were sort of friends."

She was aware of tears rising—not quiet, sad tears for a sort-of-friend, but great wrenching sobs—and she was aware of holding them down, concentrating very hard to keep the tears back as if she were desperate to pee and trying to hold it until she got to the bathroom. She would hold the sobs until Katharine went away and she even said, very faintly through her closed-up throat she said, "Go away," but Katharine didn't hear her.

"What?"

Tina just shook her head.

She saw him in the Mercury, his flying boat car sailing off the cliff into the sunset, with his foot pressed flat to the accelerator, and he didn't fall, didn't nosedive into the rocks at the edge of the surf in bloody annihilation,

296

but rather moved quietly out over the sea like a great white blimp, his momentum carrying him to the middle of the Pacific where he would finally fall from the sky and sink ever so gently into the deep sea. There was a little puff of sediments as the Mercury settled onto the sea floor. Garrett turned on the lights, but there wasn't much to see on the floor of the north Pacific. An occasional fish. He would be bored.

Tina looked at the syringe in her hand. Her face was dry. Katharine had left the lab. The sobs had fallen back into her chest, an aching tightness just below her throat. The HPLC was pumping away, waiting for the injection. She raised the syringe and looked at the sample she had drawn—no bubbles, so she inserted the needle into the injector, slowly depressed the plunger.

He must have taken the curve too fast, Katharine said they were saying. Well, of course he had. He was speeding. On the curve. He was always speeding, curves or no curves. *You can cry all you want in this car. All you have to do is find the Mercury, let yourself in. It's never locked.* Find the Mercury. At the bottom of the cliff, at the bottom of the sea, nestled like a lost treasure chest on the floor of the lonely north Pacific. Did she know what cliff, which curve?

They would have pulled the car up, taken it to a wrecking yard. *It's probably a better place for crying than the library. Feel free to use it any time.*

Sort of friends. They had sort of been friends.

Maybe she wouldn't even have heard, she thought, if not for Katharine. She would have called him eventually, this month or next, or maybe not until November or December to make plans for the conference—and found someone else installed in his office, his lab, because surely they wouldn't waste time reallocating his lab space. Who would take care of his files of papers, his notebooks, his meteorite samples? What would happen to his house—all those records, his knickknacks, the photographs?

She walked down the hall to her office and called the Chemistry Department secretary at the university. Tina said she was a colleague of Garrett Thomas's down at BIO, a friend, and she wondered if she might be of help sorting through his things. A good friend, Tina said.

It was all being taken care of. A memorial service was planned for the following afternoon. They had sent out notices to the faculty and staff at the university but they hadn't thought to send them down to BIO. The secretary gave Tina the details, sounding a little weepy herself, an older woman. It was such a shock, she said, sniffing. But what about his stuff? Tina asked, feeling foolish. Who was taking care of that? Oh, his brother, the secretary said, his brother had flown out from Chicago. There had been a will, she confided, but apparently everything was left to a friend in France who had passed away that winter. It was a good thing, said the secretary, that the brother was a lawyer. Very convenient. Right, Tina said, and hung up, thinking of the photographer who had died on the street in Paris, the friend who had got the last word, the long-distance lover, who had up and died and made Garrett sad.

She hadn't known there was a brother. What would a lawyer know about meteorite samples? And his notebooks, what about his notebooks? She supposed the Chemistry Department would be taking care of all that.

She went to the library. She wandered through the stacks, tears leaking quietly down her face while she gathered up armloads of journals, and then she stood at the photocopy machine copying every paper she could find by Garrett Thomas, beginning with the ones that had won him the Nobel Prize in 1952. She found his two books on the shelves, the first published in 1960, its pages well-worn and stained, the card in the front covered with stamps that ended on June 4, 1978; and the other, published five years ago but looking brand new, its binding a smooth satiny brown with the title in gold letters, only two stamps on the card, the last that same day in June, the year of its publication. She wiped her face on the sleeve of her sweatshirt and went downstairs with her pile of photocopies and checked out both books.

When she called her father the evening after the memorial service, Tina didn't tell him that her heart was pounding with fear and dread while she waited for him to pick up the phone. She hadn't talked to him in weeks, and she wanted to ask him why he hadn't called, but he answered so matter of factly, so cheerfully, that she felt ridiculous. It had always annoyed her that he felt compelled to talk to her every week; she couldn't very well complain because he'd taken to calling her less. They had a brief conversation, and Tina didn't mention that she had just gone to a memorial service for a colleague whose car had flown off a cliff, and that the colleague had been her friend, and that the friend was a man about his age, a lonely man with a dead lover and no daughter to love and care for him. She didn't tell her father that the death of this colleague in an accident had filled her with superstitious dread and concern for his safety. Her father was not, after all, a reckless driver. In fact, he was careful to a fault, the type that held up lanes of traffic because he insisted on maintaining the speed limits that everyone else ignored. Nor did her father sound sad or lonely today. Indeed, he seemed unfailingly cheerful, and once he'd asked about Chip and realized that she hadn't called him with any momentous news, he was eager to get off the phone and go about his business, whatever that might be at eight o'clock on a Saturday evening.

She left Garrett's books on the easy chair. She left his papers scattered across her desk along with the wayward chromatograms and unopened mail and yellow note pads. They were at once penance and consolation, strewn about her office, waiting to be read, touchstones to a pain the memorial service did nothing to ease—the single brother, dry-eyed and expressionless in his black suit, the esteemed colleagues eulogizing Garrett Thomas, talking about his work, his contribution. When Tina knew, and they knew, when everyone knew that none of it mattered or would matter, that Garrett Thomas had disappeared without a trace and all claims to the contrary—his books in her chair, his papers strewn across her desk—were but flimsy consolation.

Chapter 27

The data trudged slowly and meticulously into Tina's charts and onto her graphs, and summer stretched into fall, and she never did hire a technician to replace Michael. Garrett's papers shifted about her desk like dusty heirlooms with no display case or context, their title pages stained with the dull green of spilt *mate* as Tina worked over and around them, always planning to read and file them, putting it off. Her NSF proposal scored high and was selected for funding. The days got shorter and cooler, and in November it started raining. Chip stopped fretting about irrigation water in the pond and started worrying once again about slugs and snails, about the river rising, the creek flooding, the lettuce crop lost. . . . It rained so hard the last two weeks of November that the road to the farm became impassable to all but Jorge's four-wheel-drive truck, and then even that got stuck and Meche had to walk back to the house in the driving rain with their three kids. Chip was stranded at the farm then, busy digging drainage ditches so the road wouldn't wash out altogether; and Tina stayed in town, where she hardly noticed the rain as she struggled to complete the work she wanted to present at the conference.

Two things were abundantly clear in Tina's new data: that during the last half of the Cretaceous and once during the early Eocene, the CO_2 content of the atmosphere had been over three times its modern-day value; and that CO_2 had been a major, if not the dominant, driving force in the climate changes from the mid-Cretaceous through the mid-Eocene. The correlation between Tina's CO_2 data and sea surface temperature over some eighty million years was more conspicuous and more consistent than she or anyone else had expected. It was only natural, given such data, that she would want to quantify the relationship. Only natural, that it would put her in mind of a certain gray day spent at the library trying to decipher William Cox's misguided reference to her work, reading about problems with climate model predictions of the effects of anthropogenic CO_2. . . . Waiting for Garrett. Feeling a little queasy. It was back in March, and she had been pregnant, when it first occurred to her that her ancient sediments might provide what the climate modelers needed to assess the "Great Experiment." But she had never dreamed that she would be able to calculate the temperature sensitivity to CO_2 with such confidence and precision. Until she saw her amassed data.

By the end of November, that data had mounted a campaign for explication on every front, drafting into service whatever neglected and half-forgotten ideas it could summon—dream epiphanies, intuitions, beer-fortified rants on a moonlit Pacific stage, and off-on-a-tangent library queries, all the wild and untamed riffraff of Tina's questioning soul transmuted into the solid and reasonable stuff of science. The correlation between picoplankton productivity and temperature that had baffled Tina since she first started analyzing the cores was now easily explained by the close correlation between CO_2 and temperature, which longstanding theories of chemistry and physics accounted for, and by the negative correlation between CO_2 and picoplankton productivity—which not even the most radical of recent hypotheses could account for. Roy's work failed to shed any light on this latter. The picoplankton did not grow faster with more CO_2, or slower with less, and it was unlikely that changes in CO_2 had caused their productivity to vary. That the inverse might be true, however—that the picoplankton might have had an effect on the CO_2 content of the surface waters of the ocean, and thus the atmosphere—was something Roy had no way of assessing. And the numbers in Tina's charts, the forms of her curves, every way she found to analyze her data indicated that changes in picoplankton productivity were the driving force behind most of the fluctuations in CO_2 from the mid-Cretaceous until the end of the Eocene.

The best way to explain a clear result that no permutation of established theory or hypothesis could account for was, of course, to make up a new hypothesis. The picoplankton were apparently responsible for locking carbon away from the atmosphere-ocean cycle on timescales of several thousand to millions of years. But how? And where? Where did they put it? Tina turned to an oft-forgotten and neglected stash of carbon, the dissolved organic carbon, the DOC, that was the residue of life in the ocean. This deep sea cache of dissolved organic compounds was amorphous and elusive, infinitely more varied and complicated than the dissolved nitrate, phosphate and CO_2 that were life's raw materials, and attempts to characterize it were fraught with problems—but there was no denying that it contained a lot of carbon, at least as much as was in the atmosphere. Tina's hypothesis maintained that the picoplankton were somehow locking carbon away from the atmosphere in the DOC. Somehow. The hypothesis could explain her curves and Zhang's benthic foram record of organic carbon storage, which Orloff had dismissed as unreliable—she could even find a tidy way to account for the periodic dark bands of black shale and the undulating temperatures of the Cretaceous—but she couldn't do anything about that big gaping Somehow. Roy was working on it with his cultures, but they needed more than that. They needed shipboard studies, they needed biological oceanographers, she needed to figure out ways to analyze the DOC . . . they needed help before they could even give a name to the Somehow. And so, the first week of December, just three days before the conference, Tina decided to include the fledgling hypothesis in her talk. She would toss that big Somehow out to her colleagues as a challenge, get them interested in the picoplankton, provoke them into action. That's what conferences were for, after all—new work, fledgling hypotheses.

The day before Tina was to leave for San Francisco, the rain let up and Chip and Jorge finished repairing their road. Chip called to tell Tina he'd be coming down to Brayton, and they made a date to go out to dinner. It was a little before noon when he called, and Tina was drinking *mate* and planning her talk, her desk a chaos of notes and transparencies, all waiting to be ordered into the folders she'd laid out. The problem was that she couldn't figure out how to fit everything into a twenty-five-minute talk with five minutes for questions.

There were three folders: one for the materials she would present during her talk; one for her reserves, to include anything that might come in handy for answering questions and objections afterward; and one with reprints of her papers for anyone who was interested. Only the folder of reprints was full. Tina fished the transparency of Orloff's strontium data out of the mess and set it in her presentation folder. Fortunately, their paper was still in press. She was going to be in the odd, uncomfortable position of naysaying her own paper, but at least no one would have read it yet. And, ironically, the star by Orloff's name meant she would have to handle the complaints and queries when the paper appeared.

Tina found the three transparencies she'd made of her own core data. One showed sea surface temperature, the curve and the temperature scale on the axis drawn in red; another showed CO_2 in black; and she'd drawn the picoplankton productivity curve in a cool blue-green. She laid the three graphs one over another the way she planned to do for her talk, and stood above her desk with her *mate* gourd nestled in one hand, looking at them. She was going to talk about the long uneven heat wave of the Cretaceous, and about the resilience of the picoplankton during the KT holocaust at its end; she would refer to the spike in CO_2 at the beginning of the Eocene, an event that spanned two million years, as "abrupt," and discuss the ten-million-year decline that came after it. She would talk about the relationship between CO_2 and sea surface temperatures, about the sensitivity of these ancient climates to changing atmospheric CO_2, which the good resolution and detail in her data allowed her to quantify. And then, with these eighty million years and thousand meters of sediments in evidence, she was going to leap blithely upcore to talk about a time so insignificant that it hardly registered a skin on the surface of the slowly accumulating sediments of the deep sea.

It almost seemed indecent, Tina thought, to view these curves that rose and fell with the slow grace and considered pace of geologic time, ponder the long magnificent reigns of dinosaurs and cyanobacteria—and then jump scales to the short lurid reign of man. But it was also exciting, like a short circuit in time, as dazzling and unnerving as an arc of lightning between clouds.

Tina caught herself toying with the *mate* straw, dredging it through the *yerba* in a violation of *mate* etiquette that would have sent her father up the wall. She set the gourd aside and stretched. Then she picked out the transparency she planned to open her talk with and held it up to the light.

It was one of Roy's electron micrographs of the three species of cyanobacteria, two blue-green spheres and an ovoid huddled together in the middle
like teammates debating their next move. Tina had printed her title across
the top: "Midget Plankton Tell it Like it Was: Climate and CO_2 of the Mid-
Cretaceous and Early Cenozoic." There was nothing wrong with the
title . . . but it seemed incomplete.

Tina retrieved the Chemwipes and some methanol from the lab and
rubbed out the title, changing it to read: "Midget Plankton Tell All: Climate and CO_2 of the Mid-Cretaceous and Early Cenozoic, and New Figures for Temperature Sensitivity in Contemporary Climate Models." She
wondered if any of the carbon-cycle modelers would come to her talk, or
even some wayward atmospheric scientists. Would Harper Gibson be
there? Conroy Decker? What would they make of her picoplankton now,
when they saw this data, heard her new hypothesis...? Not much, Tina
thought, staring at the mess on her desk, if she didn't get it organized. She
looked at the clock. She'd been   daydreaming for the past hour,
and she felt tired and dazed, the mate doing no good whatsoever. She
glanced at the easy chair. It had been months since she'd napped there.

She had to clear the chair of its accumulated junk—her knapsack and
jacket, a change of clothes, a lunch bag with an uneaten apple . . . Garrett's
books nesting in the little cavity where the cushions came together at the
back. She picked up the books and dusted them off on her sweat pants.
The Origin of Life Session at the conference was being dedicated to Garrett. There was a dinner planned later that evening, also in his honor, and
Tina thought she might go, though she wouldn't know anyone. She slipped
the books into her knapsack and set it on the floor next to the chair. She
didn't have to return them until someone requested them, and no one
had—but she would drop them by the library on her way home. Maybe
they would catch the eye of someone walking past the QE300s, the gold
letters on the spine of the one, or the faded cloth binding of the other.
Maybe she would take them off the shelf occasionally and leave them out
on a table by the new journals where a passing scientist or student might
pick them up, curious—not looking for anything in particular, but wondering what was in the books, if there might be something worthwhile
there, something he might not need, but would like to know. . . .

She's wearing a suit. And a tie, and big black shoes with wedges in the
bottom. She has these ribbons that she's trying to hang up for everyone to look

at, red and black and blue-green ribbons that she's trying to tack up on the pro-
jector screen, but they won't cooperate, won't stay where she pins them. There's
a Mahler symphony playing, the andante movement—very serious and dra-
matic music that Garrett is conducting with his eyebrows, his face tilted down
for all to see—but the ribbons won't go for it, won't wave in time to this sober
symphonic beat. They want to boogie. In fact, that's what they're doing, they're
dancing up a storm and there's nothing for it but to kick off the shoes with the
wedges, throw off the suit jacket and dance. They're dancing around the may-
pole, wrapping it up in red and black and blue-green, all boogying to the tune
of some old rock 'n' roll song from the sixties. It's fun. But then the music
changes again and the dance changes and now Tina doesn't know the moves.
She doesn't know how to dance to this music, there's just no keeping up as they
slam dance their way through the eighties, piercing nipples, growing mohawks,
turning off the lights and leaping into the dark uncertain future of the next mil-
lennium— She grabs for the pole. She wraps herself around it, arms and legs,
hugging it tightly, like she used do before sliding down the pole in the play-
ground she played in so fearlessly as a child. But this is no Jungle Jim pole, and
she is not fearless. This is a great, swaying tube of sediments, wrenched from
the earth and suspended in dark space, and she squeaks along inch by inch,
clinging with sweaty hands and legs. She loosens her hold for a second, just to
see what will happen, and the core suddenly tilts like a seesaw and sends her
sliding, not down-core but up, and she is gaining speed, swooshing along in the
fast lane, where the rules are different and unfamiliar, where she never learned
how to play—

What the hell? What the hell is she doing here, hanging like a fool, clinging
to such an infinitesimally narrow band of sediments at the end, the wrong end,
of this core? She looks up: the core rises reassuringly above her. She looks
down at her dangling feet—nothing to see down there, it's dark. Why, then,
must she look, and look again, must she contort her head and strain to see out
past her feet into this dark unborn time? It's dangerous, perhaps foolish. And
exciting. And illicit and slightly obscene, like peering into the future of a fetus
with no future.

Chip was so exhausted from digging drainage ditches that Tina thought
he was going to nod off right there in the restaurant, keel over into the
kung pao chicken and braised bean curd with mandarin sauce while she
talked. By the way she talked, one would have thought that she was the

one who'd been stranded for the past two weeks, shipwrecked with this pack of ideas that she was preparing to present to her colleagues but hadn't yet shared with anyone, had hardly spoken aloud. They had finished eating and were sipping tea when Chip finally interrupted her monologue.

"Is it news yet?" he said, suddenly looking wide awake and ready for action.

"Huh?"

He pushed his tea away, folded his arms on the edge of the table and leaned toward her. "Seems to me it's news now," he said.

"What's news?" she said, like a fool.

"That billions of years ago there was three times as much CO_2 in the atmosphere as now."

"Millions, not billions."

"And that the earth was a hothouse because of it. And that you can tell how the climate is responding to the carbon dioxide from—"

"No, they'll have to feed my temperature sensitivities into the models to get an idea of—"

"Seems to me there's a *lot* of news here. Like that the fecundity of a teensy weensy algae that stashes carbon away in the deep sea controls how much carbon dioxide remains in the atmosphere—"

"That's just a hypothesis, Chip."

"And that those same little algae are probably responsible for hiding away part of the man-made CO_2 that scientists can't find—"

"That's pure, unadulterated conjecture."

"—and that since we don't know much of anything about the ecology of these algae, we can't know what will ultimately happen to all this hidden CO_2, which could at any moment be released from its cache and belched back into the atmosphere, thus accelerating global warming—"

"You *would* choose the most speculative aspect of this very solid work to glom onto, wouldn't you?" Tina looked at him in wonder. She had been talking to him about her work, and now here he was spewing it back at her. How strange it was to hear it from his lips, so concisely framed, his clear and simple summing up of the point he saw, his description of the forest where he so effortlessly ignored the trees.

"Does the press come to these conferences?" he said, breaking open the fortune cookie the waiter had brought and popping half of it into his mouth.

"I don't know. I think a few science writers come. But I doubt they'll be at the Paleoceanography and Paleoclimatology Session."

Chip glanced down at his fortune. "It wouldn't kill you to go to them," he said, crumpling the slip and tossing it onto his plate.

"Chip, I'm giving a talk. I'm going to write a paper soon. The people who need to know will—"

"Christ, Tina, what a snob you are." He picked up the other cookie and the bill and stood up.

"I'm not a snob," Tina said in a surprised, high-pitched voice. But even as she said it she wondered if he might be right. She knew that her colleagues looked askance at scientists who dealt with the press, as if it were indicative of science that was less than rigorous, a certain laziness or paucity of ideas. She had never given it much thought before, but now it seemed to be a perception she shared, something bred into her in graduate school.

Chip was looking at the slip from the cookie he'd just broken open. "This was supposed to be yours," he said, grinning.

She looked at the fortune he handed her: "One evening's conversation with a superior man is better than ten years of study." She followed him over to the cash register and waited while he paid the bill.

He was still grinning into his mustache and looking smug when they got back to the apartment, and later, when the phone rang and he picked it up and started chatting with her father, Tina thought for sure Chip was telling him about the stupid fortune cookie. She was in the bedroom packing for her stay in San Francisco, but she went and stood next to him, waiting for him to hand her the phone. Her father was apparently doing most of the talking, obviously in no hurry to talk to her. She knew he liked Chip, but what was he going on about? She hoped he wasn't depressed. Sometimes he got depressed around the holidays. Chip, however, was smiling, nodding and interjecting an occasional "¿verdad?" and "That's great."

Tina sat down on the couch to wait. Maybe he'd changed his mind and wanted to come up for Christmas after all. She'd splurge and buy him a last minute ticket. If they planned it right she could pick him up at the airport when the conference was over; maybe they'd even spend a couple of days in San Francisco. She hated to think about him down in L.A. all alone, going out to some chain restaurant for his Christmas dinner. He'd said he couldn't get away, but she didn't see why. She supposed if he'd pushed a little she would have gone down there . . . though now that she thought about it, he hadn't even asked her to go down to L.A. for Christmas. Chip finally relinquished the phone. "It's about time," she said, taking the receiver he held out. "Hi Dad."

"Hi sweetheart. *¿Todo bien?* I have some wonderful news for you."

"You're coming up for Christmas?"

"I went to the graveyard last week. *A hablar con tu mamá.*"

"Oh." Tina picked up the phone, stretched the cord over to the couch, and sat back down.

"We had a long talk. You know it's still there, our little cross for Canela?" Her father chuckled. He didn't sound depressed. He had been telling her this about the cross every time he went to the graveyard for the past twenty years, and every time he told her he sounded equally surprised and pleased that the dog's illicit grave had not been desecrated. "I wanted to wait for you and Chip," her father was saying. "But then we decided it was better this way. Tina, sweetheart, *tu papá se va a casar.*"

Her father stopped talking, waiting for her response, and Tina felt as though her senses were suspended, frozen in confusion, as though she couldn't understand his simple words.

"Tina?"

"Yeah, Dad. But . . . I mean, that's wonderful, I guess, but . . . Uh, who . . . ?"

"Jackie. Jacqueline Spitzer, *¿sabés hija? La que vive abajo.*"

"She lives in the building there? I've met her?"

"No, I don't think so. When you were here? Two years ago? She moved in after that."

"Are you sure about this, Dad? I mean, it seems sort of sudden."

"Sudden? You think? It's one year and a half. And twenty since—"

"No, I didn't mean that. You've known her—Jackie—a year and a half?"

"Yes."

"When—?"

"January two. For the New Year. We are going to do it at the courthouse. Now, hija, that doesn't mean you and Chip should do it that way. *Es que nosotros somos viejos. Y una boda, pues . . .*" There was a pause, and then her father said, "*Tina, tu mamá—Me deseó—felicidad, tu mamá.*"

"Well of course, Dad. I mean, I don't think she ever expected . . . " Tina didn't finish her sentence. What did she know. Her mother's ghost had never talked back to her.

"Now you will have someone to help with your wedding. Jackie is very excited to have a daughter. She has two sons, but she never sees them. She was divorced a long time ago, but her husband died so now you might say she is a widow too."

Her father went on about Jackie, and Tina wondered, tried to remember if he'd talked about her before and she hadn't been paying attention, or if he was only now talking about her—maybe he'd had to get permission from the ghost to even talk about her. She questioned him, trying to sound enthusiastic, trying to sound happy. Well, of course she was happy. She had wanted this for years, wanted it all her life, hadn't she? *Una mamá. Su papá feliz, independiente, sin ella.* Happy without her.

Chip was in the bedroom when Tina hung up.

"He's getting married," she said to the empty living room.

"I know." He came in from the hall with a huge smile on his face. "It's great. No wonder he didn't want to come up for— Oh, Tina," he said then, laughing. She was crying.

"I just hope he knows what he's doing," Tina said, as if this had anything at all to do with her tears.

"He's a grown man," Chip said, still laughing as he walked over and reached down to hug her.

She stood up and buried her face in his belly and cried like a little girl, glad that he didn't say anything else, didn't ask her to explain. What could she explain? That when she should be pleased that her father was happy, that he would have company in his old age, that she was relieved of the full burden of his attention and expectation . . . she felt hollow and disconnected instead, as if she were still a child tugging at his hand and he had suddenly let go, leaving her to float away like an unattached balloon, without purpose or direction? That the suitcase she had just been packing, the clothes she was choosing, this conference where she would stand up in front of her colleagues and present the work she was so excited about seemed suddenly insignificant and pointless, that she felt like a performer abandoned by her best fan?

She pulled away from Chip and wiped her face on her sleeve.

"At least I know this Jackie's not marrying him for his money," she said, forcing herself to smile. "I guess I should be hoping *she* knows what she's doing."

"He didn't tell me much about her. Just that she lived there in his apartment building."

"She's from New York. A school librarian . . . Can you imagine? My dad with a librarian?"

"Sure. Why not?" Chip smiled. "It's a lot easier to imagine than a farmer with a snobby chemist," he said. "Your dad reads. He likes books."

"Yeah." Tina nodded. "He said they have a lot in common."

Chapter 28

On the first day of the conference, Tina went shopping. At four o'clock in the afternoon there were no more talks she wanted to hear and she was in the city for the first time in she couldn't remember when, and the dress she'd brought to wear for her talk the next day was the same dress she'd worn at every presentation she'd given since her doctoral defense four years ago . . . so she went shopping and bought herself a new outfit. A suit, of all things, she bought herself a suit. She found it in the juniors department and it was very stylish, a parody of a men's suit—at least it felt like a parody to Tina, who was feeling vaguely uncomfortable in the midst of her suit-bedecked male colleagues at the conference; there were also people wearing jeans and Birkenstocks, but not when they were giving presentations. Tina's suit looked respectable enough, once she got it out of the juniors department, but the cut was fitted and just a little sexy, the material a soft, cream-colored rayon. The next day, as she was standing off to the side at the front of the conference room, waiting for the person before her to finish answering questions so that the moderator could introduce her, Tina was aware of this, that she looked pretty and respectable at the same time, and she was glad she'd bought the suit.

Five minutes into her talk, however, it didn't matter what she was wearing: her audience was already raising a ruckus.

Tina had shown the picture of the cyanobacteria and briefly discussed the *Rover* results that she, Roy, and John Carr had published back in March, the high values of primary productivity in the North Pacific gyre when the picoplankton were included. She wanted to waste as little of her twenty-five minutes as possible explaining her methods, so she'd raced through a description of the Saturation Index—which was a published, if not long-established technique—slapped a map of the cruise sites on the projector for two seconds, and then rushed headlong into her results.

The buzz started as soon as she put up her red graph, the sea surface temperatures. Tina kept talking.

"The positioning of the continental landmasses during the Cretaceous has long been the most accepted explanation for the warmth and equability of its climate, but in recent years this explanation has lost, rather than gained, credibility. The Saturation Index temperatures for these sites allows us to lay to rest doubts about whether the climate really was warm and homogeneous." She was using the end of a pen for a pointer on the overhead projector, and she ran it back and forth along the Cretaceous section of the temperature curve. "As you can see, average sea surface temperatures in the late Cretaceous were six to twelve degrees Centigrade higher than in the modern oceans. Our friends the dinosaurs were living in a virtual sauna—though note," Tina indicated the undulations in the curve, "that there was some disagreement about where to set the thermostat.

"With these high temperatures and the similarity of temperatures for sites from the equator to forty degrees south, it seems safe to say that ice did not exist even in the interiors of the northernmost continents. A comparison of the O-18 and Saturation Index data supports this conclusion, as you'll see in a moment." Tina paused. She knew she was talking much too fast. She inhaled slowly, filled her lungs, exhaled. Then she moved her pen along the curve to the end of the Cretaceous, stopping at the KT boundary.

"There is a little dip here at the KT boundary, but you can see that temperatures didn't begin a steady downward trend until well into the Paleocene. That trend was interrupted by a sudden heat wave in the early Eocene," she indicated the spike at the beginning of the Eocene, "after which the downward trend resumes, a little more gradually, and then, toward the end of the Eocene, we begin to see an increase in the range of temperatures between mid and low latitude sites."

Tina picked the graph of O-18 temperatures out of her file and laid it on the projector over her own. "Here we have temperatures from the oxygen isotopes in surface forams for the same series of samples, work done by Katharine Cline, Janice DeWitt, and Sylvia Orloff. As you see, the two curves diverge in the late Eocene," Tina said, raising her voice as the buzz got louder and more unruly, "indicating that a permanent ice cover has begun to form— Hold your horses!" She turned to face her audience and held both hands up to quiet them. "A paper on this is coming out in *Geochimica et Cosmochimica Acta* next month. I've got preprints here to placate the skeptics." She slipped the O-18 curve off the projector leaving her red Saturation Index curve in place. "But right now, I have something new I want to discuss."

There were some snickers, and Tina realized that everything she'd shown so far was new. She paused and peered out at her audience, but she couldn't see much beyond the ring of light she occupied with the projector. People came and went between talks, going off to another session or to view the exhibits or posters, and she had no idea who was out there now. She'd seen Orloff's new grad student floating around earlier, but no one else she knew from BIO had been at the morning paleoclimate session.

"The most plausible explanation for this Cretaceous heat wave," Tina went on, "requires an elevated level of CO_2 in the atmosphere, but until now there has been no real evidence for this, and no reliable method for obtaining it. Nor can climatologists agree on just how much atmospheric CO_2 is needed to produce such elevated temperatures."

Tina went on to give a brief explanation of her paleo-CO_2 technique— too brief, as it turned out. When she laid her black CO_2 curve over the red temperature curve, the buzz started up again, louder and more insistent, inexorably skeptical.

She had misjudged. She had not explained enough about the method to convince them that they were really looking at a graph of CO_2 for the eighty million years spanned by the cores. She'd been hoping they would suspend their disbelief until time for questions, cut her some slack.

She should have known better.

Tina glanced toward the back of the conference room, where she could make out the dark forms of people standing in the open doorway to the corridor. No one seemed to be walking out. And no one was actually interrupting her, the way they would have at a BIO seminar. But she knew that if she ignored their objections and went on as planned, they would spend the next twenty minutes grumbling and planning out arguments, rather than listening to what she had to say. That's what she would have been doing, anyway.

"Okay," Tina said. She was standing balanced on her toes, like a dancer in mid relevé. "Let's back up." She forced her heels down firmly on the floor, set aside her graphs, and opened up her folder of reserves.

She was fully armed. She'd known they would question the method eventually, and she had transparencies that summarized the work she and Roy had done to develop it. She went through them as quickly as possible, explaining how Roy had grown cultures of picoplankton at varying concentrations of CO_2 and she had extracted the lipids and analyzed for carbon-13; she showed a graph of the results, and explained the equation relating CO_2 and isotope fractionation that she'd fit it to, citing the studies that had been done on corn. She showed how well the lipid C-13 in picoplankton from water samples replicated the measured CO_2 concentrations, and how the lipid C-13 in a thirty-year sequence of surface sediments reproduced Keeling's atmospheric CO_2 curve for the same period. Finally, she explained how Zhang's isotope analyses of surface forams in the cruise cores provided the background C-13 for the paleocean.

When she finished, Tina paused and glared at the dark room full of her colleagues, challenging them to object. When the room remained quiet, she quickly set aside the folder of reserves and replaced her temperature and CO_2 graphs on the projector.

"As I was saying . . . " she went on, with an air of tried patience that drew a few laughs. She set the tip of her pointer on the transparency, sliding it back and forth along the Cretaceous section of the curve. "One of the most obvious and dramatic results is this outrageously high CO_2 concentration in the Cretaceous—more than three times the modern level." She froze the pointer on the vertical scale to emphasize the values. "Sylvia Orloff has suggested that CO_2 released by hydrothermal activity might have been responsible for these high Cretaceous temperatures, and she and Katharine Cline used the strontium isotopes in the carbonate as a proxy." Tina laid a graph of Orloff's data, done in orange, over her black CO_2 curve. "This is the hydrothermal activity derived from that data, which is described in our paper in press," she said. "When that paper was written, we only had the temperature curve, but now we can compare the hydrothermal activity with our record of atmospheric CO_2.

"You can see some general agreement, a relatively high level of activity for the mid to late Cretaceous, and a general decline throughout the Cenozoic. But the decline is not enough to account for the attendant decrease in CO_2, and none of the finer detail of the CO_2 curve—these undulations in the Cretaceous, this dip at the KT boundary—are evidenced in the hydrothermal input. Clearly some other factor or factors were playing an important role in modulating CO_2."

Tina removed the orange graph from the projector, leaving the CO_2 and temperature in place. She laid her blue-green curve over the black and red ones, and carefully aligned the three graphs.

"Given our evidence that the picoplankton play a substantial role in the ecology of the open ocean, and that their lipids are so ubiquitous in deep sea sediments . . . I decided to take a look at picoplankton productivity in these cores." She turned to look up at the screen. "Actually, these data were a byproduct of the Saturation Index study, and, if the truth be known, I thought maybe I could get something for nothing."

No one laughed. They were too busy staring at the interplay of red, black, and blue-green lines projected on the screen.

"The blue-green curve," Tina said, "shows the ratio between lipids specific to the picoplankton, and a broad group of common phytoplankton lipids. In other words, you're looking at how picoplankton productivity *deviated* from overall marine primary productivity . . . and the correlation with the CO_2 curve is absolutely amazing." A murmur went up from the room, and Tina smiled: this was a murmur she had anticipated. She tilted her watch to the light and took a deep breath, reminding herself that she was not on her death bed and she did not *have* to "tell all" in the next eight minutes. "It appears that changes in the composition of the marine plankton were somehow driving shifts in atmospheric CO_2 concentration, with a change toward higher picoplankton production relative to other phytoplankton—like this dramatic one at the KT boundary—leading to a decrease in CO_2. And a relative decrease in the picoplankton, like here in the Eocene, leading to a rise in CO_2 . . . " Tina moved her pointer along the blue-green curve, lingering in the Eocene ravine, which was mirrored so perfectly by a slightly offset spike in the black CO_2. "But how? By what mechanism could picoplankton affect CO_2 concentration so dramatically?

"According to conventional wisdom, most of the organic carbon produced by phytoplankton in the surface waters of the open ocean is rapidly recycled in the water column, with only a small percentage reaching the sediments, and an even smaller percentage escaping remineralization by bottom-dwelling bacteria. For atmospheric CO_2 to be affected—for it to be drawn down, say, like it was in the mid and late Eocene, or here in the valleys of these Cretaceous undulations—either the total productivity of the ocean would have to have increased; and/or sedimentation rate would have to have increased; or the organic matter reaching the sediments would have to have been better preserved. According to conventional wisdom. We might even go out on a limb and postulate that the composition of organic matter buried in the sediments changed, the ratio of carbon to nitrogen and phosphorus. These are all changes that we should be able to detect in the sediment record—and don't. Yet, Zhi-Jiang Zhang at Wood's Hole analyzed the carbon isotopes in benthic forams for these same cores and concluded that the proportion of carbon tied up as organic matter did indeed change in concert with the atmospheric CO_2."

Tina paused and took another breath. She knew she was talking too fast again, but there was nothing for it now if she was to get through everything—and suddenly it did seem imperative that she get through it all, not in the papers that would come out of this work months and years down the line, but right here, right now, at this conference in this room full, or half-full or quarter-full, she couldn't tell how full, of her colleagues. She wanted to set these new ideas free in the world, send them home with these scientists, let them get to work.

"I would like," she went on, "to hypothesize that organic carbon can be stashed not only in the sediments, but in the oft-neglected dissolved organic carbon, the DOC, of the deep sea. And that the picoplankton, with their unique physiology and environmental adaptations, make a larger and more refractory contribution to this deep sea stash of DOC than do other classes of phytoplankton. A shift in plankton ecology that favors the picoplankton would then result in an increase in this persistent portion of the DOC and a draw-down of pCO_2, and so forth.

"We're not likely to find direct evidence for such a mechanism in the sediments, but we may garner some clues from study of DOC in the contemporary ocean, and we can learn more about how and what the picoplankton might contribute to it by studying their ecology and biochemistry.

"Which leads us to our next question: what environmental factors would have favored or hindered the growth of the picoplankton relative to other classes of phytoplankton? What caused these fluctuations in the late Cretaceous? This spike at the KT boundary? This decrease in the Eocene and its reversal?"

Tina slipped the water column profile from the *Rover* study back on the projector. "At this point," she said, "we can only look at how the pico-plankton differ from other phytoplankton and speculate. Notice the deep water maximum in picoplankton productivity in this profile from the North Pacific. I don't have time to show you, but Roy Shimohata has been doing culture studies on the picoplankton's response to various environmental factors, and they are remarkably tolerant to low levels of light and nutrients. We might imagine that this was what allowed the picoplankton to thrive during the catastrophe at the end of the Cretaceous—that spike in relative productivity at the KT boundary—while other phytoplankton would have suffered from a decrease in sunlight caused by the gases and dust of an asteroid impact." Tina stopped. The moderator was already moving out of the shadows, a young graduate student timidly asserting the rule of the conference. "Three more minutes," Tina told him, and he nodded and stepped back to the side of the room. She hadn't meant to get into speculation about the KT boundary. She cleared the projector and turned to face her invisible audience.

"In my remaining three minutes," she said, "I'd like to talk about how this new knowledge of paleoclimate and CO_2 both aides and inhibits our understanding of contemporary climate—specifically, the effects of CO_2 released by human activities."

Tina took the last graph out of her presentation folder and slipped it onto the projector. "For the first time, we have independent measures of paleo-CO_2 and sea surface temperature that can be used to test and constrain contemporary climate models. Global temperature sensitivity to atmospheric CO_2 concentration has been one of the most elusive and controversial elements of the models, and this data gives us our first empirical measure of it. Here you see CO_2," she said, running her pen along the vertical axis of the graph, "versus temperature"—she indicated the horizontal axis—"for our entire data set from these cores. We can obtain an average temperature sensitivity by simply fitting a straight line to the data and finding its slope—about eight-tenths of a degree per hundred ppm change in pCO_2. Or we can refine the approximation by dividing the curve into small linear sections, producing a series of "temperature sensitivities," each valid for a given range of CO_2."

Tina replaced the graph with the color picture of the picoplankton she'd opened her talk with. "Even as these temperature sensitivities promise to improve our confidence in predictions of the climate's response to future levels of atmospheric CO_2," she said, "I'm afraid we must be more skeptical of attempts to predict what those levels might be." She turned so that she could admire the picture up on the screen in all its blue-green glory. "If these tiny plankton played such a significant role in the carbon cycle for so many millions of years, and if they are still as prevalent in the vast open reaches of the modern oceans as our study indicates, then it's likely that they will continue to play a significant role in the future. And until we know how and in what form they monitored removal and release of carbon to the atmosphere for so many millions of years, we cannot say with any certainty what atmospheric CO_2 will look like in a hundred or five hundred years. And I'm out of time. Thank you."

Tina was standing balanced on one toe, as if she were about to lift off. Instead of the usual polite applause, the room erupted with the buzz of arguing scientists. The lights came on and she squinted out at a sea of waving arms, each a question or pronouncement. The room was overflowing. There were people standing in back, spilling out the door, lining the walls, squatting in the aisles. She saw Katharine in the front row, talking with Orloff's new graduate student and a man Tina didn't recognize. Two rows back she saw Katharine's cruise flame, Nigel, his arm in the air like all the others, with a question.

The young moderator had stepped up next to her and was trying to bring the room to order when Tina noticed Orloff sitting by the aisle halfway back, about to fire off a question, her colleagues' heads already turning en masse, like the starlings in flight over Chip's farm. Tina tried to look past Orloff to acknowledge a young man in the row behind her, a graduate student, certainly, in a denim shirt, tentatively raising his arm—but when Sylvia Orloff spoke, he snatched it back as if he'd raised it by mistake.

"This hypothesis," Orloff said with an air of impatience, though the room quieted almost instantly. "You propose the removal of carbon from the cycle as some sort of unspecified dissolved organic material. This is very hard to imagine, on these timescales. Take that spike in CO_2 in the Eocene—you are looking at a change over, what, two million years?"

Tina nodded, waiting.

"So you're saying that this organic carbon stays in the deep sea for millions of years? And yet the age of the DOC in the contemporary ocean is only six thousand years—"

"*Average* age," Tina interrupted her. "Which means there could well be components that are much younger, along with ones—contributed by the picoplankton—that are much, much older."

"And you think these cyanobacteria cause fluxes in this 'older' fraction of the DOC?"

"One could imagine," Tina said, "that the fluxes are dominated by the rate of input, which would be controlled by fluctuations in the size of the picoplankton population, whereas the remineralization of the DOC is so slow that—"

"I fail to see how remineralization takes place at all if this material is so resistant to bacterial breakdown."

"*Chemical* remineralization, not biological. There are myriad spontaneous but very slow organic chemical reactions whose rates are affected by physical and chemical factors such as water temperature or pH. If you look at petroleum formation in sediments, for example . . . " Tina paused, annoyed that she was getting sucked into an even more radical-sounding speculation. "Until we do more studies on the DOC," she said, "we really have no basis for talking about a mechanism. And I'm sure that one might come up with a different explanation altogether for these correlations that would be equally believable and equally incredible—"

"Such as that your 'paleo-CO_2' curve is just an artifact," Orloff interjected. "That these picoplankton are just recording uptake and production of CO_2 at the base of the photic zone, where, as you pointed out, they are capable of active photosynthesis."

Tina felt the fire rising in her face, the dark, burgundy-red fury of her sepia-skin blush. She slapped a transparency onto the projector. "They *can* function at very low light levels," she said. "But if you look at the water column distributions you see that they are distributed pretty evenly throughout the photic zone. In no case did we find them below the thermocline—even in areas where the surface layer was only seventy or eighty meters deep, they collected at its base rather than move into the cold water below, presumably because they're too small to penetrate the density gradient. Certainly," Tina said shortly, "the *Rover* study was limited, and all of this needs more work." She swapped the water column data for the black and red graphs. "But I'm afraid it's a little hard to swallow a correlation like this one between temperature and CO_2," she said, swinging her arm toward the screen where the graphs were projected, "if the lipid data is only recording local water column changes in PCO_2, as you suggest." She turned quickly and gestured to the man sitting next to Katharine, who was waving his arm insistently. "Yes?"

"A look at the carbon isotopes in another biomarker would clarify some of these questions," he said. "There's a series of alkenones made by coccoliths, which might make better paleo-indicators, since we know more about them, and they can be counted on to stay close to the surface."

"It would be interesting to develop other biomarkers," Tina said. "But we'd still need to explain *this* correlation. . . . " She added the blue-green curve to the graphs on the projector and turned to look at it, trying to regain her composure.

"Another biomarker isn't going to change that data," a voice boomed from the back of the room, and Tina turned in amazement to see Harper Gibson leaning against the wall in back, wearing his usual khaki uniform and looking more disgusted than usual, his arms folded across his chest. "Anything you come up with now is going to have to take those pico-plankton into account, I don't care what timescale you're talking. Look at the correlation she has there. You couldn't ask for a much clearer record."

Thank you, Harper, Tina thought, trying not to smile. She nodded at an older gentleman she didn't recognize, sitting up front.

"The correlations are certainly convincing," he said sympathetically. "As for this hypothesis . . . It raises all sorts of questions about the DOC, which we've been pretty much ignoring in carbon cycle discussions at all levels."

"We've been ignoring it for a reason," Orloff interjected. "It doesn't play an active role in geochemical cycles."

"But that's precisely the point, isn't it?" The gentleman in the front row turned to address Orloff. "We're not talking geochemical cycles in the sense of Urey's early studies, the two decades of work that Holland summed up in his treatise on chemical oceanography. We're talking about *biogeo*chemical cycles."

"Which are regulated by nutrient supply from hydrothermal and terrestial sources, in other words by tectonic forces—"

"That depends on your timescale, of course."

"Which is the problem here."

"If you will," he said amiably, turning back toward Tina at the podium. "The range of timescales is indeed one of the most interesting things about this picoplankton-DOC hypothesis. What you're doing, in effect, is introducing a whole new mechanism for change operating on what appears to be an intermediate timescale, linking fast biological and slow geochemical processes—"

"It's actually superimposed on the large scale tectonic activity," Tina said, glancing at Orloff.

"Of course. But what I was going to say is that it will be very interesting to look at Quaternary sediments and see how this fits with the biological pump theory for the ice ages. The way I understand your hypothesis and the little you've gleaned about picoplankton ecology, the environmental changes that fuel the pump would produce a contrary effect in these cyanobacteria. In other words, when nutrient supply and overall productivity were highest and the rest of the phytoplankton were actively pumping CO_2 out of surface waters, the picoplankton would have been in relative decline, partitioning *less* CO_2 into the DOC; and when other phytoplankton were stressed by nutrient deprivation, your picoplankton would have been thriving, partitioning *more* CO_2 into the DOC. And this translates into a *negative* feedback on orbital cooling and warming as we understand it."

"Right," Tina said. "Except I'm guessing that the picoplankton effect was relatively minor during the Quaternary—that any changes in the amount of carbon they were funneling into the DOC would have been overshadowed by large changes in total productivity during glacial periods. I doubt we'll see this correlation between picoplankton productivity and CO_2 in the Quaternary."

"The effect might be minor," Harper fired from the back, "but that doesn't mean it can be ignored. What we've got here is a whole new paradigm. What you're saying is that we can't look at organic matter production and export as black boxes with arrows going in and out. You're saying that a mere shift in the *distribution* of that production affects export."

During this entire exchange the room had been quiet, no arms waving, no argumentative buzz. But now, in the wake of Harper's pronouncement, the arms reappeared, all angled insistently toward Tina, who was suddenly wishing everyone would get hungry and go to lunch. She glanced at her watch and looked for the young moderator, but he had retired in confusion. It was ten past twelve. "I have reprints of papers here," she said to cut the questions short. But instead of moving toward the door, they flocked to the podium to talk to her.

Everyone was wearing a name badge, but Tina was so caught up in the stream of questions and requests for reprints that she hardly noticed who she was talking to. She didn't notice the black ribbon that said PRESS hanging from the badge of the science writer from the *Chronicle* until he requested an interview. Without thinking, she agreed to meet him in the exhibition hall for a few minutes before dinner, and then she turned her attention to the silver-haired gentleman from the front row, who was carefully extracting reprints from the piles she was juggling.

"It's really unconscionable of you to make the DOC your storage facility," he said, smiling amiably. "Especially if you have no evidence, except lack of other possibilities. But it's certainly a provocative hypothesis. Zhi-Jiang Zhang has been talking about this work."

"Oh, yes, Zhang did the foram C-13. Are you from Wood's—" Tina looked at the man's name badge. "Oh! Professor Maitland. Hi." She had been reading his papers for so many years that she felt as if she should know him. She left her reprints out on the podium and stepped aside to talk to him.

"I like this link you're trying to forge between biological oceanographers and us geochemists. It's long past due. Who's this biologist you've been collaborating with? Shimohata? I don't suppose he's here."

Tina shook her head. "I tried to get him to come, but he didn't have the funding. He's at the University of Illinois, a botanist—this isn't the sort of conference he usually schedules for."

"Well, I'm sure you'd both be interested in the new work the biological oceanographers are doing at Wood's Hole, working with marine microbial communities—though I don't know how aware they are of your photosynthetic cyanobacteria."

"There've only been the two papers," Tina said. "Roy Shimohata's identification of the species in 1980, which was pretty much ignored. And an in situ study that we published earlier this year."

"I've got a lunch date," Maitland said. "But I would like to talk to you more. All speculation about the DOC aside, your paleodata looks very solid. As do your temperature sensitivities for the predictive models. We've been thinking a little along these lines at Wood's Hole also, using CO_2 data from the air in the ice cores, but of course that's only good for the Quaternary." He paused and glanced at his watch. A small group of young researchers and students had gathered about them, but people were beginning to leave, worried about having time for lunch before the next series of talks. "I'd better go. But perhaps we can meet for dinner tonight? Or lunch tomorrow? I'm flying back to Boston tomorrow evening."

They made an arrangement to meet for lunch the following day, and feeling a little dazed, Tina started to gather up her notes and transparencies. She picked up her knapsack from the floor next to the podium, but one particularly persistent and earnest grad student was still plying her with questions about the Saturation Index.

"I know a great place for lunch," Katharine said, coming up behind Tina and taking hold of her arm.

Tina smiled apologetically at the student, handed him a reprint, and let herself be whisked away by her friend. "I'm glad you made it," she said as they stepped out of the conference room into the hall.

"Are you kidding? I wouldn't have missed this for the world." Katharine glanced around and lowered her voice. "Can you believe the way that bitch lit into you? After you went out of your way to be so tactful and not come right out and say that you're dumping a bucketful of ice cold water on her pet theory? Listen, Tina, that guy who was talking about coccoliths being better paleo-indicators than your picoplankton? He told me he's been offered a postdoc in Orloff's lab. He's an organic chemist, and as far as I can tell, she's hiring him to work with biomarkers, to set up an instrument like yours. A man!" Katharine said, her voice rising. "Sylvia Orloff has hired a man! She must be really desperate!" She clapped a hand over her mouth and looked over her shoulder, but they were out of the crowded hallway now, crossing the cavernous foyer of the convention center, and there was no one around.

"I always used to think you were exaggerating about Sylvia," Tina said. "Something you said once, about her being 'power hungry.' I thought that was ridiculous."

"It *is* ridiculous. But it's also true. You just saw it in all its naked glory.

What just went on in there between Sylvia Orloff and Harper Gibson? That was about power. And Sylvia lost." Katharine threw back her head and laughed. "What a riot. Harper Gibson, of all people, rushing to rescue the fragile damsel in distress. Not that the damsel wasn't doing a good job of rescuing herself, but still, it added bite to Orloff's defeat, having Harper Gibson chime in. And then just to add insult to injury good old Maitland makes it abundantly clear that he likes your outrageous hypothesis."

"I didn't even know that was Brian Maitland," Tina said. "We're meeting for lunch tomorrow."

"I bet he wants to offer you a job. And ten to one it'll be tenure-track."

"Oh, right." Tina laughed. "People don't just go creating tenure-track jobs out of the blue because they hear an interesting talk."

"People don't, but Brian Maitland might. That's the thing about power. It's all about manipulation—of people, funding, image. Brian Maitland, by all reports, is adept at all three. Especially image, which is where Sylvia is beginning to lose ground." They had arrived at the front exit, and Katharine pushed open the glass door and stepped outside. "Speaking of image," she said, holding the door for Tina, "I like your outfit. Though you do know, don't you, that if you weren't doing such blockbuster research you could never get away with looking so pretty. I do believe Harper Gibson is smitten, by the way."

"I hate to disappoint you, Katharine, but I think Harper is smitten with the picoplankton, not me."

"Everyone is smitten with the picoplankton," Katharine said. "They're all the rage. Even before your talk everyone was gabbing about some paper of yours that came out last spring, wondering what you were going to come up with. And now . . . It's exactly what you want, isn't it, when you come up with ideas like this? Everyone talking about them, jumping on your bandwagon. BIO had better get moving with a decent job offer if it expects to hang on to Cristina Arenas . . . though I have a feeling that Sylvia plans to make things difficult."

There was a chill wind that made Tina wish she were wearing more than a rayon jacket, but the sky was clear, the downtown office buildings sparkling in the winter sun, the street bright and bustling with lunch-bound pedestrians. Tina's post-presentation daze was beginning to give way to elation as she walked alongside her friend. They hadn't seen each other since August, but Katharine was jabbering away as if it were just another Friday afternoon at BIO and she was dragging a recalcitrant Tina off to go dancing, or down to the pier for TGIF. Today, however, Tina was not reluctant. She was pleased to be going out to lunch with Katharine, glad for the news and gossip, the exposé on power and manipulation.

"You know what?" Tina said, stopping in the middle of the sidewalk.

"What?"

"It's good to see you." She reached up and gave her friend an awkward hug. She had never expected this friendship to outlast Katharine's move to San Diego. But it had, it would. "You look good," Tina told her. "Being away from the bitch seems to suit you."

"It's funny," Katharine said, as they continued walking. "Even at the Navy lab, mentioning that I did a postdoc for Sylvia Orloff at BIO is like pushing a button and getting instant respect. It's like you've dropped down from some higher plain that they all aspired to but couldn't reach. Little do they know . . . They already want to promote me. I'm going to be supervising *four* people, one of them twenty years older than me. All men, of course. It's kind of scary."

She didn't look scared. Katharine Cline looked perfectly capable of dealing with anything the Navy gave her to deal with. She recounted her success in her new job without the affectation, the self-conscious upward cant of chin, that once would have embellished such a report. She'd had her hair cut stylishly short, precluding the arrogant flourish she used to achieve tossing it back from her face. She looked tough, capable, and professional, dressed in a wool skirt, matching jacket and silk scarf; indeed, despite Katharine's claim that she'd been disowned, she was so clearly one of Sylvia Orloff's women that Tina had to smile.

The restaurant Katharine had picked out was eight blocks from the convention center, and it was full of locals, not scientists. They ordered from a menu of gourmet Mexican dishes—tacos stuffed with corn fungus and shrimp, tamales with mole, six kinds of salsa, and papaya margaritas, which Katharine insisted on ordering for both of them. Tina ate, and Katharine talked about her job—the trips to Washington for meetings; the odd, not entirely unpleasant way the men had of respecting her; the work in the lab trying to optimize an incredibly slow and inept process for cleaning up contaminants in the bay sediments. Her biggest problem, Katharine told Tina, was a middle-aged scientist who was shunted from lab to lab because no one wanted him, but they couldn't fire him; he had just been shunted into her lab because she was new. All in all, Katharine told Tina, the Navy people were rather boring. They were all married and there were no graduate students to spice things up, no cruises to keep their juices flowing.

"Speaking of cruises," Tina said, smiling slyly. "I saw Nigel in there, at my talk."

"I know. I'm having dinner with him tonight."

"You are?"

Katharine laughed. "You should see your face, Tina. But don't worry, I am happily married. There's a group of oceanographers getting together. I was going to invite you, but you said you wanted to go to one of the awards dinners. Though—" Katharine's face lit up. "Maybe you want to reconsider?"

"No. Thanks. The dinner is in Garrett Thomas's honor. I don't suppose I'll know anyone besides Mark Jenner, but I want to go." She glanced at her watch. "Which reminds me, I wanted to go to the Origin of Life Session this afternoon."

"Nigel, you know, is not married."

Tina laughed. "Right. Just living with his girlfriend. And I, I'll have you know, am practically living with Chip."

"The farmer?"

"Right. Organic farmer extraordinaire, active in various and sundry environmental and political issues that I cannot keep track of, president of the Brayton County Association of Organic Farmers, and respected member of the community."

"I guess this is serious. Do I have to wait for you to get married to meet him?"

"Who says we're getting married? Whatever happened to good old just living together? This is the eighties, right?"

"Affirmative. And that was the seventies."

"We'll visit you in San Diego," Tina said, pushing the last bit of rice around her plate. "I'm thinking we'll be down that way this summer, spend a week or two in L.A. with my father, if Chip can get away from the farm. He really likes Chip . . . And he's getting married, and we've never met the bride," she added, rushing the words out, still trying to assimilate the fact of her father's impending marriage.

"Your father's getting married? That's so cool! How old is he?"

"Uhh . . . fifty-six?"

"You see? Everyone gets married now. Speaking of which, did you hear about your technician, Michael Moore?"

"Michael? Michael just started grad school in the chemistry department at MIT." Tina held up her hand, trying to get the waitress's attention. She looked back at Katharine. "You mean Michael's getting married?"

"Got married. They're pregnant."

"I didn't even know he had a girlfriend."

"Not only that, but they think it's going to be twins."

"Twins?" She dropped her hand and looked at Katharine's face. "Come on, you're pulling my leg. Where'd you hear all this, anyway? You hardly even know Michael—do you?"

"No. But my boss just went to this big meeting about sediment clean-up, and he was telling me that he met this geologist from Petron who had a guy in his lab who happened to have worked at BIO and it turns out that—"

"Never mind. It doesn't matter."

"Well, at least he won't have any trouble supporting twins, working for Petron— What's wrong?"

Tina toyed with her margarita glass. "I don't know. I think he's working on a project we started in my lab. The one that got me funded last year—"

"Oh lord, Tina, don't tell me your technician is trying to scoop you too!"

"No, no. I was never too thrilled about that project. He's welcome to it." Tina shrugged. "It's just that Michael didn't tell me he was going to continue with it. He told me he was going to MIT."

"Well, I don't know that he's *not* going to grad school. There's some kind of exchange thing, I think—"

Tina held up her hand. "I know. Between NSF and industry. You see, I'm not entirely uninformed. Though I'm beginning to wish I were," she mumbled.

"What?"

"Nothing. I'm just trying to figure out if there is anything that I should do—besides feel bad and slightly stupid—about the news that my ex-technician has run off with this sleazy geologist from Petron without telling me, to continue work on a project of my creation . . . " Tina sighed. "I'm sorry, but all this news is a little overwhelming. I've gotten out of touch the last few months, without you around to keep me informed."

"Ha! I hate to break it to you, Tina, but you've always been out of touch. Even when I was around."

"I know," Tina said. "I'm trying to make up for it. I *am* giving careful thought to the meaning of power and Orloff's hunger for it; I *am* carefully considering what her venture into biomarkers intimates for any future I might have imagined for myself at BIO, such as that I might be offered a permanent position someday; I am appropriately suspicious that her new interest has something to do with the fact that I haven't heard from the director about finding me some lab space of my own when Max Lindquist returns next month, a request I made back in October when my grant was approved. I am even attempting to confront and analyze my current pissed-off, vindictive feelings toward our foremost Woman of Science. My good friend and stalwart feminist Katharine Cline—who I am now listening to *very* carefully—has been trying to convince me for some time that such feelings are a matter of self-defense and survival . . . " Tina grabbed the check as the waitress set it between them on the table. "That such pissed-off feelings are not traitorous, or ungrateful, which is how they might seem when you think of the ground-breaking role that Sylvia Or—"

"Hey. Give me that."

"It's on me. Counseling fees."

"At least let me pay my half."

"Can't," Tina said, rummaging through her knapsack pocket for her wallet. "Goes against my upbringing. Sitting in a restaurant, dividing up a check—it's unseemly."

"I guess the fact that I'm being paid per diem is beside the point then."

"Right."

"You know," Katharine said, watching Tina count out the bills, "we're thinking about it too."

"You're thinking about what? Setting up a biomarker lab?" Tina glanced up doubtfully.

"No, dummy. About having a kid."

"Oh." Tina lowered her eyes to the buttons on Katharine's jacket.

Katharine giggled. "We just started trying."

"Oh. Well, that part sounds like fun." Tina put her wallet away and stood up. "Keep me posted."

"Don't I always?"

≡   ≡   ≡

She missed the dedication of the session. Mark Jenner was just sitting down, and the first speaker was arranging his notes, when Tina slipped into a seat in the back row. The room was only about half-full and except for a couple of graduate students who were sitting down the row from Tina, they were all established scientists, middle-aged or older. No student moderators at this session, she noticed. Garrett's cronies introduced each other with a familiarity born, she supposed, of the marginal nature of their inquiry. She couldn't help but wonder about the power Katharine talked about, the hunger for it. These men, here in this room, didn't care about power any more than Garrett had, though certainly they'd all had their share. At one time or another they'd had funding and image and the ability to manipulate people if they wanted, and now they didn't care. Perhaps that was it, Tina thought, they hadn't had to scratch and fight for it, the way Sylvia Orloff had. Perhaps it was privation that created this hunger for power, a privation Garrett had certainly never known. Power had fallen into his lap with the Nobel Prize when he was twenty-eight. Easy.

Tina turned her attention to the speaker. He was giving a rehash of the "RNA World" theory, and she crossed her arms and leaned back in her seat, marveling at the irony of starting a session dedicated to Garrett with the theory he most reviled.

She sat there for the entire three-and-a-half-hour session without asking a single question or offering a single comment.

The only new idea in the batch almost made her laugh, and she wasn't sure if the tears in her eyes were tears of mirth or grief as she imagined Garrett good-naturedly tearing it to shreds. The scientist was one he had been doing battle with for years, now proposing that life had begun deep in a hydrothermal vent. He had some impressive slides of life around the vents to spice up his talk, and a dubious claim that bacteria could live deep inside, at temperatures of two hundred and fifty degrees Celsius. Tina imagined Garrett down there on the floor of the north Pacific. Revving up the Mercury, heading south to the East Pacific Rise to check it out.

They would give him a grand welcome. The giant crabs would dance and the bacteria would gyrate and brilliant orange tube worms would wave their tubes in celebration of Garrett Thomas's arrival in their midst. He would be so dazzled that he'd forget why he had come. He'd aim the Mercury's lights at the plume of hot sulfur gas rising from the vent, and then he'd remember. He'd get the thermometer from the glove compartment.

Climb out of the car and dig some string out of the cavernous trunk. Tie the string to the thermometer and drop it into the vent to prove his point. The crabs would line up to watch, the tube worms lean forward eagerly. Maybe he would drop a vial of amino acids and peptides down there too, show them what happened.

Everyone knew the temperatures were so high down there that not even the simplest organic molecule could survive degradation. Tina almost broke her silence to point this out, but someone else beat her to it—also noting that the bacteria referred to were mere artifacts, chemical etchings in the stone.

She didn't pay much attention to the last two talks. By the time the lights came up, she was deep in conversation with Garrett. They were talking about all the things they'd never talked about. About power and responsibility. About the value of science and the value of art, the value of science as art. She had a headache from fighting back tears of frustration and remorse. It was an oddly familiar feeling, this talking to the dead, as if she'd known it all her life. All those visits with her father, perhaps, to her mother's grave, talking to Mamá. She'd been too young for remorse then, when her mother died, but this frustration she knew well: you had to make up all their answers yourself.

She was glad she hadn't gone to the graveyard when they buried Garrett. She preferred to imagine him down there on the sea floor—somewhere off the coast of Peru now, with all that bright and lively company. Even if he wasn't likely to find out what he wanted to know there. How life had begun.

Tina left the conference room, her head down so that her hair fell over her face and she wouldn't have to talk to anyone. There were a lot of things she wanted to know that she would never know. How life had begun was probably one of them. Why Garrett had died was another. If there was a why. Though she wasn't so sure she wanted to know that. How could she bear to think that she had turned away from her friend when he might have needed her, when he had been in despair? Better to believe in events with no why, random events without rhyme or reason, events that not even chaos mathematics could describe.

Chapter 29

Chip held the folded newspaper out at arm's length, admiring the article that dominated the *Chronicle's* science and culture section. He was amused. He approved. It was Sunday morning and they had walked the two miles out to the main road to get the paper, walking fast because it was clear and cold, between storms. They had come back and built a fire and made pancakes, and now they had both read the article, sitting at Chip's big kitchen table, eating the pancakes and drinking coffee, but he read the headline aloud again in a dramatic voice, teasing her: "'Microscopic Algae Hold Key to Global Climate. A group of little understood marine phytoplankton may control carbon dioxide responsible for global warming.' How long was the interview?"

"I don't know. Twenty minutes? We had a beer." She'd gone for a walk after the Origin of Life Session and almost forgotten her meeting with the reporter, but he'd been waiting for her when she hurried back to the exhibition hall, fifteen minutes late. They had sat at one of the round tables near the refreshments, and Tina had carefully and thoroughly answered all of his questions. At least, she thought she had.

"'A study presented by Brayton Institute of Oceanography researcher Cristina Arenas at the annual conference of the American Geophysical Union offered new evidence for theories of global warming.'"

"Chip. I just read it, thank you."

"'Dr. Arenas showed that high levels of carbon dioxide were responsible for warm temperatures during the Cretaceous period, a hundred million years ago, as well as for a brief warm spell in the Eocene period about forty million years ago.'" He paused, skipping over a few paragraphs, then read on. "'Dr. Jeremy Hoffman, speaking for a group of scientists at the Center for Atmospheric Research, says that the study supplies data they need to check their climate models, and that the global temperature sensitivity to carbon dioxide determined by Dr. Arenas is thirty percent higher than the one they have been using in their models. Dr. Arenas's study also showed that increases and decreases in carbon dioxide levels corresponded to decreases and increases, respectively, in the population of a little known group of phytoplankton, recently discovered by Dr. Roy Shimohata of Illinois State University. According to Dr. Arenas these tiny plankton, known as picoplankton, siphon carbon dioxide out of the air and cache it away in the deep sea, in the form of dissolved organic molecules—'"

"God. He makes it sound like that's a result of the study, instead of a hypothesis to explain the unexplained."

"You should have told him about the picoplankton munitions cache," Chip said, looking up from the paper. "Remember? That dream you told me a couple weeks ago? This journalist would have loved it—I bet he wouldn't even have bothered to call Cox if you'd told him something that juicy. It was the perfect metaphor, better than what you usually come up with when you explain stuff to me. Just think, Tina, you dreamed the perfect metaphor for your work!"

"I did not. I dreamed a bad science fiction movie."

"But maybe it was the truth. Didn't you tell me once that you sometimes dream solutions to your problems in the lab?"

"No. I did not tell you that. I don't dream solutions to anything. I dream weirdness and then I wake up and think of solutions. Once in a while. Usually I just dream weirdness." She did not tell him how careful she'd been with the reporter, how she'd been afraid that she would get carried away and do just that—use some odd metaphor to explain her work and have it reappear as literal, absolute fact in the newspaper.

He turned his attention back to the paper and read on. "'The picoplankton are still prevalent in the open ocean today. Scientists concerned about global warming from the burning of fossil fuels may need to consider their caches of dissolved organic carbon in the deep sea when they estimate future levels of carbon dioxide, Dr. Arenas says. She would not, however, say whether ignoring them would have caused estimates to be too high or too low.'"

"I did not say that! About the DOC—"

"'Dr. William Cox at the University of Arizona, however, said that the new study proves that estimates of future global warming have been too high—'"

"Where Cox comes up with this stuff, I don't know. If anything, it seems to me the estimates would have been too low."

Chip looked up from the paper. "So why didn't you say that when the reporter asked you?"

"Because I don't know. God, Chip, this is a *hypothesis* we're talking about, and a pretty far-out one at that. The reporter twisted it all around."

"He didn't twist it. He just left out a few of your ifs buts and maybes so that people could understand it. It's too bad he had to talk to Cox. Listen to this: 'Dr. Cox claims that the new study proves that climate models which have been predicting doomsday scenarios of global warming are based on erroneous assumptions about the carbon cycle.'"

"Chip. I read it."

"'He said that it's now clear that there have been natural fluctuations in carbon dioxide—'"

"Oh yeah, right. Over thousands of years, not decades."

"'And that the current rise is well within the range of these natural fluctuations and thus poses no serious threat—'"

"Except of course that the 'natural fluctuations' caused acute global warming and cooling and associated readjustments in the species composition on the earth."

"'This is just further evidence that plants adapt to, and even thrive on, an increase in atmospheric carbon dioxide, said Dr. Cox.'"

"Oh god, this is utter nonsense. How convenient that he neglects to comment on the temperature sensitivities, which, as Hoffman pointed out, are higher than the ones they're using in the models—fifteen times the ones Cox came up with."

"What about this," Chip said, "did you see this? Cox says they might be able to add some nutrient to the open ocean that will encourage the picoplankton to grow faster and cache away more carbon dioxide. He says that we might be able to control the climate with 'picoplankton farms.'" He lowered the paper and looked across the table at Tina.

She laughed. "There you go, Chip, a farmer's dream. They can do away with El Niño year rains so the creek won't flood your lettuce field."

"But that creek is *supposed* to flood now and then. I figure we're just paying dues for planting the lettuce down there—hell, we had over a month of good harvest off that field. Farmers shouldn't be greedy," he added.

"That's not what you were saying a few weeks ago, when the field flooded."

"Well, I know, but . . . Jesus Christ. I don't think," Chip said slowly, "that I'd really want us to be in *control* of the weather. It would take all the excitement out of farming. And what could we blame when things went wrong?"

"I wouldn't lose sleep over it, Chip. It's absurd. Misses the point entirely. My whole shaky hypothesis relies on the connection to the deep sea, on a huge volume of very dilute solution—you're not going to hook into that with an aquatic farm. I can't believe they're still quoting this guy."

Chip tossed the newspaper onto the table. "I've told you. They quote this guy because he's on the list of people to call whenever anyone wants a statement to spice up an article about global warming—"

"This reporter said he wanted to write about my talk. He didn't say he was doing an article about global warming."

"If global warming is mentioned, Tina, then it's about global warming. This is the part that's news. Not what happened a hundred million years ago, interesting as you may find that, but what's happening now, next year." Chip gestured at the newspaper. "William Cox is always ready and willing with a nice, simple, absolute statement that is easy to put into a newspaper article. Unlike Cristina Arenas, who refuses to compromise even the smallest detail to get a point across, or tell these great stories she tells off camera—who refuses to take sides, even when she knows one side is nonsense—"

"We're talking science here, not politics. He wasn't interviewing me about a presidential candidate."

"But government policy needs science, should be based on science—"

"Government policy, not politics."

"Oh, Tina, you don't have one without the other. And you don't have either without sides."

"The science doesn't take sides. The science just is whatever it is, and if I'm going to communicate with the press then *that* is what I have to communicate. I can't say I know, when I don't. I can't make knowledge absolute, when it isn't. It doesn't matter what I might imagine or dream or even feel is true. I can only repeat what the data says, what the science is—" She broke off. Suddenly it seemed that they had had this argument a million times, in a million different forms, that it was somehow woven into the fabric of their relationship, inherent in their love . . . and that despite Chip's perennial complaint that it was impossible to win an argument with her, he was definitely winning now, without ever making any of the points that Tina would have made if she were having his argument with herself . . . which she supposed she was. Which, perhaps, was why he was winning: she was on his side.

If she were he, she would argue that there is no absolute until you define it; or she would point out that if there is more than one way to interpret a set of data, which as often as not there is, then the science does indeed have sides; or she would say that the data can't really talk by itself. . . . But Chip didn't say any of these things.

He was watching her face, looking at once smug and sympathetic, a smile hidden in his mustache. "Tell me something, Tina," he said. "Are *you* always so sure of the difference? Between what your data says, and what you dream or imagine—what you *feel* is true?"

She blinked. She would never have said that, never admitted that beyond all the protective layers of reason and analysis, she harbored such a shockingly alinear, nonreductionist paradigm of thought. And yet he knew. She got up and poured herself more coffee. Where had it come from, this empathy of the mind, of two such different minds? Was it born, as it were, of pure sympathy and love? Of whatever this thing was, that they called "love"? She took her coffee back to the table and sat down. She watched the steam curl up from her cup, looking for a pattern in the way it broke loose from the liquid. She didn't say anything.

She thought about the lunch she'd had with Brian Maitland. They'd talked about his theories of the ice ages, about how the picoplankton might fit in, about problems with the existing data, problems that Tina's methods and the Quaternary segments of the *Explorer* cores might solve. They had talked about ways to test her hypothesis, and he had laughed when she pointed out the cruel joke she had played on herself: that she should have spent the first five years of her career developing techniques for the analysis of organic compounds in sediments, only to invent a hypothesis that could not be tested in the sediments. Their lunch had lasted two hours, and Tina had left it dreaming of miraculous collaborations. Only now, back at the farm, sitting at Chip's rough wood table, watching him drag a cold wedge of pancake across his plate to scour up the last bit of maple syrup . . . having spent the morning walking on his newly ditched road, and the night in his bed beneath the tree that creaked and scratched against the roof all night. . . . Only now did she pause to wonder what she would have done if Katharine had been right about Brian Maitland wanting to offer her a job—and feel a strange sort of relief that he hadn't.

The article in the *Chronicle* seemed to have triggered a chain reaction. In the two weeks before Christmas, reporters from all over the country called Tina to ask about the picoplankton and the greenhouse effect . . . and about sunspots and clouds and the day's weather. Tina tried to be amenable. She answered the relevant questions as best she could, deflected the others. She tried to speak clearly and simply about her work, but what she was quoted as saying never sounded at all like what she'd thought she'd said. She didn't know *how* to talk to the press, she told Chip. It wasn't taught in graduate school—how to translate her work into words they could not misconstrue, or exaggerate, or twist. They would never get it right.

"How can they get it right?" Chip said, when she complained. "When you're always pointing out that there's no 'right' to get? You have to simplify it more."

"But it's not simple. What am I supposed to do? Exaggerate? Lie?"

"I didn't say that. It wouldn't be lying to just come out and tell them what you think."

"What I think? But they ask me the most ridiculous questions. 'How high do you expect temperatures to go in the next ten years?' How would I know? I'm not a climate modeler, and even the modelers don't know. Who could answer a question like that without explaining all the uncertainties of the models, without giving a range of possibilities? 'Will the picoplankton exacerbate the problem of global warming?' Or the opposite—'Will the picoplankton limit the rise in CO_2?' I say I don't know, and they make it sound like I'm harboring some secret. Why can't they just say I don't know? Period. No idea."

"Just give them a scientific opinion, Tina. That's all they want."

"I think that's an oxymoron—a scientific opinion. We're not supposed to have opinions."

"But you do, don't you? Have opinions." And he gave her his new I've-got-your-number look that made her want to curl up and bask forever in the weird empathy of his love.

They spent a not-so-quiet Christmas at the farm with Jorge and Meche and their kids. On January 2, 1984, Alberto Arenas Rosenfeld married Jacqueline Grace Spitzer at a courthouse in Los Angeles, and Tina spoke on the phone with her stepmother for the first time. Even after twenty years of living in Los Angeles, Jackie sounded like a New Yorker, at least to Tina's unaccustomed ear. She knew all about Tina. She always enjoyed reading the science section of the *New York Times*, she told Tina, especially since meeting Alberto and hearing about his daughter the scientist. She mentioned the name of a writer there, asked Tina if she'd read his articles. Tina said she didn't recall, but that Chip would probably know of him. Jackie knew all about Chip, too. She told Tina how much her father liked him, as if it were a great secret. She talked about Alberto, and about how happy she was. It would have been hard not to like the woman, who was clearly—to Tina's utter amazement—head-over-heals in romantic love with Tina's father. When she told Tina about the plan she and Alberto were making to go to Uruguay for a belated honeymoon in February, Tina was speechless. She could not remember her father ever having mentioned wanting to go to Uruguay. She had been thinking of inviting them to Brayton.

Two weeks later, when James Walker called Tina wanting to do a telephone interview for a feature article in the science section of the *New York Times*, Tina remembered Jackie mentioning his name and went out of her way to be cooperative. His questions were astute and well-informed. He was genuinely interested in the workings of the carbon cycle, in the important but enigmatic role played by the picoplankton in the Cretaceous and early Cenozoic. He seemed to understand that the temperature sensitivities Tina had derived from the paleo-record were the only part of her work with direct implications for contemporary climate predictions, and he had plans to talk to the climatologist in Colorado who was working them into his model. He did not ask Tina what she thought of picoplankton farms. Tina actually enjoyed talking to him and was looking forward to seeing his article. She imagined her father and his new wife reading it . . . but the article never appeared. A week after the interview, James Walker called Tina to apologize. He said that temperatures in New York had just plummeted to record lows and his editors refused to run anything that had to do with the greenhouse effect when it was cold. Tina laughed when he suggested that he might call for an update the next time there was a heat wave, but he was serious.

Tina's colleagues were slightly less fickle about their interest. By the time she wrote up her results and got a paper off to *Nature*, she had received so many inquiries, requests for reprints, and suggestions for collaborations that she figured the actual publication would be anticlimactic. She sent an unsolicited copy of the paper to William Cox and told him that his "pico-plankton farms" were ridiculous. She suggested that he stop confusing the public with such nonsense. She told him that there was no evidence what-soever for a direct feedback relationship between CO_2 and the pico-plankton, that the relationship was more complex than that, and that if he was so interested in her work he would do well to read the enclosed preprint of her paper.

By the end of January the press had pretty much lost interest in Tina, except for the local television station, which wanted to feature Tina in a "profile of the scientist." Thinking of what Chip had said to her about being a snob, Tina reluctantly agreed to the Brayton station's request to interview her at BIO . . . only to end up with a television crew crowding into the lab with their cameras and microphones, just two days after Max Lindquist returned from Sweden. She felt ridiculous posing next to the floor-to-ceiling maze of the vacuum line in her lab coat and gloves while she answered their questions. Lindquist didn't comment, but Tina could tell that he wasn't happy to find his lab at the center of so much contro-versy and publicity. Her colleagues' censure seemed to ripple through BIO's halls and labs, casual allusions to Tina's new fame biting into greetings and post-seminar chats. Tina was embarrassed, and then surprised when she began to understand that the censure was tinged with jealousy. In some cases. Not all. Sylvia Orloff's disdain was pure and untainted. She and Tina exchanged their usual polite nod when they passed each other in the hall the day after the television fiasco, but Sylvia's disgust was palpable, her cool greeting loaded with contempt—as if it were tiny Cristina T. Arenas who had failed to live up to Sylvia's Orloff's expectations, rather than the other way around. Tina told herself it didn't matter, that she didn't care.

But it did matter.

Tina was now a guest in the labs she had been running for the past two years, and though Max Lindquist was too polite to say anything, it was immediately apparent that she was in his way. He needed room in the freezer, which was packed full of Tina's samples. He needed office space for his Swedish post-doc, which meant evicting Tina's easy chair and moving a second desk into her office. He wanted to rearrange the instrument lab, use the chart recorder with the GC. Tina had funding to do the work she wanted to do, attention and respect from the wider scientific community, samples in plenty, but she was still a soft money researcher vying for a more permanent encampment at BIO, and Sylvia Orloff's disdain mattered. BIO politics and gossip mattered. Tina no longer needed Katharine to point this out. She badgered the director about her laboratory situation, but he kept putting her off. He told her that he was working on it, that he would let her know "soon," that the holidays had slowed things down. She talked to him just after Lindquist's return, and he mentioned that there was some interest in moving the Mass Spec to another lab since Lindquist wasn't using it. Tina knew what the "interest" was. She knew that Sylvia was lobbying to install the instrument in the little lab where her postdoc had taken up residence. She also knew that, though Max Lindquist would be happy to move the instrument—and her—out of his instrument lab, he wouldn't relinquish the Mass Spec to Sylvia Orloff without a fight. Over the next two weeks of tripping over each other in his labs, it also became apparent that Max Lindquist held Tina's work in genuine high regard; that he felt responsible for her presence at BIO; and that despite her bad taste in dealing with the press he thought that—given some lab space of her own—Cristina Arenas was more of a reinforcement than a threat, and he should be congratulated for having brought her to BIO to begin with.

When the director finally called Tina into his office and made his offer, Tina knew that in a subtle, we-won't-say-anything way, she had won out over Sylvia Orloff's objections. The offer was as good as any Tina had hoped for, given that none of BIO's tenured professors had retired or died. The lab was one that the biologists had been using for storage since before the new biology building was built. It was on the first floor of the chemistry building, a room about half the size of Lindquist's wet lab, with lab benches on three sides and two sinks and a hood that might or might not work. Lindquist had agreed to move the HPLC-Mass Spec down there, with the stipulation that he have free access to it, which was fine with Tina. Some grad students down the hall could be paired up to free an office for her. Tina accepted the director's offer on the spot and went home to tell Chip . . . who was less enthusiastic than she had expected.

"But you mean, it's not really a job? It's just a lab they're giving you, and when your grant runs out you're back to square one?"

"Well, yes. I'll have to write another grant. That's the name of the game."

"Christ," he said, chewing on his mustache. "Here you are, a successful scientist with a Ph.D and a hot theory that everyone is interested in, and you've got less job security than our two farmworkers."

"Yeah, but I've got a lab all to myself," Tina said. "That's no easy feat at BIO. And they're giving me some money to get set up, even funds for a new chart recorder."

He looked at her for a moment, and then he smiled and drew her into a resigned embrace. "So I guess that's as good as it gets, huh?"

She nodded, her cheek chaffing against his shirt. But, as it turned out, it wasn't.

Tina was in the process of ridding her new lab of the various strange and odoriferous objects the biologists had stored there, when Brian Maitland called and offered something much better.

A real job. Tenure track. A wet lab and an instrument lab at her command. Her own group, a post-doc, and two grad students already interested in working for her, replete with their own fellowships. They had acquired a Mass Spectrometer. There was money for an HPLC, engineers and chemists to build the interface. Zhang's isotope lab around the corner. It was a sudden thing, or so it seemed to Tina, the possibility not existing, then existing in the short space of a telephone call. Though of course there was more to it than that. There were Tina's papers, which Maitland had been reading. Maitland's papers, which Tina had come of age reading. The collaboration with Zhang. Maitland at the conference, their lunch together. Just as Katharine had predicted, Brian Maitland had created a place for her, used his power—easily, it seemed, deftly, invisibly—to create a job for a young scientist he wanted at his institution on the Atlantic shore. She couldn't think of anyone she would rather work with.

She told Maitland that she would think about it, that she needed to consider. He thought that BIO had offered her something comparable. Brian Maitland was a brilliant man, but he wouldn't know about farmers. How they built their soil, year by year. How they took root in their land, like the trees they planted, how they could not even pick up and move across a valley or a hill, let alone to the other side of the continent. To a place where they didn't know the weather. Or the soil. Or the slant of light on a hilltop. Where the birds were foreign. The sunset all wrong. She told Maitland she would think about it. She could not imagine saying no. She didn't see how she could say yes.

There were farmers there, after all, in Massachusetts, weren't there? Inland, perhaps, upstate New York? What did it matter, really, west coast, east coast? She would ask, it wouldn't hurt to ask. Hadn't Chip been the one to criticize her job at BIO? Apples? Hadn't he told her about some kind of apple he liked that grew better back east? He could grow apples.

She put it off. For days, a week, going on two, she put off talking to Chip about Maitland's offer . . . until one day in late February she went up to the farm to see him in the afternoon, and it was clear that she couldn't put it off any longer.

He was out in the orchard doing the last of the pruning, up high on the ladder with the loppers draped across the back of his neck, clippers in hand. He said he was almost finished, and she stood a few feet away, watching him prune. He told her his strategy for coaxing fruiting spurs out of recalcitrant pear trees, pointing out some young spurs as evidence of its success, and then he was silent as he made the last few cuts, leaning out from the ladder at precarious angles. When he finished, he slipped his clippers into the holster on his belt, and Tina waited for him to come down, but he stayed up there on the third rung from the top of the pruning ladder, looking out at the sun setting over the hills. There were wisps of white clouds flying in on the wind, turning pink now. It was a beautiful sunset, and Tina stepped away from the tree for a better view. She almost didn't hear when Chip started talking again. "Maybe we should make your Dad happy," he said quietly.

"Dad?" She moved closer to the ladder trying to make out the expression on his face. "Dad seems to be doing a fine job of making himself happy."

"Well hell, then maybe we should just follow suit and go down to the courthouse." He kept his gaze fixed on the hills and clouds, turned slightly away from her.

Tina looked at the loppers draped so casually across his thick neck, the curved blades open, sharpened and dangerous-looking. She wanted to take the damned things off his neck, but she couldn't reach. She thought of him falling from the ladder, injured, hurt . . . she couldn't bear it. He must know, she thought, that he would be better off with someone else. Someone who would love his babies, fill his farm with kids and go to meetings and write letters and save the world for them. Someone who would never leave, never even think about leaving, no ifs, buts, or maybes. She should have said so a long time ago, set him free. She ought to say so now.

She reached up and laid her hand on the back of his blue-jeaned calf— tentatively, as if it were the first time she'd ever touched him, the time she called him back into her apartment to make love. She felt him flinch. She did not want to say no, could not say no. "Dad didn't want that," she said.

He came down from the ladder then, lifted the loppers off his neck, and hung them over a rung. "So we'll do it big, then," he said. "We'll have us *una gran boda*." And before Tina could say anything, he had stepped behind her and wrapped his arms around her middle and was hunched over whispering in her ear all his plans for this *gran boda* to top all *bodas*. "A big celebration, here at the farm. In June, once everything's in the ground. Under the bay tree. Jorge as best man. The girls as bridesmaids. Your friend up from San Diego—Katharine, as best woman or whatever it is they call it. And, of course, your dad and Jackie. Hell, we'll invite all of Brayton, everyone you know at BIO, have a band. Meche can sing—have you ever even heard Meche sing? Oh and tons of food, a pig, we'll roast a pig!" He went on and on, and Tina knew she should make him stop, but he had her in his arms, pressed into the solid mass of his body with his voice in her ear, describing this event she had never envisioned or desired for herself in such a way that she found herself wanting it as much as she wanted his hands on her, there, at that moment, in his orchard next to the pear tree he'd just pruned for fruit.

"Chip . . . " She twisted herself around to face him, to talk, to try and be serious about this thing he was proposing, but instead found herself caught in a kiss, swept into it like a grain of sand in a breaking wave and the best she could do was remind him that she had no birth control, to which he said not to worry, and proceeded to make love to her with a gravity and fervor that belied all the visions he'd just conjured of light-hearted June *bodas*.

It was cold, the sun down behind the hills, the full moon rising, casting light but no warmth. They had tumbled into the grass of the orchard, were lying in a damp tangle of jeans and sweatshirts. "Chip," Tina said, rolling away from him and pulling her clothes into place. She sat up and hugged her knees, looking uneasily at the dark trunks of the trees in the orchard, as if their very presence were a rebuke, as if they were even now warning her not to ask what she was about to ask, admonishing her to make her decision one way or the other and leave them all in peace. "Chip," she said for the third time, and this time he rolled over onto his side to look at her, his jeans hanging open.

"I've been offered a job," she said, and his eyes narrowed, and then he rolled over onto his back and tucked himself in and buttoned his jeans and sat up on his knees while she told him about Brian Maitland's offer.

"What did you tell him?" he said.

"I said I would think about it."

"What's wrong with staying at BIO? You said it was a good offer. Good enough, considering . . . "

Considering. Considering what there was to consider. She had not told Brian Maitland that his offer was ten times better than anything BIO had offered. That what she had to consider was a boyfriend. A lover. These were not things one said. If a man had a wife, he would take her with him, they would go off together to meet this opportunity. It was only natural. And a woman? If she had a husband would she take him with her? Why was it so much harder, so unnatural to want this?

"I thought maybe Jorge and Meche could buy you out. We could buy a farm in New York," she said lamely, and saw the intake of air and the pained surprise on his face, and felt as though she'd stabbed him in the back with his own carefully sharpened clippers. She looked down at the ground, where his hands had curled so that his fingers dug into the soil as if of their own volition, as if his body would cling there, even if he tried to make it move.

And if the husband were this man sitting next to her with his fingers clinging to the soil of his Brayton County orchard, looking off toward the dark tangle of blackberries that was the creek that led to the fields he had cultivated and nurtured and protected from pigs and slugs for ten years now, this man now swiveling his head in a slow semicircle to take in the lumpy shadows of the hills he had reseeded with native grasses where the full moon was rising with such pure and glaring clarity? What then? Did the woman stay, let the opportunity slip past without regret and dig into the soil by his side?

She had a job, a good enough job. For now. She loved him. If she loved him she would stay and marry him. It was the natural thing to do. A job was a job . . . like a farm was a farm.

Chapter 30

She was as empty as the shell she kicked across the sand. As sad as the deserted beach. As lonely as she'd ever ever been.

The wind was picking up and she wondered if it could actually lift her, sweep her back into the dunes. She stopped walking and looked out at the horizon, this strange horizon where the sun always seemed to be on the wrong side, black with clouds now, the beach deserted because there was a storm coming in. Hurricane force, they said. She turned around and started back the way she'd come. She could just barely make out the Institute buildings off in the distance, the cluster of cottages where she lived. She had walked farther than she'd intended.

She thought of Chip reading about the Congressional hearing. Her words in the newspaper. If he would see himself there. If he would realize. Or if he would be disappointed. She hadn't talked to him since she left, eight months now. She had resisted the temptation to pick up the phone and call him. It wouldn't be fair. He'd told her that. Told her to be gone and have done with it then. Perhaps he would not want to see her name in the paper or otherwise. Perhaps it would hurt.

She hadn't thought it possible that she could be so content, and yet so miserable. The work was going well, her fledgling lab group off to a good start. At her urging, Maitland had invited Roy Shimohata to join the biological oceanography team. The botanist had just moved out with his wife and two children. They were renting a house up the road in the town. Now

Tina had only to walk to the adjacent building to consult with Roy. She'd made some headway in developing a method for analyzing the DOC, concentrating on deep water samples, the oldest, most refractory components of the DOC. She was a long way from being able to trace anything back to the picoplankton, but there was a plethora of new information about their ecology, thanks to Roy and his newly inspired colleagues. It was exciting, fascinating work and it seemed to Tina that they were learning in leaps and bounds. Not that any of it had mattered much at the hearings she'd just come back from.

She'd thought of Chip when she'd first agreed to testify, she and Maitland and six other scientists, including, to Tina's horror, William Cox. She'd thought of him while she was preparing her talk, while she was sitting on the panel answering the congressmen's questions, listening to her colleagues, to the politicians, the administration bureaucrats. She thought of him now, how right he'd been. How much he'd known, her farmer.

Just tell them what you think. Choose sides. Give your scientific opinion. Come on, say it.

She'd told them precisely what she knew, and she'd told them what she thought. But it hadn't been enough. For all they'd learned in the past year, for all Tina's hard work, she still could not fit the picoplankton into a carbon cycle model or say how they might affect future levels of CO_2. They were as much a wild card as when she first proposed her hypothesis. But she did say that this very uncertainty was worrisome. She did say that whatever questions remained, the dramatic rise in atmospheric CO_2 created by the burning of fossil fuels was indisputable—because to her amazement, one of the agency chiefs said this was still in question, this single, absolute, well-documented fact.

An old argument with Chip came to mind. She had not understood the extent to which science could be manipulated out in the world. She had not understood that uncertainty could be used to cover up what was more certain, what was unknown used to deny what was known. She had not realized that bad science would be given as much heed as good.

Come on, Chip, no one would say that atmospheric CO_2 is not increasing, or that global climate is not going to change in some—

Yes they would. That's what they're saying.

You're talking politics again. Not science. No scientist would—

And Cox and his clique? They're not scientists?

It's arguable.

Well, argue it, then.

And she had. She'd stood her ground, argued her case. She had stood fast by what she did know, what was as solid as anything science had to offer, the temperature sensitivities she'd derived from the sediment records. The climatologist from Colorado explained how he'd used the data to calibrate his model, how it increased the degree of certainty in the predictions he was offering. But he was still talking in probabilities, of course, nothing absolute about his predictions.

You have to be specific. Absolute. Strike fear into their hearts.

Fear?

It's the only thing. It's the only thing that will move them to do anything. You've got huge industrial interests working against any move to curb use of fossil fuels. Big corporations, lots of money. Like Petron.

She'd always thought he was exaggerating, when he said things like that, that he was just a zealot flinging rhetoric. But there was a letter still sitting amid the litter on her desk, an invitation to coauthor a book for the "general public" that would "set the record straight" on global warming, to be published by an organization called the National Research Institute. There was the implication of a large "advance against royalties." Tina had no idea why she should have been singled out for such a book; she was only on the periphery of the field, and a newcomer at that. But a little investigation revealed that the National Research Institute was an ultra-rightwing think tank, publishing such an insidious and convoluted mix of propaganda that even Chip couldn't have imagined it—the environmental movement was a communist plot, the ban on DDT an attempt to depopulate the world, radiation leaked from nuclear power plants was good for one's health, the hole in the ozone layer was an optical illusion—and Petron Corporation headed its list of sponsors.

Absolute. Tina had not been absolute at the Congressional hearing. She had not compromised the truth of what wasn't known. Nor had Maitland. Nor the climatologists from Colorado. Only William Cox had done that, and one other scientist, a physicist she'd never heard of before. Those two had gone all out, claimed absolute faith in conclusions that no one else in the scientific community could verify or support. The Congressmen, of course, were confused. They were trying to decide whether to mandate a major study of the impacts of global climate, reviving an American Academy of Sciences proposal that had been discarded when Reagan first took office. There was also some talk of legislation in the making, an energy bill designed to mitigate the source of the climate change, while they studied its potential impact.

Tina looked out at the uneasy sea. The horizon seemed to be moving in, shrinking. She had never even seen the Atlantic coast before she'd moved here, but she had seen Atlantic sediment cores, some of the oldest, most undisturbed sequences in the DSDP collection. It was a passive margin, the sediments in orderly layers, accumulating conveyor belt style as they moved away from the mid-Atlantic ridge, so different from the chaotic California coast she knew, with its maze of faults and jigsaw of tectonic plates. Tame was how she'd imagined the east coast, older and calmer than the west, even the waves smaller, more civilized. But there was nothing tame about these waves today. They were huge, churned up by the storm, crashing in a roiling froth that moved erratically up and down the tidal zone. Tina worked her way farther up the beach to walk in the soft, uncertain sand above the high tide line.

One of the congressmen had turned to her and asked why they should worry about this problem, or allocate funds for its study, when there was a good chance that some unforeseen behavior by the picoplankton would save the day. Tina was tongue-tied, at a loss for what to say, how to point out the obvious. Finally she found herself saying that if there was any chance that the picoplankton would "save the day," then there was just as much chance that they would exacerbate the problem and the predictions he was hearing for CO_2 build-up and climate change were *under*estimated. Then Cox had somehow turned the discussion to his research showing the beneficial effects of CO_2 on agricultural crops, and the next thing Tina knew, they were bandying about the costs of super-engineering feats to reroute irrigation projects and high tech levees to protect coastal areas and unheard of new advances in weather manipulation . . . until the congressman who was pushing the energy legislation interrupted and asked the scientists to offer an opinion. All of them said that caution was definitely in order, except for Cox who said that the CO_2 from fossil fuels was a boon to agriculture and would feed the world's hungry, and the physicist who said that there was absolutely no need for energy conservation based on greenhouse emissions, and then the discussion deteriorated completely with the administration people calling for "proof" from the scientists, who could not offer the sort of proof called for, and the congressman who'd brought up the energy legislation being called an "alarmist" as if it were a dirty word. . . .

Her afternoon with the leaders of the nation made the dinnertime discussions she used to have with Chip seem like enlightened, sophisticated, and well-informed debates.

Next time, mi amor, she whispered to the wind. *Next time I'm going to do better.* Was it compromising her science? To simply state the obvious that had been lost in all its uncertainty? To come up with better metaphors? Was it compromising the truth of what wasn't known, to emphasize what was? She thought of Garrett, dear Garrett, perched on the hood of his Mercury. Garrett would never have made that sort of compromise, would he? But then, he wouldn't have needed to. That was one of the attractions, after all, in origin-of-life research: its pure irrelevance.

The light went out of the sky suddenly, and Tina looked up from the sand, startled. The black clouds that had been on the horizon just moments ago had closed in overhead. There was not another soul in sight—no person, not a single gull or sanderling, the Institute still a tiny smudge of buildings in the distance. The storm had come ashore, a rage of a storm, and she was all alone in her thin west-coast jacket and jeans, her tennis shoes. She shivered and felt a little afraid, tried to hurry in the soft sand. She'd never been in a hurricane.

Could they really stop it now, this experiment they had set in motion? This dangerous and useless experiment that mocked its subject and tempted fate, that offered no chance at verification, no repeat run? Chip was right: no one was even trying to stop it. She did not have Chip's passion and faith or, ultimately, his hope, but she would say a thing or two next time around. She could feel her colleagues coming around as well—Maitland and the climatologist from Colorado. All of them horrified, frightened, intimidated by the responsibility they suddenly realized was theirs. At a loss. Out of their realm. And, like her, thrilled by the whole mess of an experiment.

Who wouldn't be thrilled? A geological event of such magnitude occurring before one's very eyes, all the power and grace of the earth condensed into a few puny decades, a century or two! How would it be? The climatologists were trying hard to predict that. Greater storms, bigger hurricanes, ever-more-erratic weather. More and bigger heat waves, waves of fire, drought, all the random events of weather that only chaos mathematics could describe. And what else? What subtle, sinister changes were even now under way, what not-so-random surprises were in wait? Would she live to see the deepest, most stable currents of the sea slow to a halt, the ocean stratified completely, the warm cap of surface water thickening and spreading like putty, sealing off the polar seas, no cold water to sink and none to rise again with its rejuvenating store of nutrients? Imagine the positive feedback of that! No more CO_2 being ferried into the deep sea, no marine plants to suck it out, Keeling's curve veering upwards, rising to what limit? What would survive, what would die? Which species expand, which contract? Would the picoplankton thrive, a few species of tiny cyanobacteria returned to their glory, shedding jacket after jacket, slurping up CO_2 and frolicking in the tepid waters of this swollen and stratified sea, surviving against the odds like they had survived at the KT boundary . . . until the nutrients had dwindled to nothing and even they succumbed? Would life retreat to Garrett's vent, to tubeworms and crabs and sulfur-eating bacteria, to its origin, if his colleagues' theory were correct? Oh Garrett, all those years, your entire existence spent imagining the unimaginable, the impossible miracle that was the origin of life—and look how simple, how easily construed, how immediate and very possible its demise!

Not likely, Tina thought. Life wouldn't end with this. She didn't believe that. But Homo sapiens? Would they thrive in new agricultural climes, migrate to Canada and Siberia, new promised lands? Was there any decent soil up there? Or would they race along with their technology, adapting to the changes they'd wrought, keeping in step with their ludicrous out-of-control experiment. That was, apparently, what they were going to try to do, and perhaps they would succeed—though Tina didn't have such blind faith in technology to think it could happen without a lot of death and mayhem. A sad day for science, she thought as the first few drops of rain fell on her head, death and mayhem aside. If the earth's most essential and all-intrusive cycle were of their own construction . . . ? What joy, what glory would there be to understanding that, what ballast for a questioning soul? What in the world would be left to explore?

Maybe she should have been an astronomer. They couldn't control the luminosity of the sun. Its growing heat. They couldn't control the asteroids spinning across space, the tiny probabilities that they might meet up with one, probabilities as small, perhaps, as the probability of their own existence . . . though there was talk of even that. Something about putting atomic bombs in space to intercept and blow up an asteroid that came earth's way. Should they do that? Would that be okay, Chip? Would that be fucking with God? To avert certain doom and demise?

Oh, how she yearned to ask him that. To see the look he gave her, hear what he had to say.

Who would have thought that in the end they clung to the same God? That it was this idea of an earth where man was small, insignificant, a nick in time, that they had shared? Who would have thought that it would be in this feeling or place in the mind or soul or wherever it was, this most unlikely place, arrived at by two such different paths, that they would connect . . . only to part ways?

It was pouring. Tina lifted her face to the flooded air and braced each step against the wind, making her way back down the beach to her office and labs. Wet. Cold. Miserable. Filled with this profound loneliness, and with the thrill of this spectacular Atlantic storm.

Author's Note and Selected References

The discussions of geochemical processes in *Carbon Dreams* are based on those prevalent in the scientific community in the early 1980s, though I have taken liberties with the exact timing of certain discoveries. Basic principles of the earth sciences are presented as reliably as possible within the novel's historic and aesthetic constraints, with many omissions and oversimplifications. I took much of my information from papers in scientific journals, but several general texts were also helpful. *The Sea Floor* by E. Seibold and W. H. Berger (1993) gives a readable and concise treatment of most of the novel's scientific themes. Stephen Schneider's book *The Coevolution of Climate and Life* (1984) is a thorough and well-written account of the history of the planet. *The Earth Through Time* by Harold L. Levin (1991, 1998) is a readable and up-to-date textbook that I found useful, and *An Introduction to Organic Geochemistry* by S. D. and B. J. Killops (1993) is a good overview of this field. I was helped in my thinking about paleoclimates and productivity by the collection of review articles in *Productivity of the Ocean: Present and Past* edited by W. H. Berger, V. S. Smetaek and G. Wefer (1989).

Tina's actual research projects are fictional, based on sound scientific principles, but with no exact analogues in the real world. They are, in essence, armchair experiments, developed in a credible manner, with results that fit plausibly into gaps in our knowledge and highlight the real trends and upheavals apparent in the scientific literature of the past two decades. The idea for using lipid biomarkers as paleotemperature indicators came from reading articles by S. C. Brassell, et. al. (*Nature* 320 [1986] 129-133) and G. Eglington, et. al. (*Nature* 356 [1992] 423-426). Tina's idea for using the carbon-13 of biomarker lipids as an indicator of paleo-CO_2 was inspired by an article by J. Jasper and J. M. Hayes (*Nature* 347 [1990] 462). Papers by G. Rau, et. al.(*Nature* 341 [1989] 516-518) and by K. H. Freeman and J. M. Hayes (*Global Biogeochemical Cycles* 6 [1992] 185-198) were also particularly helpful. The ubiquity and importance of photosynthetic picoplankton in marine ecosystems first became apparent in the early 1980s (T. Platt et.al. *Nature* 301 [1983] 702-704; for an overview see J. G. Stockner *Limnology and Oceanography* [1988] 765-775). Roy Shimohata's three species and their unusual ecology are modeled on the chroococcoid cyanobacteria that constitute a major component of this small size-class of phytoplankton. I have taken great imaginative liberty with all of these ideas, assigning coccolith biomarkers to cyanobacteria, using a different analytical instrument, and generally dramatizing, extrapolating and inventing results to the point where Tina's research bears only a basic conceptual resemblance to its models; her hypothesis is entirely a product of these fictional results. Charles Keeling is the only real scientist who appears in the book; his work, like that of Urey and Holland mentioned toward the end, forms part of the book's historical framework.

Books about the greenhouse effect and global warming range from sound scientific treatments to insidious sociopolitical treatises masquerading as science. Stephen Schneider's *Global Warming: Are We Entering the Greenhouse Century?* (1989) gives a reliable and accessible treatment of the science, but is somewhat outdated. A brief but well-referenced overview by the same author is *Laboratory Earth* (1997). The US Global Change Research Institute Office (www.gcrio.org) was helpful in providing me with bibliographies and historical material and offers up-to-date publications about global warming science and public policy. *Climate Change 1995: The Science of Climate Change* is a complete and reliable treatment of this subject (Cambridge University Press) by the Intergovernmental Panel on Climate Change (www.IPCC.ch). I did not come across Ross Gelbspan's book, *The Heat is On* (1997) until *Carbon Dreams* was completed, but it is a well-documented journalistic account of the campaign by oil and coal interests to confuse the public about the science of climate change.

PHOTO BY JAMES LUGO

Susan Gaines's short stories have been published in various literary magazines and selected for the anthologies *Best of the West* and *Sacred Ground: Writings About Home*. She was educated in the sciences, with degrees in chemistry and oceanography. Though she considers northern California her home, she has lived in a variety of places, most recently in Uruguay, where she has been at work on another novel.